"Alan Jacobson builds an unrelenting, fast-paced, global-stakes machine of a thriller out of many intense and moving personal stories. Start it and hold on."

—Thomas Perry, *New York Times*–bestselling author

"Set in the darkened corners of the world stage, where operatives navigate a confusing, deadly world, *Die Trying* tells a riveting story of highly-placed treason and heroism. Fast-moving and sometimes frightening, it's an outstanding read."

—Stan McChrystal, four-star general and commander, Joint Special Operations Command (Ret.)

DIE TRYING

The Works of Alan Jacobson

NOVELS
False Accusations

KAREN VAIL SERIES
The 7th Victim
Crush
Velocity
Inmate 1577
No Way Out
Spectrum
The Darkness of Evil
Red Death

OPSIG TEAM BLACK SERIES
The Hunted
Hard Target
The Lost Codex
Dark Side of the Moon
Die Trying

MICKEY KELLER SERIES
The Lost Girl

ESSAYS
"The Seductress"
(Hollywood vs. the Author, Rare Bird Books*)*

SHORT STORIES
"Fatal Twist" *(featuring Karen Vail)*
"Double Take" *(featuring Carmine Russo & Ben Dyer)*
"12:01 AM" *(featuring Karen Vail)*

DIE TRYING

AN OPSIG TEAM BLACK NOVEL

ALAN JACOBSON

OPEN ROAD
INTEGRATED MEDIA
NEW YORK

All rights reserved, including without limitation the right to reproduce this book or any portion thereof in any form or by any means, whether electronic or mechanical, now known or hereinafter invented, without the express written permission of the publisher.

This is a work of fiction. Names, characters, places, events, and incidents either are the product of the author's imagination or are used fictitiously. Any resemblance to actual persons, living or dead, businesses, companies, events, or locales is entirely coincidental.

Copyright © 2025 by Alan Jacobson

ISBN: 979-8-3372-0083-5

Published in 2025 by Open Road Integrated Media, Inc.
180 Maiden Lane
New York, NY 10038
www.openroadmedia.com

For Paul Knierim

While researching my novels over the years, I've been asked why I don't hire someone to do it for me and focus solely on writing. The short answer is that I would not get to work with people like Paul Knierim.

In 2008, after being granted clearance to work with the Drug Enforcement Administration (a process that took six weeks), I was assigned a public information officer. But my detailed questions required a field agent who did the things my characters would be doing.

I soon received a call from Paul, an agent who was again returning from a multiyear stint to stem the drug trade in South America. He was at headquarters awaiting reassignment. I became Paul's assignment.

Paul's honesty, integrity, insight, experience, case stories, and depth of knowledge gave me a behind-the-scenes understanding of the dangers and challenges DEA agents face—on a level impossible to achieve by having a research assistant ask a list of sterile questions in my stead. Moreover, our give-and-take discussions led to a sixteen-year friendship that we both cherish.

While *Die Trying* is not about the world of illicit drugs, it *is* about people who put the needs of others ahead of their own, just as Paul did every single day.

AUTHOR'S NOTE

Nearly every time I write a novel, at least one reviewer notes that my fiction appears to be "ripped from the headlines"; however, I conjure most of these ideas before those headlines occur—sometimes years prior.

I believe that the best fiction is propped up by facts—which is why I do so much research for my novels. This increases believability since real-world associations enable the reader to relate to, and connect with, the story and characters. If my fiction is forward-looking and well-grounded, it increases the odds it will intersect with reality.

To me, sprinkling in truth is like a chef's use of truffle oil: a little bit makes the other flavors explode. I always add a few drops to enhance the verisimilitude.

In *Die Trying*, the challenges to the Constitution and the desire to call a Constitutional Convention are true, and the numbers I cite are real.

That said, I don't mix in truth to make political statements. *If there's nothing else you take away from this note*, it's that. Polarized readers will claim that I'm anti-Democrat or anti-Republican—but my only goal is to tell a highly entertaining story.

While some actions taken by President Nunn in *Die Trying* might evoke those espoused by President Trump, the concept behind Nunn's actions—and those of his predecessor, President Rush in *Hard*

Target—came to me in 2000. Trump was a real estate developer and owner of Miss Universe pageants . . . not a former US president.

Finally, I finished the first draft of *Die Trying* just prior to Hamas's October 7, 2023, massacre. I decided not to change anything significant relative to the story, characters, or setting.

DIE TRYING

"Iran's use of [US] institutions of religious worship for illegitimate foreign influence operations threatens our national security, and intentionally threatens our Constitutional order."
—REP. DOUG LAMBORN (R-CO)
July 28, 2023

China's efforts "target our freedoms, reaching inside our borders, across America, to silence, coerce, and threaten our citizens and residents."
—FBI DIRECTOR CHRISTOPHER WRAY,
testimony before the House Select Committee,
January 31, 2024

"We don't take an oath to a country . . . we don't take an oath to a religion . . . to a tyrant or dictator or wannabe dictator. We do not take an oath to an individual. We take an oath to the Constitution, to the idea that is America. And we're willing to die to protect it."
—GENERAL MARK MILLEY,
retirement speech, September 29, 2023

"As chairman [of the president's Joint Chiefs of Staff], you swear to support and defend the Constitution . . . but what if the commander-in-chief is undermining the Constitution?"
—LIEUTENANT GENERAL H. R. MCMASTER,
National Security Adviser for Donald Trump
(*The Atlantic, September 21, 2023*)

"Today we live in a world where the absurd regularly becomes real . . . We must focus on the urgent problem of what to do about the likely unraveling of democracy in the United States . . . by fully recognizing the magnitude of the danger."
—THOMAS HOMER-DIXON,
founding director, the Cascade Institute
at Royal Roads University

1

COMBAT READINESS TRAINING CENTER
GULFPORT, MISSISSIPPI

A dense fog hung low, early morning dew clinging stubbornly to the tips of the grass surrounding the training complex. Single-story mud-brown stucco buildings speckled the verdant pitch, with massive oak trees lining the periphery.

Karen Vail steadied her M4 rifle and adjusted her tactical helmet, which was hard and heavy and fitted with articulating ear flaps. Lexan goggles overlaid a compact black gas mask that contained filters protruding from her cheeks like tumorous growths.

At least it was January. Wearing these uniforms layered with thirty pounds of equipment in Mississippi's summer heat and humidity would truly suck.

Vail, backed by similarly outfitted OPSIG, or Operations Support Intelligence Group, operators Hector DeSantos, Troy Rodman, Zheng Wei, and a handful of trainees entered the mock building via the well-worn metal staircase.

One of only four such training centers in the country, the Combat Readiness Training Center was a facility used by tens of thousands of Air National Guard and Air Force Reserve Command personnel annually. In addition, special operations forces trained there to practice close quarters urban combat and total force, multiservice training exercises in simulated asymmetric warfare scenarios involving ground forces and combat and mobility air forces.

That's what Vail was doing on this chilly morning.

She had been participating in quarterly drills to introduce her to the tactics she never learned as a member of the NYPD and FBI. Much as SWAT units in smaller cities employed part-time officers culled from patrol, Vail's as-needed work for OPSIG Team Black provided the clandestine unit with unique abilities and experience that its operators did not possess.

Conversely, covert ops missions required an expanded skillset that complemented her Academy training and prepared for missions where life-and-death situations were a regular part of any day. It was an unconventional model for covert ops, but OPSIG made it work.

Ironically, she had joined the Behavioral Analysis Unit a gazillion years ago as a means of getting out of the line of fire that a field agent could face. But that was when her son, Jonathan, was young—and his father was an unreliable parent. She needed the safety and security of cases where drawing a handgun—or being the target of one—was less likely.

Jonathan was now a senior in college and Vail's fiancé, Robby Hernandez, was as stable a parent as they came.

When pressed to admit it, her OPSIG work afforded her the opportunity to use a different part of her brain and get the adrenaline flowing. She was never bored with her criminal investigative analysis work, but there was something about having the freedom to think on the fly, to problem solve without the weight of a thousands-of-pages rule book that governed every action you took. What's more, you got to stop extremely bad guys the world over—and save a great many lives in the process.

Hundreds? Thousands? Millions? Depending on the mission, yes.

As Vail crept up to a door on the second floor of "apartments," she was prepared for anything. She had been through such training before in Hogan's Alley at the FBI Academy—so, on the surface, this drill was not foreign to her. But it increased her heart rate, dilated her pupils, and heightened her senses—a perfect exercise designed to reproduce what an operator could experience in the field.

Rodman blasted open the door and Vail led the way inside. As she started down a hallway, she saw a flash of movement to her left. She turned and came face-to-face with a large man clad in black tactical clothing, wearing a balaclava.

Ah, the close quarters in "close quarters combat."

And, oh yeah—the combat.

He had several inches and at least seventy-five pounds on her. And the look on his face said that he intended to use every unit of measurement to his advantage as he stepped toward her.

But Vail was accustomed to men throwing their weight around.

My ex-husband learned the hard way that doesn't work with me.

She shifted her M4 rifle and swung the barrel into the man's face, momentarily stunning him and standing him upright.

And that left his balls exposed.

Which brought to mind the first lesson Vail had learned.

Never let a set of unprotected testicles go unkicked in hand-to-hand combat.

Vail unleashed a powerful kick with her tactical boot, dropping the guy to his knees, her Glock 19 swiftly drawn and pushed against his forehead.

"Karen," DeSantos said in her ear over comms. "Karen, he's down. Take a breath."

She took that breath and straightened up, secured her pistol, and repositioned the rifle.

"Copy that."

"You good?" DeSantos asked as Rodman pushed past Vail to tend to her "victim."

She faced DeSantos, her breath still rapid and shallow. "I'd say that qualified as . . . short duration, high intensity conflict . . . with sudden violence at . . . close range. Yeah?"

"Yeah," DeSantos said, wide-eyed and nodding animatedly. "Why don't you take five? Get some air."

"I'm good, Hector."

"Take five, Karen."

Even through the two sets of goggles between them, she saw the intensity in his gaze.

Vail turned and pushed past Zheng and another couple of geared-up operators, then ran down the metal staircase, pulling off her tight helmet as she went.

Guess I do need some air.

As she reached the bottom, she looked out at the stand of trees fifty yards away, her kinky red hair blowing in the gentle breeze. She felt DeSantos beside her.

"What?" she asked. "Feel better?"

"A little. That air thing . . . that was a good idea."

"Uh-huh." He turned to face her.

She could not ignore her friend, so she met his gaze.

"So what was that back there? Picturing Deacon in front of you?" Vail narrowed her eyes. "Damn. Was it that obvious?"

He shrugged. "It got a little intense, you know? This is an exercise. And you beat up that dude pretty good. Probably broke his nose. Burst a testicle. Or two."

Vail looked back at the building. "Seriously?"

"A guy wouldn't joke about that."

"Well, shit. I didn't realize." She looked back at him. "Really?"

"Really."

"Maybe I should go apolog—"

"Let it go. For now." He placed a hand on her shoulder. "Should I be concerned?"

Vail rubbed at her forehead with her black tactical glove. "I'm good. I'm fine. I've *been* fine. But I do think you're right. Still." She shook her head. "It's been years since Deacon . . ."

"The trauma never really goes away. Like PTSD, it can trigger."

Vail nodded. *Like PTSD. Deacon's abuse probably* did *cause PTSD.* She never looked at it that way, but shame on her. She should have. "Probably hasn't been an issue because Robby couldn't be a better partner. I thought I put Deacon, that part of my life, behind me."

"Hey, you're the one who studies the mind, not me. But do we ever really leave our past in the past?"

Too early in the morning for something that profound.

He gave her a tap on the shoulder. "That was rhetorical, Karen. Get your head straight, get your shit together, and get that helmet back on.

We're just getting started. Southern Strike's next. Lots more exercises planned for the weekend."

"Awesome." Vail took another deep breath, then seated her helmet and turned to face the building. *Can't wait.*

2

29th & N STREETS NW
WASHINGTON, DC

Aaron Uziel lay in bed panting heavily. "What got into you?"

Dena took a deep breath. "You did. Quite deep, I might add."

Uzi looked up at the ceiling and laughed as hard as his oxygen-starved lungs could manage. "Yes . . . I did."

"I was worried Maya was going to wake up and come in."

"I think you got past it," Uzi said.

Dena giggled.

Uzi reached out and curled her hair around her ear as he rolled onto his right side to face her. Then—

Uzi winced. Sirens rang out. The air was dank, his throat full of bile. Police.

Fire. Ambulance. His small apartment was strewn with debris.

Stout body, in silhouette. Its back to him: Gideon Aksel.

Intense fear exploded through Uzi's torso like a jolt of electricity. "Dena!"

He yelled his wife's name as he staggered down the hallway, his legs heavy, as if stuck in knee-deep mud.

"Maya?"

Add it up, Uzi!

Police. Fire. Ambulance. Mossad Director General Gideon Aksel.

His brain couldn't put it together, his vision mentally fogged.

DIE TRYING

He reached the bedroom. Darkness. In the sparse moonlight, two bodies. Dena?

Maya?

Throats slashed.

Blood everywhere. In the bed, covering their faces.

"No!"

"Uzi. Uzi. Wake up!"

He sat up, arms thrashing. Yelling. *Shaking.*

Someone was shaking him.

"Uzi, you're dreaming again. Listen to me."

Eyes open. Heart bashing against his sternum.

I'm home. DC. No Dena. No Maya.

Emma, his girlfriend, stroked his cheek and brought his moist face against her breast. "Are you okay?"

He cleared his dry throat. "Yeah. I, uh, I need a moment."

"You want me to tell Hector and Maggie we can't make it?"

He took a deep, uneven breath, closed his eyes. "I want you to meet them. We'll go." He sat up and pushed off the bed. Felt a little dizzy. "Gonna take a quick shower and throw on come clothes."

Uzi used the five minutes alone to clear his mind, flushing the nightmare from his thoughts, sending it down the drain along with the shampoo suds.

They left his townhouse five minutes late but arrived at the DeSantos's Adams Morgan place on time.

Uzi introduced Emma to Hector and Maggie and vice versa, then handed DeSantos the bottle of Valley of the Moon cabernet sauvignon he had procured a couple of years ago.

"This is that bottle we were supposed to drink after the whole Moon thing, right?"

Uzi grinned. "It is."

"Moon thing?" Emma asked as she helped Maggie set out the cheese plate and crackers.

"Inside joke," DeSantos said, giving Uzi a wink. He leaned back. "You okay?"

"I'm . . . yeah. I'm good. Nightmare." He sighed deeply. "They'd gone away, but I've had a few the past couple of months."

DeSantos lowered his voice. "Guilt over your relationship with Emma?"

"Let's not psychoanalyze." Uzi waved a hand. "How was your training weekend with Karen?"

DeSantos laughed as he cut the foil seal on the wine bottle. "Well." He snorted.

"That good, eh?"

He pulled the cork and set down the cabernet to breathe. "Started off a little rough, but we had nowhere to go but *up* from there." DeSantos held up the wine. "Kind of like a rocket."

"Ah," Uzi said, nodding slowly. "Moon. Rocket. I see what you did there."

"Well, I don't see," Emma said, coming behind them. "Want to share that inside joke?"

Uzi and DeSantos looked at each other and laughed out loud.

"Not really," DeSantos said. "No!"

Emma was a well-proportioned brunette with a law degree from Hastings in San Francisco and a job in one of the legal departments at the Department of Defense. Five years younger than Uzi, she had been dating him for four months. Her introduction to DeSantos was long overdue.

As they ate dinner, Emma and DeSantos got along well, trading barbs about the military—a favorite topic of his given his own career as well as that of his father, a retired and highly decorated four-star general.

While Emma and DeSantos went at it, Maggie flirted with Uzi, as she often did. The DeSantos marriage was one not rooted in tradition—or exclusivity—by design. It made Uzi uncomfortable, but he had learned over the years to accept it and make sure nothing came of Maggie's overt advances. The last thing the best friends needed was to share a woman.

Maggie invited Emma to join her in the kitchen to put the final touches on an apple crisp Maggie had baked an hour earlier. As they both cleared the dining room, DeSantos leaned in.

"I like her. Seems serious."

DIE TRYING 13

Still bothered by his dream, Uzi shrugged. "Yeah?"

"Yeah. Is it?"

"Yeah."

"Good. I think." DeSantos eyed him, clearly sensing something was up.

"How do *you* feel about it?"

Uzi had lost Dena and Maya—his wife and daughter—thirteen years earlier in what was coldly described in the Mossad field reports as "collateral damage" related to Uzi's prior work as a covert operative for the intelligence agency. As he later learned, there was a lot more to it. Regardless, Uzi had an extraordinarily difficult time getting past their deaths. He went through therapy, which helped, though it ended disastrously and resulted in more pain and suffering.

Uzi had been through what DeSantos once described as "the ringer," a hackneyed expression, the origins of which involved physical torture. But Uzi's hurt was emotional. It affected him deeply and led to many sleepless nights and stress lines carved into his face. Physical manifestations, yes, but as he reminded DeSantos, at least he was alive. A tortured soul, yes, but here he was, having made it through the seemingly unending tunnel of grief and misery and finally, finally emerging on the other side.

His wife and daughter would forever be in his memories, but his therapist, Dr. Len Rudnick, told him he had a right to be happy. It took a while for that concept to get through his dense skull, but he had come around to understanding what Rudnick meant.

After all, he had a lot of life left, and he had better start living it.

That particular morsel of wisdom had been imparted to him by another emotionally tortured mind-bending student of the human psyche, FBI behavioral analyst Karen Vail.

"Yo," DeSantos said, "Alpha Male One to Alpha Male Two. How do you feel about that?"

"Huh?" Uzi looked up and realized he had been lost in thought. "I, uh, I'm good. Yeah, I'm finally good with it."

DeSantos studied his face a moment, his mouth contorting, his eyes squinting and traversing Uzi's. After a moment, he nodded. "Okay then. I'm happy for you. You two look good together."

14 ALAN JACOBSON

"I know. I haven't felt this way since, well, since Layla."

"Now that was a disaster."

"But before *that*, last time a relationship felt this right was with Dena. And that ended bad, but not because of us. We had a great marriage."

"Whoa." DeSantos scooted his chair back, the wood legs scraping against the polished concrete floor. "Marriage? You uttered the word marriage."

Uzi's face shaded red. "I did, but I didn't mean th—"

"Freudian slip?"

"I was talking about Dena."

DeSantos chuckled. "Giving you shit. I'm happy for you, boychick," he said, using his usual Yiddish term of endearment for Uzi. "You deserve it. And I like Emma. A lot. But what is it with you and finding beautiful women—intellectually and physically?"

"Is there a law against that?"

"If there was, we'd ignore it!"

Uzi and DeSantos laughed and gave each other a high five.

"What trouble are you boys planning?"

The voice came from behind them. Maggie wrapped her arms around DeSantos's neck.

"Trouble," he said. "Yep. That's what we do best, isn't it?"

Maggie and Emma took their seats.

"Unfortunately," Uzi said with a glance at DeSantos. "Yes."

The following morning, Uzi walked into the Washington field office, took the elevator to the fourth floor, and waved to his newly promoted special agent in charge, Marshall Shepard. As he approached the cubicle of Special Agent Hoshi Ko, she handed him a manila envelope stamped TOP SECRET.

"We ready to start?" Uzi asked. "Everyone's here, waiting for you."

"I'm early."

"They're earlier."

"Damn overachievers," Uzi mumbled as he walked down the hall and entered the room where the Joint Terrorism Task Force worked.

"Morning everyone," he said, wandering into the room with his eyes on the folder he was pulling from the packet Hoshi had handed him.

A wave of applause rippled across the large, open room. Uzi lifted his gaze and jutted his chin back in surprise, then realized why they were clapping.

Uzi raised a hand and nodded. "Okay, okay." He was sure they were mocking him. He moved to the seat at the head of the conference table and tossed the folder on the polished cherry wood surface. "I appreciate the reception, even if some of you were razzing me. But let's get started. Full agenda."

The Joint Terrorism Task Force, or JTTF, was a presence in all fifty-six field offices across the FBI. Situated in the heart of Washington, DC—the target of both international and domestic terrorists—this squad carried additional importance and responsibility. WFO, as the Washington field office was known, was the second-largest division in the country, behind only that of New York City.

The JTTF was composed of representatives across federal, state, and local law enforcement agencies. As suggested by the name, it focused on investigating terrorism and terrorism-related activities. It also collected and shared intelligence and responded to threats and incidents at the ring of a phone. In short, its job was to efficiently coordinate information and act to prevent attacks on US soil.

In addition to meaningful but lower-profile members like the IRS, Metro PD, Federal Air Marshals, US Park Police, Federal Protective Service, all the expected "alphabet agencies" were represented. The CIA's seat was taken by Mahmoud el-Fahad, a rare Palestinian serving in a federal law enforcement agency. Affectionately known among his colleagues as "Mo," he sat near the near end of the conference table, to Uzi's right.

"Mo," Uzi said, "You're batting leadoff."

"Right." Mo tapped the laptop remote and the PowerPoint began. A photo of a partially masked man splashed across the screen. "The pandemic was a boon for bad actors around the world. They were all too compliant with masking, which made it tougher for us to track these knuckleheads. We had to rely less on facial rec and more on GPS tracking of known associates and HUMINT," he said, referring to human intelligence. "The Agency's using artificial intelligence to work on new facial rec algos that are more eye centric and they're making good progress. But in the meantime, we've got some gaps in our knowledge base, so we've had to fill it in using other methods, like natural intelligence."

"Come again?" a deputy US marshal said. "What the hell's natural intelligence?"

"Obviously," Uzi said, "a bad joke. Opposite of artificial intelligence. Natural intelligence." He smirked and shook his head. "Continue, Mo."

"Sorry. Just found out my wife's pregnant. Practicing my dad jokes." A round of congrats spread across the table.

"Awesome news," Uzi said, shaking Mo's hand. "Not to spoil the mood, but let's get back to the bad guys. Do we have any info worth sharing?"

"We do," Mo said, swiping to a new slide. "Al-Sharif's network has expanded exponentially since we handled the bombing in Algeria. The Agency now has information that strongly suggests Sharif has succeeded in setting up a few cells here in the US."

Uzi leaned forward. "How many operatives? How many cells? Do we know where—at least the states where they've set up shop?"

"Unfortunately," Fahad said, "we don't have any of those answers. I'm waiting to hear back from a CI who's—" His vibrating phone clattered and danced across the slickly polished tabletop. Fahad glanced at the screen as it lit up, then pressed the side button to silence the call.

"This informant is supposedly on the verge of getting the location of one of the cells. I'm not expecting an exact address, but I *am* hopeful that we'll at least—" His handset buzzed again. Fahad gathered it up and checked the number. "Sorry. This could be the intel we've been waiting for."

"Take it," Uzi said. "We'll loop back to you when you're done."

Fahad left the room and Uzi handed off the meeting to an agent with the Drug Enforcement Administration.

Two minutes had passed when Fahad reentered the room. But instead of returning to his seat, he leaned beside Uzi's ear.

"We need to talk. Now."

"Now?" Uzi glanced at the participants. "We've got an aggressive agenda," he said under his breath, "and I don't want to lose—"

"Now." Fahad nodded. "Trust me."

Uzi threw up his hands. "Okay." He stole a look at his Omega Moon watch, made famous by Buzz Aldrin on Apollo 11, an unexpected personal gift he and DeSantos received from Director Knox after their recent classified lunar mission. "Let's take our break a little early. Be back here in ten."

Uzi rolled his chair back, unfolded his six-foot-two frame, and nodded at Hoshi Ko, his right-hand JTTF agent. "Nudge me when it's time."

"Sure thing."

Uzi huddled with Mo in the corner of the board room. "What's up?"

"It's about your wife and daughter."

Uzi narrowed his eyes. "What are you talking about? You know what happened to—"

"That's what makes this so difficult for me."

Uzi shifted his weight onto his right leg. "Mo. What are you not saying?"

Fahad glanced over his shoulder, then back at Uzi. "I should not be telling you this."

Uzi squinted. "Telling me what?"

"That call. I thought it was about Sharif, but my CI had other intel. He said he heard about an unconfirmed sighting."

"Okay," Uzi said, leaning toward Fahad, who was a few inches shorter.

"Sighting of what? Who?"

"Dena Uziel. With a younger woman."

Uzi stood there, unflinching, waiting for the punchline. It'd be a sick joke, but judging by Mo's face, this was not another attempt at bad dad humor. He locked his eyes with Fahad's.

"I trust this source. And no, I obviously haven't verified. I thought about waiting to tell you—"

"Mo, this is bullshit. Someone is using you to get to me. To hurt me." He cleared his throat. "My wife and daughter were murdered in a terror attack on my apartment. I saw the—the crime scene. I—" His voice caught.

"I know the case," Fahad said. "It's—it's my job to be informed. Especially in matters like this." He waited but Uzi had gone silent, lost in thought. Finally, he said, "How sure are you?"

Uzi's gaze found Fahad's eyes. "Huh? How sure am I about what?"

"That the people murdered were Dena and Maya."

Uzi looked around the room. He was in a secure area, among colleagues—most of whom he had known for a reasonable amount of time. Some were friends. A lot of whom he trusted with his life. But it still did not feel right discussing this out in the open.

Uzi found Hoshi and touched her right elbow. "Something's come up. I'll be back soon. Resume on time. Proceed with the agenda. Brief me later on what I missed."

"Got it."

Uzi headed for the door and pushed through it into the corridor, Fahad by his side. They entered an empty conference room, activating the automatic lights.

Uzi squared his shoulders. "Crime scene was a mess. Windows blown out. Police. Fire. Bomb squad. Or—" He closed his eyes. "No, they came later. Mossad execs on-site. My friend was outside. I ran upstairs to the bedroom . . . it was dark. My wife and daughter . . . in bed." He swallowed hard. "Necks slashed. Blood. A lot."

"So there was a positive ID?"

Uzi looked at the large window and squinted, his gaze *somewhere* and nowhere. His mind's eye was in his old apartment, replaying the painful visual of his wife and daughter lying there in blood-soaked bedsheets. But was it them?

"Uzi—positive ID?"

"No. I don't know. Don't remember. I've got a block." Uzi shook his head, canted his gaze to the ceiling. "I freaked out. Ran up the stairs. Dread. Adrenaline. Anxiety. Grief? I don't know. Hard to breathe . . ." He rubbed his chin with thumb and index finger. His skin was slick. "Two bodies." He cleared his throat. "So much blood."

Fahad placed a hand on Uzi's back. "Sounds like you had a horrible—unthinkable—experience." He waited a moment. Quietly: "Did you see their faces?"

DIE TRYING 19

Uzi pried his attention back to the present. "I—yeah, of course. No." He rubbed his temples. "I'm not sure. I didn't go into the room."

"Could you swear that it was them?"

Uzi opened his mouth to answer. But nothing emerged.

"You had no reason to question that it was them," Fahad said.

Uzi's voice was barely above a whisper. "The power of suggestion?"

Fahad bobbed his head. "And grief, sorrow, adrenaline, disbelief. Very powerful emotions."

Uzi sat down uneasily.

"I'm just trying to assess what we truly know versus what we *think* we know."

"Gideon Aksel, he was there."

"Mossad director general." Fahad nodded. "Who else was there?"

Uzi's gaze rose again to the ceiling. "My friend. Nuri Peled. Outside the building. He said he was sorry. That freaked me out."

"Did Peled know your wife and daughter?"

Uzi nodded.

Fahad spread his arms. "Call him. Ask him if he saw their faces."

"He's dead." A moment passed. "This can't be. It can't be. It's been so many years. Your CI. Where—where were my wife and daughter spotted? I mean, where were they *supposedly* spotted?"

"All I know is he heard that there was a woman who matches your wife's description with a younger female."

Uzi turned to Fahad. "He can be wrong, right? He can be jerking me around. He can be—this could be a malicious rumor intended to hurt me. I've put so many ass wipes away, this could be revenge."

"All possible. Which is why I wasn't sure if I should tell you."

"I'm glad you did." He rose from the chair and craned his neck ceilingward. "I think."

"I'll treat this like any case I've got, see if I can gather more HUMINT."

"Appreciate that, Mo."

"I'm going back to the meeting. Why don't you go home?"

"No. I'll be right in."

"You sure?"

"Hell no. Can't say I'm sure of *anything* anymore."

Fahad gave Uzi a pat on the right shoulder and left him alone in the room.

Uzi stood there thinking of Dena and Maya. Questions about their murders filled his thoughts, things he had accepted at the time.

He started pacing the room. He had to know if this "intel" was bullshit. Or if there was even a morsel of truth to the shocking revelation that the two most important people in his life were still alive.

Uzi stopped, closed his eyes, and took a deep breath. He needed answers.

3

The afternoon passed quickly. Case after case was discussed, occupying Uzi's thoughts and forcing him to keep his mind on work—vitally important because of a sweeping dual-track Middle East normalization plan that was opposed by as many radical groups as it was supported by regional governments.

The first track consisted of a plethora of individual treaties designed to establish diplomatic and economic ties between the Middle Eastern Arab countries and Israel. In a perfect world, these accords—termed the Abraham Treaties—would pave the way for track two: lasting peace between Israel and the Palestinians.

But President Vance Nunn was an America First politician. Coined in the 1850s, "America First" was used by politicians for different purposes, from Woodrow Wilson's attempt to project neutrality in World War I to the Ku Klux Klan's white supremacist, anti-Semitic, and fascist rhetoric of the 1920s.

Publicly, President Nunn's purpose in adopting an America First policy was for the United States to become insular, to deemphasize US involvement in world politics.

Leaving NATO was his most controversial move, followed by declining to counter Russian aggression. NSA-intercepted intel captured President Yaroslav Pervak discussing a second act to his invasion of Ukraine: a similar attack on one or more NATO members, possibly Bulgaria, the Czech Republic, Estonia, Latvia,

22   ALAN JACOBSON

Lithuania, Poland, Romania, or Slovakia—as well as non-member Moldova.

On the campaign trail, Nunn touted his decision to divert US taxpayer dollars from endless wars toward domestic infrastructure improvements.

With America looking inward, the UK took ownership of the Abraham Treaties. The British were brokering the talks and setting the guidelines.

But with terrorists looking to blow up negotiations, sometimes literally, the United States provided the bigger bang for the buck; for the groups looking to destabilize the Middle East, there would be enormous benefit to drawing the sleeping giant into a conflict, derailing the peace process.

That put the spotlight on Uzi's JTTF and gave them threat analysis overload.

Now alone with his thoughts, sitting in the FBI parking garage beneath the large field division building, Uzi thought the most direct path to get answers regarding his wife and daughter was to go to the source. That meant filing a request to exhume Dena's body, which was buried in a cemetery in Jerusalem.

But the shortest path to the information did not equate to being the easiest. It was fraught with obstacles, a big one being religious law. More culturally than religiously observant, Uzi had holes in his knowledge of Jewish ritual. However, he was fairly certain that disinterring a body was highly restricted. If he recalled correctly, one of the only reasons for disturbing a body was to move it to a family plot or to move it to Israel if it had initially been laid to rest elsewhere. He was doing neither, so he could be facing a fight.

Uzi gripped the steering wheel. It was past quitting time but he did not want to go home. Emma was supposed to be staying the night and he did not want to get into this with her. How awkward would that be? And what if it all turned out to be bogus? He could cause irreparable damage to their relationship . . . all for nothing. Perhaps that was the purpose behind this BS. Someone did not want him getting serious with Emma?

No. Not likely. *Think clearly, Uzi.*

But he could not just stay out all night. He had to go home. He just would not share the information with her—until there was certainty.

But what if they *are* alive? What then?

Uzi rubbed his temples. He could not think that far. One thing at a time. Verify or exclude. That was his priority. Then he would deal with whatever else came his way.

Israel was seven hours ahead of DC, so it was the middle of the night. There was nothing he could do for another six hours when the municipal agencies would be opening.

Religious restrictions aside, disinterring his wife's already violated body brought a guilt all its own. He had not visited her grave in years. On one hand, that was understandable—he lived six thousand miles away. But he had been to Israel a few years ago on an OPSIG mission. He could have gone then. He was there, in Jerusalem. Not that far away. And yet it was too painful.

No. It was fear, fear of pain—not the pain itself. He was afraid of reopening the old wounds and what kind of funk that would put him in—and for how long.

He walked into the anteroom of his immediate superior, special agent in charge of the counterterrorism division, Marshall Shepard. "I need a few minutes with the SAC," Uzi told the support personnel.

"I'll see if he's available," a young man said, lifting the phone and pressing a button. A moment later he said, "Head on back."

Uzi walked in and saw his friend and boss rocking in his leather office chair.

"When'd you get the new seat?"

"Yesterday." He ran a hand over the soft surface. "It's the best. Top grain leather."

"Isn't *full* grain better?"

Shepard's lips twisted in frustration. "You have a reason for coming in here? You must have a reason. Knowing you, it's not a reason I want to hear."

"For once, Shep, I think you're right."

"Only once?"

"True. That's an understatement. I mean, even a broken clock is right twice a day."

24 ALAN JACOBSON

Shepard frowned. "What do you want?"

"What if I told you I got some intel today that my wife and daughter might be alive?"

Shepard snorted. "I'd say someone's yanking your chain. *Definitely* yanking your chain."

Uzi sat there, quiet, and pulled a wood toothpick from his pocket. He poked it through the plastic wrapper and stuck it in his mouth.

"Yeah."

Shepard studied his face. "You're serious. Someone told you that?"

"Yes."

"How do you know it's not a ruse? To get you to start looking for them. In Israel, or worse, in the territories."

"And why would somebody do that?"

"I think we both know about your previous work. Before you returned to the US."

Uzi nodded slowly. He could not deny Shepard's point: former intelligence and counterterrorism agents were targets. Uzi had been both, and more: a government-sanctioned assassin. But it was worth the risk. He would deal with anything that came his way.

"Who told you this?"

"Another federal agent who has ties to—and sources in—the Middle East."

Shepard leaned back and the chair creaked. New or not, Shepard was football player large and springs had their limits.

Uzi read his boss's face. "I know, the source is what bothers me, too. But my guy's credible. And a credible source has credible CIs. Because he or she won't tolerate any BS. You fuck with us, we cut you loose. You aren't our CI anymore."

Shepard nodded slowly. He had gone from disbelief to considering how it might be possible.

Uzi was pushing the toothpick left to right in his mouth using his tongue. "I mean, I don't know what to think. What do I do with this info? It's set my mind on edge. I'm . . . shit, *uneasy* doesn't begin to explain it. If there's a sliver of hope—"

"I hear you. Not sure what I'd do if I were in your situation."

"I'm going to talk to a judge tonight—I mean tomorrow morning,

Israel time—see if I can get Dena's body exhumed. That seems to be the quickest way to an answer."

Shepard raised his brow. "Good. Good. I think that's a good approach. I mean, if she's there, you can go on with your life and forget that this crossed your desk."

"The exhumation—not easy in the least—*is* the easy part." Uzi stopped playing with the toothpick and locked gazes with his boss. "But what if her body isn't there?"

"Then, my friend, then we have lots to think about. Their deaths were a major terrorism case in Israel and had ripples in US–Middle East policy at the time. Threw a major wrench into peace prospects. But what are we doing here? We've got no answers and lots of questions. And some what-ifs and maybes thrown in. *Lots* of what-ifs and maybes. You need to push it all aside. Go on with your life and work the case on the side. Something comes up, pursue it. But don't let your thoughts go wild with what-ifs. It'll drive you crazy. Don't give any credence to that supposed intel until verified."

Uzi knew Shepard was right. Everything he said was correct.

And yet none of it mattered. Because Uzi was not a robot without feelings. He had just learned his beloved wife and daughter could be alive. It could be bullshit. But how could he ignore that and go about his day-to-day life with that thought banging around inside his skull?

How does one compartmentalize that information and merely ignore it until—or *if*—it becomes relevant? How does one get relevant intel six thousand miles away?

"Uzi," Shepard said. He looked up. "What?"

"I've known you a long time. This is going to eat at you until you get some answers."

Uzi turned away, staring at the wall.

"You want to go. To Israel."

He swung his gaze back. "I . . . I don't know. Yes. No. I mean, how can I n*ot* go?"

"As your friend, I understand. As your boss—"

"How 'bout we stop there?"

Shepard frowned. "I'd like to, but I can't. Because I have a boss, too. Lots of 'em. And if the assistant director gets wind of the fact that you want to take personal time off after getting a big promotion, that won't sit well. And you don't need any enemies. Well, any more enemies. You may have some credit with the director, but Knox's not going to be around a whole lot longer."

"It's personal time. No one can tell me I can't take it."

Shepard got up from his chair. "Oh man. You gave me reflux, you know that? I have to take this Pepcid stuff. All because of you. You trying to give me an ulcer, too?"

"What am I supposed to do, Shep?"

Shepard groaned loudly. Slapped the desk. "Yes, you can take time—no one can officially tell you not to. But shit happens unofficially, right? We got a full workload, JTTF's plate is full with some very sensitive cases. Very sensitive cases. And this is freaking DC. Lots of prime targets. I don't have to tell you this."

"And my guys are good. Most committed men and women in the country."

Shepard shook his head. "A week. Be back in a week. I can cover for you for that long. Longer than that, Byrd is gonna get red in the face."

"Thanks, Shep."

"Hey, I'm retiring next year. What's the worst they can do to me?" Uzi shrugged. "Take your pension?"

Shepard frowned. "Get out of here, man. Make sure Hoshi is up to speed on that sheik's case. And let her in on what you're doing so she can pick up some of the slack on your active cases."

"Thanks, Shep."

"Hey, this isn't a gift. It's just me being a good boss to one of his best agents. Having you working at two-thirds efficiency is as good as most working at a hundred percent."

"You really mean that?"

"Hell no," Shepard said. "But it sounded good, didn't it?"

Uzi got up from the seat and gave his friend—and boss—a fist bump. "You know it's true," he said as he headed for the door.

"I do," Shepard called after him. "I just don't like to admit it."

4

At 1:00 a.m. EST, Uzi dialed a judge he knew in Jerusalem. It had been a while since they had spoken but there was no question he would remember Uzi. The old fart had been Uzi's next-door neighbor while growing up.

Justice Herbert Steinmetz squinted at the camera. "Do my eyes deceive me?"

Uzi turned on another light to expose his face better. Staring back at him was a man in his early eighties, Einstein-messy white hair sticking up in every direction. "Uncle Herb, how are you?"

Steinmetz was not Uzi's uncle by blood—more by closeness of relationship. His mom had told him to call him Uncle Herb when Uzi was a young boy—and it stuck.

"Eh. You know how it is. You get old, everything hurts. The hearing gets a little worse. You gotta pee more often. People start whispering behind your back that it's time to retire already."

"And? Is it time to retire?"

"This you joke about? What would I do with my life?"

"You could tend to that garden of yours."

"Plenty of time to do that on my days off. So what's bothering you?"

"You know I work for the FBI. Joint Terrorism Task Force. One of my colleagues got some intel that Dena and Maya could be alive."

28   ALAN JACOBSON

Steinmetz's jowly expression was serious—and then he burst out laughing. Loud chortling. "How'd you know I had a shitty day yesterday and needed a good joke to warm my kishkes?"

"Uncle Herb . . . I'm serious."

Steinmetz's face went immediately slack. "You *are* serious."

"Believe me, I wouldn't joke about that."

"I guess not. Forgive me."

Uzi explained what he knew—and what he did not.

Steinmetz nodded, then steepled his fingers together in front of his chin. "Well, Uzi, as you know, exhumation is not something we take lightly. Jewish law—"

"I know. I understand. But I figured that if you have doubts about whether or not someone's dead, the easiest and most direct way of verifying such information is to look at the body buried under the marker."

"Very logical. And very clinical, Uzi. But we have to check with the family. Her parents may not see it like you do."

"How so?"

"From what I remember, Dena's family was a lot more religious than yours was. Modern Orthodox, yes?"

"Yes."

"Well . . ." He spread his hands, as if that was all he needed to say.

Uzi set the phone down on his end table and angled it to face him. "I realize religious law dictates that we don't disinter a body unless there are very specific circumstances. And my reason doesn't meet any of them. But Israel doesn't operate its legal system according to religious laws. It's a democracy. Rule of law, not *religious* law."

"I'm a judge, Uzi. Excuse the pun, but you're preaching to the choir."

"Right. So religious law is not the governing principle here. The law of a government for the people is."

"You should let the judges do the judging, no? Otherwise they may get rid of all of us. Superfluous."

Uzi bobbed his head.

"As a judge, I use laws as guidance. But few legal matters are as black and white as the text printed on a page. There's nuance in just about every case. I prefer to look at all sides of an issue, particularly one that embodies emotion, family, pain, and loss. More broadly, the risk versus benefit equation bolstered by the facts of that specific case."

"Makes sense. But what are—"

"You've got no proof whatsoever that Dena is alive. In fact, you've really got nothing to bolster your need to disinter except one person's word who claims to have seen her. Or claims to know someone who's seen her? And based on this, you want to violate her family's religious beliefs and dig up their daughter's body?"

"I'm sure there has to be some case law that—"

"There is. *Rubenstein versus Selberg.* The Supreme Court denied the parents' motion to open the grave of their son, a soldier who died in battle. The court based its decision on the fact that the parents and the army couldn't show the court any sufficient or clear evidence that the wrong person was buried there. Sound familiar?"

"*Too* familiar."

"The court ruled that in order to issue a judicial order that allows opening a grave and disinterring a body, two major issues have to be considered: is it possible to take a DNA sample from the corpse to complete a genetic test; and the effect on other buried people in the cemetery, in adjacent or nearby plots—as well as what the families of the deceased think of such action."

Uzi sighed.

"The court also considers the amount of time that's passed since the body was buried. And—are Dena and Maya buried together?"

A pang of pain stabbed Uzi in the gut. "Yes."

"That makes it even more difficult. When you've got a husband and wife buried together, a mother and son or daughter . . ." He shook his head. "It's even more difficult to get the court to order the grave to be opened."

"This is not the answer I was expecting, Uncle Herb. Or hoping for."

"I know this is difficult for you—and I hope to God this informant isn't just blowing smoke. But understand it's not as simple as FaceTiming your longtime friend and getting a signature on a legal document."

"I was hoping."

"Don't hope. Get some facts. Build a case for disturbing her body. Bring me something compelling. Okay?"

"That's what I was trying to do by exhuming her body."

"Uzi—"

"I get it, I get it. I'll see what I can dig up."

"Not funny."

"Believe me," Uzi said with a sigh, "no one knows that better than me."

5

Uzi phoned Hector DeSantos, but the call went straight to voice-mail. He messaged him via WhatsApp and asked if he was in town.

A moment later, DeSantos responded affirmatively, to which Uzi replied:

Something's up and I need to run it by you

DeSantos wrote back:

Wrapping up a training exercise in shooting house then I'm free

Uzi told him to meet at the reflecting pool in front of the Lincoln Memorial.

Forty-five minutes later, Uzi was standing in Lincoln's shadow, allowing his thoughts to take him back to the country's earlier years, of a great man who did great things. Of a man whose life ended far too early. Just like his own wife and daughter.

If that were, in fact, true.

"Boychick."

Uzi turned to see DeSantos approaching. "You said by the reflecting pool."

"Sorry. Greatest president we ever had. Had to pay his statue a visit."

"Everything okay?"

Once DeSantos reached him, Uzi explained what Mo's informant told him.

DeSantos laughed. "And? What do you intend to do with this sketchy intel?"

They started walking along the east side, Uzi wondering if that was a trick question. He turned to him and shrugged. "I need to check it out."

"Kind of out of the blue, you know?"

"Mo said this guy's intel has been good. He's been his CI for years." DeSantos chewed on that a moment. "Let's go with it for a minute. Why'd he think Mo would be interested in this info?"

"Maybe he knows that Mo works for the federal government and that I'm with the FBI and that Mo could reach out to me."

"Very altruistic. But why would this CI care?" Uzi nodded slowly. "Good question."

"I try not to ask the bad ones."

Uzi looked down at the aggregate walkway as they continued alongside the reflecting pool. "Maybe he passes along anything he comes across, in case it's of use."

"Still. Not buying it. *Maybe* he wants to jerk your chain. Or whoever started the rumor wants to cause you pain."

Uzi thought a moment. DeSantos could be right. Probably was. "So you'd ignore it?"

DeSantos stopped walking and turned to face the water. After a minute of gazing at the gentle ripples on the pool, he cleared his throat. "No. I'd have to check it out. Or it'd drive me crazy."

"That's where I'm at."

"Let's go talk with Knox."

He turned to face Uzi, who nodded.

DeSantos cleared an appointment with the FBI director's new assistant. Fortunately, Douglas Knox was returning from a meeting at the White House and had fifteen minutes free before his next appointment.

They headed over to FBI headquarters, the iconic, though aging, Hoover building. The Bureau had spent years examining a move to another location and constructing a modern complex. But like anything in government, there was red tape, endless complications, and political considerations. Decisions were made and then frozen by bureaucracy and/or politics.

After clearing security, Uzi and DeSantos made their way up to Mahogany Row on the seventh floor, preferring to take the stairs for the exercise.

His newly assigned assistant informed Knox they had arrived, then sent them back.

Knox was standing at his desk talking with another agent. "Make sure the president gets that." He looked over and nodded at DeSantos, then turned to Uzi.

"You two wanted to see me?"

"Yes, sir," Uzi said.

"I've got . . ." He twisted his wrist and checked his watch. "Twelve minutes." It was a Cartier Tank, from what Uzi could tell. After being fitted with a Speedmaster Moonwatch for their last mission, Uzi started familiarizing himself with some of the well-known Swiss brands.

He recounted what he knew of the situation with Dena and Maya—which was not much.

Knox turned to face his window onto Pennsylvania Avenue. "Agent Uziel, this is hard to accept, let alone believe." He slipped his hands in his pants pockets. "From what I recall, the classified report said you saw their bodies."

Uzi stood there, his eyes canting to the right and toward the ceiling. "I saw . . . I saw *bodies*. Yeah. A woman and girl. They were in my apartment. My bed." He clenched his eyes. "It was dark, I was . . . I was in shock. It was our bed, a lot of blood . . ." His voice trailed off. "Did I actually see their faces?" He thought a moment. "I *thought* they were Dena and Maya. My mind shut down. I'd lost my wife and little girl. I wished I'd died along with them." He opened his eyes and swallowed hard.

Knox, remaining impassive and keeping his back to them, said, "According to your reports, Batula Hakim said she did it, that she was the one who murdered them. And from what I was told by directors Tasset and Aksel, that was the case."

Uzi felt a lump in his throat. He tried to clear it, but this was not a physical obstruction. "Yeah, Hakim took credit all right. An in-my-face admission, retribution for her brother. She blamed me for his death. But was she saying that because she really did it?"

"Or," DeSantos said, "because Hakim was trying to cause Uzi intense pain? He did, after all, fall for her and—" DeSantos stopped himself, no doubt concerned about overdoing it and sprinkling rock salt in his friend's emotional wound.

Uzi rubbed at the creases in his forehead, as if trying to iron them away. "Doesn't matter what her reasons were. And yeah, this new intel could all be bullshit. They could be dead like I've thought all these years. But I need to find out. I can't live like this. Wondering."

Knox turned around. "If whoever is behind this wants to cause you pain by dredging this up again, creating false hope, only to lead nowhere, they'll have accomplished their goal."

"Yes. But doing nothing and *not knowing* would be just as bad. Worse." Knox nodded. "Let's say they're still alive. Where are they?"

"I've got nothing to go on. I've got to . . . investigate."

"I can't assign any personnel. I can't give you any resources. Even though you're one of ours, this is a private matter. *If* they're alive—and that's a huge if—they could be anywhere in the world. Maybe Mossad's director general would be willing to divert some people."

Uzi almost laughed. Even though Gideon Aksel had a hand in the whole affair that led to Dena's and Maya's murder—if that's what it was—he could not see Aksel devoting any time or manpower to this.

"OPSIG is black," DeSantos said. "Our budget, our reports, everything's classified."

Knox glanced at his watch—a casual move, not one to send a message—and sat down hard in his seat, placing both forearms on the desk. "I realize the weight of this intel. And I'm well aware of OPISG's budget. I created the damn group and Secretary MacNamara and I discuss our allocation every year. But this . . . this is a personal matter. We still have a budget we've got to adhere to and manage. It's not a bottomless pit."

"Can I at least get some OPSIG or CIA support?"

"The Agency won't go near this. The Abraham Treaties. They won't do anything that'll even remotely have a chance of disrupting the negotiations."

"Why do you think that's even an issue?" DeSantos asked.

"Because people think everything that happens in the Mideast revolves around peace between Israel and the Arab nations. As you well know, that's not true, but the facts don't always matter.

"And no one wants to be responsible for doing or saying something that tanks the negotiations. I'm sure director Tasset isn't going to do anything that could come back to kick him in the ass."

Uzi and DeSantos shared a disappointed look.

"But sir," DeSantos said, "if we just—"

"I'll do what I can," Knox said, holding up a hand. "I'll make a call. See what Tasset's thoughts are on this."

Uzi ground his molars. "Thank you, sir. Appreciate whatever you can do.

Whatever you can give me."

"Us," DeSantos said. "Whatever you can give us."

Knox locked gazes with DeSantos, then tightened his lips and nodded imperceptibly. "Fine."

They stood by DeSantos's sedan, having withheld their thoughts until they were outside everyone's earshot.

DeSantos leaned back against the fender. "Went about as good as could be expected."

"Regardless of how nice Knox asks, Tasset isn't going to help us, is he?"

"Nope."

Uzi pursed his lips and nodded slowly.

"Boychick. Don't take this the wrong way, but how would you feel about dropping it? Forgetting that Mo ever said anything to you."

"How could I do that?"

"Right," DeSantos said, holding up both hands. "I get that. But where would you start? How much time are you prepared to devote to this—we both know it could take years to get to the bottom of it. If there's something to get to the bottom of."

"Maybe it'll only take a week or two. All we need is one solid lead that confirms the intel. We have that." He shrugged. "We might be able to follow breadcrumbs and figure out if it's bullshit or true. If it's true,

I take it to the next level. Who's behind it? Are my wife and daughter still alive? If so, where are they?"

"If Knox isn't willing to devote any resources, he's sure as hell not giving you the time off from the Bureau, which, unlike OPSIG, is highly scrutinized. Unless you have lots of sick days in the bank."

"I do."

"Then where would you start?"

"Where I last saw them. Israel."

"Makes sense," DeSantos said. "So you're sure you want to do this?"

Uzi thought a long moment. "What would you do if you heard a rumor that Brian Archer was still alive, that he'd survived Scarponi's gunshot and has been living in Italy under an assumed name?"

Brian Archer was DeSantos's partner many years ago, his first in OPSIG. His death was a shocking blow at the time. It's something DeSantos continued to regret to this day.

DeSantos's vacant stare at the parking garage wall in front of him told Uzi all he needed to know.

"Would you go looking for Brian?"

DeSantos finally blinked and faced Uzi. "I'd be on the next flight to Rome."

"Should this be any different?"

"No." DeSantos pushed off the car and stood up straight. "I'm gonna ask Knox for some time off—use my sick days if I need to—and we're going to fly to Tel Aviv. Together."

"We wouldn't have backup."

"Since when has that mattered? Sometimes you and I are all we've got."

Uzi spread his arms. "This may all be for nothing. The intel could be bullshit."

"The alternative is to blow it off. And then you'd wonder every single day if they were alive. It'd eat you alive."

Uzi nodded absently. *That's exactly what would happen.* "We don't have shit to go on."

"Then, my friend, we'll be in our element." DeSantos laughed mischievously and punched Uzi's right shoulder. "Never stopped us before."

6

Uzi stopped into the office the following morning, having booked his and DeSantos's flights to Ben Gurion International Airport. He would have preferred to use one of his OPSIG aliases but this was not an official, unsanctioned mission—as odd as that seemed—so he and DeSantos agreed not to use government resources to avoid getting Knox in trouble should the shit hit the fan.

And in a situation like this, there were all sorts of possibilities for crap to strike those fast-spinning blades.

He stopped by Marshal Shepard's office and broke the news to him. Uzi was not feeling well—wink, wink—and would need to take some time off. Given their prior conversation, Shepard wished him a swift recovery and told him to watch his back if he rattled any of the many hornet's nests where he was headed.

His last stop was at the desk of Special Agent Hoshi Ko. Hoshi knew when, and when not, to ask questions. Uzi appreciated that. He confided in her what he had been told by Fahad and also that unlike the usual cases they worked, he would not be calling her for support.

"I haven't specifically been told not to call you," Uzi said, "but it doesn't look like I'll be able to use any government resources on this."

"I don't mind helping you on my own time."

Uzi gazed into Hoshi's green eyes. She was Korean and Chinese, an interesting hybrid that mixed her parents' genes exceedingly well—most likely with a European ancestor tossed into the mix. She was tough and yet at times timid, loyal, and bright. He did not mind telling her repeatedly that he too often did not express his appreciation for her friendship.

"Thank you," he said, and gave her left hand a squeeze. "I'm hoping this will be a simple exercise. Find information that confirms they died thirteen years ago in that attack or confirms they're still alive. If it's the latter, I'm going to keep looking until I find them."

"When's your flight?"

"Three and a half hours. I've got one more thing to take care of, then meeting Hector at Dulles."

"Good luck."

"I have a feeling luck is not gonna be a factor. I'd better get an answer sooner rather than later. Can't lose my job over this. But I may have to if they're alive and I can't find them."

Uzi's last stop was at Mahmood Fahad's home in Burleith, a neighborhood just outside Georgetown.

"You finished the remodel," Uzi said as he stood in the family room and glanced around the ground floor.

"You should see the roof deck. I've got a gas grill up there, a view of the National Cathedral, and—why don't I just show you?"

"Can't. Got a plane to catch. To Tel Aviv."

Fahad tilted his head. "You're going to look for them?"

Uzi shoved his hands into the pockets of his 5.11 Tactical pants. "I have to. "I'd never be able to sleep again knowing they could be out there somewhere."

"You realize that this was *not* verified intel."

"Doesn't matter. I have to look into it."

Fahad sat down slowly on the nearby sofa. "Uzi, I trust my CI, but . . . what if this was just a way of luring you there?"

"I'm aware of the risks."

"It could be one of the terror groups you deal with on a daily basis. A sleeper cell here in DC. We know they're here. And they use our freedoms and protections against us. They find out your name, google it, see a news article about your wife and daughter. Pull up something about you and your work with the JTTF. Not too difficult."

DIE TRYING 39

Uzi knew anyone searching online for him would never find a photo.

OPSIG's team of hackers and cryptographers made sure that any picture of him, even one in an innocent shot he had accidentally photo bombed and snagged by artificial intelligence, was digitally shredded. He had no public-facing social media presence. Nothing about his wife and daughter or his prior life existed. Every other morsel of information that found its way to a server anywhere in the world melted into the cyber sphere within seconds of being posted, figuratively sliced and diced, destroyed for all eternity. "I can't say your scenario is impossible. But it's highly unlikely." He shrugged. "No idea how to assess those odds."

"You going alone?"

"Hector's coming. We've got a week. And we won't have any support."

Fahad nodded silently. "Man. I feel . . . I don't know . . . kind of responsible. I shouldn't have said anything."

Uzi sat down in a plush seat opposite him. "Mo, I appreciate you bringing it to my attention. I mean, shit, what if you never told me and it turned out to be true?"

"Just be careful. My people, some of them can be incited to violence." He chuckled. "What the hell am I doing, telling you what the radical Palestinian factions are capable of?"

Uzi laughed. "I appreciate your concern. Really, I do. I know you've got my back." He stood up and held out his fist. Fahad bumped it with his own and Uzi winked. "Keep your ears open. You hear anything, let me know."

"I'll keep working my network, see what I can find."

7

DULLES INTERNATIONAL AIRPORT
CHANTILLY, VIRGINIA

Uzi met DeSantos at their gate on the D concourse. "Sure you want to do this?"

DeSantos gave Uzi a look that was equal parts annoyance and disbelief. "Seriously. I'm here because I want to be here. You're family. And that's all we're going to say on the subject. Got it?"

"Got it."

DeSantos gestured over his shoulder. "I'm gonna hit the head before we board."

He returned five minutes later, just as the gate crew called the first group.

A commotion behind them drew their attention.

"Excuse us. Let us through. Excuse us."

Uzi saw CIA Director Earl Tasset approaching, flanked by two security protective service agents.

The two suited men faced Uzi and DeSantos and asked them to meet with the director a couple dozen feet away in a clear area.

Uzi squared his shoulders. "Director."

"I know what you're doing." Tasset's brow scrunched, sending his eyebrows down disapprovingly. "I spoke to Director Knox, as I'm sure you're aware."

In the background: they were up to boarding Group Four.

DIE TRYING 41

"Great," Uzi said, lowering his voice. "You know why *we're* here. Why are *you* here?"

"Because, gentlemen, you can't go. And I felt I owed it to you to tell you why. In person."

"Why?" DeSantos asked.

"The treaty negotiations. It's a very politically sensitive situation."

"And the disposition of my wife and daughter is a very *emotionally* sensitive situation."

DeSantos glanced over his right shoulder, seemingly checking on the boarding situation. "If it sets your mind at ease, we won't do anything to upset the negotiations."

Tasset laughed out loud. "I know both of you quite well. So you realize why I find that hard to believe."

"We won't be participating in the treaty negotiations," Uzi said, "so what could we possibly do to disrupt them?"

Tasset's face shaded Macintosh red. "What could you *do*?" He caught himself and lowered his volume. "Whenever you two are involved—especially if family or members of your team are involved, everyone knows what you're going to do."

Uzi and DeSantos, eyebrows scrunched downward, shared a glance.

"And what is that?" DeSantos asked.

"You'll knock down every door. Check under every rock. Blow up everything in your way. Bottom line, to get what you're after, you'll move mountains if that were possible. And if it wasn't possible, you'd die trying."

The announcement of the last call for their flight crackled through the gate's speakers.

Uzi clapped his hands. "This has been a lovely chat, sir, but the Holy Land calls. Pristine beaches, beautiful bikini-clad women, biblically rich ancient history, mouthwatering food—"

"And some extraordinary mountains that need to be moved." DeSantos winked, then turned and grabbed Uzi's arm, pulling him toward the closing jetway door.

"Promise," Uzi said over his shoulder. "We'll behave."

* * *

As Uzi fastened his seat belt, he turned to DeSantos. "What do you make of that?"

DeSantos laughed—then got serious. "For the moment, we'll take it at face value. Tasset's concerned about the negotiations. Until proven otherwise, that's the extent of the CIA's involvement."

Uzi thought a moment. "Can't blame him."

"Me neither." DeSantos, in the window seat, clicked his belt home. "So we'll have to exhibit only good behavior from here on out."

"Do we even *have* good behavior?"

DeSantos chuckled knowingly.

Uzi was alone with his thoughts while the plane accelerated down the runway. As he felt the jet's lift deep in his abdomen, he said, "I'm concerned Tasset is involved."

"Involved? In what?"

Uzi pursed his lips as he chose his words. "He—and Knox—are puppet masters. I trust Knox, to a point. I don't think he's got anything to do with this. But Tasset . . . I've *never* trusted him. In fact, when I found out he had something to do with Dena and Maya's . . . murders . . . I wanted to put him down."

"I remember."

"I trust Mo. You?"

DeSantos grinned. "I've come around." DeSantos had had a very significant issue with Fahad on a previous mission—in fact, it occurred during their last visit to the Holy Land—but ultimately, they made peace. "He's a good man."

"Not what I asked."

DeSantos bobbed his head left and right. "I think so."

"That's a ringing endorsement."

He shrugged. "He's a spook. And we've got a history." Uzi drew his chin back. "I thought you got past that."

"Guess I'm not very good at letting bygones be bygones."

"Has he done anything since then to lose your trust?"

"No," DeSantos said. "But he works for Tasset, and Tasset . . . could be another story."

Uzi ground his jaw. "So we're back to Tasset."

DeSantos fingered the tray table release knob in front of him. After a moment, he shrugged. "He came all the way to Dulles just to intercept us. That tells me our going to Israel matters to him. Or the Agency. Or it matters to the president, and he told Tasset to make sure we didn't cause problems."

"President Nunn doesn't seem interested in the treaty talks. That's why they're being led by UK negotiators. Nunn's America First policy." Uzi mulled it over. "Could it really be concern over our throwing sand into the gears? Or is something bigger going on?"

DeSantos rubbed the stubble on his chin, where he had begun growing a goatee. "I think it's fair to say that *someone* in a position of power doesn't want us going. Who that is . . . I guess we'll find out."

Uzi considered that. This could make things more difficult—which they did not need. "We could use some help."

"Knox already said no."

"Off the record help." Uzi held his friend's gaze a long moment.

"You want me to ask *my father* to help us out?"

Lukas DeSantos was more than a retired four-star general: he was a media celebrity, a highly decorated veteran, and a hugely successful entrepreneur. While he no longer commanded troops, he still commanded a room.

Uzi shrugged. "He does own a defense contracting firm."

"With lots of business in the Middle East. Not to mention that he works closely with the CIA—and often depends on working with—and through—them. I can't put him in that situation." DeSantos snapped his fingers. "But Bill Tait. Tait Protection. *He* can help."

Uzi swung his head back against the seat rest. "That name rings a bell.

Why?"

DeSantos took out his phone and started typing, then hit send. "Could it be because Tait left home at fourteen and went to live in a Tennessee monastery?"

Uzi squinted at him. "Uh, nope. That wouldn't be it."

DeSantos grinned. "He's close friends with my father. He really did live in a monastery, but after getting his bachelor's, he joined up and eventually served under my dad. Tait now owns a security and executive protection company." He glanced down at his phone and nodded. "Excellent."

"And . . ."

DeSantos shrugged. "We don't have a lot of time and, well, Tait is the real deal. He's in Paris with a colleague, so they're gonna get here as soon as they can."

"This isn't a government contract. There's no one to bill except me." DeSantos waved him off. "It's covered. My dad."

"Santa," Uzi said, using his nickname for DeSantos, "you can't speak for your dad and I can't—"

"My father owns a billion-dollar company. Accept the gift. I'm sure Tait will give him a huge discount anyway. But we'll worry about all that later."

"How do you think they're gonna help us?"

"Tait's got people who specialize in all types of shit. I know the name of the firm suggests it's all about private security, but they have teams that do more. Like fixers . . ." DeSantos lowered his voice. "Fixers. Investigators. And stuff people want done under the radar."

"Private enterprise black ops?"

"He's got full-time and part-time operators in just about every country on his payroll. Sometimes my dad and him collaborate on a job." He pulled out his Pixel and hit some numbers. "Let me make a call."

A fifty-something flight attendant with a tired, sagging face that said *I wish I was retired* appeared in front of them. Her expression definitely did not communicate "fly the friendly skies."

"Sir, put that phone away. Now. We're airborne. You were supposed to put it in airplane mode when I made the announcement. Didn't you feel us pushing back from the gate?"

"Sorry." DeSantos turned his head away from her. "I'll just be a minute."

"Sir. *End that call.*"

"We're federal agents." He elbowed Uzi. "Show her your creds."

Uzi reached into his pocket, then stopped. He faced the flight attendant, then apologized. "We *are* federal agents, but we're not here on government business."

DeSantos was already chattering away to someone.

DIE TRYING   45

The woman nodded at DeSantos. "Then why is he still talking?"

"That's a very good question. There's a long answer, but I won't bore you with the psychiatric technobabble assessment. I mean, that report went on for thirty pages. Of course, if I told you what the diagnosis was, that'd be a violation of HIPAA confidentiality laws, and—being federal agents—that'd be an egregious breach of our oath. Let's just say my partner has problems with authority figures."

"Really. Then let's see how he handles the captain." She turned toward the aisle and took a step in the direction of the cockpit.

"Wait." Uzi swung his head to DeSantos, who was ending his call. "He's off," he called after the flight attendant. "And shutting his phone down." He elbowed DeSantos, who complied.

She threw him an angry look that said, *We'll see if I answer when you hit the service button.* Or maybe it was meaner than that: *I'm going to put strychnine in your coffee.* Could've been either.

"What the hell was that?" DeSantos asked. "What?"

"I told you to badge her."

"And I almost did. But we agreed to be on good behavior." DeSantos rolled his eyes. "Oh my god. Uzi, I was kidding."

"Seriously?"

"Seriously, dude. You think we're gonna get to the bottom of what happened to Dena and Maya by following the letter of the law?"

"What about the treaty negotiations?"

"Overstated. Overreaction. Overblown."

"I see a pattern here."

"Look, we'll be careful, okay? Obviously we don't want to screw anything up. Especially a sensitive process involving a bunch of countries that've been waging a cold war for seven decades. But we're flying several thousand miles from home and eating up valuable vacation time. And we sure as hell ain't gonna see any beaches or dine on any fine cuisine."

"You left out beautiful women."

DeSantos shrugged. "Never say no to that one, boychick."

"Fine," Uzi said. "We'll stay on the right side of the line as much as we can. But we cross it when we need to."

"Like I said before. Why should this mission be different from all the others?"

8

METRO TORONTO CONVENTION CENTRE
FRONT STREET WEST
TORONTO, ONTARIO

US President Vance Nunn agreed to meet with the People's Republic of China President Jao Ping in a private room off the main hallway at the G20 economic summit.

A notetaker and translator followed half a dozen steps behind, even though Jao spoke acceptable English. It was standard governmental procedure, as was the presence of the three aides who walked just behind Nunn. All three were experts on Chinese culture and negotiation; one was a student of the president of the Communist party. All were considered vital in guiding Nunn during their negotiations.

But when they reached the room, Nunn turned and told his entourage that he would be taking this meeting alone. Their faces betrayed their shock—and concern—but no one objected.

Jao did likewise with his people. A few sentences were exchanged in Chinese; although Nunn tried to read their body language, he could not discern what was discussed. Regardless, Jao's men backed off and moved off to the side of the hall.

Nunn placed a hand on the shoulder of the lead Secret Service agent and told him to wait outside. Jao's Ministry of State Security officers looked awkwardly at their American equivalents and joined them at their side as the two leaders walked alone into the room.

DIE TRYING 47

Inside, as the doors silently swung closed behind them, Nunn and Jao strode to a small conference room table and took seats opposite one another. The surroundings had a wealthy feel, with walnut wainscotting and velvet floor-to-ceiling drapes that gave the fifteen feet an illusion of even greater height.

"Do we have a deal?" Jao said, folding his hands in front of him.

Nunn cocked his head and squinted. "We discussed a two percent share of Ganfeng Mining and Metals. I want five."

Jao was sixty years old with a full head of jet-black hair and an unusually flat face—a feature that gave him an advantage in discussions such as these: it made it difficult for others to read him. Poker players who could transform their expressions into emotionless masks often left with the winner's share.

Jao excelled not only at cards but at the art of political negotiation—a sport all its own, with vastly higher stakes.

Jao harrumphed, a confident chuckle that belied his disgust. He adjusted a pair of wire-rimmed glasses with his index finger and thumb, then made eye contact with Nunn. "I could tell you how offended I am that you would change the terms so late in the process. I could walk out and force you to come after me, concerned that years of covert discussions had fallen apart due to good old American greed." He tilted his head and studied Nunn's face.

Nunn, an equal to Jao in cunning and negotiation, sat rock still. His features remained unchanged, his mind transporting him to a beach in Southern California watching bikini-clad, plastic surgery-altered women parading around.

"But I'm not going to do that," Jao said. "I anticipated your ask and I'm prepared to give four percent. Fair, would you not say?"

Nunn made a show of considering the offer. Finally he said, "Done," and extended his hand. "This will be held in my blind trust, of course."

"Which I have heard has 20/20 vision," Jao said with a chuckle.

Nunn grinned. No response was necessary. When he had taken over the office of the presidency, his career as a hedge fund founder and manager was well-known. During vice presidential debates it became an issue for his political opponents to exploit—so he offered to place all his holdings in a trust that would be managed by a third party. The gesture worked—and although the issue of his wealth and potential conflicts of interest was raised repeatedly during the Glendon Rusch–Vance Nunn campaign, it ultimately made no difference to the electorate.

The average American did not understand investing, trusts—blind or otherwise—hedge funds, REITs, commodity markets, IPOs, or venture capital. They simply saw Nunn as a successful, wealthy individual. They wanted to be like him, took to him, and—for some odd reason—*trusted* him.

Nunn was the kind of vice-presidential candidate who did what he was supposed to do: avoid being a negative drag on the presidential candidate; instill confidence in his running mate; and rise to the task of campaigning successfully, speaking to the party base; and raising money.

When President Rush's helicopter went down, Nunn's hands were clean, and he was sworn in to lead the country.

One thing that Nunn had perfected while running his hedge fund was gaining access: to company executives, engineers, designers, data managers, chief technology officers, and manufacturing personnel across a broad spectrum of industries. He regularly met with these people, toured the facilities, factories, and research laboratories. It was the kind of pseudo insider information that caused one past US president of the opposing party to call Wall Streeters "evil fat cats."

Nunn did not care for that polarizing demonization, nor the characterization. Instead, he decided to embrace it and looked to make the leader of the free world proven right. "If I'm unfairly made out to be an evil fat cat, maybe I should do something to live up to that depiction," he told the *Washington Post* at the time.

Nunn went in search of legal insider information wherever possible: as part of his due diligence when investing clients' money, he met with these and other key employees who moved the needle for a company, not extracting special data that was not already in the public sphere, but using this information—and his intellect—to ask pertinent questions of multiple thought leaders in an industry. Then he put the proverbial two and two together.

And he was exceptionally good at math.

Nunn turned that formula into outsized returns over the next several years for himself and his clients by making prescient, timely investments—and divestments.

When he and Rush won the White House, Nunn turned his hedge fund over to his son and daughter to run and made good on his promise by placing his holdings in the kind of trust he had no control over, with no knowledge of the assets in the portfolio.

While these steps eliminated conflicts of interest, a vital, overlooked intangible remained: the high-level contacts he made during his years in business. These came in handy when he, now as president of the United States, needed a favor. He knew who to ask—and how to ask it. Throughout history, turning down a request from the president was not only difficult but unwise.

More importantly, Nunn could message someone in a company—and, unbeknownst to them, include a benign-looking, coded link that, when clicked, would install malware on the company servers, leaving a "door" through which a cyber intruder could enter and help himself to whatever information he wanted.

And that is exactly what happened.

Through that data breach—as yet undetected—President Jao's army of cyber thieves, an entire division of thousands within the Ministry of State Security—vacuumed up the detailed blueprints to McKinney-Donaldson's yearslong $549 billion project: the US NGAD, or next generation air dominance fighter jet, designed to replace the aging F/A-18 Super Hornets and flawed F-22 Raptors.

Jao's plans, however, were not limited to reproducing the plane. As when China stole the engineering designs of both the F-22 Raptor and F35 Joint Strike Fighter, he wanted his engineers to study the rumored laser weapon and smart skin technologies—and, most importantly, develop sensors that could "see" America's most advanced invisible planes. In other words, neutralize its weapons systems and virtually strip off its stealth layers—and with it, all advantages the United States would have over China, Russia, Iran, and North Korea.

In a confrontation over Taiwan, the United States would be defeated within days, if not minutes. It would be like playing hide-and-seek with someone standing in a barren field, with nowhere to hide.

And in return, Jao agreed to funnel two—*now four*—percent of Ganfeng Mining and Metals profits in a growth company specializing in copper, cobalt, rare earth metals, aluminum, phosphate, and lithium to Vance Nunn. Based on the past five years' returns, that would net him $750 million *per year* in perpetuity. And since the money would be held in an offshore account—and untraceable to him—those funds would be out of reach of US taxes.

Over the next fifteen years, Nunn would have at least $11 billion waiting for him by the time he reached sixty-five and retired to the private island he had purchased three years ago with his hedge fund proceeds.

The two men stood, and Nunn held out his right hand. Jao took it, covered it with his other hand, and shook.

"I'll be in touch as we get closer," Nunn said.

"Are you ready?" Jao pushed his glasses up his broad nose. "The data breach is going to be discovered sooner rather than later."

"I've had meetings with my people. We're ready. There'll be plenty of rhetoric. I'm going to say some tough, accusatory things. Are *you* ready?"

Jao laughed. "I've got the blueprints. Why should I care about political bluster and social media soundbites?"

9

BEN GURION INTERNATIONAL AIRPORT
LOD, ISRAEL

The 787's wheels hit the tarmac with a slight jolt as the plane rolled down the runway.

It was a long flight—almost eleven hours—and Uzi's mind had been on overdrive as he pondered possibilities, approaches, and the dangers of poking around blindly.

They carried their duffels into the concourse past the large, silver WELCOME TO ISRAEL sign and multistory water fountain and followed the directions to ground transportation.

Uzi powered up his phone. He had been waiting to make this call since halfway through the flight. He spent thirty minutes kicking himself for not thinking of it before they took off. Then again, the Tasset visit threw him off.

A groggy voice answered the call. "Uzi?"

"Hey, Hoshi. We just landed."

"I'm happy for you. But it's . . . what time is it? It's really freaking late here."

Uzi slapped his forehead. "Oh shit. Hoshi, I'm so sorry. We're what, seven hours ahead of DC? It's almost 2:30."

"What do you need?"

"You know what? I'll just call you later."

"I'm like half awake. Might as well ruin my night's sleep completely."

"Okay, if you insist. Can you dig around the CT database?" Uzi asked, using the abbreviation for counterterrorism. "Coordinate with the Threat Screening Center."

"Looking for what?"

"Exactly," Uzi said.

Hoshi was silent for a moment. "Like I said, I'm only half awake. 'Exactly *what*?'"

"Exactly *that*. Something. Anything that looks like it could be related."

"So you want me to cast a wide net."

"Yes, yes. A wide net. Not too wide, though."

"R-i-g-h-t," Hoshi said slowly, drawing out the word. "Wide, but not too wide. Looking for nothing in particular."

"I know," Uzi said, rubbing his forehead. "I'm not being very helpful."

"That's okay. I'm used to it."

"Ow," he said, feigning hurt. "Remind me not to ask you for help in the middle of the night again."

"Don't worry. I will."

"No doubt."

"What happened to not using Bureau resources?"

"I had to say that. I'm your boss. But at the moment there are only two of us working on this. We don't have time to track down every Tom, Dick, and Harry who was arrested on a CT violation. But we can't overlook something that could bear fruit." Uzi's phone vibrated. He pulled it from his face and glanced at the display. "Hoshi," Uzi said, "I'm sorry."

"Sorry? About what? Waking me up?"

"No, not that. I mean, I *am*, but—"

"I didn't bring my crystal ball to bed."

Uzi snorted. "Sorry—I've gotta go. And yes, sorry for waking you up. Just do your best. If there's nothing to find, so be it. But if there *is* something to find, make sure you find it."

10

The red light flashed on Yuval's screen in the security room behind Ben Gurion airport's screening area. His monitor lit up with a still photo of a man.

"Sophia," Yuval said to the woman to his right. "Alert. Lane Four." His Hebrew was hurried but clear. "On a UK no-fly list. Wanted by UK authorities for multiple violent crimes."

"No alert from Shabak?" Sophia asked, the unofficial Hebrew acronym for Israel's Shin Bet internal security service.

"No. There's a note to notify Mossad's director general but not to detain—as long as he's not connecting to a UK flight."

Sophia frowned. "Let him go and then alert Mossad and MI6."

"Let him go?"

"Let him go."

Yuval hit a button on his console and the red light changed to green. On his monitor, he saw the gate agent glance up, acknowledge the clearance, and wrap up his questioning of Hector *Santiago*—one of DeSantos's cover names.

"Uh, we got another."

Sophia got up from her chair and walked over to Yuval. "Another what?"

"Another one of those alerts. Aaron Uziel." Yuval pointed at his screen. "Former Shabak, Mossad, IDF." He glanced at Sophia. "He's done almost everything in the security services." He lifted his phone from its receptacle.

"Notifying the Mossad director general. And MI6. *After* I call Adam."

"Adam? We're doing what we're supposed to do. Why do we need to check with the boss?"

Yuval contorted his lips as he waited for the call to be answered. "Just in case something fell through the cracks."

"And because you're not comfortable with just letting them go," Sophia said.

"No. No, I'm not."

11

Uzi and DeSantos climbed into the airport cab. The man's taxi ID placard, mounted on the pillar of both sides of the car's interior, indicated his name was Shmuel Ellis. Shmuel accelerated hard from the curb and zipped in and out of traffic en route to Golda Meir Boulevard.

Uzi grabbed the hand grip on the door as his body jerked sideways, his left shoulder slamming into DeSantos's right. "Holy shit, this guy drives like you."

"I never drive like this."

Uzi looked at him.

"What? I don't. Yeah, I go fast, but we always arrive in one piece."

"Don't like the way I get you there?" Shmuel asked as he swerved around a slower moving van. "Always can walk. Let you out?"

"No," Uzi said, his right arm smashing up against the door. "Just get us there."

"Alive," DeSantos added.

Uzi glanced at the rearview mirror and the man was frowning. Shmuel jerked hard left—and Uzi made a mental note not to criticize Shmuel's driving again.

Uzi and DeSantos arrived on the outskirts of Jerusalem at the home of Uzi's friend and former colleague, Binyamin Herzog. They bid farewell to Shmuel, who needled them on the way out as he helped them with their bags.

56 ALAN JACOBSON

"Got you here. No pieces," Shmuel said in broken English. "And very, very fast. You don't thank me for that."

"No pieces," DeSantos said with a chuckle. "That's something."

"Thanks," Uzi said.

They slung their black, overstuffed 5.11 Tactical duffel bags over their shoulders and headed up the walk to the front door.

"How do you know this guy?"

"Benny and I served in the Shin Bet," Uzi said, referring to the Israel security agency. The US equivalent of the Shin Bet, in terms of scope of duties, was a loose amalgamation of the FBI and Secret Service. "Benny's wife was killed in a Hamas café bombing about ten years ago. His niece, brother, and sister-in-law were killed in a rocket attack on their home in Sderotfive or six years ago."

DeSantos winced. "They find the bastards responsible?"

"First attack was a suicide bombing. Second . . . no. And then his other brother and sister-in-law were murdered in a firebomb attack launched from Gaza that set their house on fire in Sderot. He's got no family left."

"Jesus."

Uzi was bringing his fist up to knock when the door flung open.

"You think you have to announce yourself? Boychick, seriously. I've got this place wired with more cameras and sensors than the PM's residence."

"The prime minister doesn't need them as much as you do."

"No shit," Benny said, ushering them inside with a waving hand. "I've made a lot of enemies over the years."

"I only had a cup of coffee with the Shin Bet," Uzi said, "but Benny's been with them for almost twenty years. An old fart who's done it all, seen it all, thinks he *knows* it all."

Benny harrumphed and elbowed DeSantos. "Is he this much of an asshole at home, or does it come out when he lands in Tel Aviv?"

DeSantos made a show of pursing his lips in thought. "I don't think it matters what country we're in."

Uzi introduced DeSantos, then they set their duffels down in the modest family room. Uzi and Benny embraced. Benny was thick and broad, a few inches shorter than Uzi.

DIE TRYING   57

Benny held Uzi at arm's distance and assessed his face. "You're aging, bro. Not the tight young skin I remember."

"Fuck you."

"And what's this boychick shit?" DeSantos said. "Come again?" Benny asked.

"You called him 'boychick' when you saw him. That's *my* nickname for him."

Benny laughed a raspy smoker's laugh. "Sorry to intrude on your man crush term of endearment."

"Well," DeSantos said, "I'm not sure I'd call it a *crush*."

"Mud on them?" Benny asked, pointing at their Keen boots. Uzi checked his. "No."

"Fine. Keep them on." He walked into his living room. "Your WhatsApp said you need some help."

Uzi lifted his brow. "Not sure where to start. You know what happened with Dena and Maya. Thank you, by the way, for the call after—"

Benny stopped and faced Uzi. "I'm here for you, brother. And remember, I owe you one."

Uzi stuck his index finger into Benny's chest. "That you do."

"Tell me what you need."

Uzi recapped what he knew, then stopped.

Benny took a seat on the couch and motioned them to the chairs opposite him. "Go on. Tell me more."

"That's the problem," DeSantos said. "That's all we've got."

"Seriously?" Benny winced in discomfort as he shifted on the sofa.

"Shin Bet deals with counterterrorism, counterespionage." Uzi spread his hands. "You've got contacts inside and outside the West Bank and Gaza. Can't you ask around?"

"Uzi . . ." Benny cleared his phlegm-filled throat. "Excuse me. Israelis smoke too much."

"*You* smoke too much."

"Yes. I smoke too much." Benny looked away, at a wall where a single photo of him with General—later to be Prime Minister—Ehud Barak.

Uzi studied his face. "It's more than that, though."

Benny kept his gaze on the wall. "Yes."

58 ALAN JACOBSON

They waited for him to continue. A moment later, he said, "I'm not doin' so good. But you know, we Israelis, we're tough motherfuckers. You gotta drag us into the coffin. We don't go willingly." He turned to Uzi. "I've got brain cancer." He removed his cap and showed a fuchsia-colored scar coursing along his shaved scalp.

"Operable?"

"It was. Got me three years. Metastasized to my lungs. So—the fat lady is singing."

Uzi fought to keep his expression neutral. In fact, he wanted to burst into tears. "Knowing you, the reaper doesn't stand a chance."

Benny picked up a blue stress ball and squeezed it repeatedly, his mind elsewhere. "Look. I know this is shocking news, but that's not why you came to visit. Let's get back to your . . . problem."

Uzi leaned forward. "Now hang on a sec—"

"No. We'll talk about my health later. Maybe. For now, you're here on an urgent matter. So we deal with that first. Okay?"

Uzi swallowed. "Okay."

"I'm still with the service. I've been working remotely three days a week, going in when I'm able to. They've been very flexible."

"Good."

"But there's a limit to how much valuable capital I can use up with informants and contacts. I ask for favors . . . those should be favors asked on behalf of the country, for the benefit of millions of people. Not one."

Uzi nodded. Slowly. Working that through his mind. He knew that what Benny was saying was true and reasonable. But was he saying it because he had to or because he really meant it? He waited, holding his tongue, hoping Benny would elaborate. He did not.

"Benny," DeSantos said. "We get that. We face those issues at home, too. The stuff we do for the United States, and often the world, they're the same type of things you do for Israel and its neighbors. But a lot of times there's wiggle room. Places where intel can be obtained. Quietly. A little here. A little there. An inquiry with someone that doesn't cost much in return."

Benny stared off to his right, thinking. "You're right. And I'll do what I can. I'll see if anyone in the Arab Department, Department for

Counterintelligence has heard any chatter. If I come up short, it won't be for trying."

"Of course," Uzi said. "I know you'll do what you can. And I hope you know that I appreciate anything you can do, any *way* you can help us."

"Fine. Then get your bags and I'll show you to your room. It's a small apartment. You don't mind sharing, right?"

"We've slept in fields and mud ponds," DeSantos said. "Same room? Piece of cake."

"Piece of cake?" Uzi chuckled. "Easy for you to say. You snore up a storm." DeSantos grinned and shook his head. He knew as well as Uzi that a covert operator could not suffer from any type of noise-producing sleep disorder.

Sawing wood, an ill-timed gasp, or a snort could prove deadly.

12

**100 S. UNION STREET
ALEXANDRIA, VIRGINIA**

FBI profiler Karen Vail walked over to the Starbucks on the corner of King and South Union streets in Old Town Alexandria—a long football toss from the historic Potomac River.

She ordered a mocha and a decaf Americano. While waiting, she glanced to her right, where a painted wood sign, hanging in front of an irregular slate hearth, noted that she was standing inside the Seaport Inn Restaurant, built in 1765. To preserve the historic nature of the building, Starbucks retained key elements of the original interior, like the original rough-hewn beams and stone walls.

Microsoft's Copilot chatbot told her that she had walked through the same entryway as had George Washington, Thomas Jefferson, James Madison, and John Adams well over two hundred years ago. She felt a gentle chill shudder her torso over the historical connection.

She put away her phone and, over the din of the grinder, watched the barista prepare the drinks.

Vail dropped some oat milk into the mocha and left the other drink black. She walked outside and grabbed a table to wait for her attorney, Dylan Price.

He arrived a moment later and thanked her for the coffee.

"How are you doing, Karen?"

"Helped Vegas PD catch a mass murderer, so there's that."

Price raised his cup. "That's why I like repping you. You may be a tough SOB, but that's one of the things that makes you so good at what you do." Vail bumped her coffee against Price's. "That and the behavioral analysis stuff."

Price laughed. "Of course. That too." He took a sip of the Americano and set the cup down in front of him.

"Where do we stand, Dylan?"

During one of Vail's previous cases, she got into a tiff with the chief of police in Oahu. To be transparent and honest, that was not the problem; but it did result in the man making her life miserable, the proverbial mountain out of a mole hill. More like a mountain *range*. She had entered a potential victim's home after hearing a noise that sounded like the woman was in danger. It turned out to be the dog, which was whining over his owner's murdered body.

It was all cool—or should have been—but the chief opened his mouth, Vail opened hers, accusations flew, sharp language followed, and then came a behind-the-scenes power play that left Vail needing a defense attorney.

This was, of course, not her former defense attorney, R. Jackson Parker. After thinking through this history, Vail realized that there might be a slight problem brewing if she had to collect business cards to keep track of her team of legal counsel.

Parker felt she would be best repped by Dylan Price, as employment law, particularly for federal agents, was his specialty. He had been hard at work on her case ever since.

"Look," he said, leaning forward in his chair.

"Uh-oh. When someone starts out with 'look,' it means he's asking for my understanding."

Price nodded slowly. "That's true. But not just that. I want you to get the full picture of what we're dealing with."

"You've explained it three times. I got it."

"So you know how bad it could be if the full weight of the DOJ's boot came down on your Adam's apple."

Vail cringed. "That's not a very appealing visual, Dylan."

"My point exactly. Could be real bad. Lose your job. Your career."

"You're preparing me for a less-than-ideal offer, aren't you?"

62   ALAN JACOBSON

Price did not answer her directly. He took a sip of his coffee. "I've spoken with the assistant attorney general—who's one of your bosses—and we did some negotiating and shouting, some name-calling and then more negotiating."

Vail chuckled. "Sounds like me talking with my unit chief."

"That did come up, actually."

Shit. Great. Fuck my life.

"Suffice it to say that I think it's best to take it on the chin and accept their offer."

"I'm not good at taking things on the chin. I tend to swing back."

Price nodded slowly. "I've heard that, too. From Jackson Parker. And . . . well, a few other people I interviewed."

I hope he's making a list. They will definitely not be character witnesses.

Vail pursed her lips and thought a moment. "And what exactly is 'taking things on the chin' composed of?"

"I negotiated a soft landing. Essentially, a figurative slap on the wrist."

"How 'figurative'?"

Price cleared his throat. "Four weeks unpaid administrative leave and a reprimand in your file."

Vail stared at the table, thinking. Shook her head. "I'd rather have my say. I didn't do anything wrong."

"I respect your desire to fight. And it'd make me a ton more money, too." He chuckled—but Vail's face did not even crease. "However, I'd be doing you a disservice. It's hard to fight the parent in court—in this case, the Department of Justice—and then hope everything will return to normal, like nothing ever happened. As hard as it may be, I think it's best to let me accept this deal."

Vail took a gulp of mocha, hoping the chocolate would calm her, open the gates of reason, and bring sense to her response.

Who am I kidding? When has chocolate ever done that for me? Even worse, when have I ever had a moment of calm reason?

Before she could stick her foot in her mouth, Price broke the silence. "If it helps—confidentially—someone high up stepped in and vouched for you, requested a light sentence. I wasn't supposed to say anything."

DIE TRYING 63

Vail dipped her chin and looked at Price sideways. "How high up?"

"Headquarters. Seventh floor."

Director Knox.

If Knox intervened and this was the best he could do, she knew she should be grateful and take the deal. Fighting it, making her employer an adversary, would get her nowhere. Just as Price said. He was giving her good advice.

"Okay," she said. "Take the deal."

Price clapped his hands. "Good decision. I know this is the right way to go. Honestly, if I thought I could do better by pursuing this further, I'd tell you. I'm not a pushover. If I think I can win a fight, I'll lace up the gloves in a heartbeat."

Vail gathered up her cup, rose from her seat, and extended her right hand. "Thanks, Dylan. I know you gave it everything you had."

As he shook, he said, "Six months or so from now, it'll be forgotten."

"My bank account balance won't allow *me* to forget. Nor will the companies I owe money to."

"Now, now—"

"No, it's fine," she said with a wave of her left hand. "You're right. I'm just bitching. I'm good. Thanks again."

She headed back to her car, wondering what Robby's reaction would be. But as she turned into the Aquia Center's parking lot, her cell rang. The number was identified by her phone as Douglas Knox.

"Mr. Director. I realize I'm not supposed to know, but I'd like to thank you—"

"Agent Vail, no need to thank me. It was a purely selfish act. Didn't want to lose a valuable agent. And I happen to believe you did nothing wrong and that this was . . . about something else."

Yeah, the chief didn't like me. Simple as that.

"That said, my opinion doesn't matter in these cases. I wasn't able to make it go away, but it was best to let it play itself out."

"Yes, sir."

"You'll report to work at the Pentagon at 2:00 p.m. Secretary McNamara has been alerted."

"So my pay won't—"

"It'll be covered by OPSIG while you're on administrative leave. And I don't have to tell you that this is confidential. You can tell Agent Hernandez, but after that it's a hard stop."

"Yes, sir."

"Just a heads-up that your paycheck will be coming from Hamilton House Cleaning, Inc."

Vail's brow furrowed. "You're making me a maid?"

"Only fitting since I've had to clean up all your messes over the years. Now it's your turn."

"That hurts, sir. But sharply funny."

"I think we'll both agree that this was the best possible outcome."

Vail hung a U-turn in the profiling unit's parking lot. "I know you said thanks wasn't necessary. But I'm grateful for everything you've done."

13

**THE OLD CITY
JERUSALEM, ISRAEL**

In addition to apartment-style housing, the old city contained an expansive marketplace, known as the shuk in Hebrew and souk in Arabic where merchants sold everything from leather satchels to woven carpets, spices, beaded necklaces, shawls, T-shirts with pithy sayings, and Dead Sea elixirs. Shop owners sat on stools or well-worn wooden chairs outside the entrances awaiting customers.

Uzi looked at the finely woven scarves hanging on a wire. "Maybe Maggie would like one."

DeSantos's eyes widened. "Heck yeah. Fire engine red." He selected one, haggled a bit with the Arab vendor, then paid him.

Dena had preferred hiking in the wooded forests to shopping, but Uzi liked to occasionally spend a few lazy hours on a day off wandering the marketplace—what Dena referred to as "shmying around"—and then grabbing an espresso or Turkish coffee and a fresh-baked pastry.

Minutes later, as Uzi and DeSantos killed time perusing the crafts, Benny showed up. They walked together a moment until they reached an empty alley. As he turned to face his friend, Benny's expression told Uzi all he needed to know.

Uzi nodded. "Counterterrorism had nothing."

"Nothing," Benny said, his shoulders rounded, his gaze on the ground.

Uzi leaned back against the brick wall—masonry made to look like the Second Temple's perimeter walls, not cinder or red brick. "Damn."

"Hey," DeSantos said, "we knew it wasn't going to be a walk in the park. We're just getting started. It's literally day one."

"And I'm not done," Benny said. "I've got a few more stones to turn over.

I don't give up so easily."

"No, you don't. But I can't just wait around. I think I should go talk with Gideon."

"Aksel?" DeSantos asked, his voice rising an octave. "Seriously, boychick. Aksel has been a thorn in your side for how many years? And he's head of a spy agency. What's he going to tell you? Nothing useful. Nothing truthful."

Uzi shrugged.

Benny coughed, somewhat forcefully, then swigged some Coke to lubricate his throat. "You really think you can trust *anything* Aksel tells you?"

"Maybe not." Uzi pushed away from the wall. "I'll read his face. Body language. That'll probably tell me more than his mouth."

14

MOSSAD HEADQUARTERS
RAMAT HASHARON, ISRAEL

The sign inside the building featured a biblical quote that supplanted the motto that adorned the entrance during Uzi's time with the intelligence agency. These days, it read:

בְּאֵין תַּחְבֻּלוֹת יִפָּל עָם, וּתְשׁוּעָה בְּרֹב יוֹעֵץ
PROVERBS 11:14

Uzi harrumphed. *Where there is no guidance, a nation falls, but in an abundance of counselors there is safety.*

He did not disagree. But with an important caveat: the better the counselors—and the counsel—the better the advice.

Uzi greeted the security personnel, provided his ID, and mugged for a visitor's badge photo when he heard his name called.

He spun around and saw his old friend Nadav. They hugged and then laughed about a story Nadav related to the intake guard about a mission he and Uzi carried out—to which Uzi said, "Almost completely went to shit. But we pulled it off and escaped with our lives."

"And the PLO bomber," Nadav said, raising a finger. "Better not leave that part out."

"You're right, bro. My bad."

68   ALAN JACOBSON

"Damn right." Nadav spread his hands. "That was the whole purpose of the mission!"

Uzi pointed at the clock on the wall behind the intake desk. "Gotta run. Meeting with the director general."

"And I'm your escort."

"Then do your job, bro."

Nadav laughed and gave Uzi a solid punch in the deltoid. A moment later, Nadav delivered him to the office of Gideon Aksel. They bumped fists and Nadav backed away as Uzi opened the door.

Aksel leaned back in his office chair. "Well, well."

"Gideon. Thanks for seeing me."

"We've had our differences over the years, but you're ultimately a brother. The brotherhood means something."

"Appreciate that." He eyed Aksel suspiciously. "Are you mellowing?"

"Not a chance." He nodded at a chair at the end of his neat desk piled with files, all stamped in large red Hebrew letters. Uzi knew the words indicated that these were highly classified documents.

"Maybe a little." Aksel shook his head in disgust. At his admission? At all the work in front of him? "What do you need?"

Uzi sat down heavily. "Good. Getting right down to it." Aksel spread his short, beefy arms. "We're both busy people."

Uzi dropped his chin to his chest, trying to compose his jumbled thoughts. "Got some intel. Unverified but . . . well, partially verified but . . . honestly, it's dubious."

"That's never stopped you before."

"Gideon, c'mon—"

He held up a hand. "Go on. You were saying it's dubious. What's 'it'?"

"Right." Uzi cleared his throat. "Uh . . . that Dena and Maya . . . um . . . weren't murdered that night at my house."

Aksel made steely-eyed contact with Uzi's gaze and held it. Poker face. "And you believe this intel?"

Uzi observed him. That was not an outright denial. *Interesting.*

"Whether I do or not, I have to check it out, Gideon. You know?"

"I'm answering as Mossad director general. That's the hat I have

DIE TRYING   69

on right now, understand? And my answer is, I saw them dead. *You* saw them dead. What more do you want?"

"Definitive proof."

Aksel sighed, flexed his thick fingers, maintaining his eye contact. "I think it best you concentrate on finding out what happened during the past thirteen years rather than trying to find *them*." He said nothing more.

What does that mean?

"Are you saying that they weren't killed in that attack and that they lived for a time after? That they *are* dead now?"

Aksel's jaw tightened, and he started shuffling papers on his desk. "I can't comment on active cases. You know that as well as I do."

Yes, Uzi knew this. He had used that response himself on countless occasions as a law enforcement officer when he wanted to dodge a question. It was also sound, if not standard, investigative procedure.

Uzi looked away, at the walls lined with framed photos of Aksel with various world dignitaries: not only the US president, secretary of state, and House Speaker, but foreign leaders across the Eurasian and Arab worlds.

"Obviously I get it." He turned back to Aksel. "But at the same time, I need to know, Gideon. Covert activities make up a disproportionate part of both our lives. We sometimes lose perspective on reality. On life as a whole. A different world exists outside our spec ops bubble. Honestly, I'm having a hard time processing this intel. Evaluating it."

Aksel leaned back in his office chair. "Very philosophical, Uzi. I'm impressed. Where did this sobering assessment come from?"

"I'm older. Wiser." He dragged his hands down his face, rubbing both eyes. "And . . . I had a very long flight."

Aksel laughed boisterously. But then he got serious. "Look. Al-Humat and its de facto parent organization, Iran, have tried a lot of things to derail the peace process, for years, and now the treaty negotiations—but we've not taken the bait.

"They've launched rockets into Sderot, sent Shahed kamikaze drones—the ones Russia used against Ukraine—crashing into our homes. Iron Dome shot down missiles over Jerusalem. And their partners in terror, Hezbollah, they've been firing missiles into the

70 ALAN JACOBSON

north. Then al-Humat kidnapped a kibbutznik in a cross-border raid. Destroyed our farms with firebombs." Aksel shook his head, the massacre's pain still evident.

Uzi wondered if Tasset had warned him about their arrival after the confrontation at Dulles.

"Each time we've shown tremendous restraint, which has gotten the prime minister in trouble with his coalition. You know Israeli politics. Deeply divided. The PM loses a few votes and her coalition falls apart and we go to new elections. We've had way too many the past few years. She doesn't want that. I don't want that. I like our government right now. Moderate, no extremist bullshit.

"These treaties will be a big deal. For her, for the United States. For the world. It'll likely lead to peace. In the Middle East? A two-state solution? Recognition of the Jewish state by the Palestinians? Trade with Lebanon and Saudi Arabia and Morocco, the UAE—Uzi, these are things that would've been considered impossible only a few years ago."

"I get that."

"Then do you understand that your . . . actions . . . your presence here could jeopardize all that."

"Me? *One guy* among billions in the region?"

"One guy among billions? Look at what Hitler did. One guy with a racist vision. Kim Il Sung, Hirohito, Lenin, Tojo. The list is long, Uzi. All 'one guy' with an agenda."

"You're comparing me, and my quest to find my wife and daughter, with evil dictators?"

"Of course not. Point is, one person can wreak havoc and change the course of history. Affect the lives of millions. Even, in your case, when he doesn't mean to."

"How does that relate to me looking for information on *my family*?"

"You, my friend, are a wild card. We have no control over what you do. Your *employer* obviously has no control over you, either—you and your colleague are in a place you shouldn't be, where you can cause great harm."

He knows about Hector. *Of course he knows about Hector.*

"I still don't see—"

Aksel slapped the table. Files jumped. His desk lamp flickered. "Dammit, Uzi. You're playing right into their hands. Did you stop to think of that? What if you're being manipulated? What if you're being used to blow up the treaty negotiations? All this stuff about your wife and daughter being alive . . ."

"I have to know, Gideon. Yes, that crossed my mind. Thing is, I miss Dena and Maya. Every day. Every. Single. Day." He teared up, swallowed hard. "I went through therapy. It helped me get on with my life. But that's not the same as forgetting. I'll never forget. I don't want to."

Aksel looked down and nodded.

"Don't you miss Devorah?"

Aksel's head shot up, his eyes moist. It was subtle—and he blinked away the excess fluid. He cleared his throat, a long, raspy, and phlegm-filled noise. He pointed a stubby index finger at Uzi. "I've known you too long, my friend. And I know that you're not going to drop this just because I tell you to. You won't be satisfied unless I get you some answers."

"Now you're talking."

Aksel sighed long and hard. Rubbed his forehead with strong fingers.

Shook his head. "I'll look into it."

Uzi felt a surge of excitement, of victory, in his chest. But it vanished instantly. He could not help but think that Aksel was lying. As DeSantos said, deception was his job. Still, they had been through so much the past two decades. Wasn't Uzi due some consideration?

"You saw what *I* saw that night," Uzi said. "You were there. In my apartment. Their bodies, their—"

"Uzi. I'll look into it. Personally. For now, as director of Mossad, I have to ask you to leave. Will you give me your word?"

"My word?"

"That you'll leave Israel. Go home."

Uzi felt like shouting at the sky. This was a reasonable offer. *If* he could trust Aksel. Was this the best he could hope for? Did he really think he could get to the bottom of this by flying six thousand miles and kicking rocks?

"You're taking too long to answer, my friend. So let me put it this way: if you don't agree to leave, we're going to have no choice but to detain the two of you."

"On what charge?"

Aksel shrugged. "Espionage."

"Spying on America's closest ally? Are you kidding me? That'd destroy our careers. You'd never do that."

"I want you to see the value of doing what I'm telling you to do. Go back to Washington."

"Can you at least make this trip *feel* worthwhile?"

Aksel shook his head in disapproval. "We're going in circles. You know I can't talk about active cases."

That's the second time he said that. "Active cases?"

Aksel slapped an open palm against the desktop. "Even if there *was* one, I couldn't tell you. You know this."

He and Aksel had their differences over the years, contentious periods where they were openly hostile toward each other. But this was not that. Aksel was not being unreasonable. Their history was not a factor. At least, not outwardly.

"Take off your Mossad hat. Hypothetically, Gideon. *If* there was an active operation, what unit would be engaged?"

Aksel leaned back in his chair. "Uzi . . ." He shook his head again. "Let's approach this a different way. Use those brains God gave you. Hypothetically or not, there's a limit to what I can tell a *current* operative—everything's need-to-know. A *retired* operative? Do I really need to answer that question?"

"*Any* information you can give me." He lowered his voice. "Off the record . . ." Uzi felt like he was begging. Only because he was. "You shouldn't have come."

Uzi sat there, staring at the photos on the wall. "I was hoping for . . . I don't know . . . *something* one way or the other. Clarity to put it to bed or . . ." He shrugged. "Breadcrumbs to send me off in the right direction. In case it was true."

Aksel stared at him poker-faced.

"Can I at least get the medical examiner's report on their bodies from that night?"

"Not my purview. But *if* this was an elaborate coverup, and they *are* alive, do you think that whoever is behind it wouldn't also fake the death certificates?"

"Good point." He ran both hands down his face. Uzi had asked every way he could imagine. He lifted himself out of the chair, then headed for the door.

"Have you checked in with your former colleagues?"

Uzi stopped, his hand on the knob. But he did not turn around. "Next on my list. Anyone in particular?"

"I can think of several. Can't you?"

"You want me out of here. I don't have time to—"

"I happen to know that she would love to see you."

Uzi turned to face Aksel, whose face remained impassive. Had he taken off his Mossad hat? For a brief moment?

"Tell you what. I know you wouldn't have left Israel no matter what I said. Or threatened. And we both know I have no right to have the two of you detained. Yes, I could do it but then I'd have to deal with your Department of Defense. I have enough problems without causing more of my own. You called my bluff."

Aksel's phone buzzed and he glanced at the display. "Leave this in my hands for now. Take some time to unwind, catch up with an old friend or two." He dipped his chin ever so slightly.

It was subtle but Uzi could swear he had not imagined it.

"Relax and let me do my thing." His face hardened and he pointed an angry index finger at Uzi. "Whatever you do, make sure you don't endanger those negotiations. Promise me."

"Okay."

"But when I give you whatever info I'm able to dig up, you'll be on your way back to the US, yes? Or I'll have to create a huge diplomatic mess and *put* you two on a plane."

"Okay." Uzi stood there a long beat, parsing those last few comments. Realizing he was still standing there with his right hand on the knob, he pulled the door open and left.

15

HA MA'ARAVIM STREET
JERUSALEM, ISRAEL

Uzi walked into Benny's apartment, where DeSantos and Benny were huddled over his desk.

"Get anything from Aksel?" DeSantos asked.

Uzi pursed his lips. "Maybe some subtle hints. Officially, he told us to back off and go home."

Benny swiveled in his chair to face Uzi. "Unofficially?"

"He suggested I catch up with some old friends. Former colleagues."

"Okay," Benny said. "Any ones in particular?"

"He *accidently* said 'she.'"

"Gideon Aksel doesn't say anything by accident," DeSantos said.

Uzi snorted. "No, he doesn't."

"So he wanted you to key in on a female operative who's a friend of yours," DeSantos said. "I didn't think Aksel would give you the time of day, let alone relevant information."

Uzi shrugged. "Don't know yet if it's relevant."

Benny's computer beeped. He swung back to face the monitor and began striking keys.

"I'm in."

"In what?" Uzi asked.

DeSantos moved behind Benny, joining Uzi. "The Shin Bet server."

"I'm spoofing my identity and location." Benny's fingers sped across the keys. "But always best to attack the weakest link."

"Hard to believe the security service has a weak link," DeSantos said. "That's kind of disturbing."

"Every agency has a weak link, Hector. Law enforcement, intelligence agency, corporation, doesn't matter. What do they all have in common?" DeSantos shrugged. "Is this a trick question?"

Benny slapped the keys rapidly. "It's an *easy* question, Hector. Think about it. What do they all have in common?"

"Humans," Uzi said.

"Humans," Benny said with a nod. "Yes!"

"People," Uzi said, "are always the weakest link in any secure facility or secure system."

"Ten-four," Benny said, tipping his head back and leaning forward to look through the bottom of his lenses at the screen. "Prison escapes? Human error, stupidity, or laziness. Cyber breaches? Same thing. An employee clicks on a link he's not supposed to. Opens an email he shouldn't." He finished typing and sat back in his seat. "Done."

"Done?" DeSantos asked.

"Done. I planted the worm that will collect the data we want."

"Plants, worms . . . can't you geeks speak English?"

"That *was* English."

DeSantos shook his head in mock disgust. "Now what?"

"We wait."

"How long?"

"Not long," Uzi said. "There's some fudge factor in here because of all the variables, but if I had to guess, I'd say somewhere between fifteen minutes and . . . maybe an hour. Benny?"

"Seems about right."

"How are you so sure?" DeSantos asked.

Benny chortled. "Because I'm very good at this."

"No." DeSantos shook his head. "Can't be this easy." Uzi shrugged. "Unfortunately, it often is."

"Remember that hack of one of the top password manager apps last year?" Benny leaned forward. "The hacker exploited a vulnerability in a media player that hadn't been updated on an employee's home laptop. The cyber criminal installed a keylogger on that laptop and recorded the worker's corporate login credentials. Bam . . . done deal. A well-respected security company—whose only job it was to safeguard millions of customers' passwords—was duped."

Uzi elbowed Benny's shoulder. "We feel kind of naked walking around without sidearms. You have access to any that aren't registered to you?"

Benny bobbed his head. "I think I know someone I can talk to."

"You got a guy," DeSantos said.

Benny drew his chin back. "A guy?"

"It's a saying."

Benny shook his head. "I don't know this saying."

Uzi and DeSantos laughed.

Uzi patted Benny's back and explained its meaning.

Benny nodded. "Ah. Okay. Then I *do* got a guy." His PC beeped a series of rapid tones. He rolled his chair to the keyboard and started typing.

Uzi got up and began pacing.

A moment later, Benny announced, "I'm in."

DeSantos looked over Benny's shoulder. "Make sure they can't trace this back to who's doing this."

Uzi laughed. "You mean us?"

"The guy whose computer you're hacking."

"Really? Hadn't thought of that." Benny rolled his eyes. "*Of course* I thought of it. Could've used Russian or Chinese hackers. Went with North Korean."

"Works for me," Uzi said.

"This is a onetime deal, okay?"

Uzi pointed at the screen. "Did you make it so they don't realize we're in the network? At least for a few days?"

"Days may be pushing it." Benny struck some keys, waited, then struck a few more. "Let's hope I'm better at this than Muskie's people are." Uzi's eyes flicked over to Benny. "Muskie?"

"Alana Muskovitz. Chief of cyber security." He chuckled. "Excuse me, *director general*."

"You know her?" Uzi asked.

"She is a legend, my friend. Retired military intelligence brigadier general who merged the Cyber Bureau and Cyber Security Authority into one integrated cyber command, the National Cyber Directorate." He shook his head. "Hate doing this to her. She's busy. Building out Israel's strategy on artificial intelligence and quantum computing. But . . . you know . . . when you're in charge of the bathroom, shit happens."

"I'm gonna make sure that's inscribed on your headstone," Uzi said.

Benny nodded slowly. "If the shoe fits."

"Should we be worried about the directorate?" Uzi asked.

"Which one? Directorate of Military Intelligence? Or the National Cyber Directorate?"

"Both."

"National Cyber Directorate protects civilian infrastructure, so they are not a problem. But the way I did it, it's gonna take them time to sort out what's going on. They will shut us down, no question. But they won't trace it to us. I taught a lot of those guys what a computer was."

"That's not true," Uzi said, half-believing his friend.

"No. Not true." Benny's fingers engaged the keyboard. "Here's your data." Text rolled across the monitor from right to left in Hebrew, populating a spreadsheet titled *Mesuveg*.

Benny copied it to a flash drive and then logged off the system.

Uzi and DeSantos leaned forward, in unison, to get a better look at the Excel spreadsheet, which was now displayed on the screen.

"What does *Mesuveg* mean?" DeSantos asked. "Classified." Uzi swallowed deeply. "I feel guilty."

"We'll use the data wisely," DeSantos said. "No one else gets it."

"We'll digitally shred it when we're done with it," Benny said.

Uzi placed a hand on Benny's left shoulder. "You sure you're okay with this?"

"If I didn't know you, *really* know you, hell no. But I trust you to do the right thing."

Uzi studied the spreadsheet, trying to decipher the information to determine what was relevant. It was a list of operations the security service had run, along with the names of those who ran and participated in the mission and any other agencies that were involved.

As he pored over the document, the door opened and in walked Benny, bracing himself against the wall to keep from falling over. He joined Uzi and DeSantos with a paper bag in hand, made a show of opening it, and held up two well-worn Taurus .22-caliber revolvers.

"Those for us?" DeSantos asked.

"Yes. From the guy I got."

"That's not how to use—" DeSantos caught himself and grinned. "Thanks, Benny, these are great."

Benny removed two boxes of rounds and handed them over. "Sorry I couldn't get you something with more stopping power. But the guy I got isn't as good as the guy you got."

"Now you're overdoing it," Uzi said with a grin, talking to Benny but keeping his gaze on the screen.

Benny grunted and crumpled the bag, then tossed it somewhere in the direction of his kitchen. "I also got you SIMs. Purchased with shekels so it's not traceable." He handed DeSantos several blister-packed phone cards to insert into their handsets.

"Considering the Agency's, and Mossad's, response to our trip," DeSantos said, "these SIMs are a good idea."

While Uzi moused through the document in front of him, DeSantos inserted the new, untraceable cards into their phones.

A moment later, Uzi sat back and studied the list of female operatives that he assembled.

"What do you have?" Bennie asked.

"Lots of names to go through. I was hoping to find a few I worked with—or who might make sense based on what Gideon said. Maybe one or two I'd have a reason to meet with. But nothing is—" And then he saw it. "Wait. Got something."

DeSantos, who had started loading the pistols, joined Benny, who had come up alongside Uzi at the computer monitor.

"Didn't know what I was looking at, so my first pass through the doc was orienting myself with the data, how it was organized, and so on. Then I looked at names. Separated out the women and made a list."

"Sounds like you found something," DeSantos said. "Hell yeah. Tamar Gur."

Benny steadied himself in the seat with Uzi's help. "Sorry, I get dizzy, lose my balance." He shook off Uzi's hand. "I'm good now. You know this Tamar?"

"Lost touch years ago, sometime after I moved back to the US. According to this, she served on a mission five years ago code-named Hachalutz."

"Interesting," Benny said. "Very interesting." Uzi's jaw went slack.

DeSantos turned to Benny. "What's so interesting?"

"Hachalutz means extraction. *Rescue*."

"Hang on a second," DeSantos said, pointing at Uzi. "I know that look. You're jumping to conclusions."

"Am I?"

"Big time."

Uzi's shoulders slumped. "Yeah, maybe I am." He craned his neck toward the ceiling. "But maybe I'm not."

DeSantos elbowed Benny. "Do you know where Tamar Gur lives?"

"No idea." He nudged Uzi aside and faced his keyboard. "But I can find out."

Uzi did not hesitate. "Do it."

16

FIVE YEARS AGO
AL-FARI'AH PRISON
THE GAZA STRIP

The sniper known as Gimmel—the third letter of the Hebrew alphabet—followed his spotter, code-named Chai. Gimmel liked his call sign, as it carried an opposing dual meaning: the giving of both reward and punishment. It was not the only word in the world's collection of five hundred languages that possessed connotations at odds with one another, but there could not be a better descriptor of his job duties: he took lives at seven hundred yards, a thousand, it didn't matter—and served as both a reward to his country and punishment to the terrorists whose mission was to murder innocent civilians.

Gimmel was tall and lanky, which enabled him to get down low and flat behind his rifle, buried under his ghillie, as he waited patiently—and sometimes not so patiently—for his target to appear in his scope and the go order to crackle over his earpiece.

In contrast, Chai was of average height and build and possessed few standout athletic traits. He was not the prototypical special forces soldier—but he excelled in math and computational skills. He could calculate windspeed and direction, distance and dew point in a handful of seconds.

And like traditional spec ops operators, he and Gimmel possessed the drive to succeed, to complete the mission, to excel and exceed.

DIE TRYING 81

Under the cover of darkness, Gimmel chose his perch and set up shop. They were there as backup, should the hostage rescue go awry: Plan D on their mission dossier. Nevertheless, his and Chai's job for Operation Savior was to be ready. He settled into his new home for the next few hours and slowed his breathing.

Lieutenant Commander Tamar Gur trained weekly for missions like this one. Her team was highly skilled and considered "the best of the best"—a hackneyed, but true, expression.

Formally known as Sayeret Matkal, or Special Operations Reconnaissance Unit 269, Tamar's group was tasked with conducting deep reconnaissance behind enemy lines to obtain strategic intelligence and carrying out missions requiring hostage rescue, direct action, and counterterrorism activities.

Operation Savior was hostage rescue, pure and simple.

The top-secret unit was formed in 1957, designed after the elite British Special Air Service, or SAS. Sayeret Matkal's first high-profile mission came nearly two decades later in Operation Entebbe, when the unit rescued ninety-one of the ninety-four hostages held in Uganda by Palestinian terrorists.

Like its contemporary US Navy Seals counterpart, it packed extensive training, planning, and preparation into every mission. Obtaining adequate intel from the Palestinian territories was a challenge, but when lives were at stake, Sayeret Matkal deployed and often accomplished its objectives.

Tamar moved her company of eight men and two women with deliberate alacrity, a balance that allowed for cautious, yet effective, penetration. The longer you remained in a location, the greater the chance of discovery—hence the need for proper intel and exhaustive training.

When dealing with subterranean tunnels, a known calling card of Hamas and its sister group, al-Humat, it was impossible to secure a map to strategize around unless you had an inside source who could draw the tributaries by memory. Palestinian terror groups were often effective in preventing such information leaks, murdering those suspected of collaborating with Israel and dragging their bodies through

82 ALAN JACOBSON

the streets as a clear signal to others in the community: if you open your mouth, this will happen to you.

Tamar's unit navigated through a mix of intuition, scientific information (moisture content of soil), humidity levels, and low-tech compass readings to find their way to where they believed the hostages were being held.

Tamar, the first female to gain admittance to the unit, spoke Hebrew into her helmet mic: "Aleph One nearing target."

"Copy," Aleph Four said. Four was Lawrence "Lev" Levy. "Aleph Six approaching from the north. Two tangos just neutralized. Won't be long before they're discovered."

"Copy that." Tamar knew their second clock had been activated—the first coming when they took out the guard at the mouth to the tunnel entrance. They hid his body well but since al-Humat had regular check-in times and patrols, the guards would soon declare a lockdown.

Trapped underground with an unknown enemy force response could spell substantial danger for Tamar's unit.

That was part of the calculus of whether to undertake this mission. But the hostages were evidently highly prized and, as far as Tamar knew—which was restricted and need-to-know information—previous recovery attempts were unsuccessful or abandoned during the training phase because of an unacceptable risk profile. Somehow the General Staff decided this mission carried better odds—which could have been an indication of the importance of this rescue.

Tamar did not question orders—at least openly—though this one did cause some raised eyebrows in the unit when they were doing the initial mission briefing. There were more unknowns than usual and they were literally trapped underground in a tunnel network they knew little about. But the unit did not choose its assignments. The General Staff dictated which were a "go" and which were not. Their jobs were to execute as flawlessly as possible, and in so doing—in this case—bring the hostages back home safe.

"Aleph Four, this is One. We're in the southwest tunnel and approaching target area A. Sitrep?"

Target area A was the first location Sayeret Matkal's intel officers directed them to search for al-Humat's prison cells—subterranean chambers with fortified concrete walls a hundred feet below the surface.

Alcatraz was nicknamed the Rock and considered inescapable because of its location in the middle of cold and choppy San Francisco Bay waters, but al-Fari'ah—*branches* in Arabic—was the rumored-but-never-seen Palestinian equivalent. Instead of an island miles offshore, incarceration underground all but guaranteed that no prisoner would gain his or her freedom.

It was the stuff of claustrophobic anxiety attacks.

Shortly after Hamas won the election to lead the Palestinian people of Gaza, Yassir Abadi, the leader of al-Humat, formed an uneasy truce with Hamas, Palestinian Islamic Jihad, and the Palestinian Authority to construct tunnels underneath Gaza. Iran's billion-dollar monetary contribution was supplemented by a hundred million dollars' worth of concrete and steel donated by other countries to benefit Gazan citizens. Instead, these materials were commandeered by Hamas and al-Humat and used per blueprints supplied by Hezbollah and its Mexican drug cartel partners—themselves expert tunnelers—for smuggling tons of contraband and weapons.

Over fifteen years, Hamas and al-Humat constructed an unprecedented network of several hundred miles of subterranean city, with bunkers, command and control centers, weapons storage depots, missile factories—and hostage/prisoner incarcerations. Toilet and waste facilities, kitchens and sleeping quarters equipped with HVAC and electricity made it possible for their armies to reside beneath the surface indefinitely.

While many tunnels traversed under the security barrier into Israel to launch attacks, the prison's subterranean location made it impossible for inmates to escape—and for anyone to infiltrate it.

Yet Tamar, Lev, and the rest of their team were trying to do just that.

"Repeat," Tamar said. "All I heard was 'again.'"

"Dense rock and electrical interference making imaging—and comms—difficult again," Lev said. "I think we've got four tangos a half click away. Preparing to engage."

"Copy. That's our way out so keep it clean."

"Roger that," Lev said. "Keep the blood to a minimum."

Tamar grinned beneath her mask; Lev's wry sense of humor provided her a brief moment of levity in a mission that allowed for none.

Tamar backed against the tunnel wall. She pulled off her mask and took a deep breath. Although they were in the desert, they were several dozen feet below the surface, which kept the heat out. However, the ventilation system could not compensate for the subterranean humidity. The odor of mildew was unmistakable. She replaced her mask.

The spider web of tunnels leading to the prison was sophisticated but claustrophobic. Anyone over six feet needed to watch his head as he moved. That was not a problem for Tamar—she was five-seven—but Lev was exactly the height of the ceiling. And outfitted with combat boots and his Ops-Core spec ops helmet—which was equipped with communications gear—he had been hunched over since entering the subterranean network.

Tamar repositioned her backpack and flashed a thumbs-up to Aleph Three, Michael Weinhaus.

Weinhaus acknowledged with a dip of his chin and removed a smoke grenade from his belt. He tossed it into the adjacent room and it exploded, filling the area with dense gas. Seconds later, three men emerged hunched over, coughing uncontrollably.

Weinhaus and his fellow operator, Eli, brought the men swiftly to the ground, disarmed them, and zip-tied their wrists. Eli dosed them with BetaSomnol, a powerful, fast acting sedative, dragged them against the wall, and covered them with a dark tarp.

Tamar keyed her mic, hoping Lev and his partner Ari would be able to hear her. "Passing checkpoint Bet Five."

Tamar, Michael, and Eli entered the west tunnel headed toward Lev's position. They planned to meet at the same place, at the mouth that led to the prison's main room. Because of its location, the prison doors were manually controlled. The terror groups had run conduit throughout, providing ventilation and electricity—but there was a limit to how much draw al-Humat could hide from the Israelis, who supplied the territory's power.

Tamar, Michael, and Eli moved in tight formation to where the tunnel doglegged left. But as they approached, an object careened toward them, bouncing left and right, off the walls and low ceiling.

"Grenade!" Tamar blurted.

Because it was spinning and heading *this* way then *that*—in low light and only partially visible even with night vision goggles—they were unsure which way to run.

Eli corralled it like a punt returner, using his body to surround a wayward football. He gathered it up and spun and fired a fastball in one motion—in the direction it came from. The device made it twenty yards before it exploded, unleashing an echoing boom that obliterated their hearing and showered them with fine particles of concrete dust.

"Sitrep!"

Lev's shout was barely audible over Tamar's headset. She turned up the gain on her radio. "Engaged tangos. Grenade exploded ten meters downwind of our position."

Tamar pushed herself off the ground and took stock of her team: they were all moving and there were no dismembered limbs—though they were clearly stunned, if not concussed. Eli was crawling along on all fours and Michael was palming the tunnel wall with his right hand, trying to keep his balance.

Tamar kicked away large chunks of rock by her feet, then adjusted her goggles, which had been blown askew. "So much for not making a mess."

"Think we got any of 'em?" Eli asked as he stumbled toward her.

"We're gonna find out."

They again moved in a tightly bunched formation, single file, as they stepped toward the bend. Tamar gave Michael a hand signal, who then tossed two flash bangs into the adjacent tunnel. They went off and released a dense cloud followed by magnesium-bright flickers. Tamar swung her Tavor rifle left and steadied it, then stepped forward and fired at the men coming toward her.

Blinded by the bright light and smoke, they never knew what hit them. Their presence was now known, so there was no need to be stealthy; their approach shifted to speed and aggression, a more dangerous and less calculated plan that raised their already high risk profile.

"Aleph Four," Tamar said, "tangos are aware. Move in!"

17

Lev cursed under his breath. The message was truncated but he got the gist. They had pinned a lot of their operational success on retaining a cloaked existence. With the element of surprise now gone, the chances they could rescue the hostages—and escape alive—had plummeted.

Lev and his team members, Ari and Ringo, moved at a trot, rifles at the ready and their rubber soles slapping the compressed gravel-and-crushed-stone floor.

Ari fired first, a short, controlled burst of suppressed rounds that struck the chest of a guard in front of a lightly rusted iron gate. He fell back into the bars but his knees buckled and he collapsed in a heap.

Ringo's follow-on shots took out a second armed man.

Lev quickly patted down both bodies and found a ring of five keys hanging on a carabiner.

Ari slapped several charges on the tunnel wall to their right. If their intel was right—a big if—that would blow a hole into an area near where Tamar and her team were approaching.

He issued a warning over their patchy comms and they sheltered as far from the explosives as possible. The controlled blast produced a jagged entry—and fortunately no tangos.

"Window ready," Lev said as he flipped through the keys looking for the correct one to open the prison gate. "Aleph Three setting a flare."

88   ALAN JACOBSON

Ringo lit the incendiary device and followed Ari as he swung open the unlocked gate wide enough for them to pass through.

Tamar saw the red light flickering dozens of yards away. They double-timed it down the tunnel and found the opening Lev had blasted for them. As they approached it, a flurry of rounds pinged off the walls and floor. Tamar felt a stab in her back—it was hot and she had difficulty getting air.

A ricochet. It had found the open area in her vest, beneath her armpit. Hit a lung, probably collapsed it. Other than that, she had no idea what damage she had sustained; truth be told, she did not want to know.

At the moment, the object was survival and completion of the mission.

She tried rolling onto her side and crawling—but felt a hot poker in her back.

"I'm hit," she gasped above the din, scraping the words from oxygen-starved lungs. "Aleph One's hit. Take cover."

Tamar knew that last order was probably superfluous—her highly trained team members had already lowered their profile and were preparing to return fire.

But two hands grabbed her and yanked her backward. Rounds were still pinging the walls around them, but Tamar was concentrating on trying to get air into her chest and remain conscious. She couldn't feel anything below her waist, which was likely a blessing, given the pain she was experiencing in her back and chest.

She located her pistol and maneuvered it into her right hand. She was down but definitely not out.

The gunfire was getting louder—their pursuers were closing in. She waited, taking aim at a spot roughly thirty meters away.

Like soldiers unknowingly wandering into a field of landmines, a group of al-Humat fighters appeared a distance away. Tamar did not hesitate, steadying her pistol handle on the ground and squeezing off three rounds.

Two of the approaching men dropped. Others kept coming, firing as they neared. Eli dodged and dropped, a bullet striking the side of his helmet. Out of the corner of her right eye, Tamar watched him disappear from her periphery.

She took aim again and fired. Whether it was her shots or Michael's, the bodies of two visible men shuddered as if struck by high voltage current and crumpled to the ground.

Tamar silently celebrated the hit—but in the next second, a concussive force struck her in the face, knocking her against the wall.

Muffled hearing.

Chalky dust and chunks of detritus floating overhead.

Explosion. Get up, Tamar.

But she couldn't.

Shouting, screaming, yells of pain.

"Tamar, lesseget! Lesseget," Ari said over the radio. *Retreat! Retreat.*

Sound advice—but she couldn't follow it since she had no feeling in her legs. She rolled onto her stomach and crawled forward, using all her upper body strength to drag herself through the detritus littering the ground, now headed in the opposite direction, moving haltingly around the large concrete hunks, twisted conduit, and exposed wires piled throughout the tunnel.

Her lungs deprived of vital oxygen, she grunted loudly, perspiration rolling off her cheeks. She advanced a foot at a time until a hand grabbed the back of her uniform and lifted her off the ground.

That was probably not the best thing to do—she figured her spinal cord had to be injured. Any jostling could make it worse.

But between paralysis and death, this was definitely the way to go.

"Smoke is making it tough to see," Eli said, rounding a bend in the tunnel. He set her down against the wall and gathered himself as he glanced around the area through his night vision glasses.

"Aleph Five," Tamar said weakly into the mic between clenched teeth. "Don't let any of these fuckers get past you into Israel."

"Copy," Gimmel, the sniper, said. "Anyone sticks his head outta that tunnel is gonna lose it."

18

Chai kept his infrared scope pinned against his face, surveying the two exits. They were well-hidden but had been found by Israel's new tunnel discovery technology, deployed last week.

Excellent timing, as it turned out.

Gimmel blinked a few times to moisten his eyes. "Anything?"

"Seriously, dude. You don't have to ask. I see something, I say something. You know that."

Gimmel grunted. He knew. Of course he knew. As he would come to learn, the hardest part of his job was not the shooting, it was the waiting. Remaining still, keeping your focus, avoiding stiffness—particularly in colder weather.

And right now, with a mild but steady January wind, his hands were in need of some movement so he didn't lose that crucial connection between brain and finger joints, the critical blood flow to the capillaries in the extremities.

A crackle broke the radio silence. "Five tangos headed toward the west exit."

"Copy that," Gimmel said, stretching out his digits and caressing the trigger.

"On my mark," Chai said.

Tunnel construction and technology had come a long way during the past quarter century: from crude single-person passageways that required slim people with the agility and lungs of an athlete to the present-day wonders that were wide enough to drive trucks through, with lighting and ventilation systems, sensors and cameras—and in some cases, train tracks and the flatbed cargo carriers that traversed them.

When terrorists and cartels needed to transport weapons, drugs, and other illicit materials out of sight of law enforcement—in this case, the Israel Defense Forces—the groups put forth the requisite effort and expended the necessary resources.

Many of the tunnels terminated inside a building to mask their existence. But finding an appropriate structure to use as a covert point of egress was difficult in Israel, where the citizenry was alert to suspicious construction activity. As a result, some exits featured brush, angled rockface, or other camouflage methods.

That was what Chai was watching through his binoculars: an area of roughened ground at the base of a hill where the natural outcropping concealed an opening in the sandstone, a layer of palm leaves draped across it.

And then he saw the false cover shift and then rise—exposing a dark-clad individual.

"Eyes on tango. Three o'clock."

"Got him," Gimmel said.

Gimmel's heart rate remained slow, a key requirement of snipers. He was ready to launch his projectile—but he wanted to wait to see how many tangos he could take out. If he eliminated the one whose body was now exposed, the others would retreat and they might never find them again.

One man emerged, then two, then three. Four. Gimmel's finger was taking out the slack of the trigger. A fifth. That was it. They began to turn toward the kibbutz across the road—a cooperative community of farmers, small business owners, and families with children.

Once they had moved ten feet from the tunnel exit, Gimmel fired. Again and again. And again.

Calm coolness as Gimmel shifted his scope to the next target.

The two remaining tangos realized what was happening. They froze.

Glanced around.

Bam. Four gone. Number two was moving, but he was unlikely to survive. If he did, Gimmel would finish him off.

The remaining black-suited al-Humat terrorist was fleeing, but—*crackle!*—and he face-planted.

Just then a large explosion shook the ground. Whatever caused it had substantial weight and power behind it.

"What was that?" Gimmel asked, waiting for the cloud of smoke and dirt to clear. "Aleph One. Check in." He waited a beat, his gaze still on the scope, seeing nothing but swirling detritus. "Four? Sitrep."

Static buzzed in his ears.

"What the fuck just happened?" Chai said. "IED? I don't know."

"I saw one of the tangos moving just before I took out the last one. Maybe he triggered it. Could've been rigged throughout the tunnel network."

"Dammit," Gimmel said, barely audible. "Aleph Four, do you read?"

As the seconds of silence passed, Gimmel closed his eyes in resignation.

Chai's voice was barely above a whisper. "וייזת יתוא."

Yeah, Gimmel thought. *Fuck me.*

19

CENTRAL TEL AVIV
UNDISCLOSED LOCATION

From what he could ascertain from an ancillary document Benny had obtained, Tamar worked for the Israel Defense Force Unit 9900, which performed highly classified geospatial mapping for the military.

DeSantos peered out at the building in the late afternoon sun as they approached. "Doesn't look like much."

"That's the point, isn't it? Nondescript. Base has been here for about seventy-five years."

"Safe to say they're like our Geospatial-Intelligence Agency?"

"Both use satellites and 3D mapping to feed intel to the military complex. But 9900's mission is geo-visual intelligence. The unit makes 3D maps from its satellites to give troops on the ground an accurate picture of the landscape before troops deploy or fighter pilots take off. Lebanon, Syria, Iran—anywhere enemy fire's coming from. But they can also digitally map building *interiors*."

"Interiors?"

"I don't know the tech behind it, but yeah. I think it came out of a program the IDF runs called Talpiot. Decades ago, they set up a training unit that takes the best of the best, the smartest outside-the-box thinkers in science and leadership—and then uses them to solve problems, develop cutting edge technology, cyber defense, that kind of thing."

"DARPA crossed with Skunk Works."

"Kinda sorta. On steroids. But their focus is always changing depending on what's needed. They've come up with some seriously awesome shit."

"Like digitally mapping building interiors from space?"

"I know of one mission a few months ago where a pilot going after an al-Humat fighter was able to target his missile through a specific window to prevent civilian casualties."

According to a call Benny made before they left, Tamar worked from home two days a week and in the unit's office the other three, residing in Lod, not far from Ben Gurion International Airport, south of Tel Aviv and about twenty-five miles northwest of Jerusalem.

Benny had texted Tamar, explained who he was, and asked her if she could meet a friend of his—someone she knew, though it would have to be a surprise. She suggested an Aroma coffee shop not far from the unit's headquarters.

As they passed the café's storefront, Uzi noticed the large red sign that read, "We've got a whole LATTE love for you." He elbowed DeSantos and nodded at the sign. "How sweet."

DeSantos laughed. "Only if you add lots of sugar."

Uzi spotted Tamar sitting at an outdoor table dressed in military fatigues. Strapped around her legs was a device that enabled those who could not walk on their own to ambulate using robotics. He had not known.

His gaze lingered on the prosthetics. He hadn't known about her . . . accident, or whatever it was that took her legs.

As they strolled closer, he whistled to get her attention.

She looked up from her phone, her jaw dropping a split second later.

"Uzi? Oh my god. What the f—"

"I know, right?" He snapped his fingers. "Out of thin air." He introduced DeSantos and they shook hands.

"Are you back in Israel? Or just a visit?"

"Just a visit. About my wife and daughter."

Tamar drew her chin back. "Say what? They're—"

"Dead. Yeah. Maybe. I don't know." He threw up his hands. "Yes. Dead. Until I hear or see otherwise."

"You're not making sense. Which—I might add—is par for the course with you."

"Tee, you haven't lost that sharp . . . umm . . ."

"Bitchiness?"

Uzi shrugged. "Not exactly my word."

"And if you said it, I'd kick you in the balls."

"Good to see that you haven't changed a bit. This is my buddy Hector."

She extended her hand. DeSantos was doing his best to stifle a laugh as he took it and shook.

"So how've you been?" Uzi nodded at the narrow wedding band. "Married, I see."

"With three kids."

"Holy shit. Who woulda thought?"

"Because I'm a tough SOB who wasn't the type to list *mothering skills* on my résumé?"

"Yeah. That."

"People change, you know? When I lost my legs, it made me realize there's more to life than carrying around an uzi and wearing tactical gear chasing around bad guys. I mean, I still do that—so to speak—but now I'm a more well-rounded person."

DeSantos elbowed his friend. "I keep trying to get Uzi to change. Lighten up."

"Good luck with that," she laughed. "Oh, look!" She pressed a button on her watch, rose from the chair, and assisted by two forearm crutches, walked several feet. A computerized pack rested against her lower back, with electric motors of the exoskeleton's compact gears strapped around her thighs and calves, whirring and whining as she moved. It sounded like an electric drill.

Uzi's bottom jaw dropped. "I knew about it but I'd never seen one. Amazing!"

She walked back to her chair with only a modest hitch in her gait.

"Invented here, in Israel. ReWalk Robotics. I can even climb stairs and curbs."

DeSantos shared an astonished glance with Uzi. "I had no idea anything like this existed."

96   ALAN JACOBSON

"We're the Startup Nation, right?" She took her seat and motioned at him. "So. You didn't come all this way to catch up. That'd be super nice, but I haven't heard from you since . . . well, since Dena and Maya. I reached out but—"

"I withdrew," Uzi said. "I lost contact with a lot of people. My dad included. I'm sorry. I won't let that happen again."

"Then what gives? Why are you really here?"

He explained what had happened and what he had learned. "I was hoping you might have a lead for me."

"On what?"

Uzi sighed forcefully. "That's a good question. Wish I knew." He did not want to mention Aksel, as that "suggestion" was provided off the record. And he certainly could not say anything about the data Benny pilfered from a secure government server. "Maybe an op you were on?"

"Can you be a little more specific? You know how many ops I've been on in my career?"

"Wouldn't risk a guess."

Tamar stood up and began to pace.

Uzi marveled at how well she moved. Slow and not at all natural, but considering she was paralyzed from the waist down, it was extraordinary. "I don't really know, actually. Never counted. A lot. You do remember I live in Israel and worked counterterrorism, right? Between al-Humat, Hamas, Palestinian Islamic Jihad, Hezbollah, and Iran, my plate was always full."

"Living in America, even working domestic terror, I forget what it's like here. What you guys deal with. Gideon once accused me of going soft when I moved to the US."

DeSantos cleared his throat. "That went over real well." Tamar chuckled. "I can only imagine."

Uzi decided to take a bit of a risk. "Did you ever run an op called 'Hachalutz'?

Tamar stopped and faced him. "Extraction? That's the op where I got paralyzed."

Uzi swallowed hard. Inched forward in his seat. He was on to something. "What were the mission parameters?"

Tamar stared at him a long moment.

"Tee. You have my word. This stays between us."

Her eyes flicked over to DeSantos.

"I work very closely with this guy. Covert ops. We share more secrets than most *married* couples."

Tamar did not laugh at the jest. Her demeanor had turned hard, whether due to bad memories or discomfort over being asked to discuss a covert operation. "We were tasked with breaking out two high-value hostages. Two women."

DeSantos leaned forward. "From where?"

"A subterranean prison in Gaza."

Uzi's heartrate began galloping. "When?"

"Five years ago. Why?"

Uzi licked his suddenly parched lips. He dragged a sleeve across his forehead, which had gone slick with perspiration. "That could've been my wife and daughter."

They sat there staring at each other. "But Dena and Maya were, um, you know . . . umm . . . killed several years before that."

Uzi heard her voice but was not processing what she was saying. *Two women. It could be anyone. Proves nothing. But it could be important. It could be* them. He figuratively slapped his face for zoning out. He had to focus and ask cogent questions.

DeSantos stepped in during an awkward pause. "You didn't know their names? The hostages."

"Need-to-know information. Forward members of my team had photos but names weren't important to mission success. If they'd told us the hostages were named Dena and Maya, I would've keyed in on that. Obviously. I knew Dena."

Uzi nodded. "And what happened? With Extraction?"

She stopped pacing and faced Uzi. "I can't—I can't say any more. Let's just say we weren't successful."

"Did you see them? The two women. If you could describe them—"

"I didn't. My team was under fire. I was dragged out of the tunnel by my BDUs. I was in a bad way. Lucky to survive."

Uzi nodded slowly, waiting for her to volunteer more information. Finally, he decided to force the issue. "You said the mission wasn't successful. How so?"

98   ALAN JACOBSON

Tamar canted her head toward the patchy blue sky.

"Aleph Two had the hostages but there was an explosion when they got out of the tunnel. I think it was an IED. And . . . people didn't make it."

"People?"

She sat down in her seat and stared into her coffee. "I lost consciousness. I mean, I remember the explosion but that's it. I was in a coma. For two months. And when I did wake up, I . . ." She squeezed her eyes tightly. "I was told I'd lost use of both my legs and was paralyzed. I was debriefed a couple of weeks later but as far as me knowing what happened with the mission . . ."

Uzi placed a hand over hers. "I'm so sorry."

Tamar shrugged. "We lost Eli, who probably saved my life by dragging me out of there. And Lev." She waved a hand. "It was a shit show."

"Sorry for your loss. And for dredging up all those bad memories."

"Yeah. Well. That's life, right?"

And death.

He sat back. "Anything I can do for you?"

"I'm good. All things considered. This contraption makes it possible to walk and take care of my kids. Play with them, take them to school. And I've got a good marriage. I'm working, doing really important work. I make a difference just about every day. How can I complain?"

"I'll do a better job of staying in touch."

She smiled. "I'd like that. Good luck searching for answers. Keep me posted on what you find out."

Given what he had just been told, perhaps their time *was* better spent finding answers rather than looking for his wife and daughter. "Any thoughts on who I should talk with next?"

She chuckled. "No one on that mission will talk to you. Me and you, we've known each other forever. But any other operative won't be giving you the time of day, let alone anything of value."

Uzi nodded. "As it should be."

"Tell you what. If I ask, it's not *you* asking." She spread her hands.

"Could work. Would you do that for me?"

She tilted her head in empathy. "Of course. I can't imagine the pain you're feeling. The uncertainty, the wild emotions going on inside that . . . complex brain of yours."

Uzi snorted. "Complex. Better than *deranged*. That's where I thought you were going."

She chuckled—knowingly. "I'll text or call you as soon as I know something."

Uzi stood up and leaned in for a hug. "Thanks, Tee. Good seeing you, even under these circumstances."

She and DeSantos shook, and off he and Uzi went.

"Impressive," DeSantos said as they walked back to their car.

Uzi glanced over at him. "Huh? Oh. Tamar. Yeah, she's got a heart of gold. And steel. Tough soldier. Tremendous will. I'd play on her team any day."

20

MA'ARAVIM STREET
JERUSALEM, ISRAEL

Uzi's Bureau phone was ringing. He was stirred from a deep slumber and automatically grabbed for the handset. But it was not where it was supposed to be . . . because he was not at home.

He opened his eyes and glanced around the darkness, saw DeSantos, and realized where he was. Jerusalem. Benny's apartment.

As he lifted the device, he caught a glimpse at the numerals: 2:24 a.m. local time. He would not have brought his work phone with him, but he didn't know when or if he would need it. He kept it charged just in case. And that turned out to be a good thing: it was Hoshi on a secure videoconference call.

"Hey. You always know how to brighten my day," Uzi said. "Or night." He paused. "You *are* calling to brighten my day. Aren't you?"

"You're in bed. What time is it?"

"Almost 2:30."

"You said that if I found something I should call you right away."

Uzi rubbed his eyes with index finger and thumb. "I don't remember saying that, but it does sound like something I'd say."

"Plus I had to get you back for waking me in the middle of the night."

"Of course. Well, I'm glad you called. Time's tight and we could use some good news. Is it? Good news?"

DIE TRYING   101

Hoshi bent her head left and right. "Well . . ."

"Ugh. Really coulda used something positive."

"I do think it's good news. I was just making you squirm."

Uzi frowned. "Consider me . . . squirmed. Disappointing day. Thought we were on to something but we hit a wall."

"This should help."

"What the hell's going on?" It was DeSantos, sitting up in bed. "Tell me you're not on a video call. It's . . . 2:30?"

"We're past that part of the conversation. Join or go back to sleep. Go ahead, Hoshi."

DeSantos threw his blanket aside and stumbled over to Uzi's side and sat on the floor facing the phone, his eyes at half-mast in the bright light of Hoshi's desk lamp.

"Right," she said. "So I got a visit from a friend of yours, out of naval intelligence. She was super helpful."

"Oh yeah?"

"She helped me key in on some important things I was overlooking. She was as good as Marlena," Hoshi said, referring to one of the counterterrorism FBI analysts who worked with the Joint Terrorism Task Force—a group whose resources were hands-off since this was not a Bureau case.

"Who came by?"

"Viktoria Hawkins."

Hawk—oh. Alex Rusakov. Jesus.

Uzi cleared his throat and glanced at DeSantos, who was grinning. He was more familiar with OPSIG's nonofficial covers than Uzi.

"Yeah," Uzi said, piping in before the silence made Hoshi suspicious. "I'd asked Viktoria to stop in and see if she could lend a hand. Forgot all about it. I'm glad *she* didn't forget."

I said nothing to her. Did Mo tell her?

"She's got one hot bod, if you don't mind me saying."

"I happen to agree. And *I* don't mind you saying that, but the *Bureau* might. And since I'm your boss, Hoshi, I don't think we should be discussing this."

"So you *are* seeing her."

DeSantos blurted out a laugh.

"What? No. I did not say that. And I'm—I'm not. She's just a friend."

"Who's there with you?"

"My buddy, Hector."

"Oh hey. Didn't realize—"

"Can we get back to what you two were working on?"

"Yes. Sorry. I'd been searching linearly, going about it very, well . . . clinically. Using my Bureau-honed critical thinking skills. And Viktoria got me thinking creatively, three-dimensionally, outside the box."

"Such as?"

"I was laser-focused on the Batula Hakim case and she expanded my approach. I know, I know, I should've been doing that. Anyway, we came up with a list of associated names. When you get so far removed, you sacrifice accuracy and risk—"

"Yes, I know. Go on."

"Right. We then cross-referenced that to all known associates who'd been involved in global terror or extremist activities and voilà! We got a hit."

He waited a few seconds for her to continue. "And?"

"And that looked like a dead end, too. But we kept working outward, going wider, which could've reduced our chances of finding something helpful, but—"

"But you got something," DeSantos said.

"Batula Hakim's sister-in-law. Well, technically not her sister-in-law because her brother wasn't really married, but let's call her his significant other. This woman had a friend who'd been arrested for involvement in a terror plot in Chicago. The friend was ultimately released on a technicality but was picked up again when he communicated with a guy in Gaza, who was coordinating a sleeper cell in New Mexico. Following?"

"Fairly well for the middle of the night—but does this lead anywhere?"

"Right to someone who'd been wanted by the CIA and FBI on suspicion of plotting an attack on US soil. Atlanta. CIA had the security service pick him up as he was crossing into the West Bank. They put him in a holding cell while awaiting extradition to the US. Fady Madari. Ring a bell?"

"Should it?"

"Not necessarily. I figured maybe you task force heads talk about this stuff over virtual Teams lunches."

"We talk about guns and women. That's it."

"Oh," Hoshi said, drawing back.

"I'm kidding."

"Anyway, Madari was extradited, then released. Turns out Shin Bet picked up the wrong guy. Same name but different guy. After the Agency interrogated him, they realized it was a case of mistaken identity. They informed the Israelis they'd grabbed the wrong guy and were putting him on a plane back to Tel Aviv. But the Atlanta field office swooped in and arrested him. Right on the tarmac."

"For what?"

"He'd been in the US two years ago and had coordinated with Hezbollah and al-Humat cells in Detroit."

"*That* I should've known about." Uzi stifled a yawn. "Hoshi, where's this leading?"

"He was arrested on terrorism charges and is being held at Fulton County Jail. He was put in a holding cell for two weeks along with a dozen accused extremists. He might know something. You JTTF heads may not talk about terror stuff in your off time, but I bet these guys do. Brag, you know? Whose you-know-what is bigger."

"It's pretty evident whose you-know-what is bigger in a holding cell," DeSantos said. "No secrets there. Your junk is on display when you use the john."

"C'mon," Hoshi said. "This could be helpful."

Uzi was not as confident, but he did know that Hoshi was right: on occasion, prisoners boasted about their conquests to cellmates. It was worth looking into.

"Neither of you two are saying anything."

"Sorry," Uzi said. "Brain's still half asleep. But this is great work. Thanks."

"Thank Viktoria."

"I will. Definitely. And text me anything you've got on this Madari."

Uzi hung up and sat there pondering the intel. "Worth looking into," DeSantos said. "Definitely."

"You realize we're six thousand miles away."

"Indeed we are."

DeSantos brought up his right hand to stifle a wide yawn.

"But," Uzi said, swinging his legs over the edge of the bed, "we know someone who's a whole lot closer. Someone skilled in the art of interrogation. And investigation."

21

**FIOLA MARE RESTAURANT
WASHINGTON HARBOUR
GEORGETOWN**

President Vance Nunn walked into the men's room of the Michelin restaurant as his detail waited outside the door. They objected—no surprise there—but the Secret Service only advises the POTUS and, if necessary, strongly discourages certain behavior. Ultimately, however, they answer to the commander in chief—and if he demands something, the agents will do their best to adapt and try to keep him safe from harm.

Nunn knew this, as he had exercised this "right" several dozen times during his years in office. His detail did their best, though Nunn imagined that when off duty they bitched to each other over a Coke about how difficult the president made it to do their jobs.

Nunn glanced at the stalls, which were meticulously maintained, and the floors, which were spotless—not surprising, given the venue's reputation of serving the POTUS, other world leaders, and A-list celebrities.

He selected the proper door and pushed inside. He put the top down and sat. "Camel C19A6B," he said.

"Canary FFFF99," a man on the other side of the divider said. Having received the correct response code, Nunn said, "Go on."

A manila folder slid in front of his highly polished, chili-colored oxfords.

Nunn bent down and flipped open the flap, pulled out the typed document. He read:

TOP SECRET
FOR POTUS EYES ONLY

Issue:
Covert DOD group is amassing information that would prove damaging to this administration.

Objectives:
a   Strike fast and hard
b   Render the group impotent before irreversible damage is done

Operational plan:
1   Leak the name of the group to the media
2   Go public with past missions
3   Leak operatives' personal information
4   Issue press release labeling it a rogue, unsanctioned group
5   Direct attorney general to build legal cases against leadership and operatives

Nunn read the page dispassionately. He knew the memo was referring to the Operations Support Intelligence Group, the black ops division that had successfully taken down his predecessor and several key administration officials who were integral to Scorpion's organization.

But like an octopus with eight limbs, only seven had been cut off, leaving one—which repropagated. Reconstituted. Grew back stronger.

It was time for Scorpion to do its own amputations. Protect its interests. Eliminate all threats.

"You realize what's going to happen to these operatives."

The voice brought back Nunn from his reverie. The man was from the Pentagon; that's all Nunn recalled—and as long as he did what was asked, that's all Nunn cared about.

"Not really," Nunn said. "Should I care?"

"That's for you to determine."

DIE TRYING   107

"I assume they'll be arrested, tried, and convicted."

"That's what the public is going to be told. But no. None of their testimony can be made public because of national security concerns."

"So?"

"So claiming that their missions and testimony would compromise national security while trying to argue, at the same time, that these missions were not sanctioned and thus had nothing to do with national security, well . . ." He laughed. "Obviously, that's a non sequitur. It won't hold up. Even if we own the judge, it would likely be reversed on appeal. At some point, the operators' testimonies will come out—or one will leave the country, go underground, and write a book."

"So what are you suggesting?"

"One way or another, we have to eliminate them. Before they realize what's happening and scatter to other countries. That said, even if one or more gets away, they'll remain in exile, on the run for the rest of their lives—because the kill order won't be rescinded. They'll know that if they post anything, send a manuscript to anyone, we'll find them."

"None of that is my problem. In fact, it'll be *theirs*. Do it."

"Yes, sir. Just wanted to make sure you were informed of how this might go down. And that you were on board."

"I am. Informed and on board." Nunn took a deep breath as he reinserted the document into the envelope. He slid it back under the stall's divider. "Lincoln 195905."

"Copy that."

As Nunn stood up, he heard the sound of a steel wheel striking flint. He smelled the scent of burning paper as he washed his hands and then exited the bathroom.

22

ALEXANDRIA, VIRGINIA

Karen Vail had just walked through the door into her house and greeted her two dogs, standard poodle Hershey and the newest family addition, a mini greyhound named Oscar.

The dogs were jumping and jockeying for attention when her Bureau phone started ringing. Her fiancé, Robby Hernandez, lifted the cell from her hand and placed it on the table.

"You're mine now. Workday is over." And he planted a kiss on her lips. "Mmm," she murmured. She leaned her head back. "Count me in."

Her phone stopped ringing. Robby led her into the bedroom and flung her playfully on the bed. Unstrapped his shoulder harness and tossed it over the bedpost.

The dogs careened onto the bed alongside them, but Robby shooed them to the floor, where they sat staring at them. Hershey jumped back up and curled against Vail and sat. Vail gave him a big hug and some kisses on his face and then locked gazes with him. "Go lie down with Oscar." She pointed. "Go."

He reluctantly listened. As Vail turned back to Robby, the phone rang again—this time her WhatsApp tone.

Vail looked at Robby, then at the handset.

"Don't," he said. "Don't even look."

"What if it's Jonathan?"

"He'll call back."

"He just did."

Robby sighed and fell onto the mattress, face up. "Go ahead. Check it."

"Not Jonathan," she said. "But it might be important." Before he could object, she answered it—audio only. "Uzi? Is that you?"

"The one and only."

"I'm kind of tied up at the moment."

"With Robby?"

"Yes."

"Tied up," DeSantos said. "My kind of woman."

"Is that Hector?" Vail asked.

"It is," Uzi said. "And we need your help."

"Can it wait?"

"Apologies to Robby. But we're in Israel and it's the middle of the night. And, well, it might involve my wife and daughter."

Vail sat up and took a few seconds to process what Uzi had just said.

She motioned to Robby to give her a minute.

"I'm going to kill you guys," Robby said, loud enough for them to hear. "Tell him we're sorry," Uzi said. He explained why they were there and what he needed her to do.

"I'm actually suspended at the moment. On OPSIG's dime right now. That might complicate things. Or it might make it easier."

"What'd you do now?"

Vail groaned. "Remember what happened in Hawaii?"

"Ah. So the shit hit the fan."

"It did—but looks like I'll be able to clean it up without too much of a mess. As to your ask, I'll call you as soon as I've got something."

She hung up and powered down her phone.

Robby looked at her sideways. "What if Jonathan calls?"

"He's an adult. If he really needs us, and my phone goes to voicemail, he'll call *you*." She climbed on top of him. "Now—where were we?"

23

YEHUDA HAMACCABI
TEL AVIV, ISRAEL

Tamar spent hours thinking about her conversation with Uzi. About Extraction. Eli. Her injury.

Memories resurfaced that she had forced down deep. She had not forgotten any of those things, but she had skillfully practiced the art of self-preservation and removed the index to the incident. It was there . . . it had not been deleted . . . but it was not readily accessible.

Her method was rooted in the ostrich approach: if a stray thought somehow found its way into her consciousness, she blocked it by envisioning a one-ton concrete traffic divider falling in its way, closing off access to her consciousness. The defense mechanism worked.

She once asked a psychiatrist friend and found that there was a chemical explanation for it: a brain chemical called GABA—some kind of acid with a long name—suppressed unwanted memories.

Whatever the reason, it helped her get on with life. She knew it was not a smart way of dealing with the trauma and that chances were good it would return one day. That was a problem for another time.

As she pondered what to do about Uzi's ask and the effects it would have on her . . . deactivating the GABA blockage and reopening the proverbial wounds . . . perhaps it was time to rip off the Band-Aid and lay bare the weeping wound.

DIE TRYING   111

Tamar poured herself a whiskey, added a couple of clear ice cubes, and began sipping it. She set it down, then lifted her iPhone to call the lead sniper on Extraction, Gimmel Levy. But she had not kept in touch with him after leaving the service and thought it would seem odd after all these years to ask about an op neither of them wanted to remember.

Before she could change her mind—and although it was a bit late—she instead phoned the commander, Michael Weinhaus, on an end-to-end encrypted WhatsApp connection.

She and Weinhaus had maintained a professional relationship through the years, which saw him earning one promotion after another. He had an impressive position now, securing and maintaining the nuclear weapons cache that Israel officially did not possess.

"Mike. Long time no speak."

"Saw those photos you posted on Facebook. Of your little girl. She's a cutie."

"Sometimes I want to eat her up." Tamar waited a beat. "And then there are the other times."

He laughed. "Been there. Fortunately done with that."

"Got a question. It's a bit sensitive, but we're on a secure line. Still, if you want to handle it in person, I can—"

"Tell me what it is and I'll let you know."

"Not to dredge up bad memories, but . . . Extraction."

"Ugh," he said in disgust. A long moment passed. "Consider the bad memories properly dredged up."

"The two hostages. Do you remember their names? Ages?"

"Why? And why now?"

"Former operative asked. May've been his wife and daughter."

There was another lengthy pause.

"Mike? You there?"

"I'm here. I'm . . . here. Give me a sec."

Tamar heard clacking keys and then a grunt. "I don't remember their names. But two females. Ages were . . . thirties and ten or so."

"Ages seem about right. Did they survive the blast?"

"That's not—hang on." More clacking, then silence. And more keystrokes. "Undetermined . . . Hmm. Looks like one did for sure. No known disposition on the other. But as you know—or maybe you don't because you were out of it for a few months—the mission was a failure. We didn't secure them."

"Figured. No names?"

"Not listed. Need-to-know."

Tamar chortled. "And no one reading this report needs to know."

"Exactly."

"Okay. That gives me—"

"Hang on a sec, Tee. You can't give this guy this information."

"Then why did you just t—"

"Because I trust you. And you're my friend and you asked. But this was a classified mission."

"Yeah, I know that. It's just that—"

"No. There's no justification for releasing this info, *especially* if it's this guy's wife and daughter."

"He used to be one of us."

"I don't care. We don't know what the ramifications would be."

"Then what should I tell him?"

Weinhaus groaned. "Give me few. Don't call anyone. Don't talk to anyone until I get back to you."

Twenty minutes later, Tamar's phone rang: another secure call.

"Hey, Mike," she said with a relieved chuckle. "I was beginning to think you forgot."

Weinhaus was clearly not in the mood for humor. "Let's rewind about half an hour, okay?"

"Rew—"

"Rewind. Yeah. So you called me, right? You asked me for something and I typed on my keyboard for a minute and said, 'What do you know, Tamar? I found the mission report. Got it right here. Says the two women were older females. In their fifties.'" He waited a beat to let that sink in. "You understand what I'm saying?"

"Loud and clear. But—"

"No buts. This comes from—I can't tell you where it came from. High up. And this is the way it's gotta be."

"If the situation were reversed and you were that guy—"

"But I'm not. And I've got a sworn responsibility to protect this information. We don't know what can happen if you tell him what I told you earlier. So, to be clear, this is the official mission transcript. Two women in their fifties. Got it?"

Tamar was quiet as she processed this. "You want me to lie to him."

"Do you trust me or not?"

"Dumb question, Mike. Of course I do. But I also know you'd tell me what's best for the *agency*, not my friend—"

"Not the agency, Tamar. For national security. You hear me? We don't know what he might do with this info. Shit, he could sue the IDF, allege misconduct, that we should've known there was an IED there and . . . then we'd have to make the records public—or they'd try to force us to."

"That's not what this is about. He's not like that."

"Who knows where it could lead? Can you give me all the permutations? No. Can you guarantee what will happen? No. Besides, I've got my orders. You don't listen, some . . . people will talk to your boss. You get what I'm saying?"

"Yes."

"Go with the cover story I gave you."

Tamar had little choice—not if she were to keep her job and career. Even though she now knew the truth, she had her orders.

Tamar sat down at her desk. She had waited until she was certain that Uzi and his friend were asleep.

It also gave her time to consider her options before she acted. When in the army, she often did not have the luxury of having minutes, let alone hours, to clear her mind, evaluate, gain distance. Remove the emotions from the equation, if there were any.

In this case there were.

Still, Tamar's orders were unambiguous—and although she no longer worked for the IDF, she was still a government employee and part of the military complex. She wanted to help Uzi but there were limits to what she could do.

Tamar texted Uzi, anger raising her blood pressure as she typed the words.

checked into it
source said the two women were in 50s

not your girls
so sorry

She tossed the phone on her desk and rested her head in her hands. *There. Followed orders and did the deed.*

And she felt worse than awful about it.

24

TATTE BAKERY & CAFÉ
515 KING STREET
ALEXANDRIA, VIRGINIA

The following morning, at an Old Town café nursing a cup of house latte with coconut milk, Vail reviewed the material Hoshi Ko had compiled.

Fady Madari was a twenty-four-year-old radicalized by his grandfather, a former PLO organizer and compatriot of Yasser Arafat. He spent his teen years in Lebanon under the tutelage of a Hezbollah lieutenant who saw the promise in the young man: a fervent belief system and an impressionable learner who did not question his elders. The man cultivated Madari's malleable personality and returned him at age nineteen to Gaza, where he was deemed too important to strap an explosive vest on his torso. Martyrdom was for expendables.

Instead, Madari was put in charge of organizing independent terror groups in other countries—the United States included—known as sleeper cells due to their modus operandi of blending in with society and remaining operationally independent, and dormant, until given their assignment to act.

Vail had seen such a dossier before. Madari's had been curated from various sources and interviews with him, though he was not particularly forthcoming with information. That wrought creative thinking by the FBI: they arranged for an informant to become his new

116   ALAN JACOBSON

cellmate and had the guy secretly record conversations with Madari, until the informant was discovered and murdered in a prison shower.

Vail sat down at the table knowing that she did not have to tell Uzi that to truly utilize her talents as an interviewer she would need weeks—if not months—of regular visits with the target to build a relationship. Uzi had heard her disclaimer before. As she once told him at a black site buried in the English countryside, the most effective interrogation was not about cutting off fingers—or threatening to do so—but establishing trust and commonality. The goal was for the suspect to want to, consciously or subconsciously, lower his or her guard, to open up and talk honestly.

That was not going to happen here. In fact, though she hated to admit it, there was only one approach that had a minuscule chance of working: a CIA-endorsed approach in which the interrogator identified a subject's vulnerabilities and motivations. Madari was a young man, so his vulnerabilities and motivations could be *assumed* to be rooted in standard heterosexual male fare.

To that end, Vail was a not-really-that-young-anymore woman . . . a mother, married and divorced . . . and on the wrong side of forty. Although she was fit and took care of herself, and men found her attractive—if their reactions were taken at face value—she was not a hottie that would cause Madari's hormone levels (and certain body parts) to rise. Beauty, of course, was in the eye of the beholder—so one guy's cup of tea might be a mug of castor oil to another.

And yet perhaps Madari fancied older women. Or men.

Vail set her musing aside and concluded that she had nothing of value to offer: no deals to cut with prosecutors, no promises to make, no transfer to better facilities. The lack of official capacity did provide some freedom: since she was not there on a legal matter or as a law enforcement officer, she was free to tell him whatever she needed to.

She was, if anything, a ghost . . . a Department of Defense black operative with few rules to follow. Although it contradicted everything she had devoted her life to, she was growing accustomed to switching personas on the fly when she was summoned to her part-time, occasional gig of covert operations.

Complicating matters, this was not an OPSIG mission, either.

But if she promised Madari something bogus and he insisted on verification as a condition to providing information, she would be exposed as a liar . . . and what little trust she might have earned would vanish faster than she could snap her fingers.

And that brought Vail back to the one tactic she believed could yield results, which involved asking a colleague to join her. Alexandra Rusakov was—or was accused of being—bred to be a honey trap: a body sculpted from muscle and bone, shaped by the almighty with longish brunette locks and a face exuding classic beauty. She could hold a man's gaze—and interest—with her eyes, boobs, legs, buttocks—or the total package.

Considering a target like Madari, Rusakov possessed so many tools that it was hard to choose one.

It took Vail the better part of a day to find Rusakov, who she learned was on vacation at a bed and breakfast in the Shenandoah Mountains. Vail called under the guise of a neighbor who observed a broken pipe at her neighbor's apartment. Using one of Rusakov's aliases—supplied by OPSIG colleague Troy Rodman—the man confirmed that *Viktoria Hawkins* was staying there. Vail left a message for her to return her call ASAP.

But Vail understood Uzi's urgency and chose not to wait. She got in her car and started driving, arriving at the property as the sun was sinking behind the mountains. The sky was orange and purple against a charcoal background that darkened as the seconds passed.

Vail turned on her tactical flashlight as she climbed out of her car and scanned the gravel parking lot. Signs denoting reserved spots for specific units were posted; Rodman told her that Rusakov was driving a black 2012 Porsche Boxter, which was slotted into the assigned space for room four.

Vail tried her mobile one more time—got voicemail—and texted her. While awaiting a reply, she walked into the front door of the Victorian-style bed and breakfast. Vivaldi's *The Four Seasons* was playing gently from invisible speakers.

Vail helped herself to a chocolate chocolate-chip cookie that was laid out on a credenza alongside a breathing bottle of Muse Vineyard gamay. While chewing, she thought about pouring a glass and sipping it with eyes closed while nibbling on the sweet as the violins put her into an alpha wave meditation state.

But Uzi needed answers. Madari might be in a position to provide them. Rusakov was the best chance of getting them.

Vail jogged up the three flights and found the correct door. Knocked.

Waited. Nothing.

Pulled out her phone and called. She heard the vibrating handset on the other side of the door—until it went to voicemail.

Vail squinted, then knocked again. Rusakov's car was there. Her phone was there. Could she have gone hiking? And left her phone? Possible, though knowing Rusakov, unlikely.

She could have forgotten it.

Vail sighed, then sat down in the hallway, back against the wall, to wait. How long? She had no idea.

Checked her G-Shock, cringed at how much time had passed since Uzi had called, and had a thought: check the knob. Just as it would have been unusual for Rusakov to have gone out without her cell, leaving her place unlocked would have been equally surprising.

And yet she had done just that.

Vail pulled her OPSIG-issued SIG Sauer P365XL and opened the door slowly, unsure what she was going to find. It was dark, the sunset's fading light now only a memory. She stood there a moment, wondering if she should proceed or turn on a lamp. This was not TV, so she reached for the switch.

The room came to life: beautifully appointed with rough-hewn paneled walls and rustic raw wood furniture, the floral scent of unlit candles laid out on a dresser. A fluffed queen bed with a down comforter dominated the long wall.

And no sign of Rusakov.

"Alex," Vail said. "Alex, you here?"

Nothing.

She cleared the closet and anteroom, which had a bay window that looked out onto what was likely forested mountainside.

DIE TRYING 119

Last unchecked area was presumably the bathroom. *Simple deduction, Watson.* Classy place like this, likely five hundred bills per night, did not feature community commodes.

If Rusakov was inside, she would have answered. And given all the variables, she *should* be inside. But if she is and she's not answering . . . *Damn.*

Vail inched back against the wall, reached to her right and turned the knob, pushing the door open in the same motion.

She waited a couple of seconds, then swung into the entrance—and came face-to-face with the barrel of another SIG, the P365, a more compact version.

Rusakov was naked and dripping wet, white AirPods protruding from her ears.

"Karen? What the f—?"

Vail blew raspberries from her lips and slumped her shoulders. "Jesus, Alex. We almost shot each other. Why didn't you answer?"

Rusakov pulled out her left earbud. "I was relaxing, taking a warm bath with the Rolling Stones playing."

Vail holstered her gun. "I like my bluesy Mick tunes, too. But is that . . . relaxing?"

"It is for me."

Vail took a thick lavender towel from the rack near her elbow and handed it to Rusakov. "Cover yourself up, would you?"

Rusakov took the luxurious cotton in her hands and swung it around her body. "Sorry. Didn't realize you were such a prude."

"I'm not. I just . . . my boobs don't look like that."

"These aren't real."

"No shit," Vail said. "But the rest of you is." Rusakov shrugged. "Hard work."

"And genetics." Vail turned and headed for the bed. "Have a seat. I've got a favor to ask."

Rusakov joined Vail, her brow bunched in concern. "You drove all the way down here to ask a favor?"

"Uzi needs our help. Well, he asked *me*, but I need *your* help to have a shot at getting what *he* needs."

Rusakov started patting her skin dry.

"Sorry to ruin your vacation."

Rusakov laughed. "I was starting to get bored. I'm not the type who can sit around doing nothing. I went hiking, did some meditating for the first several hours. Thought I could unplug."

"And now?"

She tossed the towel over the side of the tub. "Now I'm ready to kick some ass. Let's go."

"You don't even know what Uzi needs."

"I assume it has to do with what Hoshi was working on. Whatever it is, I'm on board. I need to mix some adrenaline with all this red wine and mindfulness shit."

Over a glass of Argentinean malbec and dinner at a nearby restaurant, they discussed Uzi's ask and the challenges with obtaining that information.

Rusakov did not flinch as Vail bluntly laid it out for her. "Obviously, I get what needs to be done. What've we got on this Madari? Is he heterosexual?"

"Don't know. Maybe I should've asked Robby to join me." Rusakov lifted her brow.

"Eye candy." Vail waved a hand. "Don't tell him I said that."

"What else do you have?"

"I've got a dossier with me."

"The stuff Hoshi and I found?"

"I think she added to it."

"Great." Rusakov nodded. "I'll take whatever you've got. And, of course, I'll do my best."

Vail held up her glass. "Our best is all that Uzi expects."

"Bullshit. He wants the info. Anything less, he'll consider it a failure." She clinked Vail's glass. "But that's how *all* of us roll."

Vail laughed. "You got that right."

25

MA'ARAVIM STREET
JERUSALEM, ISRAEL

When Uzi saw Tamar's 1:00 a.m. text, he fell into the soft couch, his shoulders slumping visibly.

"What's up?" DeSantos asked, nodding at the handset.

"Tamar. She was told that the two women were older. In their fifties. Which means we're back to square one. I really thought we were on to something. I had that feeling."

"Me, too," DeSantos said. "Especially considering the source."

"The source." Uzi nodded slowly. "Gideon. Yeah, how 'bout that? Sure seemed like he was guiding me to her."

"He didn't actually say her name."

"No. He wasn't telling me *anything*, you know? Innocuous, oblique suggestions to provide deniability. But he basically eliminated all the male spec ops friends I had here."

DeSantos thought a moment. "He likely knew about Extraction, right? And that Tamar was on that op. And that you were friends with her, so she'd talk with you."

"Right."

"Could it have been another female operative?"

Uzi shook his head slowly. "I looked over that list. I don't think so."

"And Tamar's source is saying it was two older women. It's not adding up. Why?"

122　　　　　　　　　　ALAN JACOBSON

Uzi sighed deeply. "Because nothing's ever straightforward in covert ops, is it?"

"Could Aksel have been steering you to Tamar knowing the op involved two older women, so you'd chat with her, find this out, and conclude that it wasn't Dena and Maya. And that you'd—"

"Give up? Go home?" Uzi shook his head. "Gideon knows that would never happen."

"So then . . . what?" DeSantos started pacing. "Let's step back. It's possible Gideon only knows about Extraction because of coordination among agencies. It wasn't a Mossad op, it was IDF. Right?"

"Right."

DeSantos stopped and spread his arms. "Maybe he was read in verbally and it was years ago and all he remembers is an op involving two women. He legitimately suggested you check into it."

The front door opened and Bennie walked in. "Find anything of value while I was out?'

"Yeah," Uzi said. "Where'd you go?"

"Walking my dog."

"Benny," Uzi said, "you don't have a dog."

"I used to. Pilot. Golden retriever. I still take walks around the park even though he's gone. With my balance problems, I probably look like a drunken sailor." He chuckled. "Anyway, you said you found something."

Uzi briefed him on Tamar's text.

Benny grabbed a bottle of arak from the fridge and poured three glasses. "We both know the details of these ops are compartmentalized and need-to-know." He took a sip and smacked his tongue against the roof of his mouth. "I'm surprised she was able to get that info. And I'm very sorry it wasn't what you were hoping."

Uzi rubbed his face with both hands. "Should've known better than to think we'd hit on something so fast." He sat up and turned to DeSantos. "Any news on your dad and Bill Tait?"

DeSantos examined his drink. "My dad was going to make the call. Haven't heard anything since."

"So," Benny said, "where do we go from here?"

Uzi swallowed some arak, the licorice taste soothing as it spread across his tongue. "We move forward. I think Churchill once said, 'Continuous effort, not strength or intelligence, is the key.'"

"As long as intelligence isn't required," DeSantos said, "we've got nothing to worry about."

26

FULTON COUNTY JAIL
ATLANTA, GEORGIA

Due to the amount of time it took Vail to locate and drive to Rusakov, they decided to maximize their time by driving through the night. It was a nearly nine-hour jaunt to Fulton County Jail and if they took turns behind the wheel, they could each get four or five hours of shut-eye before they arrived.

Vail started the excursion, her mind wandering with no music or podcast playing in her ear. If anyone else had asked her to do this, she would have politely—or as her boss would say, not so politely—declined. But Uzi had asked. He always had her back—and she his.

Her thoughts turned to the inmate. Before getting on the road, Vail had called the prison and left a message requesting that they have Madari ready for a visit from law enforcement at 9:00 a.m. This helped the staff ensure that the convict was not eating or otherwise engaged, such as at an appointment or on a work detail.

That done, and now on the highway, Vail pondered the approach they would take with Madari. Rusakov had seduced targets before; Vail had personally witnessed a few, and there were likely dozens more she had not. She knew Rusakov was at her best when she was underestimated. The exotic-looking young woman had a drop-dead gorgeous exterior, yes, but she was bright and creative, determined and devious.

Men who judged this book by its cover were quickly dazzled by the heroine and her seductive dialogue. But by the time they turned the last page, they realized the story had ended a long time before.

When they rolled into town, Rusakov had already consumed two cups of coffee and had a filled thermos for Vail. They stopped at West Egg Café for a meal and to freshen up. Truth was, it did not matter what Vail looked or smelled like. Rusakov, however, was a different story. She needed to be fresh, vivacious, and alluring—without being obvious about it.

They split sour cream pancakes and Georgia Benedict, more java—something called Dancing Goats Coffee—brewed from organic Peruvian "sweet cake" beans. And damn, if Vail didn't get cinnamon and sweet cream on the palate. She felt like she was back in Napa with Roxxann Dixon trying to see if she could experience the listed tasting notes on her own tongue.

Arriving at the jail without an appointment was a huge risk considering how far they had come. They were relieved when Fady Madari granted them permission to meet, helped along by the suggestion that two women wanted to speak with him—and, by the way, one was an absolute knockout "who could have won the Miss World contest."

As they entered the facility, they went through the familiar process—for Vail, at least—stowing their sidearms and showing their identification . . . which were expert OPSIG fabrications.

They waited in a holding cell that doubled as an interview room. Madari was led in wearing handcuffs. He sized up the two visitors, his eyes taking in Vail before moving over to Rusakov and lingering on . . . her perfect face.

She was wearing a blousy running suit that revealed nothing as to what lay beneath.

"Mr. Madari," Vail said, "we appreciate you meeting with us." It did not matter what she said, really. His gaze was riveted by Rusakov's plump, bright red, intricately outlined lips.

Rusakov was holding his gaze, having visual sex with him. The twenty-four-year-old man was all too willing to go along with the tease.

"Do you know why we're here?"

126   ALAN JACOBSON

"Nope," he said, answering Vail but looking at Rusakov.

"Do you care?"

"Nope."

"I'd like to ask you about two women who went missing in Israel several years ago. Dena and Maya Uziel. One was in her thirties, the other was three years old."

Madari turned to face Vail. "Why do you want to know about them?"

"*Why* isn't important. To you. Tell us what you know about them."

He shrugged. "Nothing."

"That's not true," Vail said. "I *know* that you know who they are." Actually, she did not know. But reading his body language, the subtly narrowed eyes and furrowed brow at the mention of their names, made it clear he knew them. Or something *about* them. Vail was sure Rusakov picked up on it, too.

His gaze wandered back over to Rusakov.

"Mr. Madari," Vail said firmly. "We really need to know about them. Like how they're doing."

"No idea. Like I said, I don't know who they are."

Fine. You want to play this game, asshole? Well, we've got a game for you.

Vail pushed her chair back with a screech. "I'm gonna get some coffee. Looks like we're going to be here a while." She rose from her seat and knocked on the window. The guard—who had already been briefed on how this interview was going to be conducted—opened the door and allowed Vail to exit.

The corrections officer was not technically on board with what Rusakov was planning, but a box of freshly baked muffins from the café convinced him that he needed to go to the head around the time Vail left the room.

Rusakov stood up and casually unzipped her loose jumpsuit and stepped out of it, revealing form-fitting yoga pants and top.

Madari's jaw went slack, his eyes lingering on every inch of her skintight clothing.

Rusakov expected as much. On a psychosexual analytical level,

DIE TRYING

this outfit communicated that a woman was fit, healthy, and fertile. In this case, that was putting way too much thought into it. Her message to Madari appealed to him on a primal instinct that was likely baked into male DNA.

She slid back into the chair and reached forward, placing a hand atop Madari's. His wrists were chained to a steel anchor in the center of the table between them.

He looked at her red-painted nails. The slender fingers that were subtly, slowly, stroking the back of his right hand.

He swallowed hard.

"You do know about those two women my partner asked about." She left it hanging there, a stated fact without dispute.

He nodded imperceptibly.

"I want you to tell me more," she said, her voice bordering on a whisper.

Sensual.

He kept staring at her fingers, which suddenly went still. Madari lifted his gaze and met her eyes.

"You want more?" she asked, leaning forward, the low-cut top moving lower, allowing her cleavage to push up and out.

The young man took a deep breath.

Rusakov had no doubt that Madari had been taught how to resist difficult interrogation techniques in the event of capture. How to survive waterboarding, electrical shocks, even physical mutilation by knife.

But she was willing to bet he had not been schooled in what she was about to do to him.

She removed her hand and leaned back. "You'll help me out here, right?"

"Umm. I—I don't . . . I don't know much."

"Tell me what you do know." She pushed her chair back and walked around the table, resting her firm buttocks on the edge. She leaned forward and placed both hands on his thighs, inches from his groin. Her stretchy top had given way to the weight of her breasts, treating Madari to quite a show. For a guy who had been locked up for months in prison, and who had been a strict religious zealot prior to that, this was something very nearly impossible for him to ignore.

He swallowed. Hard.

And that was not the only thing that was hard.

She moved her right hand to his chin and lifted it. Looked into his eyes.

"You give me something, I'll give you something."

His Adam's apple rose and fell.

Without looking, she dropped her fingers to his groin, groped, and found what she wanted. Squeezed.

"Okay?"

He cleared his throat. "Okay?"

"You give me . . ." She squeezed again. "I give you."

He closed his eyes and threw his head back. Groaned. "What do you . . ." scraped from his suddenly dry throat. "What do you want to know?"

"The woman and her daughter. I want to know if they're alive. And where they are."

"I . . . I heard some things."

"Like?"

Swallowed. "No. You first."

Rusakov tilted her head to the side, grinning slightly, seductively. She squeezed harder, felt him respond, and then, with her left hand, pulled down the orange prison scrub pants, then grasped the waistband and ripped it open. His erection stood there, waiting.

Madari's breathing quickened.

"Changed my mind," she said. "You first. Or I stop. Right here."

His mouth dropped open. He licked his lips. "I heard some things."

"You already said that. What'd you hear?"

"That they're alive."

Rusakov drew her chin back. She had told Vail over dinner that she strongly doubted the veracity of the intel about Uzi's family. Now she was not so sure.

"Where are they??"

"They were moved around. But I haven't heard anything in four, five years. Something like that."

"Moved around? Where?"

He looked down and nodded at his penis.

DIE TRYING 129

She took the shaft in her hands, massaged it a bit—and he moaned, his head arcing backward again—but she did not want to go too far because she doubted a young guy—particularly in this situation—would take very long. And she needed to know that she had obtained all relevant information before he came. She would then get nothing more of value.

She stopped. "You're not telling me everything."

Madari's head snapped up, face red, breathing rapid. Eyes squinting, like, "How dare you?" He would slap her face, or worse, if he could.

"Tell me more," she said in a near whisper. "Now."

"That's all I know," he said quickly. "They were—they were holding onto them till a time when they could be used—leveraged. High leverage situation. That's—that's all I know."

"Did you actually see them alive?"

"No."

"Who's holding them?"

"Al-Humat. That's all I know. Now—finish."

"You keep saying 'that's all I know,' and then you tell me more. How do I know you're telling me the truth?"

Madari's mouth contorted in anger, as if she had nerve asking him that question. "Why would I lie? I want you to finish."

There were so many things wrong with his statement, but she concluded that Madari was probably telling her the truth. She just could not prove or verify it.

"Who can I corroborate this with?"

"I told you. Al-Humat."

"Names."

Madari flexed the muscles in his jaw. Thinking. Frustrated. Realizing he had to give her more to get something very special back.

"Omar Abdallah bin-Sahmoud. Used to be the main bombmaker for al-Humat. Now he's third in line of the entire group. Heads up their military planning division and their West Bank weapons smuggling department. And a guy I worked with."

"Worked with?"

Madari leaned forward. "Is this being recorded?"

"No. We wouldn't let them." Rusakov gestured with her chin for him to continue.

"I ran a sleeper cell in DC. One of the guys I worked with, he knew, too. About the two prisoners."

"Name?"

"Don't know."

"You worked with him and you don't know his name?"

"We all have aliases. We work in cells. The idea is we can't give up our people if—"

"I understand cells," Rusakov said. "What was his alias?"

"Batman."

Rusakov frowned and leaned back. "If you're lying to—"

Madari's brow scrunched in feigned innocence. "That was what we called him. I only saw him like four or five times each year."

"How old was . . . Batman?"

"Forty-two."

"You don't know his real name, but you know his exact age?"

"No harm in telling each other how old we are."

"Anything unusual about him? Weird hair, beard, tatts?"

"Beard. Trimmed, so he wouldn't look like a Muslim. No tatts. But a scar on his neck." He gestured with his chin, which was useless. "It was big. Across the jugular and carotid."

"Anything else?"

"His eyes were real weird. Wore sunglasses a lot so no one'd see it."

"Real weird? How?"

"Different colors. Made him look crazy. One eye was brown, the other blue. Like that guy who used to pitch for the Nats and Dodgers. Mets, too, I think."

Rusakov had no idea what he was talking about, but she would look into it.

"Good. That it?"

"That's it." Madari looked at her, then at his penis, which had gone limp.

She knew that would not be a problem. A moment later, order was restored and seconds after that, a cascade of fluid shot up.

Rusakov ducked and dove to avoid the spray. Except for her hand.

She stood up and banged on the door using her clean arm. The officer had returned from his bathroom break.

Rusakov did not look back—but she did not need to. It was a scene she had witnessed many times. Like a videogame, men were easily controlled by their joysticks.

27

Karen Vail did half the driving back to Virginia while Rusakov napped. The women stopped in Greensboro, North Carolina, for a meal and a restroom break. They washed up and stretched their legs, and then Rusakov took the wheel. It would be another five hours to Vail's home.

At this point, it was evening in Israel, so Vail dialed Uzi. She put the phone on speaker and waited for it to ring.

"Hey, Alex is with me in the car."

"And I've got Santa here," Uzi said. "I just want to tell you how much I appreciate you taking the time to do this. Both of you. It means so much to me."

"We know you'd do the same for us," Vail said. "And we did get potentially useful intel."

"We'll run with whatever you've got," DeSantos said.

Rusakov glanced over her left shoulder and changed lanes. "Good news is that the guy we met with, Fady Madari—you know who he is?"

"Hoshi sent over the stuff you put together with her. Thanks for going by my office."

Rusakov laughed. "I'm told that Viktoria was quite impressive."

They recapped what Madari told Rusakov.

"Sounds like Mo's source may've been telling the truth," Uzi said. "The bodies I saw in my apartment weren't my wife and daughter. But

DIE TRYING 133

these are all *unsubstantiated* sightings. No direct/first person confirmation or knowledge."

Vail shifted in her seat and tucked a curl of red hair behind her left ear. "We'll look into that sleeper cell bozo named Batman. But what about this Omar Abdallah bin-Sahmoud?"

"Could be significant," Uzi said. "I wonder . . ."

Vail and Rusakov shared a glance as they waited to see if they had lost the call.

"Uzi," Vail said, "you there?"

"Yeah. Sorry. Thinking. This Sahmoud guy could be related to the asshole we went up against a few years ago."

"Kadir Abu Sahmoud," DeSantos said.

Vail nodded. "Founder of al-Humat."

"*Co*-founder, yes," Uzi said. "They split off from Hamas. Can you two run by the Threat Screening Center? See if you can find anything in the CT database. If he's on a watchlist, the TSC may give us more info on why—and that can lead us to where he's been, what he's done, known associates."

Vail laughed. "In other words, start shaking the tree."

"*Quietly*," DeSantos said. "There are concerns our work here will disrupt the treaty negotiations."

"Copy that," Rusakov said. "We'll tread lightly. And maybe Veronika will pay another visit to Agent Ko, see if *she* can help *me* this time."

Uzi hung up and leaned back in his bed. "Interesting." DeSantos fluffed his pillow. "But."

"But it doesn't fit with what Tamar found out."

Uzi crossed his legs, staring at the ceiling. "Unless her mission had nothing to do with my girls."

Benny walked in and reached for the arm of a chair, then sat down unsteadily. "Just wanted to say goodnight."

"Omar Abdallah bin-Sahmoud," DeSantos said. "You know him?"

Benny harrumphed. "I know *of* him. Son of a terrorist who broke off from Hamas to form al-Humat. Kadir Abu Sahmoud. Lots of blood on his father's hands. And the younger Sahmoud's learned well. He's a chip off the old block of Semtex."

"Think we can track him down?" Uzi asked. "We've got unproven and unconfirmed intel that he may know about Dena and Maya's disposition. I want a face-to-face. I *need* a face-to-face."

Benny snorted a laugh, looked at Uzi and then DeSantos. "You're serious."

Uzi did not need to answer.

Benny yawned and rubbed his eyes with two knuckles. "I'll look into it tomorrow morning. See what we've got on the guy. If he's got a security detail—which is likely because of his father—we need to know. If we have recent intel on where he hangs out, who he hangs out with and when . . . you might have a shot. But it won't be without serious risk."

"I didn't fly all the way here to play it safe." Uzi sat up in bed. "Five or six years ago, my wife and daughter were supposedly still alive."

"Which we've now heard from two potentially independent sources," DeSantos said.

Benny slowly pulled himself up from the chair. "Who heard it from someone else."

"I know," Uzi yelled, punching his pillow. "Doubtful—at best. So frustrating. And we're running out of time."

"And yet," DeSantos said, "we're finally getting somewhere. Keep your chin up, boychick." He held up his phone. "My dad just texted that Bill Tait and his colleague, Phil Sanfilippo, are on a plane. Tomorrow's a new day and I have a feeling it's going to be good."

Uzi chuckled wryly. "From your lips to God's ears."

Benny turned and headed out of the room. "You are definitely in the right place for that."

28

JERUSALEM, ISRAEL

Uzi, DeSantos, and Benny met with Bill Tait and Phil Sanfilippo at Independence Park in the heart of Jerusalem.

The grounds, like so many locations in Israel, boasted a history dating back centuries. Christians, Muslims, and Jews all had remains buried there: the Jews killed by the Seleucid Greeks in 175 BCE were interred there; eight hundred years later, the bones of Christian monks who were murdered by the Persians in 614 CE were placed in the park's "lion's cave." Sometime after 630 CE, sacred Muslim bones were transferred by Allah to the western portion of the Mamilla cemetery to rescue them from a fire.

In the present, however, the park's focus was on the living, with a large swath of sculpture-adorned landscaped greenery and a walking path that meandered among pine trees. Daytime workers from surrounding businesses ate their lunches there and families picnicked. Under cover of darkness, the park transformed into a meeting place for the LGBTQ+ community.

Today, this ancient, hallowed ground served as a convenient spot to strategize. When Uzi, DeSantos, and Benny arrived, they found Tait and Sanfilippo standing in the shade of a tall pine where no interested ears resided. Despite the partly sunny day and stratocumulus-dotted blue sky, the park was sparsely populated.

DeSantos made the introductions—except for Sanfilippo, whom he did not know.

"Phil is one of my key men," Tait said.

Sanfilippo bore the stature of a former powerlifter or linebacker, someone who was hard to miss in a crowded room. He had the look of an Irishman from Italy . . . ruddy complexion with some hint of red hair, thick facial features, and a full black beard. His demeanor, Uzi decided, was that of a guy ready for action.

Sanfilippo gave his hand willingly to Uzi, DeSantos, and Benny. "Good to meet you guys. Everyone's got a story. I know we don't have time to hear yours, but . . . maybe someday over a beer."

"Amen to that," DeSantos said. "Thanks for helping us out. You've been briefed?"

"I've told him what I know," Tait said, "which isn't much. Lukas only had a thin dossier, some facts from several years ago."

"My dad didn't have much time to dig around," DeSantos said. "Uzi, let's bring them up to speed."

Within two minutes, Tait and Sanfilippo were read in.

"There are things I can do here and things I can't do," Uzi said. "Mossad, and I'm sure Shin Bet, knows Santa and I are here. We're probably being monitored—which is why we left our phones in Benny's apartment."

"We won't set off any alarms here," Tait said. "But if you've got a burner SIM, we should use that to communicate on Signal or WhatsApp. Already on WhatsApp, if that works for you guys."

"Perfect." Uzi held up a well-worn iPhone. "Our Israel mobiles. Old-time SIM cards. Ready to go."

"I'll set up a group chat." Tait motioned for Uzi's device. "I'll enter our numbers and enable disappearing messages at the twenty-four-hour mark. Just in case."

"Perfect," Uzi said. "First order of the day is to find Sahmoud, get him in a room for a face-to-face."

Sanfilippo whistled. "Okee-dokee. We're starting off with a bang. Word gets around you're on his trail, and I'm him? I go underground or I cry to my daddy and he beefs up security. Or moves me. Or both."

DIE TRYING 137

"I don't see a way around that," DeSantos said. "We can't go through official channels to find out what intelligence agencies have on him."

Benny groaned or growled—it was not a sound of joy. "I might be able to poke around. Let me see what I can find."

"Without exposing yourself?" Uzi asked.

Benny bobbed his head. "Yes."

"You're lying."

"Yes."

"We have our sources—and resources—too," Tait said. "Let's go about our business, keep a low profile, and see where it leads us in . . . twelve hours—no, let's say 10:00 p.m. tonight. Then we can reassess." He looked at Uzi, DeSantos, and Benny. "Good?"

"Good," DeSantos said.

"We should get out of here," Sanfilippo said. "We've spent enough time standing and chatting. We're lucky the place is empty. Next time we bring a hacky sack ball so we don't stick out like a sore thumb."

The two groups split up and headed off in their own directions, Benny walking home and Uzi and DeSantos heading to Benny's car.

"If we really want to go after Sahmoud," DeSantos said as he settled himself into the passenger seat, "we find out if he's got family. If he does, we go there and make *him* come to *us*."

"We're trying to keep the volume low. That's like using two stadium style loudspeakers and a bus-sized subwoofer." Uzi started the engine and pulled away from the curb. "It's the kind of thing everyone wants to keep us from doing."

DeSantos shifted in his seat to face Uzi. "Aside from Benny digging something up without anyone knowing—unlikely since Sahmoud's the son of a prominent terrorist—anything we do is gonna draw attention. And we're running out of time."

"If we had time," Uzi said, "we could sit on Sahmoud's house. Wait for him to return. Everything changes when you're up against a deadline."

"So what are we going to do if the timer goes off and we haven't gotten answers? Just board our flight and return home?"

Uzi navigated the streets of Jerusalem as he spoke. "Haven't thought that far."

"Bullshit."

"Fine. I've thought about it. Haven't reached any conclusions."

DeSantos shook his head and glanced out the passenger side window.

"Where are we going?"

"Old City."

DeSantos pulled on the shoulder harness and repositioned himself in the seat. "To do what?"

"Get answers. Before that timer goes off."

29

The Old City. It was a nondescript moniker that not only belied its complex history and age but did not do justice to its melting pot of religious and cultural milieus.

The "modern" walls and city gates were built by the Ottoman Turks in the 1530s, and in the nineteenth century it was divided into quadrants: the Armenian, Christian, Jewish, and Muslim quarters.

Detailed documentation in the Hebrew Bible and ancient maps of Jerusalem reached back over four thousand years to the Bronze and Iron ages, with boundary adjustments north, south, and east depending on the millennium. The current layout has existed for approximately fifteen hundred years.

For their purposes, Uzi and DeSantos were making their way toward the Muslim Quarter, where they would be focusing their efforts. It was there, during his years under the employ of various intelligence agencies, that Uzi spent considerable time meeting with informants and shop owners whose relatives in Lebanon and Syria had provided vital information that aided in heading off terror attacks before—sometimes *just* before—they were launched.

He figured that many of those sources had since moved on, sold their shops, or retired. Uzi hoped to find one or two key individuals still around who knew something he and DeSantos could use.

As they moved through the Jewish Quarter, they made their way past old buildings that lined an alley. A sign with Hebrew lettering

140 ALAN JACOBSON

included an English translation that read, "Institute for Talmudic Commentaries."

"Now *that'd* make a worthwhile visit," Uzi quipped. "On another trip."

DeSantos glanced at his friend. "Huh?"

"The Talmud is commentary on Jewish law, morals, and philosophy by rabbis spanning thousands of years," Uzi said. "You need scholars to give perspective and linguistic analysis to understand it. Dense stuff, but it can be interesting."

"Yeah," DeSantos said with a snort. "Sounds *super* interesting. Definitely next visit."

Today the sprawling marketplace was packed with masses of shoppers, from stooped-over elderly people shuffling along leaning heavily on canes to youngsters of three or four jumping, singing, and swinging arm in arm.

After passing through several narrow pedestrian-only walkways and making their way to the Muslim Quarter, Uzi stopped by several stores, inquiring about people he knew—and getting the response that he or she no longer owned the place, was on vacation, or was visiting family. As Uzi's shoulders slumped in frustration, he noticed someone at a distance—an old friend who had been one of his most reliable assets.

DeSantos hung back, a store or two away, to avoid the appearance of an official government visit.

"Bassam," Uzi said, a smile broadening his lips and a hug overcoming any concern Bassam might have had about Uzi's sudden appearance. "Good to see you."

Bassam Doka was a few years Uzi's senior, a full salt-and-pepper beard and hair rounding out a sun-creased face. He had a jovial disposition and an open demeanor.

"You have not been around, sir. I was beginning to wonder if you would ever come around again."

"It's been a long time, I know," Uzi said. "Moved back to the US. After—well, after a family tragedy."

"I heard," Bassam said, "about the tragedy." His gaze remained locked on Uzi's. Saying something without speaking.

DIE TRYING   141

Uzi cleared his throat. "How 'bout I buy you a Turkish coffee?"

Bassam glanced about. Uzi was unsure if he was checking on people in the area who might overhear or if he was assessing prospective customers.

"I have something better in the back. Come with me."

They moved through the single-aisle shop, scarves and women's dresses hanging a dozen feet off the ground. Not an inch of wasted sales space. Bassam passed through a divider of hanging beads into a cramped back room. He motioned Uzi to a small card table and a couple of chairs. Uzi sat so close to the beads that they brushed against the back of his head and settled an inch from his shoulders.

Bassam opened a shallow cabinet. A bottle of arak followed two small glasses. He poured both, then held his up. "The milk of lions."

Uzi tipped his glass and said, "*Fe Sahatek.*"

"*Fe Sahatek,*" Bassam repeated.

After taking a sip, Uzi set his drink down. "I'm looking for Omar bin-Sahmoud."

Bassam looked at Uzi over the rim of his glass. "You know who he is?"

"Yes."

"You can find him in Jenin. Sometimes in Nablus." He lowered his voice. "He likes women."

"So do I."

"No, I mean *women.* Women who sell their bodies."

"Prostitutes?" Uzi said above a whisper.

Bassam nodded.

Uzi drained his glass.

Bassam sat down slowly, poured more alcohol. "I think I know why you are here, my friend."

Uzi studied his drink. "Tell me."

"Your wife and daughter."

Uzi hesitated, realized he had already ventured down this road. Made no sense to turn back now. "Right so far. Go on."

"I heard something, from my son. Ghaffar. He's . . ." Bassam waved a hand, his face sagging. "His friends . . . they are not good people.

142 ALAN JACOBSON

I talked to him, but . . ." He shrugged. "You can't tell these kids anything nowadays. They know better. They're signed up for the cause, as if that's going to solve everything. Or anything."

"I can't imagine how difficult that is. Knowing the danger. Being unable to do anything about it. You think he's—you think these people are planning an attack?"

"Let me ask you this. Are you here as an—"

"No. No, I don't work with them anymore. But if your son and his . . . comrades are planning anything," Uzi shook his head. "Damn. I don't know, maybe I can talk with him."

Bassam laughed. "You still think you can solve everything?"

Uzi grinned. "I do. Dena used to get so ang—" He stopped himself and looked down, then slung his drink back. The burn was all he felt. The licorice of the arak was easily overpowered. "Sorry. You were saying. About something your son told you."

Bassam studied Uzi's face a moment. "Ghaffar asked me if I still saw you. I asked him why. He said one of his bosses was bragging that they had taken your wife and daughter hostage and that no one had any idea. They were holding them until the time was right. When they could use it. Leverage it."

"When was this?"

"A long time ago. I figured you'd come by at some point, I'd tell you. But . . ." He shrugged. "You never did. I tried calling your phone, but some guy answered. Wasn't you. I hung up."

Uzi nodded. "When you say, 'a long time ago,' are we talking months? Years?"

"Years. I can ask Ghaffar if—"

"No. No, don't say anything to him about me, about me being here, asking you about my family. Nothing. Okay?"

Bassam shrugged. "Okay. Yes. Whatever you want."

"Who's Ghaffar's boss? Who does he work for?"

Bassam leaned forward a bit and lowered his voice. "Al-Humat. He does computer programming. Hacking, I think. Maybe. Something like that."

Uzi clenched his jaw. The hacking claim was dubious—but he had a strong sense that he was on to something here. And he had to tread

DIE TRYING 143

carefully. He did not want to involve or endanger Bassam's son, no matter how poorly chosen the young man's allegiance was.

"Has he said anything more about . . . my family since then?"

Bassam shook his head. "I'm sorry to tell you this. I can see it's very disturbing."

Uzi dropped his chin and nodded slightly. "It's a mixed bag, my friend. I'm glad to hear they're alive—I've lived for many years thinking the opposite—but now, hearing they may be alive but not knowing where they are, *how* they are, if they're well or sick, being cared for or . . . or tortured. That's where it's difficult. I'm here to find answers to those questions." *And to get them out.* "But I don't have a lot of time. I have to go back home in a couple of days."

Bassam stood up quickly, spilling the arak. Uzi swung his head around and saw someone behind the divider.

"Ghaffar," Bassam shouted.

Uzi grabbed at the man and got a handful of glass beads—and Ghaffar's wrist. He twisted and Ghaffar yelled out in pain before falling backward and knocking merchandise off both sides of the store's single aisle. He gathered himself as Uzi was fighting through the tangled nylon filament.

"Santa! Santa," Uzi yelled. He dove forward like a running back crossing the goal line with the football—and saw a cell phone on the floor. Probably Ghaffar's. Uzi scooped it up to prevent him from alerting his al-Humat buddies to Uzi's presence. Who knew what he had overheard before Bassam noticed him standing there.

DeSantos had to hear Uzi yelling. Would he have noticed a man fleeing from the same location?

Probably.

Uzi pushed through the crowded market. At six-foot-two, he had a decent view over the tops of heads—and he caught sight of someone shoving customers to the side.

Ghaffar? DeSantos.

But dozens of feet ahead of his friend, Uzi saw the outline of Ghaffar silhouetted against the glary sky.

Uzi could not let Ghaffar get away. If he did reach his al-Humat compadres, Dena and Maya—if they were still alive—would be in

144   ALAN JACOBSON

grave danger. And it would likely blow up the one thing Aksel, Tasset, and Knox had admonished him about . . . the Abraham Treaties.

But Uzi's relationship with Bassam prevented him from doing anything that would endanger Ghaffar's life.

And yet . . . what if Ghaffar and company were planning a terror attack and Uzi's lack of action cost innocent people their lives?

He pulled out his cell and dialed the number he knew by heart. Aksel answered seconds later.

"Gideon, in pursuit of Ghaffar Doka, member of AH. Five-nine, a hundred seventy or so. Unknown if he's armed. But he knows I'm looking for my family. I think he overheard me talking about why I'm here. In the Muslim Quarter in foot pursuit. Headed west."

"Stay on the line," Aksel said, "putting out an alert."

Uzi could no longer say he had eyes on Ghaffar.

Likewise, DeSantos appeared unsure of where their "suspect" went. Seconds later, Aksel returned.

"Gideon, listen to me. Please—exercise caution with him. He's a friend's son."

"Some friends you keep."

"My friend's a CI. For a really long time. He's helped us a lot over the years. Just don't hurt Ghaffar."

Aksel harrumphed. "That's up to him, isn't it?"

"Gideon—"

"You know how it goes, Uzi. We catch up to him and he surrenders? Of course. I'll make sure he's treated well. But if he's armed in a crowded area and won't surrender his weapon . . . I cannot protect him from himself."

"I understand."

"Knew you would."

Uzi hung up and continued moving forward, following DeSantos's lead. He called Tait and Sanfilippo and left a voicemail reporting their status and location. He had no idea where they were or what they were doing, but wanted to alert them in case they were nearby and could assist.

As Uzi hung up, his phone vibrated: DeSantos.

"Shit," DeSantos said. "Excuse me, ma'am. Sorry." There was some commotion and then DeSantos returned to the call. "Got him."

"Where?"

"Thirty yards ahead of me, two o'clock."

"Got him."

"Who's this guy we're chasing?"

"My friend Bassam's son. Involved with al-Humat. Deeper than Bassam would like."

"Hmm."

"Hmm?"

"Got an idea."

"That's one more than I've got," Uzi said. "Let's hear it."

"We hang back and follow him instead of grabbing him up."

"And see where he goes," Uzi said. "A place where he can get some help. Security. Strength in numbers. He may not know who's really after him. He may think it's the security service."

"Exactly."

"I like it," Uzi said. "Let him think he's lost you. But keep an eye on him."

"Oh, sure. Piece of cake."

"Hey," Uzi said, catching a glimpse of DeSantos slowing his pace. "If what we did was easy, we'd have gotten bored years ago."

30

MUQEIBILA, ISRAEL
NORTH OF THE WEST BANK BORDER

Thirty-six minutes later, Uzi and DeSantos were in the back of a cab. They had WhatsApp'ed the group to keep them informed and had paid the driver generously. They told the man, identified by his posted license as Naim Zeedan, to follow a gray Fiat—and to keep the journey to himself after he dropped them off.

This was not an unusual request in these parts.

Ghaffar's vehicle slipped into line behind a few cars at Emek Harod border station, which sat outside the Muslim neighborhood of Muqeibila.

Speaking Arabic, Uzi told Naim to pull over.

"¿Cuál es el problema?" DeSantos said in Spanish, reasonably certain the Druze taxi driver did not *habla español*.

"Nuestro sospechoso está pasando por un puesto de control." *Our suspect is passing through a checkpoint.*

DeSantos glanced down the road at the complex. "Then let's go. Follow him."

"Normally, it shouldn't be too difficult to get through, but we could be flagged."

"Why?"

"Aksel could've alerted the security service to keep us out of the Palestinian territories. Or we could be on some other list." Uzi pursed his lips. "Could be how E Squadron found us."

DIE TRYING   147

DeSantos spread his hands. "So that's it?"

"When have you known me to give up that easily?" Uzi thought a moment. "I'll bet he's headed for Jenin. That part of the West Bank's got a history of terror activity. IDF's had to root out terrorists a few times over the years. Last year, the army found a weapons manufacturing factory there and cleared out several hundred large bombs."

DeSantos peered out at the area in front of them. "Maybe our driver knows another way in."

Uzi tapped Naim on the shoulder. In Arabic, he said, "You know how to get in there?"

"Not really."

DeSantos cocked his head. "You either do or you don't." He asked Naim if he spoke English—DeSantos likely wanted to avoid any miscommunications because of his vastly improved, but imperfect, Arabic.

Naim nodded. "People talk. Passengers."

"And what do they say?"

"Couple years ago. A man tell his friend there is tunnel. Want to move things in and out of Jenin. But there was problem with tunnel. He want to show him."

"Why would he do that?" DeSantos asked. "Makes no sense."

"No." Naim looked at DeSantos in the rearview mirror. "His friend was . . . contract."

"Contractor?" Uzi asked.

Naim tilted his head. "Yes. Contractor. He knew . . . um . . . how do you say in English? Engine?"

"Engineer?"

"Yes, yes. Engineer."

Uzi gestured to the road ahead. "Show us where the tunnel is."

Naim glanced left and right. "I maybe can find it. Drive around some."

"Then drive around," Uzi said, dropping three hundred shekels in the front seat. "Find it. Show us."

It took forty-five minutes, but Naim finally pulled across the street from a nondescript building. It was officially a used auto parts store that also

148 ALAN JACOBSON

appeared to perform body shop repairs. Several vehicles in various states of disrepair sat in the sun, a couple of workers busy with tasks.

Uzi messaged Tait's group and sent them the address, what they suspected, and what they were planning to do.

They asked if Naim was willing to wait for them here—they would compensate him properly—and he said he would be able to remain there for an hour.

Uzi and DeSantos got out and headed toward the business. They had agreed on a visible approach with a cover story and then would improvise as they went, depending on what they found and who they encountered.

Uzi entered first and took a quick glance around to assess threats in the vicinity. There were two men behind a counter seemingly doing normal things he would expect body shop personnel to be doing: one was digging through a toolbox and another was talking with what appeared to be a customer, going over a service estimate.

DeSantos stood to Uzi's right, conducting his own surveillance and analysis.

He and DeSantos were armed, but not with confidence-inspiring weapons. The calculus was different when the rounds you fired would not put down your enemy unless you hit him in key areas—with multiple shots. In close quarters combat, there was little room for error. Perfection and luck were preferred, if not required.

The man poring over the invoice looked up. "What do you need?" he asked in rapid Arabic.

"Car needs work. Accident."

"Yeah, yeah. Be with you soon."

"Got a bathroom?"

He jerked a hand over his left shoulder, directing Uzi off to his left, and went back to chattering with the customer.

Leaving DeSantos to wait in line, Uzi headed off to the hallway the employee had indicated.

But he would only end up at the water closet if forced to maintain his cover. His singular task was to find the hidden entrance.

Known as "Lower Gaza" and "the metro," the several hundred miles of tunnels constructed beneath Gaza served as a way for terror groups to surreptitiously move weapons, money, and supplies. A one-time technological collaboration among Hamas, al-Humat, Hezbollah, Iran, and the drug cartels of Mexico, these underground networks had become more sophisticated as engineering and materials improved.

The passageways were constructed from concrete and iron, with some sized to accommodate weapons factories and even prisons. Many featured lighting, ventilation, elevators, tiled bathrooms with showers and kitchens; bunkers for storing weapons and artillery; command and control centers and missile launching facilities; data centers with servers, electronic surveillance equipment, and communications gear. Some contained tracks for rail transport of heavy equipment.

Other tunnels were equipped with large rooms for keeping hostages and prisoners—where no one could find them and where rescue was nearly impossible.

The West Bank also had these subterranean passages—on a much lesser scale—but excavation in places like Jenin proved more difficult because of its stone substrate. Digging required patience and enduring will, as well as construction expertise—which could have been why Naim overheard the need for an engineer.

Regardless, Uzi had watched a few tunnels being built on stakeouts and had been through several on post-raid seizures. He felt he could identify even well-disguised entrances.

The hallway opened into a larger unfinished, high-ceilinged warehouse-style space. Vehicles were parked in two rows, covering much of the concrete floor. He pulled out a tactical flashlight and shined it underneath the cars as he moved left to right, looking for abnormalities. Uzi had once seen radial cracks emanating from a hole that had been excavated. In other cases, tunnels with square openings sported extraneous saw marks at the corners.

As the seconds ticked by in his head, he found what he was looking for under a 1980s Volkswagen, the fifth car he checked.

He glanced around at the walls to get his bearings and extinguished the flashlight. Seconds later, he joined DeSantos and nodded. They slowly moved toward the exit and as Uzi was about to push through the door, turned back to the counterman. "Saoud la tuklaq." *I'll come back, no worries.*

150   ALAN JACOBSON

"You find it?"

"I did." Uzi crossed the street, headed toward Naim's taxi. "And we *will c*ome back. Tonight. When no one's there."

They climbed into the taxi and thanked Naim by handing him another five hundred shekels.

"You know who Omar Abdallah bin-Sahmoud is?" Uzi asked. "Of course." Naim looked in the rearview mirror at Uzi. "Why?"

"Interested in where he might live. Or hang out."

Naim averted his eyes and cleared his throat. "Forget. I do not want to know."

"Where can we find him?"

Naim was quiet.

"You take fares to Jenin?"

"Yes. From Old City. Damascus Gate. I pick up fares, take them to Ramallah. From there, to Jenin. With proper ID at the security checkpoints."

"Do you know where Sahmoud lives?" DeSantos asked firmly, dropping two hundred more shekels on the seat.

Naim took a quick glance at the cash then clenched his jaw. "I know where his . . . his how you say. Deputy. I know where deputy lives."

"What's his name?"

"I do not know name. But is the man we follow."

Uzi and DeSantos shared a glance.

Ghaffar is Sahmoud's deputy.

Uzi pulled up his phone and tapped and swiped and found Jenin on Google Maps. "Show me where."

Naim zoomed in, moved the screen left, then right, and found the street.

"Here. This house." He showed Uzi and returned his phone.

DeSantos tapped Naim's right shoulder. "Thank you."

31

NORTH CAPITOL STREET NW
WASHINGTON, DC

Karen Vail and Alexandra Rusakov had canvassed areas known to be frequented by radical types in the district. They were going off intel provided by the FBI's Threat Screening Center, the Agency's known associates, and the NSA, to see if the "Batman" nickname had been used in international communications, particularly with Middle Eastern countries on the "not huge fans of America" list.

When that failed to yield any direct hits, Vail checked with a contact at the Anti-Defamation League, or ADL, which the Bureau worked with on a regular basis—particularly the counterintelligence and counterterrorism divisions at the Washington field office. ADL was not bound by the same federal restrictions that often constrained the FBI's ability to gather information on a suspect.

ADL's sole lead involved a man known as Haydar Tahan. Vail was directed to speak with its domestic terrorism expert, Karl Ruckhauser, who was putting together a dossier on Tahan but needed to confirm a couple of pieces of information. Once it was completed, he was planning to pass it on to the FBI for informational purposes.

As was so often the case, Vail was being pressured to "produce" under suboptimal conditions. Trying to find someone who did not want to be found was difficult enough. But when that individual had the skills and training to remain hidden in a city, it would be very tough, if not impossible—with no time constraints. Doing it in a day, without a network of confidential informants . . . Vail could only shake her head at the poor odds.

Unless something intervened to improve those odds.

The unusual scar, eye color disparity, and nickname were all stacked in that column.

"You ever seen a guy with two different eyes?" Vail asked.

"It's called heterochromia iridum," Rusakov said nonchalantly. "It has to do with the pigment, the melanin in the iris. Lots of causes. Genetics is one of them. But no, I've never seen it."

"You know a lot about it."

"I googled it on the drive over after Hoshi forwarded Ruckhauser's report."

Vail grinned. "I'm still impressed you could pronounce hetero—*hetero automatic dumb dumb*?"

They laughed.

"Heterochromia iridum. I studied to be a nurse. I was a couple courses short of finishing when I won a beauty pageant. And my dad saw dollar signs. In Russia, nurses earn the equivalent of a thousand dollars a month. But you win a beauty pageant and lots of things open up. Modeling is a big one. And he thought we could take that to the US and make a lot here."

"Probably right."

"He was right. But a few months after my visa expired, I was still here. Living in New York. I did a late-night shoot in Brighton Beach with a Russian photographer who got me drunk and . . ." Rusakov took a deep breath. "He raped me. I walked into a police station and next thing I know the FBI wanted to talk about a human trafficking ring run by that photographer. I didn't know anything about it, but the agent took an interest in me and thought I'd make a good counterintelligence analyst. Director Knox found out about me and had other plans."

"OPSIG."

Rusakov nodded. "I apparently scored high in critical thinking, problem solving, math, and science."

"Uzi told me you're very bright. Nothing's given to you at the Bureau—or the Pentagon. You earn it. And you have."

"So *you* earned your reputation at the Bureau?" Vail laughed out loud. "Hell yes."

Vail pulled the black Suburban over to a curb just off North Capitol Street. It was fairly safe to walk around the area during the day—but definitely not once the sun set.

"So Ruckhauser's report," Vail said, "fingers this Haydar Tahan as Batman?"

"Sixty percent certainty."

Vail bobbed her head. "That's not nothing."

If Haydar Tahan was Batman and if he was involved with Middle Eastern terror groups, this was where they would set up shop. An apartment in this neighborhood would likely not receive much law enforcement scrutiny—unless they created trouble. And that was the first rule of a sleeper cell: keep your noses clean at all costs.

They got out of their SUV and blew on their hands. It was glove weather—but neither of them came properly equipped.

"Looking for Batman," Vail said to a man bundled in a ratty parka sitting on a broken and bent metal chair. She hoped not to sound like a nut job, but she had to admit, that's exactly how she felt.

Then again, the area was rife with mentally ill people and those high on illicit drugs—so she probably fit right in.

The guy provided nothing of use, but neither did anyone else. Truth was, Vail and Rusakov did not expect cooperation. If anyone knew Tahan, there would be no incentive for him or her to rat on him.

Asking questions out of the blue—as they were doing—spelled "fiveoh." Police. No one in these parts wanted anything to do with cops.

Until they found a gray-haired woman in her sixties wrapped in a shawl, shuffling down a dirty apartment hallway.

"Looking for a friend of ours," Rusakov said. "He goes by Batman." She pointed to her neck. "Scar right about here. And weird-colored eyes. Seen him around? Got some money I owe him."

The woman studied Rusakov's face for a few seconds. Then, without uttering a word, gestured toward where she had come from.

"Which apartment?" Vail asked.

154   ALAN JACOBSON

The lady leaned closer—and Vail smelled an odor that caused her throat to contract. "Three-twelve," she said by Vail's ear, and then continued down the corridor.

There was no peephole or doorbell cam. They decided that Rusakov would knock and Vail would be off to the side, out of sight, gun drawn with her back to the wall.

Rusakov tousled her hair, pulled the top of her blouse down about two inches, then rapped three times with her knuckles.

"Who is it?" a muffled male voice asked.

"Vicky. From downstairs. Got water flooding into my place. From the ceiling. Gotta be comin' from your place."

Pause. Then, "Ain't no leak in here."

Rusakov glanced at Vail, who gestured for her to continue.

She moved closer to the door. "Can I come in and look? Could be in the pipes. Sometimes they get these little holes and you can't see 'em unless you look real careful. My brother had that once and when we—"

The door pulled open. Vail could only see a man's nose and mouth.

"I know what to look for," Rusakov said. "Please, just a minute or two and we'll know."

"A'right. Fine."

"Like I said, my name's Vicky. You?"

"DeAndre."

"Hey, neighbor." Rusakov slipped into the apartment and the door clicked shut behind her.

"Shit," Vail muttered under her breath.

Rusakov glanced around, taking in everything she could without being obvious.

"Never seen you before," DeAndre said.

"Moved in a couple of months ago." She made an effort to appear as if she were trying to figure out where the leak might be located, moving from room to room. "Water is funny. It doesn't go straight down. It can run along pipes or wires and then come out."

"Uh-huh."

She passed into the living room—and stopped in her tracks. Sitting there was a man in his forties rushing to slip on a pair of sunglasses.

DIE TRYING 155

"Oh hey," Rusakov said, moving across the room with long strides. "Nice to meet you." She stuck out her hand as she approached the guy she was fairly certain was Tahan. Sunglasses? Indoors?

"I'm Vicky from the second floor." He shook. "You must be Batman."

Tahan's face went slack. He stood up in one motion—but Rusakov already had him in her viselike grip and was drawing him toward her while pulling out her SIG with her left hand . . . a move that prevented DeAndre from doing something heroic.

"DeAndre. Over here. *Now*. Have a seat."

She used the tip of the pistol to flick the shades off Tahan's face, revealing two miscolored eyes.

Hell yeah. Heterochromia iridum.

"What the fuck, lady?"

She twisted his arm behind his back and pulled it up . . . an extremely painful, disarming position.

"Yo," Rusakov shouted. "KV! Get in here."

Seconds later, the apartment door blasted open and Vail stepped across the threshold. She corralled DeAndre and immediately secured him with flex cuffs.

"Now," Rusakov said to Tahan, "we're going to have a chat. And I'm gonna be straight with you. Answer our questions truthfully, everything will be fine and we'll leave like we were never here. You don't . . . well, *nothing* will be fine. And you'll *wish* we were never here."

Tahan tilted his head. "Who are you two?"

"Let me set the scene for you," Vail said. "We've got the guns. We ask the questions. Clear?"

Rusakov dug the tip of her pistol into Tahan's soft cheek. "Yeah," Tahan said. "Got it."

Rusakov pushed him down into his seat.

"Now. We know you're a sleeper cell for al-Humat."

"Hang on a s—"

"Not interested in your bullshit denials," Vail said. "We know who you are. We're not here to arrest you. We just need information."

"Information that *you* have," Rusakov said. A statement, not a question.

Tahon studied Vail's face, then Rusakov's. "Go on."

156   ALAN JACOBSON

"Several years ago a woman and her daughter were murdered in Jerusalem. It was made to look like a terror attack carried out by Batula Hakim."

"Don't know anything ab—"

Rusakov slapped him across the face with an open palm. "Don't fucking lie to me. I told you, we don't give a shit what you're involved in. We just want information. No reason to lie. Get it?"

He looked away from her and licked his lips. "Got it."

Rusakov knew a slap wasn't as physically painful as a punch with brass knuckles—or a right cross leading with the butt of her SIG. But it sent a message and likely bruised Tahan's male ego for being dominated by a woman. She could always turn up the heat a bit with a more forceful beating, but she doubted that would be necessary.

Vail noted the clock on the wall and felt her blood pressure leap. Uzi and DeSantos's time in Israel was dwindling and they had failed to deliver answers of substance.

She took a deep breath and refocused.

"So like I was saying," Rusakov said. "We know that was a setup and that the woman and girl were taken hostage by al-Humat."

"What we want you to tell us," Vail said, "is where they are now."

Tahan glanced at DeAndre, who remained poker-faced.

"Nothing to think about," Vail said. "No reason to stall. Just tell us."

"Or what?" DeAndre said.

"Trust me. You don't want to find out." Vail lowered her pistol to his groin. Pressed firmly. "Lots of blood and screaming. And when we're done, we'll call in an anonymous tip to the FBI's counterterrorism office. If you don't bleed out before they get here, we'll let the Feds sort out whatever you're doing here."

"Tell us what we want to know and your sleeper cell remains intact." Rusakov shrugged. "We leave here and your lives can go on as if we never came."

There was silence as the men appeared to be thinking.

"How do we know you're not Feds?" Tahan asked.

"Seriously?" Rusakov laughed. "Do we look like cops?"

DIE TRYING   157

His gaze traversed her face, her perfect eyebrows and nasal structure, clear blue eyes, high cheekbones, and subtle accentuating makeup. "No."

"You can think of us as private contractors," Rusakov said. "I don't have any arrest powers. I don't know if that puts your mind at ease, but it's the truth."

Those *were* truthful statements; she did not say they *were* private contractors. It was a subtle difference, though omitting information and using clever phrasing did leave room for moral debate as to what constituted "lying." But did it matter?

"How'd you find me?"

"It's what we do," Vail said. "And we're good at our jobs. Now— you've asked more questions than *we've* asked. That's gonna stop right here. Tell us about that woman and girl's kidnapping."

He cleared his throat. "I wasn't involved, but . . ." He shrugged. "It was talked about. I heard things around the time we got them." Vail continued the questioning. "Are they still alive?"

"Been in the US five years. I'm out of that circle. Last I heard, the girl was alive. Don't know about her mother. They separated them because my boss thought it was too risky keeping them together. All your eggs in the same basket."

Eggs? It was a mother and her young child.

Vail realized she was clenching her molars. She squared her shoulders and took a breath. "Where are they being held?"

"They'd move them around. Another security measure. Also fucked with their heads. They didn't know what was happening to them. Couldn't let 'em get comfortable, you know?"

"Yeah. Especially the little girl. Why give her any sense of stability? Play mind games with a child." Vail winked at him. "Awesome strategy."

Scumbag.

Tahan drew his chin back. He clearly was not expecting sarcasm, let alone criticism.

Vail admonished herself for getting personal. It *was* personal—but she should not have let Tahan know that.

Not surprisingly, Rusakov also picked up on that and took over the questioning. "You said your boss thought it was too risky, so he separated them. Who's your boss?"

Tahan hesitated. Then he looked at DeAndre, who shook his head.

"Don't look at your friend," Rusakov said, poking the SIG's barrel against his temple. "*I* asked the question."

"Omar Abdallah bin-Sahmoud."

"Sahmoud gave the orders on what happened with the woman and daughter?"

Tahan nodded.

Rusakov dropped her chin and hardened her brow. "You said you didn't know if the mother was still alive. Why? Why'd you put it that way?"

"Got in the way of a prisoner fight and got stabbed. Some kind of infection. They didn't treat it, the infection got real bad."

"Where was she being held at that point?"

"Which one?" Vail asked. "Where?"

"In the beginning, Jneid prison. West Bank. After she was stabbed, they moved the mother to the Reform and Rehab Centre for Women. Also in the West Bank. Like I said, infection got bad." He shrugged. "All I know."

"And the girl?"

Tahan shrugged. "May've been moved to Jericho prison." He thought a moment. "There's another prison, a secret one. Underground. You can only get there by tunnel."

"West Bank?" Rusakov asked. "Gaza."

Vail took a step forward. "Name?"

"Al-Fari'ah."

Rusakov squinted. "The refugee camp?"

"Same name, but no. Al-Fari'ah means 'branches.' I guess because all the tunnels converge on detention rooms. Branches of the main trunks."

Vail absorbed that. Seconds passed. "Why an underground prison?"

"Impossible to escape. And it sucks being underground all the time. No light, no sun. They use a lot of torture on the inmates." He shrugged like that was expected.

DIE TRYING 159

Vail wanted more—not that she would share it with Uzi, but she needed it for context. "What other kinds of torture do they use?"

"Enough," DeAndre said.

Vail elbowed him hard in the face and his head snapped back. "*We* say when it's enough." She wiggled her free hand at Tahan to continue.

He took a deep breath. "Stripped naked, beat with sticks or clubs. Electrical shocks. High frequency sonic noise while blindfolded. Tied up with a hood soaked in urine over your head for hours at a time."

"They did this to women?"

"Anyone."

Vail checked her watch, then glanced at Rusakov, who pulled a flex cuff from her pocket and tightened it around Tahan's wrists and the metal chair.

"What are you doing?" he said, twisting and pulling—to no avail. Vail checked the restraint on DeAndre. "How long?"

"Probably about five," Rusakov said. "We cut it close."

"How long?" Tahan asked. "'Till what?"

"Okay then," Rusakov said, joining Vail at the other end of the table. "We're outta here."

"Wait," DeAndre yelled. "Cut us loose!"

"Can't do that, guys. The FBI's gonna want to know what you've been doing here, what you've got planned."

"The F—you said you weren't cops."

"That's right," Rusakov said. "I was telling the truth. You can call me a concerned citizen who doesn't want pissant terrorists blowing shit up and killing innocent people in my country."

Vail started for the door. "Can you blame us?"

Tahan tried to stand but the restraints went taut and he fell back into the seat. "Fuck you. Allahu Akbar!"

"Yeah, yeah, yeah," Rusakov said. "Allahu Akbar."

32

Vail and Rusakov drove to a Tatte Bakery & Café in Clarendon and started making calls to tie up loose ends and fill gaps in their knowledge base before providing Uzi and DeSantos with a report.

Ninety minutes later, while Rusakov visited the restroom, Vail stepped outside to make her call. It was late in Israel—something her friends had no doubt become accustomed to.

"Did I wake you guys?" she asked.

Uzi chuckled. "We're sitting outside Jenin waiting to enter one of its tunnels."

"Uh . . . that sounds kind of dangerous."

"Danger is our middle name."

"Weird that both of you have the same middle name."

No response.

They're on edge. Understandable.

"Okay, message received. I'll give you the info Alex and I tracked down. It's good stuff. Well, all of it may not be *good*, but . . . you get the idea."

"Let us have it," DeSantos said. "Bad first."

"Our source, Haydar Tahan, a.k.a. Batman, had intimate knowledge of the kidnapping. Claims he wasn't involved. Your girls were held in a West Bank prison." She explained the details.

"So Tahan doesn't know if Dena survived," DeSantos said.

Vail waited for Uzi to comment, wondering how he took the

news—but forged ahead and provided more of the intel they had gotten out of Tahan. A few moments of silence followed.

"What's the good news?" DeSantos asked.

"We found out who gave the orders as to what was done to Dena and Maya—Omar bin-Sahmoud."

"Bastard," Uzi said. "Son of a bitch. I'm gonna kill him."

Well, now I know how he feels.

"I get it," Vail said. "But Hector, making Sahmoud disappear is not a good idea."

"Copy that. We'll take things as they come. That's about all I'm willing to commit to."

Vail could have argued and—in those milliseconds of thought—debated whether she should. But she did not know the facts on the ground. And telling skilled operators how to handle themselves in hostile territory, with emotions running high, was likely to be ignored—if not resented, friends or not.

"I asked Mo to get us what he can from the Agency on Sahmoud and correlate it with the TSC," she said, referring to the Threat Screening Center. "And Hoshi did some digging as well and talked with the JTTF. Bottom line, they ended up with a decent backgrounder on Sahmoud. I'll give you a verbal. If you want anything in writing, I can WhatsApp a report to you once I've put it all into one doc."

"Verbal is good for now," DeSantos said. "No time to read anything."

"Omar's the son of Kadir Abu Sahmoud," Vail said. "Kadir had Omar before he was twenty—likely eighteen—so that puts Omar at about thirty-five, maybe forty. Married. No kids that we know of."

Vail scrolled down the document on her phone. "You know the father's background, so I'll hit the highlights. Kadir was a violent psychopath—and I don't use that term loosely. When he was a teen, he killed a family on a kibbutz that was out in the field farming—just to prove he could do it. They were Jews and he thought it was his calling since *his* father was a religious zealot who interpreted the Koran as a violent call to arms. Kadir must've picked up on that and it shaped his worldview.

"He later joined Force 17 in Lebanon to work with Yasser Arafat but ended up joining Hezbollah and training in Iran with the Revolutionary Guard, where he hooked up with the Muslim Brotherhood,

162   ALAN JACOBSON

which gave birth in '87 to Hamas. Kadir continued his work planning and committing murders of Israeli citizens, including some high-profile attacks. He eventually split off from Hamas and formed al-Humat. Their first attack involved sending a teen into a Tel Aviv school wearing a suicide vest. Fourteen kids killed, sixty-nine injured, seventeen lost limbs."

"Kadir also personally trained Batula Hakim," Uzi said. "The terrorist who kil—who *supposedly* killed Dena and Maya."

"Focus, Uzi. I know this is still a lot for you to absorb, but from everything we can see, they were not killed in that operation. They were kidnapped."

"Right. Taking me a while to adjust to that. Sorry, Karen. Go on."

"Anyway, this was the environment Kadir's son—and your suspect—Omar, was raised in." She scrolled to the next page, titled OMAR BIN-SAHMOUD. "Here's what we've got on Omar. He never held a job outside of al-Humat. Worked for his dad and his cronies and trained with one of their leading bombmakers. Showed an affinity for designing lethal suicide vests and, we're told, got his kicks out of watching one of his devices detonate.

"When they moved away from using vests in suicide attacks, the leadership noticed he was getting restless, so they had to figure out ways of keeping him busy. We've got some holes in our intel around this time, but it looks like they promoted him and gave him more tactical responsibility. When Kadir died, his name carried him all the way to third in line of al-Humat, heading up the Gaza and West Bank weapons construction and procurement department. He designed and oversaw many of the manufacturing factories the IDF recently took out in Jenin."

"That it?" DeSantos asked.

"No," Vail said with a long yawn. "Sorry. *You guys* are the ones burning the midnight oil. Wanted to give you some input as a behavioral analyst. If Kadir was in fact a violent psychopath, it's likely Omar inherited that wonderful trait from his father. Strong genetic links there. And the more severe the psychopathy, the stronger the links."

"So Omar is likely a psychopath."

"Best guess, yes."

"Not a surprise," DeSantos said. "Good to know if we end up finding him."

"Great work," Uzi said. "Thank you—and please thank Alex for us."

"No thanks necessary," Vail said. "Just make that intel actionable."

"We're all over it," Uzi said.

33

YEHUDA HAMACCABI
TEL AVIV, ISRAEL

Tamar tossed her covers aside and glanced at her husband, who was not bothered by her movement.

She had not slept much since texting Uzi the lie she had been ordered to tell him. Deep guilt tugged at her, sending her on an emotional trip without a navigational aid.

Tamar had no idea how long it would last, but she could tell this was going to be another night where she would lie in bed for hours until sleep finally took hold.

Her husband asked her when she would get past it. She wondered the same thing. How long would it take before she arrived in the land of redemption?

There was one way to accelerate that process. Tell Uzi the truth.

What was the harm? Eddie's voice echoed in her thoughts. He was not wrong. But as a mother, she knew the pain any parent would feel in Uzi's place.

And knowing Uzi as well as she did, her telling him the women in Extraction were older than Dena and Maya would not stop him from continuing to dig until he found answers. Like the attack dog that grabs the criminal's leg and won't let go, Uzi did not give up. It was not in his nature.

DIE TRYING 165

She related to him so well because she was the same way. It was an integral ingredient in the recipe that made them both so good at their jobs. Tamar hobbled into the study, grabbed a sweatshirt and a phone, and then made her way into the backyard. She sat down, canted her face toward the stars, and felt the cool breeze on her cheeks.

What was more important? Being a true friend or following orders regarding an op that occurred years ago? Besides, she didn't know—and they would not disclose—if Dena and Maya survived the blast. In balancing out the risks involved—which appeared to be minor—she did not feel right keeping the truth from Uzi. She could not continue living this way. She had been a bear to be around, which was not fair to her husband and children.

What's more, Uzi had always been very good to her, a standup guy who went out of his way to help her when necessary. After meeting Dena, that had not changed, as they often invited Tamar on outings with them—and they never made her feel like a third wheel.

Tamar rooted out her burner phone, booted it up, and sent him a disappearing WhatsApp message:

hey tee here
can't sleep
sorry I wasn't honest w-you
it likely was your girls in the op
pressured to keep that quiet so im not telling you this

She looked up at the night sky again, wondering if she had done the right thing or had set in motion something that would ruin her friendship with Eddie, get her fired, or even put her on trial for treason.

She had not considered these consequences before sending that text . . . which was probably a good thing because she might not have gone through with it.

Someone once said the truth will set you free. She did not know who had coined that phrase—but in this case, the truth could have the opposite effect.

34

Uzi and DeSantos went on foot to get some food because they knew this was going to be a long night—and on these types of operations, you ate when you could eat, you slept when you could sleep, and you used the bathroom when one was nearby.

After finishing their plates of shawarma with hummus and Israeli salad, they walked outside. As Uzi stretched his hamstrings against the nearby wall, a text hit his phone. He showed the screen to DeSantos.

His lips parted. "Well, shit."

Instead of replying, Uzi called Tamar. She answered immediately.

"Thanks for telling me, Tee. Appreciate it. And I understand."

"I'm so sorry for lying to you. It was . . . strongly suggested that I tell you it wasn't Dena and Maya. Came from my boss, of all people. He was called by my former unit chief. One cog applies pressure to another, and so on . . . until the wrench finds the right bolt."

"And you're the bolt."

"I'm not telling you this, but there was one person who was there, in the prison when we went in, who got away. If you can get to him, he might know where they are."

Uzi pulled DeSantos close so he could hear.

"And who's that?"

"Omar Abdallah bin-Sahmoud. The head of al-Humat's military planning division."

Uzi and DeSantos shared a look.

DIE TRYING 167

"That name's already come up," Uzi said. "Any thoughts on how to find him?"

"Even if the IDF knows where he hangs out, I doubt they'd move on him because sometimes the devil you know is better than the one you don't. Plus, it'd be a diplomatic problem if we grabbed him up or assassinated him. Might cause a collapse of the Abraham Treaties. Any major move, by them or us, could make years of work evaporate."

"Aksel warned me about that."

"It's a real concern. But if you do it quietly, without any telltale sign of it being an IDF op, grab him up and no one knows what happened to him . . ."

"And then what?"

"Question him. Get what you can."

"And then?"

"And then." Sigh. Silence. "Give him Actinocyde to wipe his short-term memory. Leave him on the side of the road in the middle of nowhere. He won't remember what happened and no one can get in trouble. And hopefully you get the information you're looking for."

DeSantos pursed his lips and nodded approval.

"Tee, I appreciate this."

"I shouldn't have waited. Luckily, you're still here."

"I'll keep you posted."

Uzi ended the call, then leaned back against the storefront behind him, thinking.

"I like her plan."

"I like it too," Uzi said, nodding slowly. "But how do we get to him? A guy like Sahmoud, he's got security. We'd have to find out where he lives. Dispose of his guards. Leave no sign it was an organized op."

They were each alone with their thoughts.

"What if . . ." DeSantos started, then bit his bottom lip and cogitated some more.

"Go on."

DeSantos started walking down the street, which was shiny from a brief thunderstorm while they were eating. His breath vaporized in the cold humidity.

"Al-Humat and Islamic Jihad are at each other's throats when they aren't conspiring to blow up the US and Israel, right?"

Uzi nodded. "Fighting for control, relevance. Yeah. Why?"

"What about a false flag op?"

"Could work," Uzi said, glancing over his shoulder as they walked. "Would have to be very, very subtle. Leave only *one* thing that suggests Islamic Jihad hit the house. Like a mistake, something accidentally left behind. A clue to who did it."

"We can figure out those details later," DeSantos said. "Bigger issue is, we don't know how many security personnel he's got. When is their shift change? What's the layout of the house?"

Uzi blew air through his lips. "Not sure we have enough to pull this off."

"Enough what?"

Uzi rubbed his face with both hands. "Everything."

DeSantos checked his watch. "How long you think we have until we can hit that tunnel?"

"Another couple of hours to be safe." He twisted his torso and checked the street behind them. "I'm thinking 1:00 a.m. would be good. Won't be anyone around and it'll give us time to do what we need to do."

DeSantos tapped Uzi's elbow. "You've glanced over your left shoulder one too many times. What's wrong?"

"I think we've got company."

"Tail?"

"Think so. Could be that we've overstayed our welcome and Aksel's got someone watching us."

"He did warn you. Let's find out. Hang a left." They turned down the next side street.

There were small storefront shops—but being so late in the evening in a commercial area, few people were around. They began jogging down the center of the road.

Uzi turned and took a quick look behind them. "Clear."

"Hang a right at the corner. Find a place we can duck into."

"Too bad there's no metro here. We could drop down into a station and disappear."

DIE TRYING 169

Mass transit was an efficient way of putting distance between yourself and someone following you—if you could time it properly. As it stood, they would have to jack a car or find a residence they could talk their way into.

As they approached the corner, eight men appeared. They were dressed casually. All but two were linebacker-big. And they were armed.

"I usually like our odds," Uzi said.

DeSantos glanced behind him. There were more unsavory types at the other end of the street.

"Someone's definitely very angry at us."

"Still think it's Aksel's doing?"

Uzi cricked his neck. "Seems heavy-handed even for him. Shin Bet wouldn't come at us like this."

"Face down on the ground," one of the footballers yelled as their posse approached.

They did as instructed. Uzi expected to feel flex cuffs scrape his wrists. Instead, he got a sharp prick in the neck. Seconds later, like the end of an old movie, everything faded to black.

35

Uzi gradually became aware of his boots slapping down a flight of stairs as his mind started to clear. He realized his hands and feet were tied up. He was blindfolded.

"We know why you're here and what you're doing."

Uzi shook the cobwebs from his brain. He had been drugged.

A hand gave a not-so-gentle slap to his face. First the left cheek, then the right.

"Wake up. Hey. C'mon, dude."

Uzi took a deep breath and squared his shoulders. "American. From the south. Texas. Dallas or Fort Worth."

After a beat, his kidnapper continued. "Your parlor tricks are impressive. But fact is, we're here to deliver a message."

"So there's, what? A dozen of you?" Uzi made a show of looking around, even though he was blindfolded and could see nothing. Moisture and a smell of mold irritated the back of his throat. A basement of some kind. "I'd say you guys are professionals. Intelligence service. Probably spec ops. Black."

"You done?"

"Just getting started."

A blow to Uzi's left cheek stunned him. Being blindfolded sucked. You couldn't see the punch coming so you couldn't prepare yourself in that split second. Who knew a split second could make such a difference. Same result, but—

"My message is short and sweet. Go home. You and your friend are to stand down."

"CIA, eh? SOG," he said, referring to the Agency's special operations group.

Silence. Then:

"Do you understand what I'm saying?"

"I do. But I have to say, that punch scrambled my senses a bit. I'm not hearing you so good. My left ear's ringing."

"You want one on the other side so they match?"

"One will do," Uzi said. "I'll be sure to tell Director Tasset you've got a good right cross. What was your name? Didn't catch it."

"This is not a laughing matter, Uziel."

"No. It's not." His tone turned serious. "I'm trying to find out if my wife and daughter are alive."

"And you can do that. Just not right now. After the treaties are signed."

"I missed that part," Uzi said, yawning to stretch his sore jaw. "When will that be? Months? A year?"

"Can't say."

"Or never," Uzi said, wriggling his torso, trying to loosen the ties around his extremities.

"Anything's possible."

"Then fuck you," Uzi said, the strength of conviction behind his words. "And you can pass that feedback on to the Agency's customer service department."

"You're making this harder than it needs to be."

Uzi snorted. "I've been stuck on that line before. For the covert activities division, press one. For the drone assassination division, press t—"

Another punch collided with the side of his face.

He spit some blood randomly in front of him. "Fuck, man, that hurts."

"So I've been told. Now—let's try this again. I strongly urge you to reconsider your activities in Israel."

"Or?"

"Or you and your friend are going to spend a long time in a sedated state somewhere in a neighboring nondemocratic foreign country."

"Kidnapping American citizens? Who haven't broken any US laws? That won't go over very well."

"You're leaving me no choice. Hate to do this to you guys. We're usually on the same team."

"Fine." Uzi gave him a mock sigh. "We'll stand down."

"Do we have your word? Because if not, we'll find you again and pick up where we left off. Only we won't be so nice next time."

"Didn't realize this qualified as nice." Recognizing that sarcasm might buy him another unfriendly whack upside his head, he nodded. "You've got my word. Will you do me one favor?"

There was no reply. He heard some shuffling, rubber-soled shoes scraping against a dirty, unswept floor.

Uzi braced himself for another blow.

But none came. A minute passed. Then two.

They're gone.

Uzi immediately began working on the bindings. How he was going to free himself without a knife—or any sharp object—was something he needed to figure out.

36

Hector DeSantos was awoken with electrically-induced nerve pain delivered by a stun gun. Just enough to restore consciousness.

"What the hell's going on?" he asked, eyelids at half-mast.

One of the two men in front of him menacingly held up the twelve-inch-long tool. "You're in no position to ask anything."

The memory of the shock was fresh. He did not disagree. "Coulda just used smelling salts."

"Not as enjoyable."

"Fair enough," DeSantos said, trying not to look at the wand, not wanting to indicate any sense of fear—or give his captor any greater control than he already had.

Consciousness slowly returning, he realized these blokes were British.

And suddenly it made sense.

He felt a draft—and realized he was naked, his clothing in a pile to his right. His legs and arms were spread wide, fastened with nylon rope to the ceiling and floor. He was angled forward, his lower back bowing toward the ground. He tightened his abs, attempting to reduce the arch.

He was in an abandoned building of some sort. An old house. Dried dirt atop discolored, torn linoleum. From what he could see in the darkness, most appliances were long since removed, save the square, grease-caked oven.

174   ALAN JACOBSON

DeSantos cleared his dry throat. "What are you doing in Israel?"

"That's my question."

He moved the device close to DeSantos's exposed groin. His testicles were hanging there, swinging vulnerably in the cold air.

"Remember what I said about ques—"

"Yeah. Okay, okay." DeSantos refocused on his captor.

"Answer the question. What're you doing in Israel?"

"Vacationing with a buddy of mine." He squinted. "You're British."

"That's right, mate. Name's McGill. And my being a Brit should be your first clue that you're in deep fucking trouble. That and the fact that I've got some Irish ancestry."

"Well," DeSantos said, struggling to focus on the guy's face, "*that* and the fact that I'm stripped naked and tied in a stress position. What are you, E Squadron?" Also known as the Revolutionary Warfare Wing/RWW or the Increment, E Squadron was a British SAS branch analogous to OPSIG: deniable ops performed by highly skilled, expertly trained operators selected from the best of the best. E Squadron worked with MI5 and MI6, the Secret Intelligence Service, to carry out missions worldwide.

In the fictional realm, James Bond's employer was MI6, though in reality E Squadron was the division that performed "license to kill" operations, deploying Bond-like gadgets developed by a real Q Section and a unit chief known by the initial C.

DeSantos did not have to think too long or hard about what was going on here. Even with his brainwaves scrambled by the shiny lightning rod of torture, he keyed in on what this was about.

A few years ago, he and Karen Vail were in England on a covert mission and found themselves at the home of a prominent member of Parliament—the result of an unfortunate setup by a British colleague they had trusted. A politician many considered likely to become the next prime minister had been murdered, a hunk of high-velocity lead placed in a rather unfortunate location in his body.

Officially: shot dead in his home. Unofficially: by Hector DeSantos.

DeSantos—and Karen Vail, who was also present—had escaped the crime scene. Apparently the arm of British law was long, with a memory of equal reach.

DIE TRYING 175

"I think we've got a misunderstanding," DeSantos said. He had to say something because, as McGill said, he was in rather deep shit.

McGill laughed. "Oh no, no, no. Our intel is solid. And our main mission is to prevent you and your wanker friend from—how is it you Americans put it? Fucking everything up?"

"Why would you care what we do here?"

"Clearly you haven't been following the news. The British government is hosting these treaty negotiations. The prime minister is looking for a win here, and since the Americans wanted no part of this—seems like you're only interested in your own arses these days—we stepped up."

"I think you guys got your knickers in a twist," DeSantos said, hoping he got the expression right. "We're not here to cause any problems. The treaties are a good thing. I'm here only because we need to find my friend's wife and daughter. They're . . . missing."

"I don't give a monkey's about your needs, mate. We're here to do a job, and that's to make sure you keep your noses clean. You go mucking around in things you're not supposed to and Bob's your uncle. Operational failure. We've made a right pig's ear of this mission and the PM is asking for our arses."

DeSantos wanted to reply but he was not sure what the man had said. He remembered some idioms and sayings from his previous trips to the UK, but like any language, if you didn't use it, you lost it.

"There's another part to our mission."

A different voice, to DeSantos's left. He swung his head in that direction, but the man was standing in the darkness. "Anything I can help with?" DeSantos asked into the black hole. "You know, I scratch your back, you . . ." He shrugged. "Let me go."

Or at least let me put my pants on.

"Yeah, now that you mention it, there is something you can do. You can jump off the top of this building."

DeSantos did not like talking to someone he could not see. Especially when the guy just told him to go kill himself . . . a guy who had likely carried out missions for the UK dressed up to look like suicides. "Come again?"

"We know what you did last time you were in England. Your people did a good job scrubbing your visit. But our intelligence service is a wee bit better, I'd say." The man stepped forward, into the light. He had blunt features, a thick brow offset by a sharp but squat nose.

DeSantos squinted, trying to focus on—and remember—his face. "And you are?"

"Can't see where you need that info, but no matter. Lackwood. Arlo Lackwood."

DeSantos was under no illusion. That was not his real identity.

"But," Lackwood said, "the name we're most interested in here is Basil Walpole."

DeSantos cleared his throat. He did indeed know that name. "And who's that?"

"The man you murdered. In his own home."

DeSantos maintained his best poker face and shook his head. "Don't know what you're talking about."

McGill and Lackwood shared a glance, then the former withdrew a handgun from a holster under his concealed carry shirt. He took a suppressor from his pocket and screwed it on.

DeSantos felt his pulse quicken. "Hey. What do you think you're doing?"

"We've got mission A and mission B," Lackwood said. "We can carry out both by getting rid of you. Avenge the murder of a member of Parliament and future prime minister. All the while making sure you don't fuck up the treaty negotiations." He turned to McGill. "Two birds, one stone."

McGill. "No one'd have a problem with that approach."

"Look," DeSantos said, swinging his gaze from Lackwood to McGill. "There's a way out of this—for all of us."

"We'll still have to deal with his partner," Lackwood said, ignoring DeSantos.

McGill held up a hand. "One thing at a time."

"I know something about the incident you're accusing me of. And I can tell you that a man named Hussein Rudenko is responsible. Ring a bell?" McGill laughed. "I know a bit."

Which meant he knew a lot, in British parlance.

"*That's* who you want for the murder."

"And you know this, how?" Lackwood asked.

DIE TRYING   177

"You've got intelligence and we've got intelligence." DeSantos shrugged. "Ask your people about Rudenko. He was in England at that time. He was responsible for the ricin attack that my team and I stopped."

"You?"

"That's right." DeSantos hoped the truth behind his statement would be evident. "So you should be *thanking* me. We downed that crop duster in the field before—"

"You're quite the storyteller," McGill said with a chuckle.

The squeak of a rusted hinge caught their attention. They all swung their gazes toward the noise.

"Go see," McGill said.

But before Lackwood could move, there was—

Shouting.

Several suppressed gunshots.

And the thump of multiple bodies hitting the floor.

The linebacker-turned-interrogator Lackwood and skilled stun wand operator McGill stiffened and crouched as they watched the wall for movement.

DeSantos leaned forward and peered as far left as he could. "Problem?"

"Quiet," McGill whispered.

"So polite you Brits are. I would've told you to shut the fuck up."

Growl. "Shut the fuck up."

Noise from the corner behind them.

McGill and Lackwood—and presumably their compadres—spun in the direction of the noise. Then discharged their pistols.

The cacophony in the small house was deafening.

McGill—and then Lackwood—dropped harmlessly to the ground. Bill Tait appeared, tranquilizer gun in hand.

"Bill?"

"And Phil," Sanfilippo said, emerging from the darkness. "How'd you guys find me?"

Tait grunted. "I promised your dad I'd keep an eye on you. I'm keeping my promise."

"Grateful for that," DeSantos said, suddenly realizing his very naked and vulnerable position. "But you didn't answer my question."

"Tracking device. An app I put on your burners."

"And how'd you manage that?"

Tait bent down to gather DeSantos's clothing while Sanfilippo used his tactical knife to slice DeSantos's bindings. "This is what we do for a living, Hector. I'm not gonna disclose *all* our secrets."

And then he remembered Uzi handing over his cell phone for them to set up the WhatsApp group. *Clever*. "Whatever. Just glad you're here."

"That's the spirit."

DeSantos pulled on his underwear, followed by his shirt and pants. "That was a very unpleasant experience."

"They're only tranquilized," Tait said. "We need to get out of here and put some distance between us. Those guys are dangerous."

"Sounds like a plan. They're E Squadron."

"I know of them," Tait said. "Never met any of their operators."

"Now you have."

As Sanfilippo gathered up their darts, he paused to look at DeSantos.

"What do you say we go get Uzi?"

"You know where he is?" DeSantos shook his head. "Of course you do."

"Even experts like Uzi are susceptible to malware when they trust the sender."

"I'll have to thank my dad next time I see him."

"You should," Tait said. "He told me you're overdue for a visit."

DeSantos rolled his eyes and followed Tait and Sanfilippo out the door, grabbing his Taurus revolver that was nestled on the ground behind the bodies of the sleeping operators.

Moments later, DeSantos burst into the room and found a light switch.

"Am I glad to see you," Uzi said, still struggling to free himself. "How was your visit?"

"Ton of fun. They injected me, put me down for a nap, stripped me naked, and woke me with a stun wand."

"Ow."

DIE TRYING   179

DeSantos knelt to cut away the bindings. "From outward appearances, looks like you had a more difficult time of it." He eyed Uzi's face.

"Who were *your* hosts?"

"E Squadron."

Uzi jutted back his chin. "E Squadron. Why would—oh shit. Not the Rudenko case."

"Yep. And they were very nasty blokes. Things were *not* going well when Tait and Sanfilippo showed up."

"Seriously?"

"Took them out with tranquilizer darts, then broke me out. That's how I found you. They put some kind of tracking app on our phones. Promise to my dad."

"You *kidding* me?" Uzi asked, his brow turning hard.

"Whoa. Boychick. Can't get too angry. Saved my life." DeSantos found Uzi's handgun and handed it to him. "How about you? What'd they want?"

"Pretty sure they were SOG," Uzi said, referring to the CIA's special operations group. "And they delivered a message. Stand down. Go home. Wait till the treaties are signed to resume our search."

"Oh yeah. That was part of E Squadron's reason for grabbing me, too. But at least one of 'em was chomping at the bit to get a bit of revenge over Basil Walpole with a suppressed forty cal."

"Jesus." Uzi rubbed the marks on his wrists. "How'd they make the connection?"

DeSantos shrugged. "That's the least of our problems."

Uzi stood up and stretched his back. "You think grabbing us up was a coordinated effort between the Agency and SAS?"

"E Squadron has been known to operate alongside the SAC and SOG ground branch," DeSantos said. "So yeah. But that would really suck."

Uzi nodded slowly. "Even if it didn't come from above, there was definitely joint planning and mission cooperation. Wasn't a coincidence they both showed up at the same time and place."

"But SOG? Grabbing you up had to come from Tasset."

"Him or one of his lieutenants. Not surprisingly, they didn't admit to being Agency operators."

"But you're sure they were?"

"I'd bet my life on it."

DeSantos winced. "Let's not put it that way, okay?" He placed a hand behind Uzi's shoulder and led him out. "You know how this shit goes. Could come to that."

37

ALEXANDRIA, VIRGINIA

Vail and Rusakov grabbed pizzas on the way back to Vail's house. Rusakov lived in Arlington and Vail was now in Alexandria, so they decided it made more sense if they crashed at one place tonight, and Vail had a spare bedroom with Jonathan no longer living at home.

They were both exhausted from several hours of driving and the lack of physical activity from sitting all day.

While eating dinner—a bottle of Raymond Oakville cabernet in the center of the table and their glasses nearly empty—Vail's phone rang. She glanced at the display and sent it to voicemail.

"Telemarketer?" Rusakov asked.

"Probably." Vail filled Rusakov's glass, then her own. "So where's your fiancé?"

"Mexico," she said, dropping another slice on her plate. "A case he can't talk about."

"DEA, right?"

Vail sprinkled on some red pepper flakes. "Yep."

"You guys have a date yet?"

"Wedding? We've been talking about next May. Before it gets hot."

"Local?"

Vail laughed. "Depends who you ask—and when. Me, I want somewhere special. Robby? He's all over the place. We've talked about

New Orleans, Napa, and yeah, even somewhere in the DMV," she said, referring to the DC/Maryland/Virginia area.

Vail's phone rang again—her voicemail tone, followed by a WhatsApp message. "Same number," she said. "Oh crap. It's Bravo-1. Code Epsilon-5." She returned the call and Douglas Knox answered.

"Mr. Director."

"You with Agent Rusakov?"

Vail put the call on speaker. "She's sitting right here. Neither of us have had much sleep and—"

"Unfortunately, you're not going to get much any time soon. I've got an assignment for you two, maybe the most important in the history of black ops."

Rusakov leaned closer to the handset. "Sir? The most important—"

"Shut up and listen," Knox said. "We've got a huge fucking problem."

38

**IMRAN AUTO REPAIR
MUQEIBILA, ISRAEL**

Uzi sent Benny a secure message and told him that he and DeSantos were not going to be home tonight because of an op inside Jenin. Benny responded immediately:

Want help? I can meet you

Uzi could have used his expertise and assistance, but given Benny's health, he preferred to save him for a less strenuous outing. He hit REPLY.

Thanks buddy. We're good.

And then Benny's warning:

Watch six. Going into hornet's nest

Hornet's nest is right.
Tait and Sanfilippo went to the back of their SUV and returned with supplies in modest, low-slung leather packs that strapped around their waists and right thighs.

"Additional pistols," Tait said, handing them two nondescript sidearms.

"What *are* these?" DeSantos asked, turning his weapon over, back and forth, looking for identifiable markings.

"Ghost guns," Sanfilippo said. "Nine mill."

DeSantos was familiar with the term: in the United States, they were officially known as PMFs, or privately made firearms, and composed of generic parts ordered online and assembled into a deadly, unregistered, and untraceable weapon.

"Nine mill," DeSantos said. "Real ammo. I feel much better."

"But ghost guns?" Uzi snorted. "Hopefully they don't jam or crap out in a critical moment."

"Yes," Tait said. "There's that."

Uzi pulled out his phone and started dialing.

DeSantos gestured at the handset. "Who you calling this late?"

"Gideon." He frowned. "Voicemail." He waited, then said, "Gideon. Uzi. We had an unfriendly visit with E Squadron and CIA operators. Just wanted you to know they're in-country and keeping an eye on us. The Brits were here to deliver more than just a warning. We left them in a compromised position. Doubt they went home." He hung up and stowed his phone. "Wish we had NVGs," DeSantos said, using the abbreviation for night vision goggles.

"Going old school," Tait said. "Flashlights. Some of these tunnels have electricity but we should keep it as dark as possible for as long as we can." Uzi dropped the magazine, cleared the weapon, then reinserted a full magazine into the ghost. "Agreed. We've got no idea who or what is down there."

Sanfilippo made sure the car's dome light was off. "Good to go."

They popped open the doors and hoofed it across the street to the body shop. During their previous visit, Uzi and DeSantos had taken note of potential security systems—they did not see any—and decided to rely on that conclusion.

They approached from the rear and waited while Sanfilippo used his lock pick kit to open the metal door. Seconds later, they were entering the dark work area.

Muting his flashlight beam by placing his fingers over the lens, Uzi borrowed the Slim Jim tool that Tait brought and unlocked the car that was blocking the tunnel entrance. Uzi shifted the Volkswagen into neutral and rolled it back five feet.

Sanfilippo was tasked with guarding the area while Uzi, DeSantos, and Tait went in. They descended a metal ladder bolted to a side of the tunnel as it dropped about six stories to its main horizontal passageway.

Uzi was first down. After hitting the ground, he swung his flashlight from side to side. The air was dank and sickly. He scrunched his nose.

Pre-formed concrete walls converged ahead, as far as the eye could see.

"We've got about a six-foot ceiling."

DeSantos stepped off the last rung behind Uzi. "So you and I are gonna have aching necks by the time we climb out of here."

Tait, at five-foot-ten, would have an easier time of it—assuming the dimensions remained constant as they proceeded toward the exit.

Once Tait was down, they began their trek in the near darkness, again muting their lights and keeping them pointed at the ground.

Thirty minutes later, they had traversed what Uzi estimated at being a mile.

Uzi's heart rate was galloping, not because of the physical exertion of the hike, but because his body was trying to cool itself and failing; he was sweating profusely due to the pervasive humidity. Not only did they not know where the HVAC switch was, but they did not want to alert anyone to their presence.

When they reached the end, another ladder led up to a closed hatch. First person through would be in the most danger, as there was no way of knowing who or what was on the other side.

Second and third in line were sitting ducks in a pond. Takeaway message: if there was an armed individual waiting out there, they were all in a very bad way.

Uzi led the way; since this was his mission, he should take the greatest risk. After climbing the ladder, he found that the exit lid was not secured, which was not surprising: the terror group did not expect anyone to find the tunnel, so there was no reason to lock it. They

186 ALAN JACOBSON

emerged in pitch darkness. Uzi used his phone's display on low power mode to provide a sense of the immediate area around them, without risking discovery.

A modern electric winch was above him, poised to ferry supplies, weapons, and contraband into or out of the shaft. Uzi ducked under the large metal hook suspended from the spool of thick rope and ensured that the tiled room was clear. He waved DeSantos and Tait out of the tunnel then moved to the windowed door and peered out.

"We're in the back room of a mosque," Uzi whispered as DeSantos emerged.

"I guess Allahu Akbar is appropriate," DeSantos said. Uzi glanced around. "Not really. But I won't tell anyone."

Once Tait was above ground, they consulted the map on Uzi's phone, got their bearings, and saw they were in the al-Ansar mosque. Ghaffar's house was a quarter mile away. It was approaching 2:00 a.m. Later than Uzi had hoped, but they still had time to accomplish their mission, assuming everything went as planned.

They pulled on black balaclavas and walked into the large prayer hall of the mosque, the *musallah*, then quietly left through the rear exit.

They hoofed it through the empty streets, keeping close to the buildings and moving in the shadows. They walked separately, distant enough to look like they were not together but within striking distance should one get stopped.

Ten minutes later, they were nearing Ghaffar's home. It was a one-story structure, decently maintained and constructed of textured brown cinderblock.

They gathered at the back door. The house lights were off and all was quiet. No security cameras were visible.

DeSantos stepped up to the lock and used his pick kit to open it.

They proceeded inside, taking a few seconds to allow their eyes to adjust to the darkness. No flashlights. No talking. Only hand signals from this point.

They moved in single file, Uzi taking the lead with his no-brand pistol at the ready. Tait was carrying a hypodermic and DeSantos had the rear, his privately made firearm drawn.

Moments later, they were standing at a closed bedroom door. While Uzi stood watch, DeSantos slowly turned the knob and pushed, opening it a few inches—just enough for Tait to enter and inject the occupant, a male youth about thirteen or fourteen years old, with a sedative.

They continued a few feet farther down the central hall and entered another bedroom, using the same approach to sedate a slightly older girl.

The next room would present a greater challenge: their desire was to get in and make a clean exit with a drugged Ghaffar, but his wife was a complication. They had to be needled at the same time to prevent one from waking the other if startled.

Tait handed DeSantos another hypodermic and the three of them entered the room. Ghaffar was hooked up to a CPAP machine. They slowly approached from opposite sides of the bed, Uzi standing at the foot of the mattress with his pistol pointed at Ghaffar.

DeSantos and Tait stood just behind the shoulders of their targets. They nodded at each other, then plunged the needles into the skin and emptied the syringes.

Ghaffar's wife gasped and started to sit up.

39

The noise was muted at first. But Phil Sanfilippo heard it. The crunch of a boot against coarse rock or gravel. And then another.

Footsteps outside, nearby.

Sanfilippo pulled down the ski mask and glanced around the body shop. He found what he was looking for a dozen feet away, where a pegboard was mounted with a variety of task-specific tools. But what Sanfilippo needed was simple. Basic, even: a reel of fine, braided, galvanized steel wire . . . the kind used to hang pictures or bundle metal rods.

He grabbed the roll and clipped off a sufficient length. He re-coiled it and moved his back against the wall beside the hallway that entered the workshop.

The footfalls continued into the front office area. Sanfilippo could see the swing of a flashlight—perhaps a security guard making his rounds. Judging by the rhythm of his gait, he was moving quickly, going through the motions so he could sign off on his sheet that he had inspected the property at regular, apparently hourly, intervals.

Sanfilippo leaned back, melting into the wall's surface, keeping still and slowing his breathing. In his left hand was the wire, now hanging down along his thigh.

Did he need to kill?

Sanfilippo, a powerlifter, could easily overcome any resistance from the bored, overweight guard. He was also a black belt in jujitsu and knew how to employ a choke hold across the neck, forming a "V" of pressure with his forearm and arm over the two carotid arteries. Cutting off the supply of blood to the brain induced unconsciousness in about fifteen seconds.

If done improperly, however, the trachea could be crushed beyond recovery, and the individual would die.

He decided to forgo the garrote and go with incapacitation. If that did not do the job, then he could easily end the man's life. Break the trachea or use the wire . . . so many choices were available to him.

It was an odd feeling, playing God. But he mused that he was in the right place for that.

The guard entered the room and stopped a couple of feet behind Sanfilippo's location. He shined his light ahead, pausing, as if noting that something was out of place.

Sanfilippo held his breath.

The man tilted his head, then leaned forward and took a couple of steps—clearing the area Sanfilippo needed to do his thing. And that's when he struck. With alacrity, he stepped to his right and grabbed his nemesis from behind, settling the guy's neck, and thus his carotids, between his meaty forearm and biceps.

He squeezed. Held tight while the man struggled. And then he went limp.

Sanfilippo knew he did not have long because the individual did not remain unconscious. Once the pressure was released, blood flooded the brain with oxygen . . . and presto, the defender awoke . . . quite angry.

Sanfilippo used those precious moments to secure the guard's wrists and ankles with zip ties to a pipe on the near wall. He wrapped a dirty rag around the man's eyes and shoved another in his mouth.

Satisfied with his work, he glanced around and listened for any additional guards walking their beat. If need be, he would repeat the exercise.

Having completed his assessment, he returned to the Volkswagen they had moved, checked his watch, and stood sentry over the tunnel entrance as his victim regained consciousness.

40

Acting quickly, DeSantos pushed the woman's head down and she was asleep by the time her head landed on the pillow.

Tait pulled the mask and hose off Ghaffar and motioned Tait to help him lift the man off the bed. While DeSantos steadied the body, Tait pulled a burlap roll out of his backpack and unfurled it. They struggled getting a balaclava over the dozing man, then wrapped him in the jute fiber material.

While they worked, Uzi glanced around the room. He noticed a well-worn stainless steel lighter on the dresser emblazoned with the al-Humat logo and Ghaffar's initials. A second later, it was in Uzi's pocket.

DeSantos bent his knees, then lifted Ghaffar onto his shoulder, steadied himself, and huffed it out of the house behind Tait and in front of Uzi, who kept his handgun drawn.

Again moving in the shadows, they made it two blocks before DeSantos handed the package off to Uzi, who adopted his partner's lift-and-carry technique.

The three of them took turns hauling the sleeping Ghaffar until, a few hundred yards later, they arrived in a less desirable neighborhood. Some buildings were missing windows; others had rotting wooden doors with heavily rusted hinges.

They entered an abandoned single-story structure that looked to be an old café. Uzi set their prisoner down on the dirt floor against a cement wall and removed the burlap.

DIE TRYING   191

"That was *not* fun," Uzi said, breathing deeply to recover.

DeSantos gathered up the covering and tossed it aside. "Wasn't supposed to be. Not like we could've summoned an Uber with a man rolled in a carpet."

"Ready?" Tait asked.

Uzi checked the position of his ski mask—Ghaffar had seen him in the shuk—then nodded at Tait. "Do it."

Tait pulled another hypodermic from his rucksack and injected Ghaffar. The man stirred and smacked his lips, rolled his head side to side—then appeared to notice his masked captors standing in the darkness. He tried to back up—but there was nowhere to go.

"Easy there," Uzi said in Arabic. "We're not going to hurt you. We just have some questions."

"How'd I get here? I was—I was home. Sleeping."

"And now you're not," Uzi said. "We want to discuss the woman and daughter who were kidnapped by al-Humat several years ago. They were taken to Jneid prison and then separated."

"Why are you asking *me*?"

"*Where* were they moved?"

"Who are you, Shin Bet?"

"That's the last question you get to ask," Uzi said. "Now. Where were they moved?"

"You're assuming I know."

"We *know* you know." Truth was, they did not know much, let alone whether or not Ghaffar was privy to that level of information. "Your boss took the woman and her daughter hostage. They staged a crime scene to make it look as if the two were murdered. But they weren't, were they?"

Ghaffar swallowed. "No."

Uzi felt emotion swell in his chest; it constricted his breathing and he looked at DeSantos, who understood.

DeSantos took a step closer. "Where were they taken?"

"Like you said." He glanced at Uzi. "Jneid. Then the woman went to the Reform and Rehabilitation Center, but she got very sick. I don't know what happened after that."

"Al-Fari'ah," DeSantos said. "She was taken to al-Fari'ah." Ghaffar licked his lips. "Yes," he said, nodding quickly. "Yes."

"So you *did* know," Uzi said, side swiping his boot against the man's bare ankles.

Ghaffar winced. "Yes."

"What about the little girl?"

He shrugged. "She might've been taken to al-Fari'ah, too, but later."

"That's very specific. Sounds like you *do* know. Was she or wasn't she taken to al-Fari'ah later?"

"She was."

"Really getting tired of this shithead lying to us," DeSantos said in Spanish.

Uzi leaned closer to Ghaffar's face. "Where are they now?"

He shrugged.

"Bullshit," DeSantos said, punching him: a right cross that landed on Ghaffar's left cheek. The guy never saw it coming and his head whipped to the side. His eyelids shuddered a couple of times.

"We know who your father is," DeSantos said. "Bassam. We know where your family lives. You want to drag them into this?"

Ghaffar shook his head, blinked, and tried to focus on DeSantos.

"I, uh . . . I heard some things."

They waited a moment. Uzi spread his arms. "And?"

"I want something."

Uzi laughed. "You. Want something from *us*."

DeSantos got in Ghaffar's face, his jaw muscles flexing. "You're not in a position to negotiate, dipshit."

"I've got things *you* want. You have things *I* want. We talk. Reach a deal."

"There's only one thing we're interested in." Uzi held up his phone showing a photo of Dena and Maya. "This woman and this girl."

Ghaffar groaned. "I've already told you what I know. My info's very old. Haven't heard anything about them in five, maybe six years."

"Your boss," DeSantos said. "He'd know."

"Omar would know. Yes. But he'd never tell you. No matter what you do to him."

"Let us worry about that," Uzi said. "You're going to take us to Sahmoud's house."

"Listen to me. I've got other information that's a lot more valuable. A lot more valuable. Trust me."

"Nothing to do with the woman and girl?" DeSantos asked.

"No."

Uzi scoffed and turned away. "Not interested."

"Might help with the Americans," Ghaffar said, struggling against his wrist restraints. "Valuable info. Might help Shin Bet and Mossad *protect themselves* from the Americans."

"What the hell are you talking about?" DeSantos asked. "Why would Shin Bet and Mossad need to protect themselves from Israel's closest ally?"

"Because we're working with a group that's infiltrated the US government."

Uzi chuckled, shook his head, and walked away. It was a plot Uzi and DeSantos dealt with years ago. "Old news, pal."

Ghaffar's face shaded red. He tried to stand up, but the cuffs made the move awkward and he fell back against the hard wall. "It's not! I heard Omar say so last week. He was talking about it with Yassir Abadi."

Uzi froze near the back door. *The head of al-Humat. You got our attention.* DeSantos pulled over a rusted five-gallon paint drum, swung it upside down in front of Ghaffar, and sat. "Go on."

"First, my deal."

"Here's your *deal*: give us something worthwhile, actionable, and you're free to go. But it's got to prove out."

Ghaffar bit his bottom lip. "This group. They work with lots of others. ISIS, al-Qaeda, al-Humat—"

"We know that already."

"You know that Iran and Russia are involved?"

Uzi swallowed deeply. Russia? Yes. *Iran? No, we did not know that.* "What group is this?" His question came out in English—a rare slip.

The man squinted, then said, "I do not know how you say it in English. In Arabic it's *Sikorbion*."

Uzi clenched his hands. *Scorpion.*

He and DeSantos shared an uncomfortable look . . . the kind when both parents know the baby has pooped in his diaper but the first to acknowledge it has to do the cleanup.

194   ALAN JACOBSON

After Uzi's Joint Terrorism Task Force cleared the Armed Revolution Militia case, during its investigative write-up, it discovered references in the ARM electronic communications to the term "Scorpion" as well as sterling silver pocket watches among the leaders who had been captured. The timepieces were all engraved with the image of a scorpion.

"Outside," DeSantos said to Uzi.

They left Tait with the prisoner and exited the back of the dark building. Rain was converting the dirt parking lot to mud.

Uzi looked around, seeing nothing, his mind trying to process the meaning of what Ghaffar had just said. "You believe him?"

"Hell yeah," DeSantos said. "You?"

Uzi shrugged. "He knows things he couldn't know unless he's got insider knowledge. And we know he does. So he's credible. He's—dammit. Yes, I believe him."

They stood there in silence, the pitter patter of precipitation slapping against the broken slab of soaked pavement and puddling water.

Despite the slight overhang, they were getting wet.

"The next question is obvious," Uzi said.

DeSantos shoved his hands in his jacket pockets. "Now what?"

"Exactly." Uzi pulled out his phone, powered it up, and texted Benny, asking him to poke around, see if there was any classified mention of Sikorbion. He turned it off and shoved it back in his pocket.

"We know we can trust Knox," DeSantos said. "That's who we tell."

"But what do we really know?"

DeSantos looked up at the night sky and opened his mouth, catching the raindrops. He swallowed, then turned to Uzi. "We have credible information that's not been verified—but if true, could be of vital national security significance. Time sensitive."

"Too bad we can't line up another source that confirms or refutes this."

"What about Aksel?" DeSantos asked. "If he knew this, he'd have told . . . who would he have told if he couldn't trust the US president and his secretary of state?"

"His counterpart. Earl Tasset. They go back years."

DeSantos nodded. "So it's highly unlikely Aksel has sniffed any of this. But can he help us get that second source?"

DIE TRYING   195

"He *can*, but . . ." Uzi's voice trailed off as he replayed his visit to Aksel. "But he's gonna be pissed at what we've done tonight. Masquerading as Shin—"

"We didn't."

"We didn't, but we didn't deny it, either. Gideon told us to stand down—leave the country—and we did the opposite. We snuck into Palestinian territory and stirred the pot of a very violent terror group."

They were silent a long moment as they each processed the mess they found themselves in. In military parlance, it was FUBAR. *Fucked up beyond all recognition.*

A moment later, DeSantos sighed. "I shouldn't be the one to remind you of this, but we *are* here for a different reason."

"Are you saying we should ignore this?" Uzi snorted. "That's not an option. We can't do nothing. We're not here as federal agents, but we *are* Americans. We put our lives on the line for our country every time we spin up. How can we not help root out those who want to take down our democracy?"

DeSantos looked out at the rain, which had picked up. "You don't have to convince me. Just wanted to make sure we're on the same page."

"We've got two missions now."

"No offense, boychick, but that first one was . . . bad enough."

They both laughed, nervous energy shooting out an escape valve.

Raindrops blown by the gentle breeze dotted Uzi's ski mask. "Let's get back to it. We've got a lot to do and only a few hours before the sun comes up."

41

DeSantos paced the building line, staying out of the rain but getting wind-wet while he waited for Knox to answer. Since he had a burner SIM in the handset, he did not expect the director to answer. Voicemail clicked on seconds later.

"It's Bravo-1. Code Epsilon-5." After disconnecting, he and Uzi stared at each other in silence, the moonlight reflecting off the prickles of perspiration beading their faces.

A moment later, DeSantos felt his hand vibrating. "Yes, sir," he said to Knox. "This is not secure so I'm going to call you on WhatsApp."

"Copy that."

A moment later, they were speaking. Uzi joined DeSantos and moved close to the receiver while keeping an eye on their dark surroundings for unwelcome movement.

"We've got some intel from a source we were questioning on the wife and daughter situation." Even though they were on a secure, end-to-end encrypted conversation, DeSantos still felt safer avoiding the use of names. "Source is reliable, a significant player with the group we battled a few years ago . . . the ARM case. And he says that Scorpion is still active. Iran and China are now big players. Russia's still involved."

"Yes," Knox said.

"Yes?" DeSantos asked incredulously. "You knew this?"

"OPSIG has a division very few know about. Team Grey. They've been looking into Scorpion."

DIE TRYING 197

Uzi pulled back slightly and looked quizzically at DeSantos.

"Why?" DeSantos asked. "I mean, suddenly?"

"At least three years," Knox said. "There've been some . . . questionable actions taken by the president and there was insufficient evidence for the attorney general to take any action."

"Legally," Uzi added.

"Yes. And that's why Team Grey was brought in."

"Nothing official," DeSantos said. "No federal standards to meet to search for, or collect, evidence."

"But not usable in court," Uzi said.

"That's not the point," Knox said. "After what happened with the ARM case, alarm bells went off after two contacts the president took. I can't say how we found out about them, but because of what happened last time, we couldn't ignore it. And we had to be extremely careful."

DeSantos did not know who "we" was, but he suspected the individuals included Knox and Secretary of Defense Richard McNamara, the man technically and unofficially in charge of the unofficial OPSIG teams.

"Then we're sorry to have bothered you," Uzi said. "We thought—"

"I needed to speak with you, anyway," Knox said. "Several hours ago, the president was briefed about Team Grey's investigation. Sounded like he already knew. This was a status update."

"How'd he find out?"

"We suspect a leak at the DOD—which would not be surprising because of what Team Grey learned. We thought we had things buttoned down. Apparently not."

"Fallout?" DeSantos asked.

"From what we can tell—and we're still doing damage control— the executive branch carried out its own covert operation. The president—probably through back channels—asked Congress to look into the 'reckless and illegal' use of black ops personnel to carry out unsanctioned special forces missions on US soil. Taylor Green, the chair of the Senate Select Committee on Intelligence. He *named* OPSIG in a hearing yesterday."

"Christ." DeSantos clenched his free hand. "Son of a bitch."

"And they're going to investigate the use of targeted killings on US soil by OPSIG operators." Uzi's jaw went slack.

"Following that hearing, the SecDef was informed that OPSIG was disbanded."

"What the hell does that mean?" Uzi asked. "We're black. We don't technically exist."

"Bottom line, we've been defunded," Knox said. "Effective immediately. As we speak, the Bureau is seizing all of OPSIG's digitized records, computers, hard drives . . . everything."

DeSantos began sweating uncontrollably. "This is a nightmare. A fucking disaster."

"I wish I could say that's it," Knox said, "but it gets worse. Arrest warrants have been issued for all OPSIG operators. They won't be able to decrypt our records so fast—but the NSA was ordered to give it the highest priority."

DeSantos swiped away the rain and perspiration from his forehead. "So it's a matter of time before they have everyone's name. And address."

"A warrant's been issued for Secretary McNamara's arrest."

"Hang on a sec," Uzi said. "Don't we have congressional oversight?"

"Technically, yes."

"Technically?"

"The Office of Special Plans oversees our missions," Knox said. "But OSP was unraveled in 2004. Officially."

"So *do* they or *don't* they sign off on our missions?"

"OSP was mothballed because they were accused of siloing raw intel, bypassing approved processes of analysis, and failing to coordinate with allied intel partners. And some thought they signed off on everything given to them."

"So they weren't mothballed?" DeSantos asked.

"Now you see the problem. They *were*. But they *weren't*."

DeSantos rubbed his left temple. "So a black spec ops group that doesn't exist—OPSIG—had its missions reviewed and approved by a disgraced government entity that was shuttered decades ago."

"Correct," Knox said. "We do *not* have a congressional committee providing cover."

"Oh, man," Uzi said. "We are so fuc—"

DIE TRYING   199

DeSantos felt his knees buckle. A second later he was sitting on the wet concrete. Uzi crouched down to check on him, then sat beside him, helped him scoot back a couple of feet onto dry ground.

"Secretary McNamara's gone underground," Knox said.

DeSantos licked his desert-dry lips, trying to focus on Knox's voice. "What about Hot Rod, Hodges, Zheng, Alex, Karen?"

"I've been making calls. I didn't reach everyone because I'm not calling on my cell or an official line. They don't recognize the number so they're not answering. I left them a Code Epsilon-5. I'm sure they had their go-bags ready. Hopefully they were able to disappear. But . . ." Knox cleared his throat.

Uzi pressed his head against DeSantos's. "But what, sir?"

"But I did talk with Agents Vail and Rusakov. They insisted on trying to fix the—"

"Fix?" DeSantos blurted. "How can they fix anything? The president's a foreign agent and he's probably filled his cabinet, hell his entire administration, with conspirators. And that includes high-ranking military officers."

"They're aware," Knox said. "Agent Rusakov felt they had some time before all the data is decrypted. Time they could use to—"

"All due respect," Uzi said. "The NSA's got the most powerful computers in the world."

"All our operatives—and sources—are held in a separate system that uses quantum cryptography with photonic encryption. Cutting edge tech. It'll take them a while to break it."

"Any kind of encryption can be broken given enough time, energy, and processing power," Uzi said. "But yeah, that's stronger than anything I knew we had. Last I heard, some of that tech was theoretical. That's not nothing."

"That said, we're talking about the NSA here," Knox said. "If anyone can break it, it's them. And if they're throwing massive processing power at it and prioritizing it . . . I honestly don't know how long we've got."

"We've got two major issues," Uzi said. "Scorpion is number one. Number two is directly related: its attempt to get rid of OPSIG, maybe the only thing standing in its way."

"Up to now," Knox said, "Nunn and company have been careful not to take egregious, bizarre actions that couldn't be explained away. There was always an alternate explanation that *could* make sense."

"How do you mean?" DeSantos asked.

"During the first couple years of his first term, Nunn quietly purged his administration of officials. Team Grey's investigation found that the people he fired weren't loyal enough. OPSIG analysts studied each employee's firing and concluded that, in their place, Nunn installed people who agreed to aggressively implement his agenda.

"Some of them were approached under the guise of an employment law attorney asking if they wanted to file a complaint. Only one talked to us. She confirmed our analysts' conclusions but had no hard proof. A week later she was found dead in her apartment. Massive heart attack. She was sixty-one. No autopsy."

"Young enough for it to be suspicious," DeSantos said. "But not so young that it's unheard of."

"And administrations replace people all the time," Uzi said. "So that's explainable too."

"But it's not just hiring loyalists," Knox said. "That's not illegal. It's not good, but it's not illegal. The policy decisions they've made have been suspect, too. Again, their explanations and reasoning have that ounce of plausibility, making it hard to prove that the administration was up to no good. Was it poor judgment? Yes. Criminal? Conspiratorial? Much harder to prove."

"Strategy makes sense." Uzi nodded. "Take heat for a day, the news cycle renews, it blows over, and everyone forgets."

"The party lines up behind their guy," Knox said. "Anything to prevent the other side from gaining power. The needs of the People are far down the list. That's Washington these days."

Anger had replaced DeSantos's shock. He got to his feet. "Destroying OPSIG has major implications for national security."

"Outing OPSIG and its so-called murdering rogue operatives would *appear* to be in the public interest," Knox said. "But other than us, no one knows it's completely self-serving. Done to prevent the exposure of their plot."

DIE TRYING 201

Uzi, also back on his feet, snapped his fingers. "Hang on a second. Last year, Nunn cut the US cyber security infrastructure budget and fired the director. Didn't appoint a new director for six months—and then he chose some bozo who didn't know his ass from his elbow. Pissed me off. Was that tied to this?"

"Right after he did that," DeSantos said, "the US was hit by a major cyber attack, which originated from an Iranian cyber warfare group."

Uzi shook his head. "Totally deliberate. Nunn laid the groundwork for the Iranian attack by deliberately weakening our defenses."

There were a few seconds of silence. "We don't have proof," Knox said. "Anyone can do basic math. Two plus two adds up to four."

"What's their ultimate goal?" DeSantos asked. "We know what President Rush and his conspirators were after."

"From the intel we've gathered, doesn't look like the group's primary objectives or MO have changed. The administration's been coordinating with violent anarchist and extremist militia groups, anti-government activists, and other domestic terror entities."

"And obviously foreign enemies," DeSantos said. "Who are trying to engineer unrest," Knox said. Uzi rubbed his forehead. "A new civil war?"

"Russian and Chinese influence campaigns have been flooding social media with disinformation, divisive language, and conspiracy theories."

"A multi-pronged strategy," Uzi said.

"While enriching themselves personally. Team Grey found evidence of Nunn trying to cut a deal with China's Jao. We were about to zero in on that when the plug was pulled."

Uzi sighed. "Jesus. International terrorism, state-sponsored terrorism, and domestic terrorism. Simultaneously. And the Bureau's hamstrung."

"Nunn's claiming that the FBI's been weaponized against him. And his followers are buying it."

"How real is the domestic terrorism threat?" DeSantos asked.

"That *I* can answer," Uzi said. "JTTF's open case load—of domestic terrorism-related cases—is up over three hundred percent since we broke the ARM/Scorpion case seven years ago."

"We've got to stop these bastards before it's too late," Knox said.

DeSantos pinched the bridge of his nose. "How are we gonna do that?"

"*You* aren't. Vail and Rusakov are our main hope. You two can't come home. You'd be arrested the second you hit US soil. In fact, I'd be extremely careful in Israel because if the US issues an Interpol red notice, you're toast."

"What about you, sir?"

"I might have to go dark. I'm at a safe house right now with my wife. I'll try to quarterback from here or wherever I end up." He laughed sardonically. "I'm usually on the right side of the law. Being a fugitive's new to me."

"Our future's in the hands of Karen and Alex."

"No, Hector. The *country's* future is in their hands. Because if they don't succeed, there may not be anyone who can stop Scorpion."

DeSantos looked toward the house, where Tait was watching over Ghaffar. "Thanks for the heads-up, sir. Watch your six."

42

DeSantos disconnected the call and walked with Uzi back to Tait. "What's wrong?" Tait asked, likely reading their stern faces and slumped shoulders.

"You don't want to know," Uzi said.

DeSantos motioned Tait away from Ghaffar. Once out of earshot, he said, "We're going to need whatever people you can spare. Your most loyal men and women who have minimal political connections."

Tait squinted and drew his chin back.

"No," Uzi said. "We're not crazy. There's a coup going on at the highest levels of the administration. We've only got two operatives who are trying to shut them down. *Two*."

DeSantos proceeded to brief Tait on the fine points of what Knox had conveyed—along with classified information regarding OPSIG that he never thought he would disclose to anyone outside the group. Information he swore to take to the grave with him.

After taking a moment to think, Tait said, "Your dad could be of enormous help, too."

DeSantos's father, a highly decorated general, owned DeSantos Defense Industries, a thriving military contractor. However, he did not have many nonmilitary, apolitical types on his employee roster. At least not people who had the training that could make a difference.

Tait bobbed his head. "We could use him for support, technical knowhow, and other peripheral assistance. Maybe some frontline muscle. Depends on what's needed."

"I'll call him," DeSantos said, "put him in touch with Karen. Let them talk about what their objectives are, what they'll need to accomplish them. My father's a hell of a strategist."

"We've still got *him* to deal with," Tait said, gesturing with his chin toward Ghaffar. "And your family."

Uzi rubbed his eyes. "We're running out of darkness. Let's get to work."

43

FALLS CHURCH, VIRGINIA

Karen Vail pulled into the compound, which was well-guarded by DeSantos Defense Industries security personnel. She and Alexandra Rusakov stopped at each checkpoint to show their IDs and were directed to park by the circular driveway.

They were escorted to the study of Lukas DeSantos's mansion by a man in his early thirties, who directed them to deposit their mobile devices in a secure locker, then showed them to their seats.

Mahogany-paneled walls provided the backdrop for an ultramodern conference table with thin-profile ergonomic leather chairs. Long, narrow LEDs hovered over them from the high ceiling, suspended by fine, nearly invisible wires. The light from the bulbs was shooting up and out at all angles, a design that to Vail—with her interpretive art history background—represented missiles soaring above a battlefield.

Vail noted they were in a windowless room, which, with the deposit of their phones outside, led her to conclude this was a SCIF: a sensitive compartmented information facility. A lot of words to say it was protected against electronic eavesdropping.

As Vail discovered during a previous case, Hector had a very interesting father—though she never got to meet him. That changed seconds later as Lukas DeSantos entered.

"General. Good to meet you. I'm Karen Vail and this is Alex Rusakov."

206   ALAN JACOBSON

He nodded at them, stopping at the head of the table, Vail to his left and Rusakov to his right. Instead of shaking their hands, he motioned them to take seats. Lukas remained standing. "Hector's told me a lot about you, Agent Vail."

Quick. Read his face. Good stuff? Bad?

"Thanks for meeting with us," Rusakov said.

"Your message was a bit cryptic," he said, grasping the back of his chair. "I assume that was on purpose."

"It was," Rusakov said. "I know you're not bound to government oaths anymore, but what we're about to discuss is classified at the highest level."

Vail clasped her fingers on the table in front of her. "General, I'm sure you heard news reports several years ago about President Glendon Rush and a group of conspirators who infiltrated the US government."

"Of course. I was out of the military at that point, but not too far removed."

"There's a lot you don't know because of its classification level. That group, eventually identified as Scorpion, was a collaboration between domestic and international terror outfits set up to manipulate US and global policy. The Bureau was confident we'd identified and arrested everyone responsible. The DOJ made a strong case against everyone we arrested and they were convicted. The major players got life without parole."

The general chuckled. "Sounds like this story didn't end there."

Vail took a deep breath. "About five years ago, Katerina Connors, an aide to President Nunn, resigned suddenly. She then sat down with a *Post* reporter, who was, unfortunately, on Scorpion's payroll. Connors's interview was buried. Never saw publication. Police found her body three months later in a ravine in the Blue Ridge Mountains. Car accident. Drove off the road."

"Accidents *do* happen," he said.

Vail smiled. "A few days after doing the interview, Connors called the FBI and asked to meet with the assistant director in charge of the Washington field office. She said her life was in danger and she needed to meet *that* day because she had evidence of the president being a foreign agent. The ADIC sent a couple of agents to escort her. They arrived an hour later. She was nowhere to be found."

"But," Rusakov said, "the agents said Connors's house had been professionally searched. Laptop and phone both missing, OneDrive and iCloud accounts deleted. Attempts to obtain subpoenas for the deleted records were delayed. By the time they were issued, thirty days had passed. And guess what? The policy for both Microsoft and Apple is to permanently erase recycle bin and trash data after . . . you guessed it. Thirty days."

Lukas nodded. Vail continued.

"Knox and a few colleagues at the Department of Justice who lived through the last debacle with President Rush were concerned. But they knew they had to be extremely careful. If there was one thing they learned last time, it was that *anyone* in the administration, in any branch of the government, could be involved."

Lukas spread his hands. "And? Not hearing anything that comes close to proof."

Vail heard Knox's words in her thoughts: *Tell him whatever you need to. Do whatever you need to do to make things right.* Whatever *you need to do.*

Vail took a breath. "There's a covert division of the military known as the Operations Support Intelligence Group. OPSIG is black." She knew that generals intimately understood special operators and how and when they were utilized. They also knew that there were times when black ops were not only necessary but vital to a nation's security—and survival.

"Your son is a member of OPSIG," Rusakov said.

Vail read the general's face: a lift of his brow, the realization of things adding up in his mind.

Lukas nodded slightly. "Makes me proud. Wish I'd known. Of course I understand why I didn't."

They proceeded to give the general a summary of what Team Grey's investigation had uncovered.

"So Team Grey has concrete evidence of this plot."

"Yes," Vail said. "They've also got audio recordings of them discussing the plan over a period of months. Messages sent between various

208   ALAN JACOBSON

members of the group, including the Speaker of the House and the Senate majority leader and their lieutenants, strategizing on how to take down the government while avoiding undue scrutiny."

"Take down the government?" he asked. "How?"

"They have recordings of Congresswoman Jolene Aswad, the House Speaker," Rusakov said. "Scorpion is working with members of the TruPatriots, which—"

"The domestic terror group?"

"Yes," Vail said. "Aswad and the head of TruPatriots were recorded discussing a plan to rewrite major sections of the US Constitution."

Lukas cocked his head. "Hang on a second. I minored in American Foundations at West Point, so I know a thing or two about this. Amending the Constitution requires approval of two-thirds of Congress—and then it goes to the states. Thirty-eight states have to approve it." He chuckled. "Those are extremely high bars. Most proposed amendments die in committee. That's why the last amendment passed in 1965."

"There's another way to amend the Constitution," Vail said. "Article V."

Lukas glanced at the ceiling, then harrumphed. "Calling a Constitutional Convention."

"Article V doesn't restrict what a Constitutional Convention can change."

He nodded slowly. "A convention can't be limited at all by Congress—or the states."

"Exactly. And Scorpion is going to take advantage of that loophole. Once you've got a convention, *anything* can be introduced as an amendment."

"Back up," Lukas said. "To force a convention, two-thirds of the states have to petition Congress. How likely is *that*?"

Vail chuckled. "Both parties agree that the Constitution needs to be fixed. They don't agree on *what* amendments should be made, but once you're in that room, anything can happen—especially when there are no restrictions on what can be proposed."

He shook his head. "The states would never let it get that far."

"Except that they have," Rusakov said. "Nineteen states have already signed CCA petitions."

"CCA." Lukas squinted. "The Constitutional Convention for Amendments?"

Rusakov nodded. "They're more than halfway to the thirty-four-state threshold required to call a convention. And seven *other* states have passed a petition through one legislative chamber. Another eighteen states have a petition pending."

Vail lifted her brow. "So, General. Still think it wouldn't get that far?"

Lukas swallowed hard. "Fuck." He cleared his throat. "Excuse me." His gaze wandered the blank table in front of him.

"According to what Team Grey intercepted through COMINT," Vail said, referring to communications intelligence, "Scorpion's US-based division convened a mock convention to role-play. They decided on several constitutional amendments. The first would make it impossible for the federal government to borrow money."

Lukas let out a low growl. "We'd default on our debt. We'd dive into recession. Our credit rating would be downgraded and the dollar would weaken. And it would get worse from there."

"In more ways than one," Rusakov said. "They also want to rewrite the commerce clause to eliminate federal regulatory bodies."

"Jesus." He sat down uneasily. "They're trying to destroy our country."

"I saved the best for last." Rusakov folded her hands in front of her. "They plan to add a clause that would allow a *simple* majority of state legislatures to overrule any federal law."

"You're shitting me."

"Their hope," Vail said, "according to the conversations that Team Grey captured, is to get rid of Social Security, the Environmental Protection Agency, the IRS, and the Department of Education."

Lukas stared blankly at the framed American flag on the opposite wall. "They'll turn America into another ass-backward Soviet Union. Degrade American greatness. Destroy the global projection of US power."

"There's also SIGINT between Nunn's chief of staff and the chief of staff of the Islamic Republic of Iran Army and an unidentified male at the Joint Staff Department of China's Central Military Commission," Rusakov said. "Discussing all of this."

210 ALAN JACOBSON

Lukas kept his gaze on Old Glory. "Verified?"

"By cryptanalysis and traffic analysis."

Vail knew SIGINT was signals intelligence—and since these intercepted communications were encrypted, cryptanalysis was needed to decode them. She could not recall what traffic analysis was, but reasoned it had to do with evaluating who was talking to whom.

Lukas shook his head, refocusing on Rusakov. "A plot like this requires regular strategizing and constant modification to adjust to the situation on the ground. It also leaves behind a trail of evidence—if you have the resources to access it."

"OPSIG had the resources," Vail said. "But with all due respect, General, you're missing the point. When a group has high-level reach into *every* branch of government, getting that evidence is almost impossible when you have to rely on those *same government agencies* to provide it. It's like the DEA asking a Mexican drug cartel to turn over the names of its cocaine and fentanyl dealers."

Rusakov spread her hands. "We don't know who's involved and who isn't. But after several years in office, we're pretty certain their reach is far and wide. Whoever got in the way was dealt with."

Lukas ground his molars. "Like Katerina Connors." Vail pursed her lips. "Yeah. Like Katerina Connors."

44

The general rose from his chair and began pacing, his eyes swinging left and then right—and then left again. Processing, plotting. Strategizing.

"Scorpion's built an extensive global network," Vail said. "Team Grey was in the early stages of identifying which individuals are part of the US-based organization. And now Nunn and company are aware that OPSIG knows what Scorpion doesn't want it to know."

"OPSIG agents are in extreme danger." Lukas cleared his throat.

"We've got two ways to address this. But the choice may not be ours."

"Go on," Rusakov said.

"I'm looking at this clinically," he said. "No emotion. Strategically."

"Okay."

"I don't make these recommendations lightly."

"Of course," Vail said. "We realize what's at stake."

Lukas folded his arms across his chest. "All known conspirators need to be removed from office. President Nunn. Vice President Andrews. Speaker Aswad and Majority Leader Conti, who's the Senate's president pro tem—and third in line for the presidency. *All* top leadership positions are involved in this coup." He shook his head. "The founding fathers never considered such a wide-ranging plot . . . or the technology that's enabled them to carry it out."

"Definitely not," Vail said. "But you said there were two ways—"

212 ALAN JACOBSON

"Yes." Lukas stopped pacing and faced the wall, put both hands on a walnut cabinet, and bowed his head. "Our checks and balances, our system of government, our democracy, it's all been undermined. We can't trust anyone or any institution to right the ship." He paused a long moment. "It's up to us to fix this." He turned to face them. "We'll lose our republic if we don't act."

"That's Director Knox's assessment," Vail said.

"Okay then." He turned back to the cabinet. "There *aren't* two ways to proceed. There's only one."

Vail and Rusakov sat there waiting for him to elaborate. A minute passed, then he faced them.

"Arresting these people and putting them before the court system may or may not work. The president's appointed hundreds of federal judges during his seven years in office. Hundreds. How many are part of this conspiracy?"

"No way of knowing," Vail said.

Lukas nodded slowly. "Because Team Grey couldn't complete its investigation."

"Exactly," Rusakov said. "Nunn cut us off at the knees. And he's about to put our premier covert ops group on public trial. Every member of the OPSIG teams has put his or her life on the line on almost every mission."

Lukas returned to the conference table but remained standing. "This is a war we're fighting for the survival of the United States. Foreign and domestic actors have conspired to take over our country. But they've got the most powerful military in the world and endless resources to stop *us* from stopping *them*. We're no match. Our only way of fighting back is asymmetrical warfare."

"General . . ." Vail studied the table a moment. "We can't have any misunderstandings here. In layman's English. Please."

"We have to cut off the heads of this monster." His eyes traversed Vail's face. "We have to take them out."

Vail leaned forward. "By 'take them out,' do you—"

"He means assassination," Rusakov said, turning to Lukas. "The president? *And* vice president?"

"And the other executives Team Grey has identified," DeSantos said. "The ones we know for sure are involved in the conspiracy."

Vail felt the back of her throat tighten. "General, that's—you're saying we should *assassinate* the top leadership of the US government. *Elected* officials?"

"I don't know how much Hector's told you about me, but I'm a straight shooter. I've always talked truth to power, whether they wanted to hear it or not. Some brought me into a briefing because they needed to hear the truth and no one else would say it."

Vail looked at Rusakov. Her body was forward, her eyes riveted on the general, head nodding subtly—an all-in posture, a "point me in the direction and I'll do what needs to be done" demeanor.

That's essentially what Knox had said to Vail: *Do whatever is necessary.* In the context of OPSIG, that meant anything goes. Anything. No rules. And yet . . .

"General DeSantos," Vail said. "This is way beyond my comfort zone. I'm a career FBI agent. I've sworn—"

"Actually, you're on leave from the Bureau." He took a step toward her and set both hands on the surface of the conference table, a few feet from Vail's face.

Normally that was not a good tactic to take with her. It often led to a reaction, like a knee to the man's—

"Right now," Lukas said, "you're a covert agent of the US government engaged in a war for the preservation of its democracy. Its very *survival* as a democratic nation. You are a key soldier in a war against enemies foreign and domestic. You hear what I'm saying?"

Yes, sir, General. I hear what you're saying, General.

"I was a good soldier," he said, straightening up. "Literally and figuratively. I worked hard for the American people, sacrificed my life for this country and later served at the pleasure of the president.

"Take my comments in that context. I'm a level-headed student of democracy and US history. I am *not* a power-hungry egomaniac who gets off on making war or disobeying the laws of this great republic. Just the opposite. I'm proposing this plan to *protect* those laws."

"Of course," Rusakov said.

214 ALAN JACOBSON

"Not 'of course,'" he said, a notch below shouting. "There have been good and bad apples in the generals corp. Just like anything else in life—fewer duds as you go up in rank, yes, but the rank doesn't *guarantee* integrity and honesty. I love my country and will do anything to uphold its principles, its Constitution, its Bill of Rights. And this cabal presents the most substantial threat to the United States since Nazi Germany."

Vail examined his face: brick red. Temporal arteries pulsing.

"Do either of you dispute that?"

Vail could not.

"Republics are not maintained by cowardice," he said. "And throughout our history, the United States of America has had heroes of all stripes step up and defend our great country." He turned to Vail. "When we leave this room, I'll send you a paragraph to read. And ponder."

Oh I'll ponder it all right. "Let's agree for the moment that what you propose is the best course of action. Who would be next in line to become president? We can't plunge the country into a leaderless crisis."

He took a breath. "There's an order of succession, laid out in the Presidential Succession Act. After the Speaker, it's the president pro tem of the Senate, the secretary of state, and so on, in a specific order. Problem is, we don't know who's part of Scorpion."

"Team Grey was in the process of extensive investigations of the administration. We have *some* idea. But Knox said their data is incomplete."

"Safe to assume the SecDef is not involved," Rusakov said.

"He's . . ." Lukas glanced at the ceiling. "Sixth in line, after the Treasury secretary. But I'll check with the director. He and I go back decades. Maybe he can get a message to Team Grey, have them keep digging. It'll be difficult and it'll be dangerous, but whatever they uncover could be critical."

Rusakov bowed her head and rubbed both eyes. "First order of business is the most difficult. The heads you mentioned. Getting to the president and veep." She sat up, her expression hard with stress. "How do we pull this off? I doubt the Secret Service has any idea what's going on, what Nunn and his group are doing."

"We've got to assume," Vail said, "that like the other agencies and branches of government, some in the service *are* conspirators. Maybe not *part of* the conspiracy, but on board with Nunn's policies. He's had years to weed out anyone who was a threat."

Lukas sat down heavily. "I need to think on this. War-game it. How many people we'll need. What supplies. What weapons. What approach. And then we need to draw up an operational plan and strategize contingencies. FUBAR moments."

Fucked up beyond all recognition.

Vail prayed it did not come to that. But she also knew that, on some level, in an op like this, FUBAR moments were inevitable.

45

JENIN
WEST BANK

Hector DeSantos zip-tied his left wrist to Ghaffar's right. Wearing ski masks and having sealed Ghaffar's mouth with duct tape, the two of them followed closely behind Uzi and Bill Tait through the Jenin streets.

Sunrise was about four hours away.

They were en route to Omar bin-Sahmoud's home, which—according to Ghaffar—had two armed men at the front entrance and a single interior guard.

The house was on a hill about half a mile from their current location. Driving there would have been preferable but they had no wheels; stealing a vehicle would only increase their risk of getting caught.

Although it was cool with a steady drizzle, the balaclavas trapped the heat and zapped their energy.

Sahmoud's house did not match what DeSantos envisioned. In actuality, it was a wall of rough-hewn Jerusalem stones fit atop one another with brush and scrub growing out between the seams. The windows were barred with metal cross-hatching. Power lines ran zig-zag routes from one building to another.

Two guards were standing by the front door, as Ghaffar had said. They were armed but standing casually and smoking, neither one holding his weapon. To operators like DeSantos and Uzi, they were not in a position of readiness or situationally aware.

DeSantos motioned his colleagues back a step, behind a corner building across the street, out of view of the men.

"Who are these guys?" Uzi asked Ghaffar.

"Who do you think? Al-Humat. Trusted soldiers."

"And how do they become trusted?" DeSantos asked.

"They prove themselves. Remember the knife attacks in Jerusalem and Tel Aviv? That was them and they—"

"Got it," Uzi said. "And the guy inside? Same kind of thing?"

Ghaffar nodded.

"You're sure?"

"Yes, yes. I know these guys."

Uzi and DeSantos shared a look of acknowledgment. "What's his name?" DeSantos asked. "The one inside."

"Abeer."

"And what's the layout of the house?" Ghaffar shrugged. "Never been inside."

"Okay, Ghaffar," Uzi said. "Here's the plan."

Before he could start the next sentence, Tait plunged a needle into Ghaffar's arm. As he crumpled to the ground, Uzi guided him down and then cut the zip tie uniting Ghaffar with DeSantos.

They moved him to an alcove and rejoined Tait.

"Too bad we can't take 'em out with a rifle," Tait said.

Uzi nodded. The noise level of a *suppressed* shot would fall between that of a motorcycle and an alarm clock. Abeer could not miss that.

Tait removed two tactical knives from his backpack. He handed one to Uzi. DeSantos volunteered to take the other.

Tait circled the block and came up behind the house from the west while Uzi and DeSantos approached from the east. Once visible to the guards, Tait adopted a wobbling gait, as if exceptionally drunk.

Uzi and DeSantos remained in the darkness, at the corner of the building. The guards would have to engage their colleague and ensure he was not a risk.

Ten more feet and the men turned their bodies toward Tait, holding out their hands and telling him to cross the street. Keeping a threat away from your protected assignment was good protocol; however, they still did not have their weapons ready.

Tait lurched forward, arms flailing and his feet scuffling on the pavement. Uzi and DeSantos left their cover and ran toward the two men—who swung back, facing them.

Tait straightened up and engaged the guard closest to him as Uzi jabbed his knife into his own target, taking out a kidney and whatever other vital organs or vessels the blade could reach.

DeSantos had the easier job, practicing the same stabbing motion while Tait held the man's arms up and out of DeSantos's way.

Uzi slammed the butt of his pistol into his tango's skull, rendering him unconscious—and thus quiet—while he bled out. Tait did likewise to the man DeSantos had attacked. They moved the bodies into the shadows, leaving a trail of blood on the pavement. In minutes, the rain should wash it away.

DeSantos glanced around to make sure the noise, although minimal, did not wake anyone in the vicinity. Most importantly, it did not appear to alert Abeer, who remained inside the house.

Sahmoud's home was a duplex, with a common wall separating an attached home. Tait worked the lock and had it picked in seconds. He took a step back and let Uzi and DeSantos enter first.

The risks were clear: they had no idea of the interior layout. Did Abeer rove or was he stationary? Was he asleep in a chair or was he attentive and prepared to address a threat?

They moved in quickly but stealthily. A few lights were on, no doubt providing Abeer with some illumination to do his job.

Uzi spied Abeer sitting in a chair in the dining room facing the hallway. An entrance to the kitchen was off to his left and slightly behind him. His face was down, staring at his phone. He was shifting left and right. Playing a game of some sort.

Uzi backed away and whispered to DeSantos and Tait, informing them of what he had seen and what strategy they were going to employ.

Moments later, DeSantos made his way around the staircase and into the kitchen. Uzi walked straight into the dining room to get Abeer's attention, which did not take long. He jumped from his seat and fumbled for his handgun.

"Abeer," Uzi said in Arabic, holding up his hands. "It's all good. I'm not here to cause problems."

As Uzi began speaking, DeSantos was behind the man. The second he uttered the word "problems," DeSantos plunged the needle containing BetaSomnol into Abeer's neck then swiped down across Abeer's forearms, which the man was raising once he felt the prick. A few seconds later, the sedative took effect and DeSantos draped the man's torso across the table. They proceeded upstairs, taking care not to make noise.

But the flooring of the older house tended to creak and squeak. Although the downstairs was tile, the steps were wood—and they did not disappoint. So much for a stealth approach.

Uzi hoped that occasionally Abeer walked upstairs and triggered these same noises—or that Sahmoud and his wife were sound sleepers.

The three men made it to the second floor and faced two open, and several closed, doors. The latter were mostly closets, Uzi figured, and he passed them on his way down the hall. There was risk in that, as the prudent method was to clear each one as he went. But doing so had its dangers, too, as an old, dry hinge could alert the very people he was trying to surprise.

At the end of the corridor was—he guessed—Sahmoud's bedroom.

He put his hand on the knob, glanced back at Tait and DeSantos, then opened it.

46

OPSIG SAFE HOUSE
CHEVY CHASE, MARYLAND

After successfully reaching Troy Rodman, Vail gave him the forty-thousand-foot view of what she and Rusakov had discussed with Lukas DeSantos.

Vail felt that burner SIMs were fine for operational comms, but they needed to meet—in the same room, where they could talk, strategize, and make decisions as a group.

Rodman offered an old safe house OPSIG utilized on occasion. "I don't think it's been used in a while. All the utilities are active, lights are programmed to go on and off in randomized schemes, and someone goes by to clean and give a sense of normalcy in case anyone has eyes-on. Place is registered to someone with an OPSIG-generated verifiable cover. Nothing's traceable to us."

"Equipped with a SCIF?"

"Dining and living rooms."

Vail pursued her lips and nodded. "That house will be our task force center. We'll have to be super careful coming and going so we don't poison our home base. I'll make sure everyone gets the address securely. Convene there in an hour. I'll bring pizza in case anyone hasn't eaten."

All the attendees arrived within a ten-minute window. Those who knew one another chatted to catch up; those who did not introduced

DIE TRYING 221

themselves. They took their plates of pizza and cans of Coke and sat around the table, which had four wooden chairs and several metal folding ones with patterned tan-and-gray fabric that Vail recognized from years-ago Costco runs.

Vail and Rusakov had been careful about who they invited, going by their gut instincts, personal experiences, and relationships to help guide them in determining who could be trusted.

Attending the meeting—with handwritten name tag stickers— were OPSIG agents Troy Rodman, Vail and Rusakov, and Zheng Wei; CIA operative Mahmoud el-Fahad, who worked with OPSIG on special assignments; newly promoted assistant special agent in charge of the FBI laboratory, Tim Meadows; Rodman's close friend from childhood—and basic training—US Secret Service agent Giancarlo Stallone and his colleague Taylor Irwin; two former special forces operators and employees of the general, Dell Christie and Neil Frazier; and Vail's fiancé, DEA special agent Robby Hernandez.

Vail popped open a can of Diet Coke and saw Robby come in just as she approached Stallone, a tall, clean-cut black man with close-cropped hair. "Good to meet you, Giancarlo. I'm Karen Vail." She took a swig of soda, then shook his hand.

"Oh hey. Hot Rod mentioned you. By the way, no one calls me Giancarlo. I go by Stallion."

Vail laughed—and nearly snorted the mouthful of Coke. She brought a hand up to her lips, then forced the carbonated liquid down her throat. "Seriously? Stallion?"

"Seriously. That's what Stallone means in English. Stallion."

"Sorry." Vail laughed and shook her head. "Just can't do it."

Stallone grinned. "Well, I'd be lying if I said you're not the only one. I go by Carlo around the office."

"Carlo I can do. Thanks for being here." Vail felt someone behind her. She turned and saw Robby. "Hey, sweetie." She pulled him close by his shirt and planted a kiss on his lips. She leaned back and saw Stallone still standing there. "Oh—sorry. Robby, this is the stallion."

Carlo's gaze bounced from Vail to Robby. "No—uh—"

"The stallion?" Robby, all six-foot-seven of him, looked down on the six-two Stallone.

"Name's Carlo," he said, shaking Robby's hand. "And it's *Stallion*," he said to Vail, "not '*the* stallion.'"

Robby smirked. "I'm sure she knows that. She's just jerking your chain, man." He shook his head disapprovingly. "Right?"

Vail grinned sheepishly and shrugged.

Stallone tilted his head and looked at Vail with a raised brow. "I won't underestimate you again."

Vail held up the red can. "Smart man."

Rodman's baritone voice filled the room. "Okay, everyone. Time to start. We've got a lot to cover. If you haven't already, put your phones, tablets—all electronic devices—in the metal locker over there. Living and dining rooms are SCIFs."

A moment later, Rodman locked the cabinet, followed Vail into the large dining room, and closed the door.

Vail stood at the head of the table. To her left sat Lukas DeSantos, followed by his two buddies, Christie and Frazier. Robby took the chair at the far end, facing Vail.

Vail noted Robby's choice of seat. *As far away from me as he can get. Coincidence?* "I want to thank all of you for coming. You're here because I asked you or Alex did, or one of the core people of this ad hoc task force trusts you with his or her life." She stopped and made eye contact with everyone. "That's not bullshit. I mean it. What we're about to discuss is something I never thought was possible.

"Like you, I've sworn an oath to protect and defend the Constitution of the United States against all enemies, foreign and domestic. We live in a region filled with history. History of our great country. Of some truly amazing things we've done and some absolutely horrendous things we've done. Fortunately, we all agree on the definitions of 'amazing' and 'horrendous' in this context."

I hope everyone here is on the same page. These days you never know.

"Democrat or Republican, Independent or undecided, it doesn't matter. We may disagree on some things, but we're all Americans. And you'll do whatever it takes to make sure our country does not fall under the influence of foreign and domestic enemies who're trying to destroy our democracy, reduce America to the history books

DIE TRYING 223

alongside the Romans and Hasmoneans. Failed civilizations that are no more."

Vail raised her right hand. "I know, these are hard-to-accept concepts. I sound like some ignorant conspiracy theorist. But there are covert operators at this table who fought back just such a plot seven years ago. They know how close we came to being unable to stop those who'd infiltrated our government." She glanced at Rodman, who nodded.

"We thought we'd arrested and convicted all the offenders. We obviously did not. This time, it's not clear who's involved. And that's why this task force is small and carefully chosen. We'll stand together and do whatever it takes to save our country."

Saying those words made Vail uneasy. She had no problem with the concept—

But. Something's bothering me.

"To my left," she continued, "is a man who you may not recognize because he's good at keeping a low profile. Unlike other military types who retire and become talking heads on TV, General Lukas DeSantos wanted no glory for the sacrifices he made to safeguard the United States. He's the epitome of the best America has to offer. He didn't just spew words like I'm doing right now. He walked the walk. General, the floor's yours."

DeSantos rose and changed places with Vail.

"Look, what Agent Vail just said—about the threat matrix we face—she's right. I've reviewed the evidence FBI Director Knox and Secretary of Defense McNamara have put together. Some of that information was assembled by a covert investigative team that was trying to get to the bottom of the group that's been infiltrating our government.

"There was still a lot of work to be done, but the president discovered what the team was up to and had arrest warrants issued for some of our most respected leaders—"

"Wait," Fahad said. "The *president*?"

"Yes," Lukas said. "President Nunn and many in his administration are involved." He gave that a moment to sink in, letting his gaze touch each person in the room. "Mr. Fahad, as a CIA officer, you'll appreciate the danger in this. The president threatened to publicly disclose

224 ALAN JACOBSON

the identities of OPSIG's covert operatives unless they comply with his group's demands."

A number of attendees shifted uncomfortably.

"What demands?" Robby asked.

Lukas looked to the far end of the table. "Robby, right?"

"Yes, sir."

"Nunn's chief of staff, Moorehead Shafik, demanded that everyone affiliated with OPSIG turn themselves in. They'll be tried for murder, even though their actions were taken in the service of—and to preserve—our republic against enemy influences."

Neil Frazier's face shaded red. "They were doing what the government hired them to do."

"And we'd be hard-pressed to prove that with deniable black ops," Rodman said.

"What's Nunn's objective?" Christie asked.

"Stop Team Grey's investigation." Lukas spread his hands. "Eliminate the threat to their power. They've given OPSIG agents seventy-two hours to surrender. To drive home his point, an arrest warrant and BOLO have been prepared for each of them," he said, referring to law enforcement "be on the lookout" alerts.

"The names on that list include FBI Director Knox and SecDef McNamara," Vail said.

Lukas nodded. "And a dozen others I served with." He banged his fist on the table. "Men and women who would never. Ever. Betray our country."

"Can the president do that?" Tim Meadows asked. "Is that—I don't know, legal?"

Lukas chortled. "Since winning his second term, Nunn's constantly pushed the envelope. Bucked the norms administrations have followed for over two hundred years. Most people don't even know that he refused to sign the oath that he won't advocate the overthrow of the government. *I* didn't know about it until Director Knox told me. This is as basic a pledge of allegiance to the US government as there is. Politicians have been signing that oath for several decades."

"Why wouldn't he sign that?" Zheng Wei asked.

Lukas threw out his hands. "Because he'd be pledging not to

DIE TRYING 225

overthrow the US government or participate in any unlawful change of the government, by force—or any unlawful means."

"I remember that," Robby said. "At the time, his press secretary said it was an insult to make him sign it."

"Believe it or not," Lukas said, "signing it *is* optional. He chose not to."

"And now," Robby said, "we know Nunn had a reason."

"But disclosure of OPSIG operators," Meadows said. "That's not pushing the envelope. That puts American lives in danger. Weakens our national security. Can the president do that?"

"Can he do it?" Rodman snorted. "Once he posts the list on his social media account, what's a judge gonna do? Order him to take it down? Demand that every foreign intelligence agency delete the list they've now got?"

There was quiet as everyone considered the implications.

"Fucking assholes," Stallone said.

"And traitors," Fahad added.

"About that," Vail said. "In case you haven't read The Declaration of Independence lately, Thomas Jefferson wrote something that speaks directly to the kind of thing we've been discussing tonight. Responsibilities—and rights—we have as a people." She glanced at the general, then held up the piece of paper he gave her containing a hastily scribbled note.

"'Whenever any form of government becomes destructive, it's the right of the people to alter or to abolish it, and to institute new government. It's their right, it's their *duty*, to throw off such government, and to provide new guards for their future security.'" She set the page on the table. "More than one domestic militia has pinned that to a wall to justify its actions, its goals—which usually include abolishing equality, ensuring white supremacy. Obviously, we are not those people," she said firmly. "We're trying to *prevent* those types of things from happening."

"So what do we do about this?" Robby asked.

Lukas dipped his chin. "I've been tasked with drawing up a strategy for us to remove those involved in this plot. Director Knox has given me a list of their names. But as Karen said, it's incomplete. That means we don't know who to trust—and *that* means none of us can discuss Scorpion's coup, *or our plans to stop it*, with anyone. Wives, husbands, partners, sons, or daughters. No one. This is an extremely sensitive, dangerous operation."

"I want to be very clear," he said. "We can't guarantee success. One or more of us could get killed. Or arrested and charged with treason. Anyone not comfortable with that? Now's the time to go. We won't judge you."

Vail let that hang in the air a minute, taking stock of everyone's reaction. No one moved. "Let's take ten to eat. There's pizza in the kitchen. Phones stay locked away. If you're leaving the task force, let me reiterate that what we discussed is top secret."

Lukas clapped his hands together. "Okay. Let's get some chow."

47

JENIN, WEST BANK

Uzi moved into Omar Abdallah bin-Sahmoud's expansive bedroom, DeSantos following and Tait bringing up the rear.

But a hard blow to Uzi's head caught him off guard. He could not see who or what had struck him. His torso hit the bed on the way to the floor, a deep ache spreading across his skull.

Yelling and screaming followed.

"Abeer!" *Female voice.* "Abeeeeer!" *Across the room.*

Uzi struggled to his knees and saw Sahmoud—the number three man in al-Humat—drawing a bat back to strike DeSantos.

Uzi dove forward and slammed his right shoulder into Sahmoud's thighs.

Sahmoud's legs buckled and he dropped the weapon. DeSantos grabbed the back of his shirt and slammed the man into the dresser.

Behind him, Uzi heard Tait struggling with the woman—although she quickly went mute.

A few seconds later, Sahmoud was likewise rendered unconscious, a syringe protruding from his left shoulder.

"Well that didn't go as planned," Uzi said, rubbing the back of his head.

DeSantos switched on his tactical flashlight and shined it on the furniture, where a smudge of bright red blood covered the olivewood surface. He grabbed a damp hand towel from the bathroom and wiped the smear away then pocketed the rag.

"Find the car keys," Uzi said.

"What about Ghaffar?"

Uzi sighed. "Give him another injection. That should hold him until sunrise. He'll wake up and go home. He won't want to explain to his wife what happened, and he sure as hell would not want to be found responsible for our snatch of Sahmoud."

"What about that drug that wipes short-term memory?" DeSantos asked.

Uzi thought a moment, then snapped his fingers. "Actinocyde. Hit him with a dose of that. He won't remember anything about the past couple of days."

"Bill—got any Actinocyde in your kit?"

"Like my American Express card. I don't leave home without it."

"Prepare a dose of BetaSomnol and Actinocyde for Ghaffar."

"Running low on BetaSomnol," Tait said.

Uzi took Ghaffar's lighter from his pocket, wiped it with his shirt, and tossed it on the floor near Sahmoud's dresser. "We've been using it like water."

Tait loaded the syringe, then checked it. "Giving the wife a dose of Actinocyde, too."

"Look what I found," DeSantos said, holding up a set of car keys. "These will come in handy."

Uzi and Tait carried Sahmoud down the stairs and through the back door, where the vehicle was parked. Keeping his ski mask on, Uzi drove along the alley on the unattached side of the townhouse. He stopped and let Tait out.

Tait crossed the street and administered the double dose of meds to Ghaffar and propped him up a bit so it looked like he had fallen asleep—in the unlikely event someone found him before he awakened.

"Anything?" Uzi asked as he tried to slow his adrenaline-infused heartrate.

"Everything looks quiet," Tait said.

DeSantos, seated in the front passenger seat, swiveled his head in all directions. "Hopefully no one heard the commotion. Still, drive normally."

"I was born in Israel and live in DC," Uzi said. "I can't drive normally."

DeSantos laughed. "Normally for *you*."

They arrived at the mosque twelve minutes later. Although it was the middle of the night, they expected it to be occupied.

After making their way to the tunnel's entrance, Uzi found stacked boxes in an adjacent room. He used the tip of his handgun to push the door open a few inches, shined his flashlight in, and then stepped in to examine one of the boxes: ammunition, improvised explosive devices, and chemicals, trigger mechanisms, and hardware for making larger bombs.

Inside a mosque.

DeSantos tapped his shoulder, then gestured with a sideways movement of his head: *we need to get out of here.*

They laid Sahmoud's sedated body on a blanket and folded it into a cradle so they could lower him down the vertical chute. They attached the ends to the winch.

DeSantos checked to make sure the makeshift hammock was secure, then studied the gear mechanism. "Awfully nice of them to install this contraption for us."

Tait examined the control panel. "I doubt they thought their enemy would use it on one of their top leaders." He pressed a button and then pulled up a wide breaker-style switch. The machine hummed to life and the cable spool began to turn.

Uzi was already down below, ready to receive the body as it was lowered slowly into the hole.

That done, the three of them began lugging Sahmoud through the tunnel toward the Israeli side. It was a long trek lugging a 175-pound dead weight in the super-humid environment. They took frequent breaks and drained the remaining water they had brought with them.

They stopped and set Sahmoud down, then dropped to the ground.

"You think they could've at least left the ventilation system running for us," DeSantos complained as he used his sleeve to mop away the perspiration rolling down his face.

"Inconsiderate terrorists," Tait said with mock disdain. "I fear for this world."

They all laughed . . . punch drunk on lack of sleep, exhaustion, low blood sugar, and the sudden loss of adrenaline.

DeSantos checked his watch. "We're getting low on time. How much farther you think we've got?"

Uzi turned on his tactical flashlight and shined it ahead. "Farther than this beam reaches."

"Once we reach the end, we'll wake him up, see what we can learn."

Tait nodded. "Sounds like a plan. I can have him conscious and lucid in about two to three minutes."

"Rest time's over," Uzi said, getting to his feet. "Back to it."

48

OPSIG SAFE HOUSE
CHEVY CHASE, MARYLAND

Karen Vail finished a brief conversation with Rusakov and turned to find Robby giving her a gesture toward a room at the far end of the house.

"What's up?" she asked.

"You have reservations about this." She chuckled. "Shouldn't I?"

Robby shrugged. "We're trying to prevent a coup. This is exactly what we should be doing as federal agents. We swore to protect and defend the Constitution." He studied her face.

Vail nodded slowly but did not answer.

"Karen, what's the alternative? Do nothing? You and your colleagues thrown in prison for life for—for doing your jobs?"

"That's not an option." She shook her head. "But . . ."

Robby folded his arms across his chest, waiting for her to finish. "Look, what if you were handed an OPSIG mission package where a group of domestic terrorists was conspiring with foreign nationals, enemies of the United States, to take down our government? Would you have any reservations about carrying out that mission?"

Vail snorted. "I'd track the bastards to the ends of the earth."

Robby nodded animatedly. "*This* is that case, Karen. It can't be any clearer than that."

Vail pinched the bridge of her nose. "I know. I know."

"It's the concept, isn't it? Of taking down the president. A legitimately elected official. It's hard for us, as law enforcement officers, to process that."

"I think that's what's been bothering me. There's no due process, which is fundamental to our DNA as law enforcement officers."

Robby took her hand. "I struggled with that, too. For about two minutes. Then I played it out in my mind. The partisan divisions in Congress."

Vail snorted. "In the *country*."

"Trying to build a legal case against Scorpion? When they've infiltrated the executive, legislative, and judicial branches of the federal government? How the hell do you deal with that? Especially with misinformation and bot campaigns coming out of Russia, Iran, China, North Korea, flooding social media. Conspiracy theories repeated on cable news without verification—going viral and causing more division."

"Our electronic voting machines were hacked, corrupted, manipulated. Remember that? Total bullshit." Vail closed her eyes. "Things would get so fucked up. Nothing would get sorted out."

"If this case was tried in court, we'd need smoking gun evidence," he said. "Video testimony naming names. Documents. Money trails."

"It'd have to be a rock-solid case. And even then, if the judge is a party to the conspiracy, justice won't be served."

Robby placed his index finger beneath her chin and gently raised it to make eye contact. "Do you trust Knox?"

"I do."

"Are you proud of the work you've done with the Bureau? With OPSIG?"

Her time in England, the incident with Basil Walpole, flooded her thoughts. She pushed it aside and concentrated on all the good they had done, the vitally important missions they had completed over the years. The killers she helped catch, the terrorist plots she helped foil. "Definitely."

"This is no different. You have a job to protect the Constitution, to serve the people, throw off attempts by foreign and domestic enemies to take over the government. *That's* what we're doing here."

She nodded, squared her shoulders, and took a deep breath. "Okay."

"You good?"

"Yeah." She turned and started back toward the group. "Let's get these bastards."

49

Vail reconvened the meeting and was relieved to see that no one had left. Then again, someone who opposed their efforts on a visceral level would remain, learn the group's timing and methods, and then betray them.

But Vail knew that each of these handpicked individuals was chosen for a reason—prime of which was that he was trustworthy and would be able to grasp the danger of what Scorpion was doing.

"Before we continue," she said, "any questions?"

Tim Meadows raised his hand. "Not to beat a dead horse—'cause I love horses and I'd never do that—but we're *not* looking to build a case to prosecute the people involved in this plot."

"In a perfect world," Vail said, "we would. But the people who are in charge of this coup have the world's most powerful army in the history of this planet at their disposal. They control . . . well, everything. And they've done a terrific job of shutting us down."

"Then what's our plan?"

The general, who was standing behind and to Vail's left, moved forward, beside her. "Tim, right?"

"Yes, sir."

"That's one reason why we called this meeting. To get everyone's input on what I'm about to propose."

Lukas laid out his strategy and the reasoning behind it while Vail assessed the attendees' reactions.

"Tim," Vail said. "Now that you've heard the general's proposal, what are your thoughts?"

Meadows squirmed in his seat. "Call on someone else, would ya, Karen?"

"I asked you for a reason. We're here for open discourse. Say what's on your mind."

He took a deep breath. "For those of you who don't know, I worked the case that General DeSantos mentioned. The one with Armed Revolution Militia, the earlier iteration of Scorpion. They realized I was on to them and tried to kill me. Almost did, but . . . I got lucky."

"Quick thinking," Vail said. "Not luck. You were brilliant." She turned to the others in the room. "He stuffed himself into a safe in his workshop a second before the bomb went off."

Meadows looked down at the table. "Thanks."

"There's a 'but'?" Vail asked.

He shrugged. "I'm not a field agent. I'm not an operator. I'm a lab geek. A forensics and cyber guy."

"So, bluntly speaking, *aggressive interventions* fall outside your comfort zone," she said.

Meadows swallowed deeply. "Yeah."

"Look," Dell Christie said. "I was a Tier One operator with the SEALs until six months ago. You people know the shit we do. Targeted assassinations, stuff we ain't never s'posed to discuss. None of *us* wants to think too much about 'em. No soldier does. Gets inside your head. But it's a fact. It's our job. When we spin up, America's safety's in our hands. We get our target package and we execute. We don't question the orders. So yeah, Tim. I get you. You ain't built for that—and that's okay. You shouldn't be doing the things we operators are trained to do.

"But as the general was laying it out, I started thinking about everything that needs to be done. We do the shooting, kicking in doors, and blowing shit up. But intel officers tell us where and when we can find our targets. Sometimes we've got guys hacking servers to turn off lights or cameras or security systems so we can get to our target. Analysts do the heavy lifting weeks in advance. Point is, it's a team effort. *You* are part of that team, Tim. Guaranteed you won't be crouching behind a rifle."

236 ALAN JACOBSON

"Thanks, Dell," Lukas said. "Couldn't have said it better."

Rodman stood up, consulting his G-Shock. "Excuse me for a minute."

He walked out and closed the door quietly behind him.

"What we're proposing," Stallone said, "is something *none* of us ever thought we'd be doing. For those of you I haven't spoken with, Taylor Irwin and I are with the Secret Service. It's not anywhere in writing, but it's widely known that we'd take a bullet to protect the president. For us to be involved in an op like this is pretty damn significant. But history will look back on tonight's meeting as historic. Brave men and women putting their lives on the line to preserve our democracy."

Rodman had told Vail that Stallone served on President Nunn's protective detail but transferred out in year one because there was something about Nunn that made him uncomfortable. He could have taken another protection detail but felt that would be a step backward. He was sent to headquarters and then assigned to CIS, the cyber intelligence division.

The door opened and Rodman reentered, followed by FBI Director Douglas Knox—uncharacteristically dressed down in a sweater and jeans. Vail could not recall ever seeing him in anything but an immaculately tailored suit.

"Mr. Director," Vail said. "Didn't know you were coming."

He faced everyone. "I'm here because it's vital you understand the importance of what you'll be doing. I wanted to drive home that point—and vouch for the veracity of the people in this room. They each have my deepest respect." He gestured at Vail and Lukas. "I know you're in the middle of a Q and A. Please, continue."

"Actually," Taylor Irwin said, "I've got a question for the director." He leaned forward and tilted his head left. "Do we have a smoking gun, sir?"

"A smoking gun," Knox said. "In terms of evidence?" He turned to Vail. "I've briefed them on everything we discussed, sir."

Knox nodded slowly, keeping his gaze on Irwin. "You're with the Service, right? Irwin?"

"Yes, sir."

DIE TRYING 237

Knox put his hands behind his back and bowed his head for a few seconds, then locked on Irwin's gaze. "This is as close as you'll get to a smoking gun. The president had a burner phone in the residence. At night he used the secure TELECRYPT app to communicate with his conspirators all over the world. Chat messages that lay out what Nunn and his cabal are trying to do."

"But TELECRYPT deletes its messages within thirty minutes."

Knox's lips thinned into a slight grin. "Let's just say they *are* recoverable. For talented people with the right skills."

Irwin spread his hands. "Then why don't we take this to the AG?"

"We did. And he tried to get warrants—and wire taps—but he was shot down by judges Nunn had appointed. He also had to be careful what they disclosed to the judge. If Scorpion found out what we were up to, we'd never find out who was involved. So the AG couldn't share a lot of the data we'd collected—and we had to bury it in a bogus investigation that had nothing to do with the president or Scorpion."

"Then we didn't get the evidence legally," Robby said.

"No." Knox glanced at everyone around the table, no doubt debating what he should divulge. "The General Services Administration's Public Buildings Service division manages about nine thousand government owned and leased facilities. Federal courthouses, FBI headquarters, federal agencies—"

"And the White House," Vail said.

Knox pointed at her. "And the White House—which is obviously a very old building. And old buildings require . . ."

"A ton of maintenance," Meadows said.

"Right. A lot of the work's done by contractors hired by the Public Buildings Service. These contractors are local businesses, including small companies. Some are having trouble making ends meet. We had an operative hack the Public Buildings system to see the repair requests as they came through. We found one that got us near where we needed to get, based on some insider info we got on where Nunn keeps that phone. With a company that fit our profile."

"You got us a mole," Robby said.

Knox bobbed his head left and right. "I prefer *useful source*. Limited in scope and access. Late last year, we took advantage of an electrician who was having difficulty paying his bills. Let's call him Hal. For a generous fee, Hal hired our operative for a few days. We backfilled his cover story to show an impressive career in electrical engineering and subcontracting work. He accompanied Hal to the White House to make those repairs. While on-site, our guy cloned Nunn's burner phone. The recovery of the deleted TELECRYPT messages was done by OPSIG's cryptography engineers."

"Definitely not something you can bring before a grand jury," Vail said under her breath—but loud enough for others seated nearby to hear.

"Any other questions about the evidence we've got?" Knox glanced around, then noticed that Robby had raised his hand.

"Hernandez."

"I'd like to get back to discussing what General DeSantos proposed before you got here."

"Please," Knox said, "I didn't intend to interrupt your meeting. You have any specific questions for me, Hot Rod knows how to get in touch." Knox gestured to Lukas, figuratively passing the gavel back to him and leaving the room.

50

Robby waited for the door to close, then turned to Lukas. "General, I want to make sure we're clear on this. Your plan is to intercept the president's motorcade?"

"That's correct, Robby. It'll be difficult but doing it anywhere else will be damn near impossible."

"That limo is hardened. How are we going to pull that off?"

Lukas nodded: this was a question he had anticipated. "I've war-gamed how I think it should be done using standard military vehicular interdiction in an urban setting. But this motorcade is a lot more complex, and specifically the limo. Agents Stallone and Irwin, this is your sandbox."

Stallone shared a look with Irwin, then leaned forward in his seat, pushed it back, and strode to the front of the room. He picked up an erasable marker and stood beside the white board. "I served on the president's protection detail, so I can give you an up-to-date assessment of what we'll be dealing with.

"As you can imagine, keeping the president alive—the service's primary mission—is an all-encompassing job. Of all the places we have to protect POTUS, the motorcade is when the president's most vulnerable. There's a joke inside the service: the safest motorcade is . . . anyone?" None of the attendees ventured a guess.

Stallone spread his arms. "The safest motorcade is *no* motorcade." Chuckles wove through the room. "That said, we do a damn good job.

The motorcade's not just a bunch of hardened vehicles. It's a mobile command and control platform—like Air Force One, but on the ground.

"First, there are *two* presidential limos—we call them beasts—the one the president rides in is code-named Stagecoach and the decoy goes by Spare." Stallone drew two rectangles and labeled them. "Both have matching license plates."

"First problem," Rusakov said, "is we won't know which Nunn will be in."

"Normally," Stallone said, "that *would* be a problem—and that's the idea. But I'm a supervisor in cyber intelligence. I've got access to the system where the schedule, itinerary, checkpoints, routes—all that data—is stored."

"Huge advantage," Lukas said. "So you'll be able to give us advance notice which is Stagecoach and which is Spare?"

"Yes," Stallone said. "But that brings us to the real challenge. We call these limos beasts because they're built like tanks. They weigh nine *tons* apiece. The president's rear compartment has its own oxygen supply and eight-inch-thick armor-plated doors that seal completely to keep chemical weapons from getting in. The windows have five layers of glass and polycarbonate—and they're bulletproof. They don't open, except for the driver's, which only opens a few inches.

"The bottom of the car chassis has a reinforced steel plate to protect against bombs. The Duramax diesel engine is coated in a flame-retardant foam—an idea taken from NASCAR.

"Body's made of military-grade armor. Five inches of steel, aluminum, titanium, and ceramic—designed to absorb up to .44-caliber rounds. The tires are puncture- and shred-resistant Kevlar filled with gel, rather than air, with steel rims that extend inside the tire so the car can still be driven at highway speeds even if the tires are destroyed."

"Man oh man," Robby said. "*Tank* is right."

"What about onboard weapons?" Rodman asked. "Anything we need to worry about?"

Irwin snorted. "Pump action shotguns and tear gas cannons. Night vision/infrared driving systems. Oh, and built-in grenade launchers in the front end."

DIE TRYING 241

"Grenade launchers?" Robby chortled. "Jesus Christ."

The general was chewing on his lower lip. "What about the gas tank?"

"Armored, too," Irwin said, "with some kind of foam inside that prevents it from exploding."

Lukas nodded. "Too obvious a vulnerability to leave unprotected."

"Living in DC," Zheng Wei said, "I've seen my share of motorcades. The two limos aren't the only vehicles."

"No." Stallone nodded at Irwin. "Tay, you want to pick it up from here?"

"You're on a roll, Carlo. Keep going."

"Fine." Stallone turned to the whiteboard and gestured toward his sketch. "There are route and pilot cars, which travel ahead of the motorcade to check the roads and provide intelligence to the trailing vehicles." He added a few R's and P's to the diagram. "Sweepers are cops on motorcycles and in patrol cars that travel behind the pilot cars and in front of the motorcade." He drew small S's for those.

"The lead car, in this case a Chevy Suburban, that's basically a buffer for what lies ahead." Stallone sketched an LC inside a rectangle.

"The limo is next, followed by the presidential security detail SUV, code-named Halfback. A heavily armed Secret Service agent sits in a rear-facing row, with an open back window." More squares and shapes with labels went on the board.

"The electronic countermeasures vehicle, known as Watchtower, comes after that. It's another Suburban with two antennas and a couple of squat black cylinders—shortwave radar sensors for picking up incoming missiles and drones. The cylinders can also deploy countermeasures, like infrared smoke and chaff, to throw off incoming threats. The car also has broad spectrum radio frequencies for jamming remote explosives."

Stallone's diagram looked like an alien spider—drawing was not one of his strengths.

"Is that all?" Zheng Wei asked with a chuckle.

"Actually," Irwin said, "no. There are control and support SUVs, which carry a top military aide with the nuclear football, the president's doctor, and members of his cabinet if they're along for the ride."

242   ALAN JACOBSON

The nuclear football, the attendees knew, was a briefcase that contained retaliatory options for launching a counterstrike, a book listing classified locations in the event of attack, and the nuclear authentication codes. It accompanied the president everywhere he went.

Stallone added these vehicles to the diagram. "Next are the counterassault team SUVs, nicknamed Hawkeye Renegade, which carry Secret Service direct attack operators. They're quick react teams if there's no advance warning of an imminent threat.

"This is a friggin' army," Rodman said.

Stallone laughed. "Next comes the Intelligence Division vehicle. It communicates with other units about potential threats along the route. And then there's the Hazardous Materials Mitigation Unit, a truck with sensors to detect nuclear, biological, and chemical weapons." He added these to the already full whiteboard.

"The remaining vehicles consist of—"

"There's more?" Zheng said.

"'Roadrunner,'" Stallone continued, giving Zheng a stern look. "It's an F350 pickup that's got a satellite comms array and antennas to provide all the cars in the motorcade with encrypted voice, internet, and video."

"All that," Irwin added, "is followed by an ambulance and a rear guard of motorcycles or local police cars."

Stallone squeezed in some tiny circles, then set the marker down.

No one spoke for a minute as they perused the mess on the whiteboard.

"Did someone say we had a huge *advantage*?" Rusakov asked.

"That was me," Lukas said. "And I stand by that. We have *several* advantages." He held up his right thumb. "We'll know which car Nunn will be in." Index finger. "We'll know the route of the motorcade ahead of time, so we can plan—and plant things ahead of time." Middle finger. "We know what each of these vehicles are capable of doing." Ring finger. "And Stallone has access to the GPS system deployed on Stagecoach."

"And if you have access to that," Meadows said, "you should be able to remotely control the onboard computers."

"Exactly," Lukas said.

DIE TRYING 243

Stallone held up a hand. "Doesn't guarantee success but improves the odds from just about impossible to anything's possible."

"We're going to need more." It was Neil Frazier, one of the retired Navy SEALs. "Someone on the inside. Besides you and Irwin. To get us more intel and help us pull strings when the moment hits."

"That *would* be extremely helpful," Stallone said with a nod. "I'll see what I can do. No promises."

"Agent Irwin," Frazier said, "what about you?"

Irwin shook his head. "I'm not in ops like Carlo. Can't help."

"Even if we have someone on the inside," Rusakov said, "what do you think our chances are of pulling this off?"

Irwin laughed wryly. "Not very good."

Stallone frowned. "Normally, I'd—"

"Look," Lukas said. "This is a difficult mission, no question. We're talking about the president of the United States. Things have changed a lot since the days of Lincoln, JFK—heck, even Reagan. Doing what we're attempting isn't easy. And honestly, that's a good thing."

"The motorcade is, without a doubt, a well-designed setup," Frazier said. "But as a SEAL, I can tell you that nothing's perfect. Nothing's impervious to attack."

"Terrific news," Vail said. "Because we're going to have to find those imperfections—and figure out how to exploit them. General, you, Frazier, Christie, Irwin, and Stallone—that's your assigned task. Gaming that out."

"Yes, ma'am," they said, nearly in unison.

Gotta love the military.

"And, Tim—can you please join them? Your skillset will be important."

He issued no retort, so common in their relationship, and merely nodded—though his face was flaccid with uncertainty.

Vail looked past him at a picture of the Washington Monument hanging on the far wall and caught her reflection. One thought filled her mind:

What the hell did I get myself into?

51

JENIN, WEST BANK

Bill Tait injected Sahmoud with a stimulant and slapped his cheek to stimulate the sympathetic nerve system.

"Hey buddy," DeSantos said in Arabic, his balaclava again pulled down over his face. "Time to get up. These masks are hot. Let's get this over with."

Sahmoud's eyelids looked like ten-pound weights. He appeared to struggle to lift them, but ultimately the meds circulated through his heart and made their way up to his brain. "Who are you?"

Tait and Uzi grabbed him under the armpits and pulled him up against the tunnel wall.

"I know, so many questions," DeSantos said. "But here's the thing. We didn't kidnap you from your house so we could answer *your* questions."

Sahmoud's eyes focused and he squirmed—but his arms were securely fastened behind him.

"My wife—"

"Yes," Uzi answered, likewise in Arabic. "You want to know if we let her live." He pursed his lips. "Tell you what. You answer a few of our questions and we'll tell you what happened to her."

"Fuuuuck yooou."

He was still partially sedated, so it came out as if he were drunk: drawn out and a bit slurred.

DIE TRYING 245

DeSantos looked at Uzi. "This isn't starting off the way we'd hoped." Without taking his eyes off Sahmoud, he reached back to Tait and held up an outstretched hand.

Tait searched his rucksack and withdrew the tactical knife.

DeSantos opened it and pressed the tip of the tanto blade against Sahmoud's right inner thigh, an inch from his testicles—a very sensitive area of skin.

"Our first question. You were one of the people in charge of al-Fari'ah. We—"

"I don't know this . . . this al-Fari'ah."

DeSantos added pressure to the knife tip. "Each time you lie I'll press harder. And I'm very close to the femoral artery. You know what that means?" Sahmoud nodded animatedly. "Let's try again. There was an Israeli woman imprisoned at al-Fari'ah with her daughter. What happened to them?"

"Don't know what . . . you're talking about."

DeSantos added weight to his arm, piercing the cloth of Sahmoud's pajamas. He turned to Uzi. "This piece of shit is worthless. I'm gonna cut the artery and let him bleed out."

Sahmoud's eyes widened.

"Give him one more chance to tell the truth." Uzi leaned closer. "*Last* chance, asshole. We know the woman had a bad infection from a fight at Jneid. Where was she taken?"

Sahmoud's gaze dropped to his groin. "Women's reform center."

"And then?"

Sahmoud clenched his jaw and shook his head.

Uzi and DeSantos shared a look. He knew what DeSantos was thinking: he had no problem keeping his promise to slice the leg, but that would not get them the answers they needed. And it could have geopolitical ramifications they could not predict or understand fully.

"I have something worth considering," Tait said. He motioned Uzi and DeSantos a few feet away. "I've got amobarbital in my kit."

"Truth serum," Uzi said.

"One of the active ingredients. It *has* been used as truth serum."

246 ALAN JACOBSON

"I used KGB-procured SP-117 once," DeSantos said. "It was way past expiration, but it still did the job. Does amobarbital work?"

Tait bobbed his head. "Depends on the person. Couple of things to keep in mind. It works on the brain in a few different ways, but we're most interested in how it inhibits mitochondrial respiration at the cellular level. Makes people weak, too worn out to think critically and creatively."

Uzi nodded. "Harder for them to make up lies."

"Right. But we've got to be careful not to lead him because it can allow false memories to be implanted. And there's also the potential for a drug-drug interaction with BetaSomnol."

"How much potential?" Uzi asked.

"Small." Tait pursed his lips. "Should be fine. I won't be giving him that much amobarbital."

Uzi gestured at Sahmoud. "Do it."

Tait reached into his bag. "It'll need to be done by slow IV drip so we can control the dosage." He extracted a glass vial and plunged an IV needle into the rubber top. He enlisted DeSantos to hold the bag to enable the gravity drip, then set the rate. He snapped on a rubber tourniquet to help identify the vein and inserted the cannula. Ninety seconds later, the amobarbital was entering Sahmoud's bloodstream. "We'll need a bit for it to do its job."

Uzi used the time to sit, clear his mind, and process what Sahmoud had told them. He might have dozed because he suddenly felt a presence at his feet. Uzi opened his eyes and saw Tait standing there.

"He should be ready."

Uzi jumped up and joined DeSantos in front of Sahmoud.

DeSantos had rigged the IV to hang from a cement protrusion. He checked the drip rate and nodded.

"I'm gonna back up a bit so he has some context." Uzi leaned closer, a foot from the man's face. "Omar, you were telling us about a woman and girl al-Humat had taken," he said in Arabic. "High-value targets. They were taken to Jneid and the woman developed a bad infection. Where was she taken?"

Sahmoud's eyelids were at half-mast. His head bobbed from the weight of trying to keep it erect.

Uzi held his chin up. "Sahmoud. Answer me."

"Women's reform center," he answered in Arabic. "And what happened to her there?"

"She . . . died six months later." Uzi swallowed hard. "How?"

"Doctors didn't treat . . . the infection."

Uzi felt a pang of loneliness seep through his body. His throat tightened and he had difficulty breathing. He realized that, despite the mask and Sahmoud's drugged state, he couldn't show this jerk wad any weakness. Or personal connection. He sucked in air through his nose and slowed his heart rate. Pushed Dena from his mind. "And the girl. Where was she taken?"

They knew the answer to this—at least initially, assuming Ghaffar had been honest with them. If Sahmoud was truthful with *this* information, Uzi had little reason to doubt his statement about Dena.

"Al-Fari'ah."

"Is she still there?"

Sahmoud shook his head.

They waited for him to elaborate, but he remained silent. Uzi clenched his jaw. "Then where's the girl?"

He did not answer.

"Your life depends on it," DeSantos said. He dug the knife tip into Sahmoud's thigh. Crimson liquid pooled on the surface of the cotton, then was absorbed into the fabric. "Tell us," he said firmly. "Where. Is. She."

"Ow." He looked down slowly at his leg. "Syria. We . . . Moved her to Syria."

Uzi's bottom jaw dropped. *Syria?* If this were true, their rescue mission—already exceedingly problematic—was now infinitely more dangerous, and more difficult . . . if not impossible.

"Where?" Uzi asked. "Sednaya?" Known as the "human slaughterhouse," Sednaya was a military prison outside Damascus operated by the Syrian government and specializing in torture, mass murders, hangings—and a crematorium to cover up the atrocities.

"No," Sahmoud said. "Built into the foothills. Can't escape. Special prisoners there. Asr Sayy."

Uzi let his bunched shoulders relax. At least Maya was not at Sednaya—about the worst place he could imagine them taking her. Then again, he knew nothing about Asr Sayy.

"Are you sure she's at Asr Sayy?" DeSantos asked.

Sahmoud grinned and looked up slowly, made eye contact. "I saw her there."

DeSantos crouched beside Uzi. "When did you see her?"

"Last month."

Uzi stood up and looked down at Sahmoud. He wanted to slam his boot into his face. And keep stomping until it was a mush of bone and pulp.

He heard DeSantos telling Sahmoud they were with Hamas and that they were going to let him live . . . implanting a manufactured memory that would confuse him and invoke uncertainty, when he awoke, as to what had happened to him—and make him think twice before telling anyone about it.

Uzi turned and walked a dozen feet away. How on earth would they get into a Syrian prison? More importantly, how would they get *out*?

But his daughter was there. The girl he thought had died years ago . . . alive. Separated from her parents in a scary part of the world, her captives speaking a language she did not understand.

Tears pooled in his lower lids. Had she been abused?

Uzi shut that out of his mind. He could not go there. All his energy, all his focus, had to be on getting Maya out of Asr Sayy . . . no matter how impossible that might prove.

52

OPSIG SAFE HOUSE
CHEVY CHASE, MARYLAND

The task force members took a ten-minute pause to clear their minds, stretch their legs, and let the previous discussion bounce around their thoughts. It was heady stuff and would require some time to process.

Problem was, they did not have that luxury.

Not surprisingly, Vail noticed the chatter was more subdued than during the last break.

She found Lukas, Robby, and Rodman in the living room sipping Cokes.

"Gentlemen."

"Karen," Rodman said. "Good job back there."

Vail groaned. "Not sure how we're gonna pull this off. That motorcade is—"

"We'll *make* it work," Rodman said. "We did interdictions like this in Iraq. The key is preparation. And timing."

Whatever you did in Iraq, this is nothing like it.

Vail turned to Lukas. "What if I could propose an alternate plan? I understand the reasons for how you've laid everything out. But can we really take out Nunn? Not to mention the collateral damage of, what? Dozens of people?" She lowered her voice. "And it won't get us any closer to rooting out *all* the traitors, let alone identifying who they are."

The general folded his arms across his chest. "Let's hear your alternate plan."

Shit. I should've known he was going to ask that.

Vail canted her head toward the ceiling. "I need more time to think it through."

"Don't worry about the execution. I'll war-game it." He wiggled his fingers in front of her. "Just lay it out for us."

Vail felt her face flushing with embarrassment. "I don't have one yet."

Robby turned away.

Lukas stared at her, a look the general must have used in years past with subordinates who did not toe the line. "Well. When you think of something, let us know. Because we don't have much time." He checked his G-Shock. "How long will you need?"

So the general can be a bit of an asshole. I'll have to discuss this with Hector.

Assuming I live to see him again.

Vail sucked at her front teeth, then nodded. "Point made. I withdraw my comment."

For now.

"Great," Lukas said, sarcasm permeating his tone. "Objection withdrawn."

"It wasn't an objection. I was just . . . expressing my concerns." Lukas crumpled his brow in disapproval. Or was it pity?

Vail heard Robby sigh.

I should've kept my mouth shut. But when have I ever been able to do that?

"Hot Rod," Lukas said, "where do you stand on procuring the two SAMs?"

Surface-to-air missiles?

"Checked with your guy. He's got *one*. Working on another two. Should have an answer within the hour."

"The other stuff?"

"Everything else was in your warehouses. En route as we speak. A few spec ops buddies of mine will go through it and make sure it's all up to snuff. They've agreed to help us on this. And I may be able to get a few more guys."

"Good. We're gonna need a lot more to pull this off. As to the equipment, it's well-maintained and ready to go."

"Awesome," Rodman said. "Then we won't find any issues when we check it all out."

The general's brow hardened. The two men stared at each other.

Vail watched the testosterone-fueled exchange and realized she needed to speak up.

"Guys," she said, holding up her hands. "We're under a lot of pressure. We're professionals and we've got a job to do. A very important one. Let's take a breath."

"You're right." Lukas bowed his head. "Sorry."

"Me too," Rodman said.

"Before we get back in there," Lukas said, "there are people here I don't know—or don't know well. We need to take the pulse of our task force members."

"Keep our antennas up," Vail said. "Observe people. Anyone displays odd behavior, we should speak up. Better to be careful and suspicious—and wrong—than to keep quiet and have it blow up on us."

"Exactly." Lukas leaned forward. "If our plan falls apart, if the administration or Secret Service finds out about what we're doing, we'll be spending the rest of our lives in prison. If we're not summarily executed without a trial. You all feel me?"

Vail made eye contact with Robby, Lukas, and Rodman. "Yes."

"Great," the general said with a clap of his hands. "Let's get back in that room and finish talking this through."

53

JENIN, WEST BANK

Uzi stood at the base of the ladder. Hopefully, Sanfilippo was up there, waiting. Sahmoud was seated twenty feet away, tugging at his bindings.

"What do we do with this guy?" Tait asked.

"Call Aksel," DeSantos said. "Tell him where he is, let them decide if they want to come get him or leave him here."

"Bill, you have any Actinocyde left in your kit?"

"Two vials."

DeSantos looked over his right shoulder at Sahmoud. "We only need one. Give him another shot of BetaSomnol mixed with Actinocyde."

Tait kinked his neck, then raised his brow in understanding. "You want to put him out for a while—and when he wakes up not have any idea how he got there."

"Exactly," DeSantos said. "Will that create a problem mixing with the amobarbital?"

"Shouldn't be a problem."

"Do it," Uzi said as he examined stacked boxes that blended in with the wall to the right of the ladder. "What the hell's this?"

DeSantos dug a knife into the middle of the tall stack and sliced a square opening large enough to get a hand in. He pulled out a clear plastic bag filled with white round pills. The bag sported a familiar

DIE TRYING 253

stylized silver and black *L* sticker. "Why would the Lexus logo be on—"

"Careful," Tait said, approaching them with the syringe still in his hand. "That's captagon."

"An amphetamine," DeSantos said, "right?"

"Huge in the Middle East." Uzi took the bag and maneuvered the pills inside the plastic. "They've got a double crescent stamped on one side. And yeah, that fake Lexus logo is used by a group in Syria that makes it. Manufacture and distribution are handled by a division of the Syrian army. Hundreds of millions of pills have been seized so you can imagine how many have gotten through." He handed the bag to Tait. "Billions of dollars in street value. At least it's not a problem in the US."

Tait took the bag and shoved it back into the hole in the carton. "Yet."

Uzi started up the ladder. "I'll make that call to Gideon."

"And boychick," DeSantos said, "Do *not* apologize for waking him."

Uzi laughed, his voice echoing down the shaft. "Gideon's up at 5:00 every morning." He texted Sanfilippo to open the tunnel cover and seconds later, Sanfilippo came into view as the door canted upward.

"All good?" Uzi asked.

Sanfilippo held out his hand and helped pull Uzi out of the entrance.

"Nothing I couldn't handle. You guys?"

"Got what we needed. Bill will fill you in."

Uzi popped out the SIM and replaced it. He dialed and waited for Aksel to answer the encrypted call. "It's Uzi. I've got a gift for you."

Aksel snorted. "You're leaving my country on the next flight out?"

"Not exactly. Know of a guy named Omar Abdallah bin-Sahmoud?"

He groaned. "I really need you on that plane, Uzi."

"We've got Sahmoud sedated in a tunnel that leads from Muqeibila into Jenin, comes out inside the al-Ansar mosque."

"You *what*? A tunnel? In Jenin? How—"

"You really want to know? Plausible deniability might be best here."

Aksel groaned again. Was he pissed or climbing out of bed?

"Did you find what you were looking for?"

Uzi took a deep breath, giving him a second to gather his thoughts. He had asked himself that same question. "Getting close."

"Status on Sahmoud?"

"Dosed with BetaSomnol and Actinocyde with a dash of amobarbital. Probably be out for another ninety minutes. We planted the thought that Hamas had grabbed him, but if all goes as planned, he won't remember the last twenty-four hours—including how he got in the tunnel. Wife was treated to the same cocktail without the amobarbital. I left a lighter belonging to Ghaffar Doka in Sahmoud's bedroom. Not sure what they'll make of that, but Ghaffar's been dosed as well and is asleep in an alley outside Sahmoud's house."

"And where exactly is Sahmoud? And yes, I need to know."

"In the tunnel, on the Israeli side, about twenty feet from the entrance."

"Tell me about this tunnel."

"Very well engineered and built. About three kilometers long. Starts in the back of Imran Auto Repair in Muqeibila. Looks like they're moving explosives, weapons, drugs, and other contraband. They've got bomb manufacturing factories in Jenin, so better to have the tunnel come out in the center of what they're doing. The mosque is typical civilian cover."

Aksel sighed audibly. "I'll get this info over to the IDF. Anything else?"

"There's a room right near the exit in the mosque that's a storage site for a large cache of munitions and bomb materials."

"Shit."

"And at least one use of the tunnel is to move captagon from Syria to maybe Jordan and Saudi Arabia. There's a stack of boxes by the entrance on Israel's side. Could be more. Wasn't our focus."

"Got it. Good work, Uzi."

"You know, Gideon," he said with a laugh, "when I worked for you, that's all I wanted to hear. And you rarely said it."

"I say it whenever it's deserved."

Uzi rolled his eyes. "I'm not gonna let you bait me."

"Getting wise in your old age?"

"Nice talking with you, Gideon." Uzi ended the call and shoved the phone in his pocket.

"Boychick."

Uzi turned and saw Benny approaching.

"Didn't have time to tell you," Sanfilippo said. "He called and told me he was on his way over."

"When I couldn't reach you," Benny said, "I was worried something was wrong."

"I told you we weren't going to be home."

"And going on an op inside Jenin." He shrugged. "I was sitting home and worrying. Couldn't sleep, so I finally called and got through to Phil."

Sanfilippo's phone buzzed. He excused himself and walked a few feet away.

"Well," Uzi said, giving Benny's left shoulder a squeeze. "I'm glad you're here. We have a lot to discuss. Including a location to check out."

"You got some actionable info?"

Uzi bit his bottom lip. "Haven't had time to process it. But Dena died in prison from an infection years ago. According to Omar bin-Sahmoud, Maya's still alive."

"He should know." Benny gave Uzi a hug, squeezed tightly, and then held him at arm's length. "May Dena's memory be a blessing."

"Always has been, Benny."

"So," Benny said, straightening up—and then grabbing Uzi's arm to steady himself. "Where's Maya being held?"

"Asr Sayy."

"No."

Uzi rubbed his forehead. "I know."

"My friend." Benny shook his head. "That's in Syria, a fortified prison built into the foothills."

"I know."

"You know this and yet you still want to try to get her out."

Uzi's gaze locked onto Benny's. "She's my daughter. I *have to* get her out. And if not . . . I will die trying. Not going to rescue her is—it's not an option."

"We will go home and talk."

"You're not going to change my mind, Benny."

"No. You are Ari Uziel. This I know. Stubborn as the day is long."

54

OPSIG SAFE HOUSE
CHEVY CHASE, MARYLAND

The task force reconvened in the dining room. There was a full thirty-cup coffee urn set out, alongside paper cups and lids. Vail was unsure where it came from, who made it or stocked the supplies, but she was grateful for it as she sipped her hot drink.

Though it was getting late and she was sure some of the people in the room would be reporting for work in the morning, there were still issues that needed to be addressed while they were all together.

Several of the attendees had also hit the urn, as most appeared to be holding or sipping java.

Vail stood at the head of the table and cleared her throat. The chatter continued. She whistled. *There we go.*

"Time's growing late, so I want to get back to it. General."

Lukas did not bother standing. "The Secret Service has had a lot of years to think through attacks on the motorcade. And with civic pride, I have to say they've done a damn good job of securing our commander in chief.

"And while they've hardened against external contingencies, there are glaring weaknesses regarding internal attacks. So as we discussed, our best option, and maybe our *only* option, is to rig the game from within." He nodded at Stallone. "Carlo's got access to some of the systems we'll need to modify, but the ones he can't access . . . he'll have to figure that out. Carlo."

DIE TRYING   257

"I've got a few colleagues at the service who'd be open to our . . . efforts. I'll have to tread carefully in case they're not as open to it as I think. But one tactical point we haven't discussed is that we're gonna have to take down Vice President Andrews as well—in a simultaneous operation. If we don't, as soon as we initiate the op on the president's motorcade, the veep will be locked down. We'll never get to him.

"Going forward, we're gonna use two reference names for our two primary HVTs: President Nunn will be *Lion* and Vice President Andrews will be *Tiger*. Most of you have intelligence or spec ops backgrounds so you know the value of subterfuge in communications. Even though we'll be using encrypted devices, another layer of protection never hurts."

Robby set down his cup. "Give us a rundown of how we're going to pull this off."

Stallone licked his lips. "There are two key aspects to our plan. And both work on the fact that all cars these days are mobile computers with millions of lines of code.

"Step one. I, or someone working with me, will insert a line or two of code that gives us a back door into the vehicular management system. There's a monitoring system in place to prevent what we're trying to do—so we'll have to circumvent that. I'll get on this ASAP so it's ready to go when we need it.

"Step two. Tim Meadows and I will access the digital control and command system for Roadrunner. When you give us the green light, we'll send a command to lock the doors on all the vehicles. This will override electronic *and* manual attempts by agents and spec ops teams to get out of their cars."

"I like it," Vail said. "That leaves the agents and officers on motorcycles—and the one sharpshooter in the back of Hawkeye Renegade with the open window. He'll obviously be able to engage with us."

"What about Stagecoach," Rodman said, "the president's limo?"

"That'll be addressed by our hack," Meadows said. "This'll all need to be timed right, but when the other vehicle doors lock, the ones on Stagecoach will *unlock*. And it'll disable the car's weaponry and countermeasures."

"Hang on," Robby said. "As soon as they realize someone's remotely taken control of their doors, they'll know something's up."

"Yes," Stallone said with a nod. "The security unit—which includes Stagecoach—will peel away to safety and let the other vehicles engage the threat. That's protocol."

"The cyber guys at HQ will notice something's wrong," Stallone said. "They'll work fast. Assess that something's hit multiple systems. They'll reboot into a safe mode-like state and use AI to examine the code. They'll find the lines we inserted."

"How much time will we have?" Rusakov asked. "For them to reboot and run the AI analysis."

Stallone bobbed his head. "We'll have three minutes to execute our plan. Maybe less."

"Lion will be vulnerable," Christie said, "during those three minutes." Lukas pointed at him. "Exactly. The rest we're still working on. Carlo?"

"As soon as they see something's wrong, they'll dispatch additional units to the motorcade's location."

Christie clenched his jaw. "We can't be there when reinforcements arrive.

"Three minutes may not be enough time," Stallone said. "We need to work on this some more."

"Assuming we *can* pull it off," Neil Fisher said, "that's *Lion*. What about *Tiger*? If we've got to hit him at the same moment as *Lion*, that could be more difficult because his situation—time and/or place— might not be to our advantage."

"Correct," Stallone said. "I've got something in mind. *Lion*'s giving a speech at District University tomorrow night and I know the route we'll be taking. It's the best opportunity we'll get. *Tiger* could be vulnerable at that time, too."

"We've got a lot to figure out before then," Vail said. "Good thing no one was planning on sleeping tonight."

55

JENIN, WEST BANK

Phil Sanfilippo conferred with Bill Tait the moment he climbed out of the tunnel. While Sanfilippo closed the tunnel entrance, Tait gave Uzi the bad news.

"Phil and I gotta get back home. Flight's in three hours. Someone's already on the way to pick us up."

"What's up?"

"That Scorpion group. Something's going down and Lukas DeSantos is designing an op and we're needed—and as many of my guys that I can recruit. I'd like to stay and help, but—"

"I get it," Uzi said. "The needs of the many outweigh the needs of the few."

Tait pursed his lips and nodded slowly. "Well said."

"Stole the line from *Star Trek*. But it's true." He shook Tait's hand. "Appreciate what you guys have done. Can't say enough. Above and beyond." He pulled Tait close and hugged him. "Go get 'em for us. If it's anything like last time, a lot's riding on this."

"Good luck locating Maya."

Uzi noticed headlights flash outside the shop windows: DeSantos had brought over Benny's car and was waiting for them.

"Benny, let's get out of here. IDF and Shin Bet will be coming very soon—and we need to be gone when they arrive."

* * *

260 ALAN JACOBSON

The ninety-mile drive back proved as fruitful as it was short. With Uzi driving, the three of them mulled the mission Uzi and DeSantos were committed to carrying out.

Uzi changed lanes on Highway 6. There was some light traffic but nothing that would slow them down. "We can't just drive into Syria and pull up in front of the prison."

"I've heard of crazier things," Benny said with a chuckle.

"Two issues," DeSantos said, stifling a yawn. "First, getting into Syria and then getting into the prison. Second, breaking Maya out of Asr Sayy. I mean, we could do it if we had weeks, key contacts, and substantial resources. But we don't."

"I might have a way to get us into Syria," Benny said.

Uzi glanced at his friend, who was riding shotgun. "Don't keep it a secret."

Benny splayed both hands. "What's Israel known for? Worldwide. Something even its enemies have to acknowledge?"

"Its high-tech industry," Uzi said.

"And its ingenuity, its creative spirit in solving an unsolvable problem. Desalinate ocean water? Check. Create wireless technology so the world can communicate with cell phones? Check. A pill containing a tiny camera so docs can see inside the body? USB flash drives? Check and check. Waze for navigation and Mobileye for self-driving. Drip irrigation, which revolutionized farming. The cherry tomato. And hundreds of other things most people use and have no idea were developed by Israel."

"What does that do for us?" DeSantos asked.

"We've got solutions that shift the odds considerably."

"Like what?"

"For one," Benny said, "SkyPak." Uzi cocked his head. "Come again?"

"SkyPak. It's worn as a backpack and lets you fly like a helicopter, but without rotors. Six mini jet engines strap to your arms, legs, and back. The army's been testing them. I think I can get us three of the prototypes."

"Three?"

"I'm going with you."

DIE TRYING 261

Uzi held up a hand. "I can't ask you to do that."

"You didn't."

"Benny, I don't know what to say."

"You can say, 'Tell me more.'"

DeSantos folded his arms across his chest. "Tell me more."

Benny turned and winked at DeSantos. "We have to get across the border by the Golan. IDF's got sophisticated monitoring devices. But if we go in the middle of the night, we'll have the cover of darkness. The electric motors on the jet packs use a muffler because there's some noise created by the force of the air. Otherwise, they're fairly stealthy." Uzi laughed. "I'm not sure 'fairly stealthy' fits the definition of *stealth*."

DeSantos rolled his eyes. "Tell me more."

Benny glanced at Uzi. "Hector's a fast learner. Okay, here's more: the IDF's using SkyPak for covert missions, surveillance and security, and testing it for rescue services in difficult to reach areas."

DeSantos spread his hands. "If *they're* using it, it works."

"More than works. It's amazing tech. Fifteen hundred pounds of thrust. Top speed of ninety-seven kilometers per hour—though they can technically top out at one hundred thirty-six." He shrugged. "Obviously the faster you go, the more power you use—so you don't go as far."

"I'm guessing radar can't pick you up because you're so low to the surface," DeSantos said.

Uzi nodded. "Sounds like a useful spec ops vehicle."

"And like all military hardware, they're not cheap—about half a million apiece—but there's another cost to all that tech: weight. Batteries are heavy. The SkyPak weighs about seventy-five pounds."

Uzi whistled. "That's about what geared-up firefighters carry."

"There's a monopod that helps support the weight if needed."

"How hard is it to learn to fly?" DeSantos asked.

"You two won't need much training. A few hours of practice. It's mostly getting used to the feel of the engines, balancing your weight and the suit's weight, controlling the flying angles with your arms, working the thruster. You fly helicopters and fighter jets." Benny waved a hand. "You'll pick it up."

"Too bad there's no autopilot," Uzi said with a laugh.

"Actually, there is. But it's very basic. It lifts off straight up, then returns to base. It's really for an emergency. Definitely not for evading enemy gunfire."

DeSantos nodded slowly, his lips pursed, thinking. "I like it. You said you can get hold of three?"

"I know the air force colonel who's running the program. That's how I did the training."

They continued discussing that approach until Uzi turned onto the city streets of Jerusalem. The sun was rising and his eyelids were falling—from lack of sleep. "Ugh. Need some coffee."

"That I've got," Benny said.

Uzi's thoughts kept coming back to one problem. He finally turned to Benny to get an answer. "You seriously think this colonel's going to lend us a million five in equipment? To fly a black mission into Syria?"

DeSantos laughed.

Benny launched into a spasmodic coughing fit. Uzi watched with concern.

He cleared his throat, then said, "I got him the funding to buy them in the first place. It's a strong card to play, yes. But depends on who he has to answer to."

"I wouldn't tell him we're taking them into Syria."

"Thank you, Hector," Benny said. "That much I figured out on my own."

56

JERUSALEM, ISRAEL

Benny emerged from his bedroom, completing a phone call. After hanging up, he sat down at his square kitchen table, which was pushed against a wall in the cramped nook.

Uzi brewed coffee and scrambled some eggs, onions, and lox. He even defrosted a few bagels he found in the freezer.

"Smells good," DeSantos said. "And I'm famished." He shoveled a forkful into his mouth. "Mmm."

Benny reached for his cup of java and grunted. "Not supposed to have caffeine. Interferes with my cancer meds."

"Crap, Benny. You didn't say anything." Uzi rose from his seat. "Let me—"

"No, no. I said I'm not *supposed* to have it. I didn't say I wasn't drinking it." He laughed.

Uzi shook his head. "What am I gonna do with you?"

"Love me. And I mean that. Because when you hear what I've arranged, you're gonna want to hug me."

"Oh yeah?"

"Yeah. But don't." He took a swallow and set his mug down. "Spoke to Colonel Halevi. He's gonna work with you two on the SkyPaks. We're supposed to meet him at Hatzor airbase in ninety minutes. We leave as soon as we finish eating."

"No rest for the weary," DeSantos said with a full mouth.

"Are you complaining?" Benny asked. "Because I've got more good news."

Uzi set down his mug. "Such as?"

Benny pushed around his eggs and corralled them against a piece of bagel. "I was thinking. The SkyPaks will get us close to the prison entrance. But then what? Without tanks, heavy artillery, air cover, and a Tier One special forces unit, we are *not* getting in. So I was trying to think of alternatives. Again, tech may have the answer."

Uzi rubbed his hands together. "You're speaking my language."

"A language I could never master," DeSantos said with a scowl. "Let alone understand."

"There are two systems that should work," Benny said. "First is something you've heard of, but I doubt you have seen in the field."

"Maybe. Maybe not. We've got Skunk Works. And DARPA."

"And that is how I am confident you have never seen one. We have been working with both to develop it."

Uzi and DeSantos shared a look.

"I'm sure our intel agencies have the Syrian prison guards' schedule. Best to go in at the end of their shift when they're tired and watching the clock to get out of there. That, plus the change of shift, should give us a window when they're not as attentive." Benny pushed his plate aside and interlocked his hands on the table. "We'll use a smart, robotic army."

DeSantos leaned forward. "A what?"

"A microdrone swarm," Benny said. "Three dozen tiny devices, each one a couple of inches long, programmed to work in unison to take out enemy combatants."

Uzi cleared his throat. "Microdrone swarms are theoretical. I've never heard of one being deployed."

"They were theoretical until a few years ago. But with the advancements in AI and machine learning, and enhanced Bluetooth, indoor positioning, and near-field communication developed by RSI—an Israeli company that came out of our Talpiot program—it's happening. Combined with three-millimeter chip fabs, we've been able to build working units."

"Prototypes," Uzi said.

"Not prototypes," Benny said, reaching over and grabbing half a bagel from his plate.

"If they're not prototypes," DeSantos said, "they've been tested. In the field?"

Benny chased his food with a gulp of coffee. "Yes." He bobbed his head. "Sort of."

"Yes or no?" Uzi asked. "There's no sort of."

"I want to say yes to put your minds at ease. But phase two of the test is scheduled for next week. It passed phase one."

DeSantos took a deep breath. "Beggars can't be choosers."

"The program's called Maccabee's Minions," Benny said, "It uses dr—"

"Judah Maccabee," Uzi told DeSantos, "was the leader of the Maccabean army. About twenty-two hundred years ago, the Maccabees defeated the much larger Seleucid army and the Jews reclaimed Jerusalem, Judea, and Samaria—and Judaism, their religion, which the Seleucids outlawed. They then rededicated the Temple—which is what the word 'Hanukkah' means. Dedication." Uzi gestured for Benny to continue.

"So the Maccabee's Minions drone sensors use the Fire Factory artificial intelligence model to identify specific handguns, submachine guns, and so on. They also use other AI models to analyze and recognize those that aren't in their database. Take a snub-nose .38 in an ankle holster. They may not have 'seen' that revolver before, but they'll identify it as a gun—and a threat—and neutralize the attacker."

DeSantos held up a hand. "So we're relying on AI to decide who's friend and who's foe?"

"The IDF hasn't gone fully autonomous. Machines locate and prepare target strikes, but humans review and approve—or reject. But we don't have the luxury of intel analysts parsing our data, so we've got to rely on AI. We'll be completely removed from decision-making."

"You said the enemies would be *neutralized*," Uzi said. "What does that mean?"

"The drones are armed with sharp, needle-like titanium projectiles. They shoot their targets at close range with extremely high velocity, penetrating facial bones and even helmets, depending on material and thickness."

Uzi swallowed hard. "Like . . . wow."

"That," Benny said, "will be our Tier One spec ops unit." Uzi and DeSantos absorbed that.

"The US has been working on these types of weapons, too—your Defense Innovation Unit's Replicator Initiative, which uses swarms of AI-powered drones and unmanned planes or boats to attack targets. Replicator was criticized as being killer robots and slaughterbots, since they can take out targets very efficiently without human approval or review."

"I know about Replicator," DeSantos said. "Pentagon policy requires human sign-off before a target's hit. But there aren't any treaties or limits on these AI weapons. NATO's drawn up standards, but even those are vague."

"And if terror groups start using them," Uzi said, "which *will* happen because they're cheap, they won't be concerned with human sign-off to prevent collateral damage."

"Their aim *is* collateral damage," Benny said.

Uzi spread his hands. "How do we get our hands on these miniature soldiers?"

"Friend of mine runs the unit that's testing them." Benny shrugged a thick shoulder. "I'm calling in all the favors that I'm owed. No point in going to the grave with uncalled chits."

"That's a helluva favor," Uzi said. "If your buddy's caught . . . that's court-martial and prison time."

"I saved his family's life." Benny coughed into his elbow. "Yitz always knew the ask would be big. Besides, the drones are programmed to RTB," he said, using the military abbreviation for "return to base."

"So hopefully his superiors never find out they were ever gone."

"But the projectiles will be recoverable," DeSantos said.

"I doubt the Syrians will know what the projectiles are from. Unless they've got cameras inside the prison." Benny stood up and stretched his back, then grabbed the tabletop for balance. "Look, no plan is a hundred percent, Uzi, including this one. Except for, hopefully, its kill rate."

"Hang on a sec," Uzi said. "Do we know they'll work inside a prison that's built into a mountainside? From what I know of drone swarms, they have to communicate with each other and their base unit. They may've solved that, but—"

"It's still a problem. And that's where the second part of my plan comes in. A BluMesh network."

DeSantos drew his chin back. "A what?"

"It's a mesh network that works off Bluetooth protocols to communicate. Tiny transponders and repeater devices transmit a signal from one node to the other to keep a communication chain intact."

DeSantos squinted. "How does *that* work?"

"It's like the Wi-Fi nodes you place in your house to get rid of dead zones. It creates a mesh, spreading out and repeating the signal to increase coverage," Uzi said.

Benny nodded. "In this case, once we're inside the prison, one of these nodes will need to be placed every thirty feet, max, all the way to Maya's cell. They use the latest protocols, so under normal conditions they should reach up to a hundred feet. But this is among the worst wave transmission environments. Definitely not getting a hundred feet between nodes. If we're lucky, we'll get thirty."

"So the repeaters receive and transmit the signal from one node to the other," DeSantos said. "What if one loses its signal or powers down? Or just fails?"

"The system's designed to hand off the signal to its closest nearby node, but this place is hollowed out of a mountain. We can't assume that fail-safe will work. We have to hope that none of them fail. If a battery or the device dies, the link is broken and the chain . . . well, breaks."

DeSantos inched forward in his seat. "And our smart Tier One drone army becomes a useless platoon of narcoleptic soldiers?"

Benny shrugged. "Pretty much."

"How long do the batteries last?" Uzi asked.

"These devices are small—about an inch square—so the power cell needs to be small and light. The transmitter and receiver chips are low power, but there are limits. I'll make sure the batteries are charged."

"Yeah, but how long?" Uzi asked again. "Thirty minutes."

268 ALAN JACOBSON

"Oh man . . ." Uzi said, his voice trailing off.

"Ah," DeSantos said with a nod, "one of *these* missions."

Uzi took a sip of coffee as he thought it through. "To be clear, we're going to have a thirty-minute clock once we set the first transponder?"

"Yes," Benny said. "When we deploy that first one, the thirty-minute timer starts counting down. These devices are designed for quick strikes. Drop and hit."

Uzi set his mug on the table. "But we're not using them the way they're designed to work. We have to get them *all* deployed before you send in the swarm."

"How exact is that thirty-minute limit?" DeSantos asked.

Benny bobbed his head. "It's a guesstimate. But the farther from the source, the more the battery drains."

Uzi turned to DeSantos. "They expend more energy sending the signal a longer distance. Since the farthest repeater, or transponder, that we place will be the last one, that's the one that'll drain fastest. That's why we need to set our mission timer by when we initialize the first one."

Benny shrugged. "Makes sense. I'll check with Yitz to be sure."

"You think anyone has a diagram of the prison?" DeSantos asked. "Ask Tamar," Benny said. "That's exactly what Unit 9900 does."

"Ugh." Uzi threw his head back. "She's already put her career in a red zone because of me."

"Should be her decision," Benny said. "What's the worst that happens? You ask, she says no."

Uzi frowned, then rooted out his phone.

"Is this gonna work?" DeSantos asked. "I mean, there are so many variables, so many ways this plan can blow up on us."

Benny grinned. "Do you ever ask yourself about the odds of mission success before you spin up?"

"Not usually."

"Take it from an old fart who's been there and done that. Your approach has been smart. Don't start asking that question now."

57

OPSIG SAFE HOUSE
CHEVY CHASE, MARYLAND

With the task force members wired on caffeine, they rolled up their sleeves, brainstormed ideas, drew up names of potential collaborators, and listed concerns.

They named their group the Countercoup Task Force and broke into small groups based on expertise. They then reconvened and discussed the solutions to the issues they had identified.

At 1:30 a.m., Troy Rodman stepped into the dining room and said that he had an encrypted videocall from Director Knox. He turned on the TSVTC, or top secret video teleconference system. Knox's face, seated in a room with blank walls, appeared. "I've got something everyone should hear."

"Go ahead, sir," Vail said.

"Members of Team Grey were able to sequester at a secure facility and captured communications between the Nunn administration and Chinese, Russian, and Iranian contacts. They ran the intercepts through AI to translate them."

"Is it as bad as we think?" Christie asked.

"Worse," Knox said, picking up a document. "The president just authorized the release of $150 billion in sanction money to Iran and another $75 billion to Russia. And he's going to sign an executive order rolling back the sanctions on China that prevents

US companies from selling them advanced AI chips. This impacts almost every sector of American business and national security. You think cyber crime coming out of China is bad now? Hook up a server farm equipped with cutting edge AI chips and we'll be hard-pressed to stop the onslaught."

"China's military has an army of over 100,000 hackers working 24/7," Lukas said. "They've been probing our critical infrastructure systems. Water treatment plants, electrical grid, oil and natural gas pipelines. And our transportation systems. They're now hiring contractors to expand their hacker army."

"He's correct," Knox said. "That's all accurate."

"What's their end game?" Rodman asked.

"Wreak havoc with people, communities, commerce. Businesses large and small. Projections we've done internally at the Bureau show that it'd hobble the United States for years and result in the deaths of millions—depending on how quickly we could get our critical infrastructure systems repaired."

"That's a much bigger deal than the release of sanction money," Robby said.

"Neither is good," Knox said. "And they're both related. Their army of hackers, fueled by an influx of high-end AI chips? It'll change the global balance of power almost overnight. Once they've hobbled every aspect of our daily lives, China and Russia will incapacitate our space-based assets. Our network of satellites, which we use for almost every aspect of our military, will be useless."

Lukas nodded slowly. "Paving the way for the Chinese to invade Taiwan without resistance from the US."

"And let's not forget what's there," Knox said. "The largest chip-maker in the world. China would then cut off *our* supply of chips. Chips for our computers, wireless and wired communications, TVs, game consoles, cars and trucks, AI—and a whole lot more."

There was quiet as the task force members absorbed that.

"What exactly are we looking at here?" Rodman asked.

"A strategic warm war designed to cripple the United States," Lukas said, nodding. "Without firing a single shot. Without launching a single missile or nuclear weapon."

"How is Nunn releasing all the sanction money?" Vail asked. "And lifting export controls on AI chip shipments? Isn't there a check-and-balance system in place?"

Knox chuckled. "Short answer's yes. But when you've got embedded conspirators infiltrating key institutions, it's easier to push things through, look the other way, falsify documents.

"From what we can tell, funds frozen to disrupt Iran's proliferation of weapons of mass destruction, its proliferation of delivery systems for WMD, and its support for international terrorism . . . they're all flagged for release. And that means a huge influx of money to Hezbollah, al-Humat, Hamas, Palestinian Islamic Jihad, and the Houthis."

"But that money's held in bank accounts," Rusakov said. "Foreign *and d*omestic."

Knox nodded. "And the banks holding the money are required by OFAC—Office of Foreign Assets Control—to lock down those accounts. Not even the banks are supposed to access them. To get sanctioned funds released, you file an unblocking application. It can take six months for OFAC to approve or reject. But OFAC approved it and unblocked the Iranian money in three *days*."

"So," Vail said, "they've got probably someone on the inside of OFAC."

"Wrong, Agent Vail." Knox leaned forward. "They *definitely* have someone on the inside. A senior licensing officer. We've got her name."

"Do we know when the money's gonna be released to Iran?" Neil Fisher asked.

"Four days," Knox said.

Lukas DeSantos sat back in his seat, cursing under his breath.

"And the Commerce Department restrictions on AI chip exports get lifted tomorrow. AI-Ware has quietly prepared a shipment of half a million AIW-900 chips that's due to hit the port of Los Angeles tomorrow afternoon."

"So we've got less time than we thought," Rodman said.

Knox cleared his throat. "General, find a reason to delay that ship's departure."

"I started my career in the Coast Guard," Fisher said. "Best to keep it simple. Something that can't be easily verified through another

272 ALAN JACOBSON

agency—or the internet. Like bad weather. Too easy to confirm. But we could use COVID."

"COVID?" Rusakov asked. "How?"

"An outbreak of a new strain at the facility that made or packed the chips. We don't know which boxes are affected, so all the containers need to be opened and tested. Those chips are huge—the size of a computer—so we're talking hundreds of containers."

"I like it," Robby said. "We can have someone with background as a medic report to the dock with NIH credentials, a hazmat suit, and testing kits."

"That'll buy us time," Knox said with a nod. "But will it be enough? We've *got to* stop these people. If we don't, they'll disrupt the global balance of power—and the safety of free societies. If we don't get this right, we could—"

"No, sir," the general said, standing up and putting his face in front of the TSVTC camera. "We *are* gonna get this right. We've got no choice. There's no room for error. Or failure."

Vail bit her bottom lip. *Definitely no room for error. But room for failure? Way too much for my liking.*

58

**HATZOR AIRBASE
CENTRAL ISRAEL**

Benny directed them to the main entrance of Hatzor airbase, a military installation with a history dating back some eighty years.

More recently, it served as the first posting of the David's Sling missile defense system when it went operational.

Benny showed his credentials and spoke rapid-fire Hebrew with base security. Their voices raised and they were shouting—not unusual in Israeli society—and then the guard pulled out his radio and shouted more angry words. He received a response, looked into the car, gave Uzi and DeSantos a toxic look, then waved them in.

"Everything okay?" DeSantos asked.

"He didn't care for our beard stubble," Uzi said. He noted his partner's furrowed brow. "I'm kidding. He didn't like being put in the position of breaking protocol. But Benny being who he is . . ."

Benny rolled his eyes. "I told him we had an appointment with Colonel Halevi. We weren't on the guest list, but Halevi confirmed. No worries. All good. We're not here to make friends."

Uzi followed Benny's instructions and drove to a parking area near a nondescript hangar.

Inside, there was a state-of-the-art F-35i fighter jet with three uniformed soldiers examining a wing.

To the far right was a stainless-steel counter supporting three futuristic looking black jet packs. A matching helmet was resting beside each one.

They approached and were met by a lanky, balding man with a military demeanor and IDF BDUs.

"Ephraim," Benny said.

"Which one's Uzi?" he asked.

"That'd be me. And this is my colleague, Hector."

"Ephraim Halevy." They shook hands and got right to it. "We don't have a lot of time, so I'm going to give you a crash course."

Uzi glanced at DeSantos—who either did not get the unintended pun or was ignoring it.

"Flying the SkyPak successfully is all about coordination and balance," Halevi said. "Two mini turbines strap around each forearm and you steer using arm movements. Thrust is regulated by a controller that fits in your hand. The two engines on the back give you lift and speed. It's astoundingly simple—and very, very cool to fly."

DeSantos leaned in close to get a good look at the suit.

"Some important things to know," Halevi continued. "You'll only have five to twelve minutes of flight time. The faster you go, the more battery power you use. Makes sense, right?"

"That's not a whole lot of time," Uzi said.

"We originally built these to use jet fuel," Halevi said, "but the turbines generated the same bright orange and blue flame you get out the back of fighter jets. Highly visible. And noisy. So we switched to batteries. The weight differential between batteries and fuel was similar but more compact. Once we figured out weight distribution, we were able to slim down the backpack."

"Just incredible." DeSantos stepped back. "It's the perfect spec ops tool."

"We recommend you max out at seventy-five kph. The helmets have a comms system built in. Since your hands will be busy, the comms channel is open by default. Anything you say on that frequency will be heard by others on your team." He looked at each of them. "Questions?"

Uzi ran his finger over the alloy housing one of the turbines. "Ready to strap them on, get some flight time."

DIE TRYING   275

*   *   *

Ninety minutes later, they removed the suits and hydrated while Halevi answered a call.

"What'd you think?" Benny asked.

"Incredible technology," Uzi said. "So many uses, from law enforcement to bridge inspection, and a ton of military applications."

DeSantos pulled off his helmet and brushed his hair back. "One issue is the flight time. Twelve minutes—if we fly slowly—will get us there but not all the way back."

Uzi checked to make sure no one was within earshot. "And we can't recharge in Syrian territory."

Halevi ended his call and rejoined them. "Thoughts?"

"Concerned about the range," Benny said.

"We intend to use this for spec ops missions," Halevi said, "so we've developed a spare battery pack that can attach magnetically—similar concept to Apple's MagSafe. Should give you fifty percent reserve power."

DeSantos gave Uzi a dubious look. "Not a lot of margin for error."

"I'll go get three packs," Halevi said, backing away. "Meet you back here in fifteen."

"Once we get these back to my apartment," Benny said, "we'll rig them with explosives. In case shit hits the fan and the Syrians get hold of them, we need to be able to destroy them remotely."

DeSantos chuckled. "So we'll have five electric turbine engines strapped to our bodies packed with lithium batteries—which are highly explosive in their own right—rigged with a bomb. Whose idea was this?"

"When you put it that way," Uzi said, "it does sound a bit wacky."

DeSantos laughed. "Just a bit. But no more so than flying into Syria and infiltrating a mountain prison to break out a prisoner."

"Won't be our first wacky mission. And hopefully it won't be our last."

59

OPSIG SAFE HOUSE
CHEVY CHASE, MARYLAND

Seated with Vail in the living room, the general looked at her over the top of his reading glasses. "I was skeptical when you said you were going to find an alternative. But I have to admit, this could work. And it minimizes loss of life."

"What we're planning is coming at a crucial time in our history. And in extraordinary times, extraordinary measures are necessary. I get that. I just thought that a different approach might get us more."

"Military people who've seen war go to great lengths to avoid it—because we've lived through it. For us, it's not an abstract concept." He held up the handwritten page she had given him. "Glad you found a better way."

"*We* did. Tim Meadows and I."

Lukas gestured toward the door. "Let's brief everyone."

The task force members were unanimous in their praise for the Vail and Meadows approach.

"Devil's usually in the details," Fisher said. "We need to hear specifics." Meadows walked to the front of the room. "We still have more brainstorming to do, especially with timing, but here's the rough order and logistics involved. And again, this is only made possible by Agent

DIE TRYING

Stallone's insider knowledge and access to the Secret Service's computer systems.

"First. The back-door Agent Stallone will give us will let me in. I'll hack the vehicles' operating systems and lock the doors of all the vehicles. I'll *unlock* Stagecoach's rear passenger door, giving access to Attack Team Alpha.

"This is the part where we left off," Robby said. "The security unit will peel off the motorcade the second they realize what's going on. And our three-minute window starts."

"Ah," Meadows said, holding up his right index finger. "Karen and I came up with a fix for that. Well, some of that. Several powerful, well-placed electromagnetic pulses, or EMPs, will disable the engines of all the vehicles."

"Disabled?" Robby asked. "How so?"

Meadows's lips thinned into a grin. "Modern cars and trucks are computers on wheels. And computers are made up of microprocessors containing silicon—and silicon-based electronics are very brittle. They spark over and fail when exposed to strong electromagnetic pulses. The cables and wires act as antennas to draw the pulses right in. So the motorcade's electronic transmission array will be fried, too. The hardware-resident operating systems will stop working. Those cars will be dead in the water."

Rusakov snorted. "Electromagnetic pulses? We have that capability?"

"We do," Lukas said.

"And the motorcade is vulnerable?"

"For another couple of weeks," Taylor Irwin said. "New beasts are built as needed and additional protections are added. But EMP level four protection can be installed as a retrofit. Most of the equipment is on-site and the upgrade work is listed on the schedule."

Vail chuckled to herself. *So the next time we have to engineer a coup to* prevent *a coup, it'll be more difficult to pull off.*

"Attack Team Bravo will deploy multiple electromagnetic pulses at various strategic points in the motorcade. And we'll have at least one messenger bag-sized antenna containing an EMP cannon that has a reach of 650 feet. It'll repeat every few seconds. A private company developed it for the Marines and Air Force for nonlethal missions."

278   ALAN JACOBSON

"I'm working on getting more," Lukas said.

"Why does it repeat the pulse?" Rodman asked.

"Some electronics will survive the pulse—they'll just stop working. But if the agents know to turn them off and on, some of the equipment might go back online."

Rodman nodded. "So repeating the pulse makes sure things stay dead."

"Right," Meadows said. "Overall, the EMPs will do several things for us."

Meadows moved closer to the diagram showing the vehicle locations. "The pulse will shut down electronics in the immediate vicinity." He started drawing X's on the board with a red marker.

"You mentioned that the vehicles will be dead in the water," Dell Christie said. "And the operating systems will fry."

Meadows bobbed his head. "Some operating systems are contained *in* the hardware—what we call hardware resident—which helps us out. But there's more: *nothing* electronic will work. No engine, no lights, no horn, no countermeasures, no encrypted comms. No backup systems." He held up his right hand. "Except—weapons that use spring-activated trigger mechanisms will still function. So our pistols will still operate—and so will theirs."

"How do we protect *our* electronics?" Rusakov asked.

"I've got EMP wraps en route from one of my warehouses," Lukas said. "You may know them as Faraday cage bags. Should protect our equipment."

Vail sat forward. "Should?"

"Should." The general shrugged. "We've never had to deploy them so I can't speak from experience. And it's not like I can call up the Secret Service or the J6 and ask," he said, referring to the Joint Staff's directorate that supports communication networks, computers, and related technologies.

"When you say, the vehicles will be dead in the water," Robby said, "does that include the motorcycle detail?"

"We've been using Harleys since just before 9/11," Stallone said. "They've got electronic fuel injection systems. So yeah, they'll be hit, too."

"But the personnel will obviously be able to get off and engage us. As will the agent who sits behind the open rear window of Halfback, the security detail's SUV."

"They'll be Attack Team Charlie's responsibility," Lukas said.

"Hang on a sec," Frazier said. "I'm stuck in my car, the doors are locked, and something bad's happening to the president? I'm finding a way out. I'd shoot out the windows with my pistol."

"Bulletproof glass," Stallone said. "Not impossible, but it'll take time. Same with trying to kick them out. Probably fits within that three-minute window."

Stallone groaned. "That three-minute estimate is my best guess. It's not an absolute."

"I think this is fan-fuckingtastic," Zheng Wei said, ignoring Stallone's comment. "We do our jobs, three minutes is enough. If we can't execute in three minutes . . ." He shook his head. "We *should* fail."

"Agreed," Lukas said. "And since we'll know the exact path and timing of the motorcade and *we* are going to choose the moment of engagement, we'll be able to pre-position sharpshooters on nearby rooftops to provide overwatch cover to our attack teams. Someone gets through, they'll be dealt with."

"Glad you brought that up," Stallone said. "Overwatch. The Service pre-positions snipers on rooftops along the route. We'll need a plan to deal with them. Anyone has ideas, let me know."

"Distraction is the best approach," Rodman said. "Had a situation like this in Syria. Shot smoke bombs and tear gas onto the roofs. Obscured their scopes, fucked up their vision, and the way we did it, scared the shit out of them."

"Lasted long enough for us to do our work down below," Zheng said. "I like it," Lukas said. "Neil, Dell, let's add that to the list of equipment and operators we'll need."

Christie scribbled a note on his pad. "Got it, General."

"Even if we execute well, we're gonna have to answer for this," Fahad said. "How do we remain anonymous?"

"Our operators will be heavily armored. Vests, helmets, gas masks. Protects our identities *and* helps keep us safe. Assuming none of us are captured."

280   ALAN JACOBSON

Vail knew the other part of that assumption was that if someone *was* captured, he or she would keep his or her mouth shut. Name, rank, and serial number approach. With this group, it did not need to be stated.

"Where are we gonna get all this gear?" Rusakov asked.

"Between my company's stocks and sources, and Bill Tait's—who's on his way here right now—we'll have what we need."

"How do we minimize collateral damage?" Robby asked. Stallone laughed. "Citizens or law enforcement personnel?"

"Both."

"By remotely locking the motorcade car doors," Lukas said, "we'll significantly reduce the number of officers who'll be able to engage us. More than that?" He shrugged. "Not much we can do."

The general read the room, where several task force members shifted in their seats. "C'mon, people. Look at our history. Efforts to protect and defend the Constitution were bloody affairs. About 650,000 Americans died in the Civil War. In this op, even one death of an innocent is, without question, unfortunate.

"But consider what's at stake. The rights and freedoms of 350 *million* Americans. The survival of our republic." He nodded at Robby. "We need to challenge each other, clear the air. Make sure we're all on the same page." Lukas glanced at everyone seated around the table. "Other questions?"

Rusakov raised her hand. "How are we getting to the president? He's the HVT of this op."

Vail laughed to herself. *"High-value target" doesn't do justice to Vance Nunn.*

Zheng raised his hand. "I spent five years with SWAT in San Diego after getting out of the Marines. Given the Vail/Meadows approach, here's how I think we should execute our objectives. I like what's been proposed. But as Alex noted, it only gets us to the critical moment."

Lukas waved Zheng on.

Zheng spent the next five minutes going through the tactical details of his plan, moment by moment and movement by movement. When he finished, Vail sat back in her chair, appreciative of Zheng's thoroughness.

DIE TRYING 281

Lukas appeared to be equally impressed. He turned to their Secret Service contingent. "Agent Irwin, this is your sandbox. Questions? Concerns?"

Irwin chuckled. "We're talking about extracting POTUS from the most secure motorcade on the planet. Concerns? You gotta be kidding. Hell yeah. I mean, I was trying to look at this with my Secret Service hat on, to see how we'd defend against it." He shrugged. "Things go as Agent Zheng's drawn it up . . . yeah, could work. But shit rarely goes as planned. Everyone in this room knows that."

Lukas again glanced at the attendees—as did Vail, playing behavioral analyst. "Other comments? Concerns? Now's the time, people."

"I was skeptical at first," Robby said. "I didn't think we had the horsepower to pull this off. That said, it's solid. A million things can go wrong, but the chances of it going right—accomplishing our objectives with minimal loss of life—are a whole lot better than I thought they could be."

Stallone walked to the front of the room. "Let's move to the next phase: when to execute. As I mentioned, our best opportunity is tonight at 8:00. *Lion*'s speaking at District University. The route he's taking will be favorable for us.

"Our strike on *Tiger* will need to be simultaneous. He'll be at a gala at the Reagan building. I've already drawn up a plan for grabbing him."

"This is a much larger op than I thought it'd be," Rodman said. "We have enough operators to pull this off?"

"Based on the teams I've sketched out," Lukas said, "we've got about half of what we need. Bill Tait and his people have been working on it. He's been out of the country but is en route to DC."

"What about the majority leader?" Vail said. "Bernard Conti."

"Conti's been assigned the code name *Wolf*. He's likewise got a security detail."

"US Capitol Police," Stallone said, "not Secret Service."

Now back in his seat, Meadows said, "So we don't have a window into their methods and procedures."

"Unfortunately," Stallone said with a nod, "no. Buddy of mine was on a congressional detail, but that was years ago. After 9/11, they beefed up security. Senate majority and minority leaders and House leadership have robust details. From five to two dozen agents."

"Two *dozen*?" Vail asked.

"Conti had twenty-three last I heard." Stallone chuckled. "He let it slip at a fundraising speech he gave last year. Capitol Police weren't happy. They're very secretive about who gets what—and how much. But since he's the Senate's pro tem—and third in line for the presidency—makes sense."

"Yeah," Robby said, "makes sense. But twenty-three. How're we gonna handle that?"

"Intelligence and planning," the general said. "An asymmetric attack. I've started drawing it up."

"Last but not least," Vail said, "what about Speaker Aswad?"

Stallone nodded. "Designated *Shark.* I've heard she's got a more modest detail of a dozen agents. She's scheduled to make fundraising calls across from her Longworth office from 4:00 to 7:00 p.m. and then get a late dinner with her husband. That's where we'll have to take her."

Rusakov leaned forward. "Bottom line, General. Do we have enough operators to pull this off?"

"We may not be fully staffed, but I was liberal in my analysis of what we'd need, so we should be okay."

Taylor Irwin rose from his chair and headed for the door.

"General." Rusakov rested both elbows on the table. "As a wartime tactician, you really think we can pull this off?"

"All the guys we've got," Lukas said, "and will get, are current or former spec ops operators. They can do this in their sleep. And that's the *only* way we could achieve mission success without months of extensive training." He sucked on his bottom lip. "I had unlimited resources and time? Yeah, I'd do things differently.

"But as I've told my soldiers time and again, we're dealt a hand. Full house or just plain crap, doesn't matter. We've got a job to do and the goal's the same no matter what we're holding."

"Losing's not an option," Vail said.

"No matter the odds, we've got a responsibility to do everything possible to turn any hand we're dealt into a win. Our country's depending on it." He made eye contact with everyone. "Anyone have a problem with that?"

No one blinked. No one spoke. No one shook his or her head.

"Then let's get on with this."

60

Karen Vail's eyes found the wall clock. She had been waiting for Taylor Irwin to return. On the surface, it was nothing of concern. Others left the SCIF, went to the bathroom, and returned.

Irwin had only been gone three minutes.

But her gut told her that something was amiss.

Vail rose from her seat and headed out of the room. She had picked up on a few things regarding Irwin—shifting in his chair, tapping a finger, flexing his jaw muscles—when the motorcade was being discussed, as well as moments ago when the specifics of attacking the vehicles were outlined. And then he walked out.

Of all the people present, a Secret Service agent would be the one to take such attack plans personally. This operation was the kind against which he trained regularly and often. It made sense he would need a moment to absorb and reconcile it.

But the general's admonition echoed in her thoughts. *Better to be suspicious and wrong.*

She stopped at the personal electronic device locker and saw that one of the doors had been pried open. The locker was empty.

Fuck.

Vail walked outside, her mind working the evidence. She drew her Glock.

Could be nothing. Maybe he had to call his wife.

In the middle of the night?

And he didn't ask permission: the lock had been forced.

This was a problem. The kind of scenario Lukas warned against.

And I was slow to see it.

Staring into the darkness: wooded area on all sides of her, no nearby houses. Her eyes adjusted as she moved forward.

Ahead, at the end of a stand of trees, along the narrow road, everyone's vehicles were parked. She headed toward them, reasoning that Irwin would likely go directly to his car, since as soon as they realized he was not returning—and seeing the ruined phone locker—they would come for him.

Vail did not know which sedan was his. She quickly eliminated a few: hers, Robby's, Lukas's—with the personalized plate "DA GENRL"—and Rodman's.

As she approached the car parked behind hers—bearing a government plate—she felt a sharp blow to the back of her head. Her knees buckled and she crumpled to the ground.

Groggy. Dizzy.

Someone was patting her down, looking for . . . something. Heard her Glock skitter across the blacktop.

Footsteps. She rolled onto her stomach and pushed herself up. Out of the corner of her left eye, she saw a blur, threw up a hand, and blocked something. Just enough to turn a direct kick to her jaw into a sloppy glancing blow off her cheekbone.

She crab-crawled backward to give herself some space and precious seconds to clear her head and shake off the cobwebs.

Ten feet away, she saw the outline of Taylor Irwin, a splash of moonlight across the right side of his face.

"I know you're gonna make a call," she said, trying to keep him from charging—or shooting—her.

"Give me your phone," Irwin said firmly.

"Left it in the locker. Use your own."

"Battery's dead. Seven hours in a metal cabinet, trying to reach a cell tower, drained it dry."

She struggled to get onto her hands and knees. "Shit happens when you're trying to screw other people."

"Fucking traitors, all of you." He picked up a heavy stick and swung it at her, slamming it into her left temple.

286   ALAN JACOBSON

Vail fell on her back. She saw stars as she stared up at the night sky, the moon suddenly splitting in two. Turned her head left and saw two Irwins walking away, along the line of cars.

C'mon, Karen. Get the hell up. Can't let him get away.

She sat up and steadied herself as the street in front of her rocked from side to side.

Vail scanned the pavement for her Glock but did not see it.

She picked up the stick Irwin hit her with, brought it back behind her right ear, and whipped it forward, sending it arcing in the air to Irwin's right—as she charged him from the left. He turned in the direction of the branch, which landed ten feet ahead and to his right.

In that instant, Vail's lowered shoulder plowed into his side.

They both went sprawling toward the pavement—but being so close to the line of vehicles, Vail bounced into the driver's door of Robby's SUV, keeping her upright. She kicked out her boot, slamming the tip into Irwin's chin, and snapping his neck back into the asphalt. It hit with a "thunk." His eyes rolled back into his head.

Vail tried to pounce on him and more or less fell atop him.

She swung wildly, trying to punch but was too dizzy for precision. Some blows landed squarely—stinging and cutting open her knuckles—and a couple glanced off his left hand, which he started waving, trying to stop the onslaught.

She grabbed a handful of his wavy black hair and yanked, lifting his head off the pavement. His left hand slapped her cheek, but it did not have much power behind it. Vail's head whipped to the side, and she knew she had to act fast before she lost the advantage.

His right hand grabbed her breast and he squeezed and twisted in one motion.

Vail would not yell out, would not give him the benefit of hearing her pain. She swallowed a yelp. And damn, it nearly made her see stars.

She karate-chopped his throat and he let go of her.

She swung her right thigh across his torso and scooted left while still tightly gripping his hair. She clumsily hooked his chin with her bent right knee. Forced her left leg behind his neck. Pulled back on his hair, exposing his neck.

DIE TRYING 287

Irwin's hands found her face. She shook her head left and right, trying not to give him a chance to grasp a nose, ear, or eye socket.

But he got hold of her wavy locks and pulled. It hurt like a bitch.

Vail couldn't help it. She yelled. Screamed. The pain focused her scattered thoughts. She had his neck between her thighs.

Squeeze!

She contracted her leg muscles, cutting off the blood supply to his brain.

With his free hand, Irwin punched blindly above his head—landing one blow that stunned her but did not lessen her resolve. He moved his hands to her pants and tried to pry her legs away from her throat.

Vail grunted and yelled and squeezed, suddenly grateful for Robby's nagging her to work out regularly at the Academy gym.

A minute later, Irwin slumped limply against her body.

61

Vail walked into task force room, her hair disheveled and her face and hands swollen, bleeding, and bruised.

The discussion immediately ceased. Robby was at her side and guiding her to a chair.

"I'll be okay," she said. "Just a glass of water. And a brain transplant. Please."

Someone left the room. Vail became aware of another man hovering over her: Lukas DeSantos.

"What happened?" he asked.

"Irwin's gagged and handcuffed to the door of Robby's SUV."

Stallone's face shaded red. "What the fuck are you talking a—"

"He was going to turn us in. I stopped him. Better get out there. He should be waking up about now."

Rodman and Stallone rushed out the door as Rusakov came in with a Ziploc filled with crushed ice. She pushed it against Vail's cheek, which elicited a wince.

Son of a bitch.

She handed Vail a couple of Motrin and a glass of water.

Setting the glass down, she leaned back in the seat and looked at Robby. Only one of him.

That's a good thing. No offense to Robby.

He shined his tactical flashlight in both pupils, which she did not appreciate—and told him as much.

"Looks good. Did you lose consciousness?"

"No. Dizzy. Double vision."

"Any confusion?" Robby bent down and studied her face. "What's my name?"

"Asshole."

Robby frowned. "I think you're fine."

She took the ice from Rusakov and held it in place. By the time she finished applying it to all the areas that needed it, she would be holding a bag of warm water.

"Let's get back to it," Vail said. "Clock's ticking."

Those who had gathered around Vail retook their seats. Several looked at her with concern, as if she were a symbol of the resistance they would be facing—or an example of what could happen to them should someone turn them in. It was reality scoring a direct hit, resurfacing the doubts they had managed to put to rest.

As Vail moved the Ziploc to her other cheek, she heard guttural moans and muffled shouting outside the task force meeting room. Vail figured that Irwin had been brought into the house and taken into the basement.

A moment later, Lukas, Rodman, and Stallone walked in and took their seats.

"You said he was going to turn us in," Lukas said. "Did he get in touch with anyone?"

"No. Phone was dead." Vail heard sighs of relief. "I want to apologize to everyone," Stallone said. Robby harrumphed. "For what?"

"For my colleague. I screened him. I made a huge mistake."

Vail waved him off. "You had to broach the subject without revealing what you were actually asking. You couldn't know what he was thinking."

Rusakov patted Stallone on the shoulder. "No harm done."

Vail moved the ice to her other cheek.

I beg to differ.

She kept that thought to herself as her bruise went numb from the cold. Ultimately, Rusakov was correct. She had prevented disaster.

Now all they had to do was execute well and beat the Secret Service at its own game.

Piece of cake.

62

HATZOR AIRBASE
CENTRAL ISRAEL

Benny applauded as Uzi touched down on the tarmac outside the hangar. "Very good, boychick. You nailed it. How'd it feel?"

"Getting the hang of it. Once you develop the muscle memory of maintaining balance, it's second nature. You just do it instead of thinking about it."

Benny grinned like a proud father. "Exactly."

DeSantos bumped fists with Uzi and helped him lift off the camo backpack.

Uzi sat down and rubbed his face. "Syria. Of all places. Why the hell did it have to be Syria?"

"Hey." DeSantos sat down next to him. "You're missing the most important point here, boychick. "Maya's alive. She's *alive*."

"Hang on a second," Benny said, shaking his head—and then grabbing the table to steady himself. "We don't know that for sure. Let's stay levelheaded. Our intel is unconfirmed. Anything Sahmoud said has to be taken with a grain of salt, even under the influence of amobarbital."

Uzi started to object but Benny raised a hand.

"I know. It all adds up, and that's a good thing. But—and this is important—it's not the only explanation here. If you look at it with a clear head, you know this."

* * *

DIE TRYING 291

DeSantos could tell his friend's mind was racing at an incomprehensible speed. Whenever he got like this, he risked losing control—and crashing and burning.

"I know you, boychick." DeSantos placed a hand on Uzi's shoulder. "Tap the brakes. Slow down."

Uzi could not think straight. Ideas, thoughts, emotions were coming at him faster than he could process them. His eyes glazed and a tear rolled down his right cheek. He was emotionally hyperventilating.

Syria. Syria!

He had not prepared himself for that. He had accepted the intel but he had not fully processed it. And it was just now hitting him. Hard. Grabbing a prisoner from a Palestinian jail in Israel was risky enough. But from a prison in Syria . . . an unstable powder keg to begin with; an enemy of Israel and the United States, a proxy of Iran and a dealmaker with Russia . . . the geopolitical stakes were now much greater than Uzi and DeSantos had calculated when they started down this path.

They would have to go in as black as possible. Would their cover stories hold up under interrogation? Syria's intelligence community and forensic labs were likely not advanced enough to be able to learn his identity should he be captured. Mossad had, as a matter of standard procedure, encrypted his records and bioforensics data, as had Knox when he was hired by the Bureau—unbeknownst to Uzi. But Knox knew what he was doing when he approved Uzi's application, and he knew what records needed to be purged and/or protected. When Uzi was onboarded into OPSIG, the records were locked down tighter.

But if what Knox told them about Scorpion was true, they were now on the verge of being exposed, along with everyone else in OPSIG and the greater US intelligence community.

Reality was setting in. Rescuing Maya successfully was something he, as her father, had to do. No one could stop him from doing everything possible to get her out. How could he live with himself if he let rational thought take hold, backed off, and went home?

He couldn't live with himself. He couldn't back off. He couldn't go home without trying.

But a successful mission was highly unlikely. Short of an IDF operation with coordinated GPS, spotters, drone support, assault weapons—and Mossad-level cover stories and IDs—they could not risk getting caught in-country, let alone crossing the border, by Syrian *or* Israeli soldiers. If Israel didn't snag him, Syrian forces patrolling the area probably would. Let alone the dangers they would face inside Syria.

With the SkyPaks they would be exposed only for about ten minutes each way, but even—

"Your mind is still racing." Uzi looked up. "Huh?"

"Take a deep breath. We need to have a rational discussion."

"Good idea," Benny said before offering up a few phlegm-producing hacks.

Uzi reached out to steady him.

"I'm fine. Fine." He stood erect slowly and cleared his throat. "I've got some cough suppressant in the glove box."

"I'll get it."

"Tessalon capsules. Far right."

Uzi walked to the car, pulled open the door, and found the bottle. A moment later, he was handing them to Benny.

"Has Tamar gotten back to you about what the prison's interior looks like?"

"Not yet. I'll call. Maybe she didn't get the WhatsApp." He poked and swiped. Voicemail. Left a nonspecific message telling her to call ASAP. "Benny. Check with your contacts. Just in case we don't hear back."

DeSantos took the SkyPak helmet in his hands and positioned it over his head. "What if *no one* responds?"

Uzi shrugged. "We go with what we've got. We've had far less."

"True that." DeSantos stepped into the SkyPak unit and positioned it on his shoulders. "Back to it, gents."

63

WASHINGTON, DC

Vail adjourned the meeting at 9:00 a.m. to give task force members time to go home, nap, shower, eat, clear their minds, and prepare.

Many remained while others arrived and engaged in task-based work: materials were assembled and weapons were received and checked; equipment was calibrated and lines of code were tested; maps were studied.

Taylor Irwin was given an extended-release sedative to keep him asleep for at least the next twelve hours.

Vail and Robby drove home separately to check in with Vail's son, Jonathan, who had slept over to take care of Hershey and Oscar. Both dogs rushed the door and jumped up to cover their companions' cheeks with kisses. Robby had to kneel for the diminutive Oscar to reach him.

Both wagged their tails so hard their hindquarters rocked from side to side.

"Hey buddy," Robby said, bumping fists with Jonathan, who followed the dogs to the door. "No classes today?"

"Did a virtual lecture this morning so I didn't have to leave these two alone."

"Very nice," Robby said with a stifled yawn.

"You guys were out all night. Big case?" He leaned right to see around Robby's large body. "Mom. Your face."

"Beautiful as always. *That's* what you were going to say. Right?"

Vail kissed her son as he studied her bruises.

"The other guy got the worst of it. Trust me."

Jonathan looked at Robby, who nodded and shrugged. "Don't worry. Looks worse than it is."

"Speak for yourself." Vail turned to Jonathan. "I'll be fine. Just a flesh wound."

Or two or three. Maybe four.

She stroked her son's left cheek. "Don't worry about your mama."

"Let's eat," Robby said, heading for the kitchen. "Omelet good?"

"If you're cooking," Vail said, "hell yeah. If it's food and it's edible, that's all I care about right now. I'm gonna jump in the shower and change."

"I'll have some coffee ready for you when you're out."

"You're so good to me." She leaned in, grabbed his face, and gave him a long kiss.

"Oh, jeez," Jonathan said, averting his gaze. "Get a room, will you?"

Vail pulled back and gave her son a look. "This *is* our room."

64

HATZOR AIRBASE
CENTRAL ISRAEL

After flight training ended, DeSantos was nominated to pick up dinner while Benny checked in with his contact, who had agreed to supply both the drone swarm—known as Maccabee's Minions—and the BluMesh transponders, or nodes.

Yehiel "Yitz" Gaon had deep ebony skin and a tightly cropped, graying afro. Airlifted from Sudan during a joint IDF/CIA rescue operation in 1984, Yitz settled into his new home with Shira, his wife—minus their infant son, Ezekiel, who died during the flight from Sudan to Brussels. Ezekiel was one of many children who, because of the Sudanese civil war and resulting famine, died just prior to, or during, the rescue operation.

The Gaons had difficulty fitting in at first and subsisted on government aid for four years until Yitz, sporting his father's affinity for engineering and computer science, caught on with the defense forces and eventually found himself writing algorithms for improving the targeting sensors on the F-15s that Israel flew.

Although much older than other attendees, Yitz went through the Talpiot program. Rather than graduating after three years, he decided to stay an additional three and started working on the Iron Dome missile defense system's early artificial intelligence architecture.

"Yitz!" Benny shouted, engaging in a rocking bear hug. "How's Eveline?"

Yitz leaned back. "If you can believe it, starting her military service."

"And Shira?"

"She hasn't killed me yet."

They both laughed, then Benny made introductions.

"And you? How's the . . ." he waved a finger in the air.

"Cancer?" Benny asked. "Now *she* is killing me." He forced a smile. "What can I tell you? Cancer's an unwelcome invader. And my defense system isn't doing its job." He shrugged. "It is what it is."

Yitz's frown and sagging face conveyed the sadness in his heart. "Shira and I are very sorry."

"Thank you."

"For what it's worth, my kids are living proof of the legacy you leave behind. They wouldn't be here if it wasn't for you, my friend."

Benny placed a hand over his heart. "That brings me to Uzi's predicament. I'll spare you the details, but we've got to deploy Maccabee's Minions. And, obviously, the BluMesh platform."

Yitz nodded. He sat down on the adjacent bench and hung his head. "I knew this day was coming."

Benny did not say anything. He did not need to.

Yitz took a deep breath. "This won't go well for me if we don't get the drones back. The mesh nodes, no big deal. But the minions, that . . ." His voice trailed off and he looked up at Benny. They made eye contact, but Benny maintained his poker face and held his friend's gaze. "What are you going to use them for?"

"Best you don't know." Benny sat down beside him. I'll do my best to get them back. And if they work as designed, we should. It'll be a good test of their abilities."

Yitz harrumphed. "There's no spin that'll work with this. Classified military tech . . . this is about the worst ask you could've made of me."

Benny turned away and coughed spasmodically. Cleared his throat. "Then blame me. Tell them I broke in and stole it, then called and told you. You tried to talk me into returning it."

Yitz shrugged, reluctant.

DIE TRYING

Benny spread his arms. "What are they gonna do to me?" Yitz sighed. "When do you need them?"

"Now."

Yitz winced.

"All I'll tell you is this has to do with Uzi's daughter. He hasn't seen her in several years. She's been in al-Humat custody. We don't know her condition, but Uzi's wife died in their custody five years ago."

Yitz swallowed hard.

Uzi knew Benny's disclosure was designed to appeal to the man on an emotional, deeply personal level. Having lost his son, Yitz would know the horror a father faced when his child's life was in danger.

"Dammit, Benny." Yitz rubbed his forehead, then tightened his lips and nodded. "Come with me. We'll leave your fingerprints behind just in case. You'll be on camera. No one'll believe it, but—"

"They won't be able to prove otherwise. It may be enough to clear you."

"I probably won't go to prison. But I'll lose my clearance."

Benny's eyes narrowed. "You and your family have your lives."

Uzi knew it hurt Benny to have to push his friend so hard, to be so overt in calling in his chit.

"That we do." Yitz forced a smile, then stood up. "Let's go get the equipment."

"Thank you," Uzi said.

"Good luck." He faced Uzi. "You've got good friends, you know that?" A slight grin lifted the corners of Uzi's lips. "I do."

65

THE WHITE HOUSE SITUATION ROOM
WASHINGTON, DC

Vance Nunn walked into a room in the recently renovated situation room—a misnomer if there ever was one: the "room" was a 5,500-square-foot secure *complex* in the West Wing composed primarily of conference rooms and offices.

Seated there were his chief of staff, Mack Stanos, Vice President Anthony Andrews, and *his* chief of staff, Russell Card.

Nunn sat down, not wasting time on pleasantries. "Where are we with Team Grey?"

"They're in the wind. As soon as the arrest warrants were issued. But realistically, sir, even if we could interrogate them, these people wouldn't talk to us, let alone turn on each other."

Nunn fisted his right hand. "Let's not wait any longer. Tomorrow I want to release all that data we seized. Make sure it includes the operatives' identities and missions. All of them." A grin teased his lips. "Shit's gonna hit the fan. Knox, MacNamara, Tasset—they're going to—"

"Sir, uh . . ." Stanos cleared his throat. "We can't do that." Nunn's eyebrows pulled inward. "Why the hell not?"

"Data's encrypted."

"So?"

"We haven't been able to decrypt it yet."

"And when were you going to tell me this?"

"I was working the problem. No need to bother you with it."

"Wrong. Bother me. I need to know this kind of crap when I cut deals, make threats and ultimatums."

"Yes, Mr. President."

"I don't understand," Andrews said. "The NSA's working on it?"

"Yes."

Andrews spread his hands. "Then how long till they break it?"

Stanos took a breath. "They don't know. Some kind of cutting-edge tech was used to encrypt it."

There was silence as Nunn thought. "They *are* going to get at the data, yes?"

"Yes, sir. Just a matter of time."

"I want that information. Fast." He waved a conciliatory hand. "As fast as *possible*."

"I'll tell them, sir."

Nunn pointed at Stanos. "Soon as they have it, release the names. And missions. Leak it through . . . I don't know, some conspiracy news site that'll report it without asking where it came from. Or try to verify it."

"Understood."

"Then leak some corroborating evidence so mainstream media has no choice but to report on it." He frowned. "Any other problems you've been working without my knowledge?"

"That's it, sir," Stanos said.

Nunn got up from his seat and walked out of the room, muttering under his breath. He had fifteen seconds to compose himself before he exited the secure complex and reentered the rest of the West Wing— where people would be reading his face and his movements would be documented down to the minute.

It's good to be president, Nunn thought. *Except in moments like this.*

66

DUPONT CIRCLE
WASHINGTON, DC

Vail was in position at Dupont Circle, near the tree-lined curb of New Hampshire Avenue, when she received encrypted communications in her earpiece from Lukas DeSantos.

He reported that all systems were go for their mission; earlier in the day, he had secured all the equipment they would need and staffed all the desired operators for the motorcade op. Everyone was in position and, owing to their preparation, insider intelligence, and experience, there had been no challenges from agents or law enforcement.

Follow-on check-ins from Giancarlo Stallone and Tim Meadows sent the most significant go signals they would receive: the president was on schedule. No changes had been implemented to the motorcade and Stallone was in the ops room.

To everyone's unexpressed relief, Meadows's hack was successful. He was at a secure offsite location, set to take control of the vehicles.

Robby had joined the operators on-site and was wearing a tactical uniform matching the ones worn by the deployed Metro Police Department officers.

Vail was dressed in a dark suit and white blouse, wearing an earpiece with her red hair drawn back in a bun. Makeup covered her bruises well enough for a nighttime mission. She looked like the prototypical female Secret Service protective detail agent.

She was waiting with fellow task force member, CIA officer Mahmoud el-Fahad. To an observer from a distance, their greeting was perfunctory and lacked familiarity.

"You good?" Vail asked. He nodded. "You?"

"A little nervous."

He chuckled. "Good. I'm not the only one. Imagine that. Of all the missions I've carried out on foreign soil, this one is giving me the most agita."

She winked at him, then they faced forward. All business. Waiting.

67

Lukas DeSantos stood in the window of the second floor of the Starbucks building off Connecticut Street, two hundred-plus yards from the Dupont Circle fountain. When the café reopened following the pandemic, the second floor remained closed—and except for the occasional cleaning crew, no one ventured up there.

The tables and seats remained, waiting for corporate to give the go-ahead to allow customers upstairs. At present, that permission had not come, giving Lukas privacy—and stellar views of the circle through the winter-bare overcup oak and bald cypress trees.

According to Stallone, in accordance with standard procedure, the Secret Service had welded closed all mailboxes and manhole covers along the motorcade's route. The task force planned around this information and made other arrangements to pre-position their equipment.

If the general's calculations were accurate, the route vehicle would be visible in a matter of seconds. He checked the focus on his binoculars and waited. "Hold steady," he said over his headset.

He watched as citizens circulated in and out of his field of vision, frequenting restaurants and businesses, or heading toward the nearby Metro station. They were shunted around by crowd-control barriers, but the large traffic circle that surrounded the Dupont statue and fountain were left untouched.

Seconds later, he saw the hoods of the black SUVs enter his field of vision.

"Route vehicles," Lukas spoke into the mic. "Let them go," he said, repeating the protocol they had already discussed ad infinitum. "No immediate threat. Stand ready. Pilot should be following in sixty seconds."

As anticipated, the black Chevy Suburban rolled into his visual field.

"Pilot and sweepers on Harleys. About ten seconds to showtime."

Lukas felt his heart rate increase. From this point on, timing was critical. He took a slow, steady breath to prevent his binoculars from "bouncing," which would make him lose his visual lock on the highly magnified landscape.

And there it was: "Lead car in sight." Thus began the core of the motorcade. "Five seconds."

He counted to himself: Four. Three. Two.

"Halfback visible." Police lights mounted inside the grille and on the dashboard: the Service's protective detail. "Remember: first direct threat sits in Halfback's open rear window."

"Meadows, Stallone. Stand ready. First Beast in view." It was the one with a slight black mark on the left headlight lens: Stallone's signal. "This is the decoy. Let it go. Repeat. Let Beast One pass."

He heard a few "roger that" replies over his headset but kept his focus on the next vehicle: the one carrying Vance Nunn, their mark.

"I have Beast Two. HVT in view. Approaching target. Sniper one, ready on my mark."

68

GOLAN HEIGHTS, ISRAEL

After reviewing their plan of attack multiple times, Uzi, DeSantos, and Benny napped for three hours because they knew there would be no opportunity to get shuteye until they returned from Syria—hopefully in one piece.

They drove an hour to the Golan Heights and parked at a kibbutz not far from the Israel-Syria border. First established in Israel in 1910, kibbutzim were self-sustaining, egalitarian farming villages where families raised their children communally. To remain relevant in a changing world, some modernized to include industrial plants and high-tech businesses.

"One of the residents is a buddy of mine," Benny said. "He's going to give us a ride to the border. He knows a place that's got some cover from the army's watchful eyes. It'll give us a window to operate covertly."

"And what happens after that window closes?" DeSantos asked.

"They'll issue an alert," Uzi said, "assuming they see us, which is not guaranteed because of the measures the engineers took to make the SkyPak as stealthy as possible. But if they do pick us up, they'll assess the threat and see we're moving *away* from Israel. They'll monitor and report. By the time they get orders to shoot us down, we'll be across the border."

"I can live with that," DeSantos said. "But on the trip back—

assuming we get out alive—we'll be headed *toward* Israel. A prime threat."

Uzi and Benny shared a look, then nodded. "Yep. Pretty much," they said, almost in unison.

Uzi opened the back seat and began gathering up his SkyPak.

"And that doesn't bother you? Boychick, look at me."

Uzi stopped and turned to face DeSantos. In the darkness, he could see the whites of his friend's eyes. "Bothers me a lot. But we've got no choice. We'll need some plain old good luck. Or divine intervention."

DeSantos groaned. "You neglected to mention that when we were planning this op."

"Nothing we can do. Control what you can, right?"

"Can't argue with that."

Benny launched into a coughing spasm and popped another several Tesssalons to calm the persistent tickle.

Choking down the small capsules, he said, "Syria built settlements along the border to put its own innocents in the line of fire. If a skirmish breaks out, the IDF is hard-pressed to defend the border without collateral damage. That might work to our advantage."

Uzi set the SkyPak on the hood of the car and pulled out his phone. "Power your cells down. Decreases the risk of an electronic signature setting off IDF sensors mounted on the top of Mount Bental."

As Benny removed his handset from his khaki-colored tactical pants, it vibrated. It was a number that made him look twice. "This is a sick joke."

"Who is it?" Uzi asked.

"Elaine." Benny showed them the screen.

Uzi squinted confusion. "Elaine? Your wife? The one who—"

"Was killed in the café bombing ten years ago. Yes." Benny answered and lifted the handset to his cheek, his jowls sagging with fear. "Who is this?" He listened, then said, "You called *my* phone. Now tell me who *the fuck* this is."

Benny hit the speaker icon so they could all hear.

The voice was calm, professional. "Tell DeSantos it's the law firm of Lackwood and McGill."

306   ALAN JACOBSON

Benny muted the mic and said, "Law firm of Lackwood and McGill?" DeSantos drew his chin back. "What the f—"

"This can't be good," Uzi said.

"Definitely not." DeSantos reached over and unmuted the microphone.

"This is DeSantos. Who's this?"

"Arlo Lackwood. And on behalf of my colleagues, I do hope your time in the Holy Land has been fruitful."

"How'd you get this number?"

"MI6, remember? I don't know about you, mate, but neither of us has time for stupid questions. And we've got someone your partner cares about. But we're willing to spare her life. A swap. You for her."

Uzi tightened his fist. *Someone I care about? A woman. Maya? No.*

"You're gonna have to be more specif—"

"Tamar Gur."

Uzi closed his eyes. "Leave her out of this. Please. She's done nothing to you."

"Ah," Lackwood said. "Uziel. Hit a nerve, have I? Hope so, mate. Well I say—to be honest, that's what we were going for. Counting on, actually." Uzi looked at DeSantos, then Benny. "Tamar's a soldier. She understands. Now go to hell." Uzi stabbed the display with an index finger and disconnected the call. He cleared his throat and swiped away a tear.

DeSantos grabbed his shoulder and pulled him around to face him. "Boychick, what are you doing?"

"They think they're in control," Uzi said, shrugging off DeSantos's hand. He began to pace. "We can't let them dictate the terms."

DeSantos followed behind him. "This is *E Squadron*," he said in a constrained yell that was barely above a whisper. "Despite what they say, they're here to take revenge for Basil Walpole. I've got no choice. Like you said, Tamar is an innocent here."

Uzi faced his friend. "I'm not gonna let you trade your life for hers. We'll find another way."

"Here? With no backup? No support whatsoever? The three of us against a team of Tier One operators who, like us, have a license to kill? If you care about Tamar, and I *know* you do, we don't have a choice."

DIE TRYING 307

The phone rang. Again.

"Probably 'Elaine.'" Benny gestured at the handset. "Better answer."

DeSantos brought the device to his ear and listened. "Where and when?" He looked up at the dark night sky. "I'm tied up at the moment. We're in the middle of—" He dropped his chin to his chest. "Fine. It'll take me a while to get there." He hung up.

"Now what?" Benny asked.

"I have to go," DeSantos said, powering down Benny's phone. "Now."

"Where?"

"Jaffa."

The ancient port city of Tel Aviv.

DeSantos took a deep breath. "You think you two can handle this on your own?"

Uzi bit his bottom lip. *Not sure we could've pulled it off with three of us.*

"We'll get her out. But I can't just let you—"

"I'm not gonna walk right into their hands. They'll have to work for their prize."

Uzi locked gazes with DeSantos, then gave him a long hug. "I'm sorry, man."

"For what?"

"If I hadn't asked you to come . . . this wouldn't have happened. This whole thing's my fault."

DeSantos leaned back. "Hey. We had no idea MI6 had identified me. Maybe we should've. But when we got back from England, Knox, McNamara, and I talked about it. Years passed. We thought we were in the clear. But even if the security service ever figured out what happened, even if they *somehow* ID'd me, worst-case scenario would be an arrest. A chance to defend myself in court. A hit squad?" He snorted. "That never came up."

"Given what we know now, my money's on a leak from Nunn and his people to the security service."

"Awesome." DeSantos laughed. "Makes sense, doesn't it? Regardless of how it happened . . . what am I gonna do? Retire from OPSIG? Never travel overseas again?"

308   ALAN JACOBSON

Uzi shook his head. "No idea. I just know that—"

"Crumple that thought and toss it in the garbage, boychick."

Benny came up alongside Uzi. "Go check your equipment. The shift change is an hour from now and we're tight on time."

DeSantos slapped Uzi's chest with both hands. "May the force be with you."

"And may you live long and prosper."

They shared a smile, then Uzi turned and headed off toward the SkyPaks. He pulled out his phone to power it down—and then stopped.

Benny shook DeSantos's hand. "It's been good getting to know one of Uzi's *mishpuchah.* Family."

"Just get his daughter out. That'll make this whole trip worthwhile."

"And you get Tamar out."

"Do my best."

Benny shook his head. "Wish we had more time. Might've been able to get a few colleagues to help out."

DeSantos slid a tanto into a sheath on his belt. "Pretty sure you've got the harder mission." He placed a hand on Benny's shoulder. "Be careful. Take care of our mish-patch. Or whatever it's called."

Benny laughed. "When you get back, tell Uzi I said he owes me."

DeSantos thought—and almost said, *I don't think he's going to be able to repay you.* But it went without saying that Benny was not long for this life.

Benny shoved a thin tactical flashlight into a back pocket. "One last mission. One last chance to do good, save lives."

DeSantos nodded. "You're a *mentsh.*"

Benny harrumphed and zipped his waist pack. "First *boychick.* Now *mentsh.*" He squinted. "*Mishpuchah* needs work. But otherwise, you speak Yiddish pretty good, my friend." Benny lifted the SkyPak from the trunk and handed DeSantos the car keys.

DeSantos grabbed Benny's hand and pulled him into a hug. "I'm gonna miss you."

Benny leaned back. "Life is short, Hector. Sometimes we're forced to go out on someone else's terms. Cancer tried to do that to me. But this? This op is me raising my middle finger and saying, No way." He placed his left hand on the back of DeSantos's neck. "Thank you for letting me go out on *my* terms."

DeSantos's eyes teared up.

Benny raised an index finger. "Saving the lives of innocents is a good way to leave this world," he said as he turned and trudged away, toward Uzi and into the darkness.

69

**RONALD REAGAN BUILDING
AND INTERNATIONAL TRADE CENTER
1300 PENNSYLVANIA AVENUE NW
WASHINGTON, DC**

Bill Tait slept four hours on his flight from Tel Aviv, after arranging to procure the operators and equipment Lukas DeSantos had requested. By the time Tait awoke and had two cups of coffee to get his brain in gear, Lukas had added to his list.

Tait called the general and they parsed the forthcoming plan in detail, then tweaked procedures to patch holes.

He went to his office and showered, then gathered his men and checked the equipment they had assembled from area warehouses and local contractors with whom they worked closely.

Tait sent Phil Sanfillipo to head up the team that would handle *Wolf w*hile he would lead the one dealing with *Tiger*.

When Tait arrived at the Ronald Reagan Building and International Trade Center, many of the agencies and businesses that resided there had emptied out and the staff was prepping for the gala—the event *Tiger* was attending this evening.

The structure was the first federal building in the district designed to house both government and private sector entities. By the time it was completed in 1998, however, 9/11 was around the corner—and

DIE TRYING 311

tight security put a crimp in the 3 million-square-foot structure's original purpose of allowing public access.

Located blocks from the White House, the trade center had grown-in power and importance, and the majestic architecture both inside and out reinforced that standing.

Tait stood in his tactical gear, off to the side of the magnetometer that protected the entrance by the Woodrow Wilson memorial plaza, in front of a colorful section of the Berlin Wall that commemorated President Reagan's "tear down this wall" speech.

Holding an SR-16 automatic rifle and wearing a black uniform emblazoned with CAPITOL POLICE, Tait was like the building itself: his appearance exuded power and importance. He looked the part and no one questioned his presence.

As the 7:00 p.m. hour passed, his right palm, resting on the stock of his SR-16, began to perspire. He took some deep breaths and did a mic check. Comms was working and the two real Capitol Police agents replied that everything was proceeding as planned.

At 7:18 p.m., he pulled out the burner and tapped in 911. He brought the handset to his face and lowered his voice, hoping to disguise it without making it obvious. He reported that climate activists had planted a bomb in the Reagan building and that Vice President Andrews was going to be blown to bits in five minutes. And there was nothing anyone could do to stop the bomb from exploding.

He cut off the call, powered down the phone, and walked over to a nearby garbage pail. He stood there thirty seconds, then casually smudged his fingerprints and covertly dropped the handset in the bin.

Havoc erupted a hundred feet away, in the indoor plaza beneath the atrium where table rounds were set up and the cavernous space was bathed in red, white, and blue lighting.

As anticipated, the security detail had surrounded Vice President Andrews and were ushering him toward the exit. Tait jogged over and joined the mass of nine men and three women. Tait knew which were his associates—Richards and Kennett—and identified them on sight as he approached.

Richards was following the plan, shouting orders to direct the agents toward a different exit: the one that would take them into the parking garage where Tait's GMC Suburban of similar model year and appearance sat idling, sporting the identifying flags on both front quarter panels and the vice presential seal on the rear doors.

The latter were magnetic reproductions and the former ink-jet reproductions on cloth. An observant agent might notice that these items were not authentic, but in the heat of the moment—ushering the VP out of a building because of a bomb threat—tunnel vision took over and such details went unnoticed.

Tait followed the tightly compressed group as they surrounded and moved Andrews swiftly into the cavernous garage. They exited into a glass-enclosed vestibule and plowed through the doors into the empty parking structure.

The Suburban pulled to a hard stop at the curb and Andrews was pushed into the back by Kennett. She climbed in with him and another agent, while Richards got into the front passenger seat.

Tait slammed the rear door, then slapped twice on the window. The driver sped away.

70

**THE CAPITOLIST RESTAURANT
1 INDEPENDENCE AVE SW
WASHINGTON, DC**

Jolene Aswad sat down in her seat and let out a long sigh. Fatigue tugged at her eyelids. After a roiling debate on the House floor, the Speaker walked down the street to make fundraising calls.

The average American did not realize that a high proportion of a representative's time was spent fundraising. After a long day haggling with colleagues and opposition party members, she had to resort to begging.

Then again, the money Aswad took in went toward getting her reelected, not to filling her personal bank account. The latter was addressed by a deal she had cut with the president and the group he had aligned himself with years ago—a group that was global and promised more assets than she could spend in her lifetime.

That made the unending meetings and events with very high earners tolerable. They wanted access to the Speaker—and her influence on issues that mattered to them and their interests. Political donations were the cost of doing business. It was the American way.

It was not what Washington, Jefferson, Hamilton, Adams et al. had in mind when they drew up the documents that would set the United States free from British rule, but the founding fathers were not around to complain. Times changed. America was a capitalist society and Jolene Aswad was focused on amassing her share of that capital.

The waiter dropped off a menu and, recognizing her, smiled and asked if her husband would be joining her this evening.

"Yes, John will be here any minute. If you could have someone bring me water, I'd be eternally grateful. My throat feels like sandpaper."

"Absolutely, Madame Speaker. Coming right up."

She glanced at the menu, but she already knew what she was going to have. Aswad was in the mood for a thick New York steak. It had nothing to do with the city, but being a native New Yorker, she felt obliged to order it—and truth be told, she felt oddly at home when she saw it sitting on her dinner plate.

A man set two water glasses down, a slice of lemon floating on top.

"This is different," she said.

"The lemon? Yes, ma'am. Locally sourced."

"Hm. Thank you . . ." She glanced at the name tag pinned to his white apron. "Mitch. You're new here."

He grinned. "Started yesterday, Madame Speaker."

Aswad nodded, Mitch moved off, and she gathered up the water— and drank deeply.

"Honey. Sorry I'm late." John gave her a kiss on the forehead.

She looked up and smiled. "Just got here myself five minutes ago. Dreadful da—" Aswad drew her chin back, then leaned forward and opened her mouth to speak.

But she could not form words. Could not breathe.

"Jolene?" John stood up. "What's wrong?"

Her face felt flush. And hot, but cold. She looked at John and felt her head falling forward.

Into the plate.

In the background, she heard John shout. "Call 911! Help. Hurry . . ."

And then, nothing.

71

DUPONT CIRCLE
WASHINGTON, DC

Snipers one, two, and three fired—not large-caliber rounds but a mixture of tear gas and smoke grenades that landed in front of, and behind, the roof-bound sharpshooters.

In that same instant, another group of operators sent the same vision-obscuring devices toward Stagecoach—the limo that transported President Nunn.

Tim Meadows locked the doors of all the Suburbans, GMCs, and Fords while Stallone unlocked the Beast's rear doors. A second later, an engineer from DARPA's adaptive capabilities office set off pre-placed devices and two messenger-bag sized "cannons" that emitted powerful EMPs, the electromagnetic pulses that fried all electronic devices in the vicinity of the motorcade.

Additional tear gas cannisters were tossed by supposed police officers along the route; in reality, they were Bill Tait's men and women who had positioned themselves hours in advance.

Three seconds after the Beast lurched to a dead stop, Alex Rusakov, Troy Rodman, Karen Vail, Dell Christie, Neil Frazier, and Robby Hernandez appeared from within the dense smoke wearing black tactical gear and gas masks. Vail grabbed Stagecoach's handle and pulled open the heavy back door.

Rusakov and Rodman tossed in a tear gas cannister and Vail partially closed the door to make sure the occupants received a proper dose. With all power off and the electronic equipment nonfunctional, the emergency oxygen tank would not dispense fresh air into the rear cabin.

Christie, Frazier, and Robby, who were watching their teammates' sixes, were equipped with Glock handguns, tanto knives, and tranquilizer rifles—which Christie planned to use to disable the tactical Secret Service agent perched in the protection detail's open rear Suburban window.

If the dart hit the officer's vest, Frazier would move to Plan B—the Glock—and if that still failed to disable him, the blade, which would penetrate the Kevlar fibers.

Two seconds after closing the door, gunfire erupted from behind them. Rounds pinged off the black vehicle's piano-glass armor. Vail ignored them, hoping and praying they would strike her vest or helmet and flatten on impact.

Vail pulled open the door again and Rusakov dove in, fighting off what seemed like at least two sets of haphazardly swinging arms—protective detail agents trying to keep their charge safe while coughing violently, their eyes too painful to open.

Vail felt a sharp punch to her back and was flattened against the car's exterior. She was hit—but the vest did its job. She fought for breath and regained her balance as someone to her left took a round and went down.

She could not tell who it was, but another operator immediately grabbed him under the armpits and dragged him into the darkness.

Rusakov backed out of the vehicle's rear compartment with a hacking Vance Nunn, yanking him toward Rodman, who, at six-foot-five and 260 pounds, had no problem manhandling the president and pulling him free of the limo.

72

WASHINGTON, DC

Vice President Andrews dabbed his forehead with a handkerchief and accepted a water bottle from Capitol Police special agent Mara Kennett.

"Sorry for all the commotion, Mr. Vice President," she said. "You okay, sir?"

"I'm fine. I'm fine. I take it that was not a drill."

"No, sir," the agent to Andrews's left said.

"You're Terry," Andrews said. "Terry Lamm, right?"

"Yes, sir. That's right. And we'd tell you if it was a drill. There was a credible bomb threat called in."

"I saw one of the devices myself," Kennett said.

"Holy mother of Mary. Well, you people did a stellar job, a stellar job."

He wiped his face. "My heart's still racing."

"Agent Kennett, can you—"

"My comms are out," Lamm said, touching his earpiece. He leaned forward in his seat and looked at his colleague. "Kennett, you have comms?"

"Negative."

Lamm pulled out his phone. "And no service. What the hell?" He tapped the driver's shoulder. "Richards, what about you?"

The agent pulled out his phone and consulted the display. "Nothing."

318   ALAN JACOBSON

"Is this a—" Andrews started to say as Kennett reached across the vice president and jabbed a hypodermic into Lamm's thigh.

Lamm started to grab for his pistol, but never made it past his suit lapel before his head fell back against the seat and his torso flopped against the door.

"What's going on?" Andrews shouted. Kennett faced forward but did not answer. "I demand to know!"

"You're being kidnapped, sir."

Andrews drew his chin back. "You're a federal law enforcement officer. You work for *me*. Stop this car right now."

Kennett did not respond.

Andrews leaned forward and pointed at Richards. "Stop this car. That's an order!"

"Yes, sir." He signaled left and drove down a side street.

Kennett yanked off the vice president's suit coat—aggressively and forcefully—and pulled a ratty sweatshirt over his torso. "Remove your shoes."

"I will not. You people won't get—"

Kennett elbowed him in the mouth—causing the vice president's eyes to water.

Andrews's mouth was both numb and painful at the same time. He remembered once slamming his thumb with a hammer—this was that kind of feeling.

He sat there stunned, suddenly becoming aware that Agent Kennett was pulling off his Bruno Magli oxfords.

From beneath the front seat she produced a pair of worn tennis shoes. "What are you . . ." he said weakly, his lips and gums beginning to ache. "Shut up."

She shoved his feet into the sneakers and then stuffed his mouth with a washcloth.

It tasted cold and dry. And dirty. He tried to spit it out—to no avail.

She slid a balaclava over Andrews's head, then she and Richards pulled on their own.

Richards found a spot at the curb and stopped. "We're here." He exited the car as Kennett pulled large flex-cuffs around Lamms's wrists and ankles, then secured his mouth with a long strip of duct tape.

DIE TRYING 319

She gathered Andrews and pulled him out of the car and wedged him between her body and Richard's.

Andrews tried to break free, but who was he kidding? Their grips were firm and purposeful.

The area was dark. Someone must have disabled the streetlights. On purpose? *Of course it was,* Andrews thought. *This was planned.*

The rag in his mouth was now wet from saliva—but his tongue felt like parched sand.

Kennett and Richards escorted Andrews by his arms through the door of the basement entrance of a dark townhouse.

Andrews groaned and writhed—as Kennett shoved him into a chair and secured his wrists, too tightly, with a pair of handcuffs.

Sharp pain.

A dim lamp came on in the corner of a sizable room—unfinished, cold, and humid. It smelled of sawdust.

The agent stood over Andrews. "My name's Jack Richards. I'm going to remove the rag. Don't scream or I'll hit you." He made an imposing fist with his right hand and held it in front of the man's nose. "Hard."

Andrews nodded and Richards reached into the vice president's half-open mouth, pulled out the rag, and tossed it to the floor.

Kennett snapped a couple of switches and bright lights turned on, positioned in front of Andrews's chair. He squinted as his eyes adjusted.

"Now, sir," she said, holding up an iPhone, "we're gonna have a chat."

"A chat?"

"Yes, sir. About Scorpion."

Andrews could not hide his fear—or the shock on his face. Perspiration streamed from his armpits and started to pimple his forehead. It was freezing in the basement, and yet he felt hot. Very hot.

"I want a lawyer."

Kennett chuckled. "And we want answers."

Andrews felt like an idiot. There would be no attorneys. No reading of his rights.

He could be a little thick at times, but everything was clear now. He knew what was happening.

Kennett held the phone in front of her chest and lined up the shot. She tapped the screen.

He heard an electronic beep. *Video*.

"Start talking, Mr. Vice President."

73

DUPONT CIRCLE
WASHINGTON, DC

Rodman maneuvered the coughing president over his right shoulder. His long strides took them across the grass-covered plaza toward— and past—the twenty-three-foot-tall white marble fountain honoring Rear Admiral Samuel Francis Du Pont.

Pulling up at the curb a hundred feet away on New Hampshire was a military green Patagonia electric vehicle, the kind the FBI used with its rapid deployment team in hard-to-reach areas of the world when rescue operations were required.

The four-seater all-terrain tactical vehicle was fast, highly maneuverable, and unusually narrow. It could go almost anywhere—which in this case was unnecessary. The driver's assignment was to get the four of them—Rodman, Nunn, the driver, and one of Bill Tait's heavily armed former spec ops soldiers—out of the area swiftly, without being tracked.

With bullets whizzing by and one man already known to be down, making it to their getaway car was no small task.

To reduce the risk of being tracked, located, or identified, the plan was to transfer Nunn to another two nondescript vehicles with covert registrations.

The handoffs would occur under overpasses or inside pre-scouted and pre-vetted parking garages so their actions would not be visible to surveillance cameras.

KALORAMA HEIGHTS
WASHINGTON, DC

Phil Sanfillipo, going by the call sign Alpha, removed his hand from the heated glove and checked his rifle for the tenth—or maybe fifteenth—time. He had lost count.

Sanfillipo and his fellow sniper, Bravo, had arrived at 5:30 p.m. under the cover of darkness and on foot.

They took their places on the roofs across the street from their target, Senate majority leader Bernard Conti. *Wolf.* The strategically selected homes sat at right angles to *Wolf*'s residence, affording them two different attack angles.

The plan was for a colleague of theirs, Charlie, to shoot an incendiary device through the rear window of *Wolf*'s home, setting off a fire. A second and third blaze would be set in the yard, leaving the Capitol Police detail one way out: the front door.

Wolf's wife had passed away three years ago and no one else lived in the house. There was ample land on both sides and behind to allow the fire department to prevent the blaze from spreading.

Because of *Wolf*'s large security detail, and the constraint placed on the task force to act at a specific time—dictated by the attack on Nunn—they had limited control over the situation. Once the motorcade was engaged, an alert would go out to all personnel, and it would be nearly impossible to get to the Senate majority leader without substantial collateral damage. Rather than risk Conti assuming the presidency—and rendering this entire operation moot—they had to force the issue and take him out while limiting risk to the innocent agents assigned to protect him.

As a result of his fine work in Afghanistan—and his ability to execute with little drama or collateral damage—Bill Tait had recruited Bravo for this job.

"Alpha to Bravo. Do you copy?"

"Copy."

"Charlie," Sanfillipo said. "Status?"

"In position. Awaiting go from Echo."

Echo was General Lukas DeSantos, who was calling the shots

regarding the president's motorcade. Sanfillipo was on his frequency and would be moving on his call because the timing of their actions had to be concisely coordinated.

"I have Beast Two. HVT in view approaching target. Sniper One, ready on my mark." Sanfillipo's heartbeat rose as he fought to keep an even keel while notifying his team members. "Charlie, on my mark." He steadied his gaze.

"Mark."

Through his scope, Sanfillipo saw the telltale glow of a robust conflagration, undulating flames spreading inside the rear of *Wolf*'s home. He counted off the seconds. Then: "Bravo, you're a go."

"Copy."

The front door opened and people in suits spilled out; they would attempt to encircle the Senate majority leader.

But the general's plan contained a stroke of genius: two dozen people could not fit through the front door at the same time. That bottleneck would leave only one agent in front and one in back—and *Wolf* exposed.

Sanfillipo acquired his target and fired: headshot. Bravo's round hit a split second later.

"Ready the smoke," Sanfillipo said.

Half the agents were still inside the house but fought their way out, climbing over *Wolf*'s still body.

Bravo shot a grenade into the front yard, reloaded, and launched another. White fog enveloped the agents as they scrambled to make sense of what was happening.

Like ants who had their nest disturbed, they scattered in various directions.

"Disembark," Sanfillipo said. "Retreat and exfil."

"Roger that."

DUPONT CIRCLE
WASHINGTON, DC

Vail saw Rodman head off into the rotunda of the circle with Vance Nunn slung over his shoulder. The rest was up to Hot Rod and the driver of the Patagonia ATV.

Vail led Christie, Frazier, and the compatriots supplied by Bill Tait and Lukas DeSantos as they melted into the cover of the dense smoke, rounds striking everywhere—mostly in non-vital body parts. While executing their exfil strategy, Vail sensed that this was akin to escaping enemy territory in a war zone.

As they reached the outer perimeter of the thick cloud, Vail saw their pre-positioned vehicles. They climbed into the GMC van and began removing their tactical uniforms, gas masks, balaclavas, and sidearms. They would be brought to a Tait facility to be purged of DNA.

Vail sighed relief when Robby joined them seconds later.

"Hang on," the driver said. As the vehicle pulled away, Vail took Robby's hand and let her head fall back against the seat.

That was enough adrenaline for a month.

Another story I'll never be able to tell my future grandkids.

74

TEL AVIV, ISRAEL

Hector Desantos took a few deep breaths to oxygenate his blood.

Adrenaline was kicking in, but he didn't want to peak too early. He had stressful moments ahead and needed to bring his A-plus game—because there would be no second chances. When dealing with professional killers, whose job it was to complete their mission at all costs, he could not afford to be a step too slow at the wrong second.

He should know. He was one of those professional killers. Then again, he preferred to think of himself as his official unofficial job title described: a Tier One special operator whose black missions permitted him the discretion to use whatever means necessary to complete his objectives, including, when required, taking a life, at his sole discretion.

It was a responsibility he took to heart. He had killed—numerous times—but nearly each occasion was necessary and required to complete the mission: ensure the safety of the United States government, its Constitution and institutions, and its people.

One of the few exceptions was the death of Basil Walpole. His was an accident. A tragedy. And it happened while Desantos and Karen Vail were in England trying to apprehend a virulent terrorist who was in the process of launching an attack on British soil.

What occurred following Walpole's death saved tens of thousands of people in and around London. But it did not diminish the heartbreak of what occurred inside Walpole's home. DeSantos understood

326 ALAN JACOBSON

that and was prepared to face a possible tribunal, knowing that the US government would not step in to intervene. That deniability was a vital part of his job. That was the reason his missions and his OPSIG division were highly classified. And deniable.

But the "law firm" of Lackwood and McGill was not there to arrest him to stand trial.

DeSantos pulled in front of a hiking, camping, and outdoor gear shop on Dizengoff Street in the heart of Tel Aviv. He had found its website while gassing up Benny's car thirty clicks ago.

At about 4:00 a.m., no one would be in the store. He picked the lock, fully expecting an unpleasant bleat from an annoying security system. He inserted a couple of used ear plugs he found in his pocket from a previous visit to a shooting range a few weeks ago.

He was not disappointed. The burglar alarm did its job—and that meant DeSantos needed to be efficient and quick. He found and filled a 5.11 Tactical backpack with lock ties, microfiber rags, climbing carabiners, pepper spray, a survival kit, an assortment of nasty-looking knives, an ice pick, a new balaclava, and various useful items.

One item he needed was not permitted in Israel: fireworks. However, because Palestinians often shot them off illegally at their weddings, they could be found in some stores "under the counter."

And indeed, crouching down beneath the front checkout desk, that was where DeSantos found what he was looking for. He reached into his pocket to pay and left three hundred shekels on the counter. On the way out, he noticed photos on the wall, including one of what he assumed was the shop's owner with former Israeli prime minister Ariel Sharon. DeSantos lifted the largest framed item off its hooks. He deftly removed the wire strung from one screw eye across the width to the opposing side. It sprung into a coil and he shoved it into his pocket.

Seconds later, he headed out the door and down the street to Benny's car.

75

GOLAN HEIGHTS, ISRAEL

Uzi stood on a rise and held a pair of night vision binoculars to his face. Fortunately, one variable was working in their favor: the moon was but a sliver, shedding minimal light on the landscape.

He identified the United Nations disengagement observer force watchtower to their south, along the border with Syria at the Quneitra Crossing. The post was equipped with powerful telescopes, but it was the middle of the night and there had been no border skirmishes and no overt threats during the past couple of months. That meant the UN guards were likely bored as hell and not on high alert.

By the time the IDF radar picked them up, Uzi and Benny would be in Syria. The military would be scrambling to investigate who they were and determine if they had done anything nefarious in Israel.

"You ready?"

Uzi shook his head, ending his reverie and focusing on Benny. "Let's do this."

Benny's longtime friend Ilan had deposited them in an area where they could wait out of direct view of the IDF. It would at least enable them to launch without watchful eyes.

They strapped on their SkyPaks, seated their helmets, and activated the microphones that were built into the mouthpiece.

"Power on," Uzi said. He flicked a safety on the right controller and thumbed the red button—much like the missile-firing safety switch on a fighter jet. "Stand by for go."

"Copy that."

The muted heads-up display glowed to life, superimposed over the landscape ahead of them. "Lifting off in three, two, one." Uzi felt the rise as his feet left the ground and the pull of gravity pushed down on his shoulders. He leaned forward and accelerated, Benny off to his right.

He kept the speed at twenty-five kph to conserve power. They were on schedule to make the shift change, so the only risk of flying slow was that they were visible longer to Israeli overwatch stationed on Mount Bental. Now that they were in the air and en route, Uzi realized how dark it was all around them. With no visible burning jet exhaust and little light pollution from nearby cities, even with infrared lenses it would be difficult for observation scopes to see them.

As they passed over the well-defined border fence, Uzi's attention shifted to Syrian air defenses. All remained quiet as the sides of Mount Hermon became visible. Despite the darkness, he thought he could make out snow capping its peaks. They turned right, following the foothill line until, just ahead, Uzi saw the lighted security fence and entrance to Asr Sayy, the secretive Syrian prison built into a mountainside.

"How close do we get?"

"Let me take the lead," Benny said. "There's a plateau and a rocky outcropping we can land behind, out of range of any cameras they may have by the entrance."

"Dropping back to your six."

"Roger," Benny said as he swung around in front.

Moments later, they were decelerating and approaching the ground. They dropped straight down and planted both feet on the rocky soil. They cut the power to the SkyPaks, slipped them off their torsos, and covered them with brush.

As Benny pulled a strap from his arm, he lost his balance and fell into Uzi.

"I got you. You okay?"

"I'm good. I'm good. Balance is getting a little dicey. That flight screwed up my equilibrium. Hadn't thought about that."

Uzi looked at him with concern.

"I've got brain cancer, boychick. Metastasized to my lung. You know the deal. And so do I. Enough of that. Now, what's your battery level?"

"Thirty-nine percent left."

"I've got thirty-seven. With the spare packs we might be okay."

It was chilly, though the rock outcropping blocked the wind. Uzi zipped his black light-absorbing leather flight jacket and checked his watch.

"Right on time."

Benny was already at work setting up the drones. He coughed into his elbow, then reached into his tactical pants and pulled out the bottle of Tessalon capsules.

"You're taking too many of those," Uzi said.

"Can't give away our position. Besides, what's it gonna do, kill me?"

Uzi frowned. *Can't argue with that.* He picked up the controller and helped Benny complete the start-up sequence.

"What do you know, it works," Uzi said, eyeing a confirmatory green light on the remote. "Let's do this. Shift change starts in eight minutes and that's how long it'll take you to get to the back door."

Benny slung the backpack holding the drones over his shoulders, then picked up the canvas pack holding the BluMesh transponders. Both were exceptionally light. He started to take a step—and almost fell over. "Fuck."

Uzi grabbed his arm and steadied him. "I know the plan was for both of us to go in, set the nodes, and lay down the mesh network for the Minions to use. But it makes more sense for me to go. No reason to risk both of us."

"Not happening," Benny said. "Something goes wrong, how are you gonna get out?"

"I'll find a way."

Benny chuckled and gave Uzi's shoulder a nudge. He sat down on a boulder, a flicker of light picking up his eyes. "I'll go. Shit goes bad, I'll find a way out. Or I won't."

Uzi studied Benny's face. That's when he realized that Benny was not planning on making it out. And his friend seemed okay with that.

Uzi knew precious seconds were passing. "We go in together."

"I know you realize this is probably a one-way mission," Benny said. "I'm the logical one to go."

"I've been on one-way missions before."

Benny hardened his brow. "I'm serious, Uzi."

"So am I. Two of us go in, it increases the odds that one of us can get my girl out of there."

Benny shook his head. "Think about it a minute. Be sure this is what you want to do. It's as tough a choice as you're ever gonna have in life."

"There's a good chance my daughter's three hundred yards away," Uzi said, picking up the canvas bag. "There's nothing to think about. Let's go."

76

JAFFA, ISRAEL

Hector DeSantos chose a dark road somewhere in Jaffa and pulled over to peruse his assembled equipment. Considering the circumstances, he felt fairly well set for close quarters combat.

Problem was, when going solo against multiple tangos, he preferred to pick them off one at a time from a distance.

Despite all the planning Tier One operators completed before going wheels up—*if* they had the luxury of advance notice—things often did not go as they had trained and drilled.

Invariably, one of the targets did something unexpected; a rifle jammed; a car alarm went off at the wrong moment; or more tangos appeared on scene than your intel had indicated.

So you relied on your knowledge, experience, and muscle memory. You did the job with what you had. If you were lucky, your team came out in one piece.

Except that there was no team here. It was him against . . . well, he had no idea how many operators E Squadron had sent. Had they requested reinforcements? That would be increasing their risk quotient, and their egos and confidence likely told them they had what was needed to get the job done.

Based on what he had heard and seen, DeSantos believed they had at least four agents. Not just agents . . . highly skilled assassins.

He did not stop to consider his odds of surviving this. But that did not mean he was unaware of what he was walking into. He thought of calling his wife and telling her that he loved her. Maggie would not ask why; she would know.

But even with burner SIMs he could not risk turning on his phone. Given the extraordinary capabilities of MI6, he did not want to take the chance of being located. Instead, he closed his eyes and sent Maggie a message from his heart. It was corny, but there was little else he could do. If he was killed, his body would never be found, so writing her a letter was a waste of vital time.

His kit assembled and organized, he started the engine and headed for the address he had memorized before setting off from the Golan and powering down his cell.

He parked a few blocks away, slung the backpack over his shoulder, and started off for the building.

77

OPSIG SAFE HOUSE
CHEVY CHASE, MARYLAND

A blindfolded, hooded, and handcuffed Vance Nunn was transferred to three different unmarked and covertly registered vehicles in seven minutes.

They were pulling up to the OPSIG safe house, confident they had not been followed by land or by air.

Dozens of roads and bridges out of the district were closed, actions that took nine minutes to put in force . . . an impressive feat, but too late to prevent the president from being whisked out of DC.

Vail knew that if federal and local law enforcement could confine their search to the district, they had a chance of finding him. Of course, the city itself was large enough, with hundreds of thousands of apartments, townhouses, and condominiums, plus tens of thousands more businesses, commercial buildings, and single-family homes.

Finding the country's chief executive would be akin to finding that needle in a haystack—but if he left the confines of Washington, it would be an exponentially more difficult task.

While being driven and moved between cars, Nunn was treated with oxygen and cold compresses on his eyes, but not out of compassion or concern for his health.

They needed him capable of thinking clearly and answering questions.

334 ALAN JACOBSON

Once inside the safe house, they pulled him down the basement stairs into another SCIF.

Vail, who had arrived minutes before Nunn and his "security team," pushed the president down into a seat.

Vance Nunn waited, his head darting left and right. He was seated in a hard chair. There were others in the room, he could tell that much. Footsteps around and behind him.

But no one spoke.

"Please—I have claustrophobia. Take off the hood."

A minute passed. Then two.

"I'm the fucking president of the United States! I demand to know what's going on."

Someone grabbed him under the arm and lifted him up. "Let's go."

"Where?"

They shoved him into another room and he lost his balance, tripped, and went down face-first. His nose struck the hard floor. "Please . . ." he said weakly. "Just tell me what you want."

Two people lifted him up and led him to a chair. He tasted blood as it dripped onto his upper lip.

Someone pulled off his hood.

Cold air snaked around his white-collared dress shirt. A dark-skinned man wearing sunglasses stood across from him, in front of two-way glass. He said something in a foreign language, one Nunn had learned years ago, though he was far from fluent.

"My Farsi is poor," Nunn said, confusion turning to fear. "Talk to me in English."

"English," the man said with an accent. "My name is Reza Soroush. President Esfahani is not pleased with you."

Nunn leaned back in the seat. "What—what are you talking about?"

"I'm talking about you've been slow-walking actions that you were well compensated for. Legislation you *guaranteed* that Congress would pass."

"No. No. I can't control Congress."

"And yet," Soroush said, "you told us you could."

DIE TRYING 335

"I—I, yes, years ago we told you that if we could make sure certain senators and congressmen were elected, we would have the numbers to pass the laws we—"

"And the executive orders you promised us?"

"I signed *seventeen* EOs to help our group. Seventeen! And Iran? You got a windfall from my direct intervention in the negotiations. You don't think *that* carried risk?"

"Really. That's not what President Esfa—"

"Oh come on." Nunn felt his blood pressure rising. "That nuclear deal was bullshit. It was so one-sided I had to have one of my PACs retain a PR firm to flood social media with misinformation just to convince voters it was to America's benefit. *My own party* couldn't believe the terms we were giving you.

"And I released a hundred billion in sanction money. Just for returning to the table on a deal that was expiring in two years. Do you know how much heat I took for that? What more do you people want?"

"You were paid extremely well for all of that, were you not?"

"It's all part of—"

"Don't forget you agreed to IAEA inspections," Soroush said. "That wasn't part of our agreement."

"Jesus Christ." Nunn shook his head. "Of *certain* nuclear facilities. And *you* got to choose when the inspections would take place! The military installations, those would never be inspected. You should be *thanking* me, not handcuffing me."

"You also did not follow through on other matters that—"

"Name one!" Nunn's face flushed. "One."

"You didn't cut off military funding for Israel. And you didn't move your embassy out of Jerusalem."

Nunn's eyes narrowed. He clenched his jaw. "As I told President Esfahani, the president has enormous power, but you've got to be patient. We've got the votes. In both chambers. As I've explained—more than once—this is a long game we're playing here. If we do too much too soon—"

"Not good enough," Soroush said. "The consortium wants you removed. And our money returned."

"Returned?" Nunn hung his head. He laughed sardonically. And then he took a deep breath to maintain control. "Please. Let me speak with President Esfahani."

Soroush grinned broadly. "That *is* why we're here tonight. You're going to be flown to a black site in Siberia to be . . . well, let's just say, questioned by both the FSB and our Ministry of Intelligence and Security. Then President Esfahani will talk with you."

"Siberia?" Nunn yanked on his handcuffs, but they were securely fastened. "Are you people craz—"

"In the meantime, with you missing, your government will have no choice but to have the vice president take over. Twenty-fifth Amendment, I believe, if I read your laws correctly."

"You can't do this."

"Maybe *he* will follow the consortium's mandate."

"This is insane."

"Once proof of your death is sent to the CIA, it will be made official."

"My death?"

"It can be faked—or it can be real. *You* will determine that, Mr. Nunn." Nunn closed his eyes. "I don't—I don't understand. I've done everything we agreed to."

Soroush rose from his chair. "We're going to debrief you. You tell us what we want to know, your death will be faked, and you'll be permitted to live in any of eleven partner countries. You refuse to cooperate and . . . well, Plan B. You will be killed, and your death won't need to be faked for the Americans." He spread his arms. "You understand *that*?"

Nunn again struggled against the restraints. "That wasn't our agreement."

Soroush leaned in close and bent forward to Nunn's level. The sunglasses made it unnerving, as Nunn could not see the man's eyes. "We don't care what you think."

"I'm the fucking president of the United States!"

"Not anymore." Soroush straightened up. "I believe you call this term limits."

"We call this *abduction*. Holding someone against his will."

DIE TRYING 337

"Humor me," Soroush said, slowly walking behind Nunn's chair. "How did *you* interpret our agreement? If you're persuasive, maybe I can convince President Esfahani to reconsider. A . . . misinterpretation."

"We both know what the agreement is. There's no misinterpretation."

"Then there's nothing to discuss. You haven't held up your end of the deal." He turned and walked toward the door.

Nunn groaned. "Working with the president of the United States, who's built a powerful operation to further our mission, is not enough for you?"

Soroush stopped. "You don't seem to have much of an operation. We've paid you extremely well. You could've used that money to bolster your influence."

"My influence?"

"Yes, your influence. We've seen how easily Congress can upend your plans. You need a *team* to execute what we want accomplished. Dozens of people across the government."

"I've *got* dozens of people. Strategically placed across the government, from the State Department to the Justice Department to the Agency. There isn't a single institution important to our goals that doesn't have at least one of our people in a position of influence. And they're all working toward our goals. Ask President Jao. President Pervak. *They* are very pleased with what we've done. Doesn't President Esfahani talk with them?"

"Give me the names of the people on your team and I will confer with President Esfahani."

Nunn stomped his right foot. "I don't have to disclose anything to you. *Actions* matter. Actions!"

"Give me names or we'll begin our journey to Siberia."

"You won't get out of the United States."

Soroush laughed wryly. "We kidnapped the US president from his motorcade. You don't think we can get you out of the country?" He shook his head in disgust. "You *are* an idiot." Soroush again started for the door.

"Hold it," Nunn said. He ground his molars. Closed his eyes. "If I give you their names, you won't contact these people. I am the sole—"

338 ALAN JACOBSON

"You, sir, are not in a position to negotiate. But . . ." He paused, his eyes roaming Nunn's face. "You have my word. Now. Let's start with Vice President Andrews."

Nunn sighed deeply. "Part of my inner circle." Shook his head. "And his chief of staff, Russell Card, and mine, Mack Stanos."

"What about Secretary of State Adelsohn?"

"No."

"You're sure."

Nunn frowned. "I've known Adelsohn since he was a senator, chair of the Committee on Foreign Relations. Definitely not one of us. I wanted to appoint one of our people, but no one had Adelsohn's experience. If I'd chosen someone who had no business conducting our foreign affairs, that would've been a red flag. And Adelsohn hasn't given us any problems." He read Soroush's face: the man appeared to accept that explanation.

"What about judges?"

Nunn cleared his throat. "Supreme Court Justice Watkins. Another two justices vote the way we want, but they're not part of Scorpion."

"Then how do you get them to vote with us?"

"Undisclosed favors. Two weeks on a superyacht with some *very* attractive women. No wives. No questions asked. No cameras, no cell phones, no tracking, no accountability. A highly effective way to a middle-aged judge's heart is through his pecker."

"We're talking about Tomas Claremont and Allen Samueli?" He nodded, self-satisfied. "They do what I ask."

"I approve of this strategy," Soroush said. "Who else?"

"Isn't that enough?"

"Who. Else."

Nunn sighed. "About a dozen federal judges." He proceeded to list them. "And sixteen senators and eleven congressmen." Nunn rattled them off. "And another thirteen who, like the Supreme Court justices, are supporters of ours."

"The same superyacht treatment?"

"As I said. Highly effective."

"Who are these supporters?"

DIE TRYING 339

Nunn canted his eyes toward the ceiling. "Off the top of my head, Caesar, Hood, Jackson, Cortes, Green, Lee, and, uh . . . Bragg." He shook his head. "Several more. Does it really matter?"

"Anyone in the FBI?"

"No."

"You said you've got someone at the CIA."

"Deputy director for plans. George Pickett."

"NSA?"

"Very difficult to recruit and extremely risky."

"Department of Defense?"

"A senior officer from each branch of the military."

"The US military is humongous. That's the best you could do?"

Nunn laughed—then realized Soroush was serious. He licked his lips, which felt dry enough to split open.

"While we're discussing the military, what was the point of seizing the data on OPSIG, the Operations Support Intelligence Group? Very risky."

"Can I get some water?"

"Answer my question. That stunt could've exposed us."

"It wasn't a stunt. They were investigating us, getting too close. They . . ." He turned away. "They knew things we didn't want them to know."

"I hope you're shutting this group down."

"That is the plan."

"When?"

"Soon as possible."

"What does the OPSIG data show? How much do they know about us?"

Nunn's left eye narrowed, the lid twitching. "It's encrypted. It's taking time to break. In the meantime, we're taking steps to eliminate the threat."

"And if you can't?"

Nunn had thought about this after the meeting with Andrews, Stanos, and Card. "If they expose Scorpion—and have actual proof?" He clenched his jaw. "We would discredit their evidence. Refute it. Deny, deny, deny. Classify it as planted disinformation."

"And if diversions and lies don't deter prosecutors?"

"We'll rely on our judges. And our team inside the Department of Justice."

"What if *they're* identified and arrested?"

Nunn's gaze found the floor. "Worst-case scenario? And OPSIG unearths solid proof?" He cleared his throat. "Prison. Sanctions. I'm not going to lie. It'd be very bad. But that's never going to happen."

Soroush spat something in Farsi, then turned and kicked a chair, sending it flying into the wall. He pointed at Nunn. "This is *your* fault. This alliance was a tremendous mistake." He headed for the door.

"You forget I handed Scorpion the detailed blueprints and engineering diagrams to our sixth-generation fighter." Nunn snorted. "Do you not understand the unparalleled value that affords you? The United States will no longer hold sway over world affairs. Israel—Israel will no longer have a qualitative military advantage over you. You could attack at will—and as commander in chief, I'll make sure the US does not respond."

Soroush snorted. "And if you and Andrews are in prison?"

"Those blueprints aren't going away. And China and Russia, hell even *your country* can now build sensors capable of reading their stealth signatures." Nunn leaned forward—as far as the restraints permitted. "Don't you see?"

"I do. We all do. Because I've made a recording of everything you've said, the very compelling case you've made. So others can see, too."

"Great," Nunn said, tugging on his handcuffs. "Show President Esfahani. Meantime, get these things off and bring me back to that fundraiser. I have a speech to deliver, money to raise. And I'll need a cover story as to what happ—"

"I don't think you have to worry about that."

Nunn harrumphed. "You kidnapped me from my motorcade, Mr. Soroush."

The mirror in front of him went clear. Nunn felt blood drain from his face and his skin turned chalk white.

78

Standing behind a two-way window in an adjacent viewing room was FBI Director Douglas Knox, Attorney General Winston Coulter, the assistant attorney general in charge of the Justice Department's criminal division, and the chairman of the Joint Chiefs of Staff.

Douglas Knox glanced to his left, where Karen Vail was seated at a computer monitor, observing the video recording they were making of the interrogation—conducted by Mahmoud el-Fahad, a.k.a. Reza Soroush.

"Did you get it?" Coulter asked Vail.

"I did, sir. Uploading now to the cloud. I'm still recording."

"Winston," Knox said, "do we have enough?"

Coulter lifted his brow in thought. "Enough for *what*? The court of public opinion? If this were released online, in today's environment, what would happen?"

"Nunn and his people would claim deep fake," Vail said. "That it wasn't him."

Coulter nodded. "Or that he was manipulated into saying these things. Regardless, even if we had a legal basis for introducing this into a court of law—which we don't—with dozens of Nunn's judges on the bench, to say nothing of the Supreme Court justices in their pocket, the legal arena is corrupt. Completely unreliable as a purveyor of justice."

Knox frowned and nodded.

"The framers of the Constitution never envisioned such a scenario," the assistant attorney general said.

"There's no way forward," Coulter said. "No blueprint as to how to fix this mess. There's zero guarantee that if we go the legal route, Nunn, Andrews, Aswad, and their dozens of conspirators would meet justice. Zero."

"I demand to be released," Nunn said, his gaze moving among the people facing him.

Knox snorted and turned to Vail. "Keep it rolling."

"I am, sir."

Knox left the observation room and walked up to the president's left side. "Vance Earnest Nunn, you are under arrest for conspiracy to defraud the United States of America. By sending sensitive military information to an intelligence officer employed by a hostile foreign state, you betrayed your sacred oath to protect our country and uphold the Constitut—"

"This is—it's absurd," Nunn shouted.

"Is it?" Knox nodded at the observation glass and someone turned on a light inside the room, illuminating the officials inside. They stared back at Nunn. "Mr. Nunn, would you like me to play the confession back for you?"

"No. Wait." He looked at Knox, then at the window. "I want an attorney. I'm not saying another word."

Knox and Coulter shared a look through the glass, then laughed.

Knox signaled to Vail, who stopped the recording. She walked into the room and stood beside Knox.

"I demand to be released," Nunn said. "I've done nothing wrong. But all of *you* have committed an egregious act."

Vail harrumphed. "What we *have* done is grown tired of your high and mighty bullshit, your lies, and treason." She replaced the hood, tightened his handcuffs, and led him out of the room.

79

MOUNT HERMON, SYRIA
ASR SAYY PRISON

Uzi and Benny made their way into the rear entrance to the prison. Whoever built it had expended considerable resources blasting the rock and then boring out spacious rooms and hallways. The walls, while rough-hewn, were of uniform height and width. This required more than moving dirt and trucking in concrete for a subterranean drug or terrorist tunnel.

Uzi was now concerned that the BluMesh system might not do the job. And if it did not work—or failed partway through—they would be turning over sensitive Israeli drone technology to an enemy state. In the wrong hands—such as a regime that used chemical weapons on its own people—that technology could have disastrous consequences.

As they hid in an alcove, Benny leaned close to Uzi's ear. "I think we're worried about the same thing."

"How do you know what I'm thinking?"

"I see it on your face. I may not have seen you for several years, but I've known you a lot longer."

"What do you think?"

"I think we're *here* and—like you said, so is Maya."

Uzi took a deep breath of frigid air and blew it out his lips. Twice. Three times. He thought of his daughter. He thought of his

344 ALAN JACOBSON

responsibility to do right by the United States. And by Israel. "You think we can pull this off?"

Benny nodded. "We'll make it work."

Uzi appreciated the show of confidence, even if he did not completely believe him.

They zipped up their flight jackets and decided to take the direct approach: it was daring and aggressive, but no one would believe that two guys would enter a secure facility and, in plain sight, attempt to do something nefarious.

And yet that's what they were going to do. "Can you walk?"

Benny snorted. "As long as I can grab your arm if I get dizzy."

"Do what you need to do. Ready?"

They moved out into a long corridor. To their left, a cell block. Was Maya there? They went right, which was the direction they needed to go, toward the main entrance and the concentration of guards and other security personnel.

Benny slung the canvas bag over his shoulder and removed one of the nodes.

Uzi pressed the power button and got the confirmatory green flashing light. "This starts our timer."

"Place it."

Uzi stuck it to a metal bar and paced off ten feet. He took another device from Benny and positioned it. "Done."

They continued on, repeating the process, and encountered two guards. One ignored them while the other watched, saw no threat, and walked on.

He and Benny moved purposefully, repeating the process, getting closer to the security desk.

"Hey!"

The shout came in Arabic, from behind them. "What are you two doing?"

Uzi turned and replied in the guard's native language. "Trying to get you guys internet service in here."

"Are you crazy? Inside a mountain?"

Uzi held up one of the tiny nodes. "New tech. Wait till you see what it can do. My uncle used this in a bunker in the Council of Ministers building in Damascus." Uzi snapped his fingers. "Now he's got five hundred megabits per second. Not bad."

The guard pursed his lips and lifted his brow, then nodded. "Good, good." He turned and walked on.

"Jesus," Uzi said under his breath.

"We lost a minute there."

Uzi picked up the pace and felt Benny grab his right arm.

"Sorry."

"It's okay, buddy. We're good."

They kept moving, placing the nodes, until they reached the front. Uzi took the lead this time, not waiting for one of the guards to interrogate him.

He held up one of the devices and said, "Internet by tomorrow! New technology."

Several of the men groaned, a few shouted something, and a couple waved it off—either they did not believe it or they did not care.

Uzi and Benny reached the front entrance and stopped in a blind alcove off to the right. Uzi pulled off his backpack and started turning on the drones. "How much time do we have left?" he whispered.

"Two minutes, eleven seconds."

"Start setting them out as I power them up."

Benny knelt down carefully, holding onto the wall as he lowered himself, then went about placing the drones a few inches apart.

"We're down to a minute thirty," Benny said. "We need to launch them now or there won't be enough time."

Uzi ground his molars. "Hope it's enough." He stood up and activated the remote. The plastic micro drone rotors spun up and began making the sound of a swarm of bees: a medium-pitched buzz.

And off the Minions went, around the corner and into the main corridor of the prison. Within seconds Uzi heard shouting, screaming, guns firing—and quiet.

An alarm sounded.

"Shit. Didn't plan on that."

"We should've," Benny said.

"We should've. How long you think we've got?"

"Alarm at a prison? Not long. But we're in the foothills. It'll take a few minutes."

"Only a few minutes?" Uzi's voice rose with anxiety. "Then I'm not waiting."

He swung around into the main corridor and stopped—surprised by what he saw. Bodies strewn across the floor, blood pooling from their heads.

There were no living guards that he could see, so he continued toward the cell block. The Minions were flying past him now, heading toward the exit en masse. Returning to base as programmed.

Now all he had to do was find Maya. If she was here.

If she was truly still alive.

80

JAFFA, ISRAEL

Hector DeSantos approached the location where Tamar Gur was reportedly being held. The E Squadron operatives had not ambushed him yet—if that was their plan.

He climbed to the roof of an adjacent building, using exterior drainpipes, brick facing ledges, and windows to make it to the top. He was a few stories short of being able to jump to the edifice where Tamar was captive—which did not have the same handholds and protrusions.

Instead, he traversed the gap using rope and a grappling hook, entering the third floor through an unlocked window. As he pulled himself in, he wondered if Lackwood and his buddies had purposely left it open.

Apparently not, since he still had not encountered any resistance.

Footsteps.

DeSantos reached into the backpack and pulled out the picture wire, which he had attached to the handles of collapsed telescoping hiking poles.

He pressed his back against the wall behind the door and waited. The knob jiggled and a man walked in, Walther PPK in hand. He saw the open window and stopped.

DeSantos pounced, swinging the wire over the man's head and wrapping it around the front of his neck.

348   ALAN JACOBSON

The agent was a couple inches shorter than DeSantos, but he was wiry and fit and wriggled his body left to right before bringing up the pistol and trying to aim it at his attacker's head.

DeSantos swung the man hard into the adjacent wall, crunching his shoulder and arm. The handgun clanked to the floor.

He leaned back with all his body weight while crossing the handles behind the assassin's neck and activating his biceps, delts, traps, rhomboids—along with every accessory muscle he could muster.

This soldier was a member of E Squadron, however—the elite of the elite—so he was not succumbing without a fight. He jammed his heel into the top of DeSantos's boots.

DeSantos preferred wearing his Keens for their all-weather hikability profile. But the steel reinforced toe feature just vaulted to the top of his list.

The operator brought his hands up to slam DeSantos's ears, his head, anything within reach—but his blows lacked strength and any oblique impact only scratched and gouged his cheeks and forehead.

After further gyrations and attempts to counterattack—including a feeble attempt to grab DeSantos's scrotum—the man's movements slowed, his brain drained of oxygen.

Finally he went limp. DeSantos lowered his adversary to the floor, picked up the Walther, then found a boot knife, a Sheffield commando dagger, a GPS-enabled watch, and a comms device.

Seconds later, DeSantos moved the dead body behind a nearby desk. It was not Lackwood or McGill—and, not surprisingly, the assassin had no identification.

DeSantos glanced around. In the predawn light he could see that it was an office building of some kind. Of course, he had no idea where Tamar was being held—though he surmised it was on the top floor, as that would likely be safest, farthest from where someone would enter the building.

He waited by the door and listened. Hearing nothing, he ventured out and tiptoed up the steps. He exited the stairwell—and was immediately engaged by another of Lackwood and McGill's team.

Damn lawyers.

DIE TRYING   349

The man pulled out a knife—and DeSantos raised the pistol he had just taken off the other sod. He waited a second for the guy to lunge at him—and then shot him twice. Once in the chest and once in the head.

DeSantos fancied the knife—a tactical job with a nasty serrated blade and a carved wood handle—so he took it.

Problem was, the gunshot not only served as an alarm to the others that he was now there, but it gave away his location—although the body, which was weeping red fluid at an alarming rate, did a pretty good job of that.

The jury will disregard those gunshots. And the bloody corpse.

He pulled out a pack of fireworks, then lit the fuses with a plasma lighter and tossed the burning packet down the stairwell toward the bottom floor. They started crackling around the second landing—prompting someone to start shooting at the phantom explosions.

DeSantos saw the muzzle flash off to the right, so he knew there was at least one operator down there.

He went up instead, as quietly as possible. And it was there that he found Tamar, gagged and bound to a chair. He watched her eyes for a signal as to whether a captor was nearby. She nodded at him to approach.

He sliced away her bindings with his fancy new blade.

"Oh my god, Hector. Am I glad to see you."

"I get that from my wife whenever she's horny. Which is quite often."

"Happy for you. Let's get out of here."

"How many did you see?"

"Eight."

"Are you screwing with me?"

"I'm not. Sorry."

"I took out two, so that leaves six."

"You've got exceptional math skills."

"My wife says the same th—"

"Hector, no offense, but shut up."

He nodded. "Maggie says that, too." He handed Tamar the Sheffield Commando blade and the .22 pistol he had brought with him.

"A *.22*? Nice toy."

"Someone hands you a gift, you shouldn't complain."

"Let's go. Help me up."

"Go? Shouldn't we have a plan?"

Tamar stopped. "You're right. What's the plan?"

"How the hell should I know? I just got here and saved your ass. The plan's your responsibility."

She shrugged. "I'll pretend I'm still tied up. I'll scream. You hide behind the door. Shoot them after they come in."

"Very original."

"You got anything better?"

DeSantos frowned. "Nope. Let's do it."

But before she could move, the door burst open.

81

MOUNT HERMON, SYRIA
ASR SAYY PRISON

Uzi and Benny made their way around still corpses to the opening of the cell block—to which one of the guards graciously provided the keys. Of course, he was in no position to withhold them.

Uzi unlocked the gate—and found himself staring at dozens of women of various ages, all held in a large room. To their right was another, similar-sized chamber crammed with men. The lights everywhere were blinking on/off/on/off, giving Uzi a headache.

"Now what?" Benny asked over the din of the alarm bells. "We don't have much time."

Uzi's eyes roamed the sea of orange jump-suited female prisoners. And then he did the only thing he could think of. He yelled her Hebrew name, then said, in English, "I'm looking for my daughter, Maya Uziel." He repeated it in Arabic.

A head near the back popped up. But she did not say anything. They locked gazes. "Maya?"

She did not respond.

"I think it's her," Benny said.

"If it's her, why isn't she saying anything?"

"Boychick, she was three last time you saw her. And she's been through hell. She's probably in shock. Or maybe she hasn't heard her name since Dena died."

352   ALAN JACOBSON

Uzi moved to the rear of the room, stepping on gray blankets and tripping on discarded underwear and sanitary pads. Many others shied away as he approached, except the one girl who was staring at him, watching him in the flashing light as he made his way toward her.

He stopped several feet away and whispered. "Maya?" She was thinner and shorter than he expected . . . but her health and nutrition were surely the bare minimum most of her life.

Uzi stepped closer and saw the thin scar beneath her right eye where their puppy had accidentally clawed her. "Oh my god." He swung around to Benny. "It's her! Benny, it's her."

He bent forward and lifted her up, hugged her tightly, and heard her whisper something near his ear. In Arabic: "Help me."

Uzi started sobbing, his body shuddering, tears dripping on his daughter's neck. He leaned back and looked in her eyes, which were searching his face, lacking affect.

"Let's get you out of here." He carried her through the room and joined Benny.

Benny gently stroked her face with an index finger, and without taking his eyes off her, said to Uzi, "Police on the way."

They left the gate open in case any of the women chose to leave, and started walking rapidly, Uzi carrying Maya and Benny holding a fistful of Uzi's jacket sleeve for balance.

Suddenly the alarm stopped.

"Thank God," Uzi said. "That was *really* getting to me."

"This is not good, boychick. Someone turned it off. Which means that—"

"We're not alone."

As they made their way around the deceased guards, they heard rapid footsteps behind them.

They started jogging, Uzi holding Maya against his torso, his left hand securing her head and neck.

They made the front gate and hit a button to open it. A klaxon sounded.

Shouting. Voices. Approaching from behind.

I didn't come all this way to find my daughter—only for the reunion to last three minutes.

DIE TRYING 353

They made it out of the mountain fortress and had run about fifty yards when gunfire rang out. Uzi pulled Benny behind an outcropping—and realized he was supporting all of Benny's weight.

"I'm hit," Benny said, leaning his back against the rock face. He looked down. His chest was bleeding, and an abdominal wound was rapidly pumping out red fluid. "Get . . . Maya to . . . safety."

"No."

"Uzi. This is . . . the end for me . . ." His respiratory rate increased. "Better to go out like this. Thanks for . . . making the . . . last week of my . . . life . . . an adventure."

Uzi wiped away tears as rounds exploded against the side of the large, bitter cold boulder. He winced and ducked, ensuring Maya was safely behind cover.

"I love you, bro."

Benny licked his dry lips, then winced. "Your .22."

Uzi dug it out of his pocket with his left hand while supporting Maya with his right. She clung to his neck.

Benny took the pistol and gestured with his chin. "Go." He reached over his right shoulder and fired off two rounds. They were not on target, but that was not the purpose. He swung back toward Uzi. "Go!"

Uzi pulled Maya tight against his body and ran toward the next outcropping a hundred yards away, where the SkyPaks should be waiting for them.

82

JAFFA, ISRAEL

DeSantos dove left—but there was no cover. Nowhere for them to hide.

Gunfire erupted.

Fuck! Burning in DeSantos's right side. He was hit. It was immediately painful. *Another. Two.*

McGill had Tamar on her back at gunpoint. He looked at her askew legs and kicked her right knee with the tip of his Salomon boot.

"Let her go," DeSantos said. "She's an innocent. She's got kids."

Lackwood stepped toward DeSantos. He was not smiling. In that second, he wished he had risked calling Maggie.

"Lookie here, mate," Lackwood said to McGill, who was standing a few feet away. "We'll get to complete our mission after all."

"Never had any doubts."

Lackwood swung his Salomon into DeSantos's ribs—and he let out a grunt that said, "Damn, that hurts—but I'm not gonna let you know that."

"That was for me." Lackwood brought up a Beretta and aimed it at DeSantos's head. "And this is for MP Walpole."

The windows shattered and in swung several men in tactical gear. They landed and fired their semi-automatic rifles at Lackwood and McGill in one motion.

Judging by how the E Squadron specialists' bodies reacted when struck, the high-velocity weapons firing extreme kinetic energy bullets at close range left the operators incapacitated and very much dead.

More gunfire exploded.

In the distance, DeSantos heard frantic calls for a medic.

Like grains of sand falling through open fingers, consciousness began slipping away and he drifted into a deep sleep.

83

OPSIG SAFE HOUSE
CHEVY CHASE, MARYLAND

Karen Vail huddled in the SCIF dining room with Douglas Knox, Alex Rusakov, and Troy Rodman. Vance Nunn was being guarded in the basement by Dell Christie and Neil Frazier.

Rusakov pulled out a seat and sat down hard. "So what do we do with Nunn?"

Vail took the chair next to her. "We should leak the video of his confession. Scrub its metadata so it's untraceable. Upload it to a dark website and leak its URL to a news outlet. Tim can do that stuff in his sleep."

Knox began pacing the length of the room. "The Bureau will have to open an investigation. A task force, vetted to be sure there aren't any conspirators. Start from square one, completely kosher and by the book."

Vail found the cup with her name on it and took a sip of cold coffee. "The most expansive, and important, investigation we've ever conducted." Rusakov spread her hands on the tabletop. "Again. What about Nunn?"

"For now," Knox said, his fingers stroking his chin as he paced, "we keep him isolated. His knowledge of sensitive classified information makes him extremely dangerous. Any disclosure could cause irreparable harm to America and its intelligence agents. He's proven that he

DIE TRYING 357

can't be trusted with that data." Knox brushed back a lock of gray hair. "Director Tasset's on his way here to discuss."

Vail believed that conversation would lead to Nunn's transfer to a CIA rendition facility—also known as a black site—in another country where Nunn and Andrews would be questioned further to confirm the information Team Grey had obtained on the cloned phone . . . and to nail down who else Scorpion was working with in the United States and abroad.

There the men would likely live out their sentences—either an official one provided by a US federal court—or a much shorter one via a bullet to the back of the head, courtesy of an unnamed member of the Agency's special operations group.

Vail hung her head in thought.

There was no way Vance Nunn, Anthony Andrews, or any of their fellow conspirators would be permitted to escape justice on an idyllic tropical island because of legal loopholes, corrupt judges, or other unforeseen political dodges.

As fourth in line, Secretary of State Noah Adelsohn would be sworn in as president. Vail knew that the job of bringing justice to all the conspirators, known and as yet unknown, was going to be a messy task.

She felt a hand on her shoulder. It was Knox. "You have every right to be concerned, Agent Vail. But our country defeated the Confederacy in the Civil War. We can, and will, find a way to survive this, too."

She nodded. However it went down, she felt solace in knowing that she had helped the United States defeat the most toxic, insidious, and destructive challenge to its existence in its long, multifarious history.

84

MOUNT HERMON, SYRIA
ASR SAYY PRISON

Uzi and Maya arrived at the location where he and Benny had hidden the SkyPaks.

Behind them, gunfire. In front of them, darkness.

Beyond that lay the Israeli border and the IDF—which would likely interpret their advance, if detected, as an enemy infiltration.

He took Benny's SkyPak and explained to Maya in Arabic that he was going to attach something to her body that was going to allow her to fly. She looked at him like he was crazy.

And maybe he was.

Although he and Benny did not speak of mission failure—as if doing so would cause it to happen—they knew the odds of making it out of Asr Sayy alive were poor. Thus, the part of the rescue that took place after breaking Maya out of Asr Sayy was short on specifics: they would get her back—somehow.

Uzi had strapped most of the SkyPak to her arms and back when he began his explanation of how it was going to work. "You won't need to do anything, honey. Just relax and the flying machine will take you to safety. Okay?" He had no idea what she understood—or what mental state she was in. But it did not matter; this had to be done and they had very little time. He seated her helmet, then gave her a smile and a thumbs-up.

DIE TRYING 359

Uzi leaned Maya against the rockface to support the weight of the contraption, then hurriedly strapped on his own SkyPak and programmed the controller. He flipped the microphone switch and said, "I'm going to fly right alongside you, okay?"

She looked at her arms, then at her father.

"You're going to be fine. You're gonna fly like a bird. And I'll be talking to you just like I am now," he said, tapping his helmet. "This is gonna be really fun, like nothing you've *ever* done before."

He immediately realized how stupid that comment was—she had been imprisoned most of her life, her mother dead and her father . . . gone. What did she know about fun?

Maya blinked at him, indicating she had some idea of what he was saying. At least, he *hoped* that's what it meant.

Uzi programmed her SkyPak using the keypad on her left wrist. Autopilot was going to fly at a low and slow, radar-evading altitude. He placed the magnetic battery packs on both motors and hoped they would provide enough power for them to make it across the border.

Muffled gunfire behind him.

Shit. Gotta go. Breathe.

"Okay honey, the machine's gonna move your arms and legs. Don't fight it. Let it do what it needs to do, okay?" As he turned to Maya for acknowledgment, he heard an explosion.

He wanted to turn around but did not need to: Benny had held off the Syrians as long as he could and detonated one of the explosive devices they had brought with them to dispose of the SkyPaks if they had to be abandoned.

Benny killed himself—along with approaching pursuers—to buy Uzi and Maya time.

Uzi was not going to waste his friend's act of bravery; he pressed the button on Maya's wrist pad and a three-second countdown lit up on the small screen.

Uzi stepped clear and fingered the thruster button on his own pack and watched Maya rise off the ground.

Rounds kicked up dirt by his feet.

He worked his own controller and lifted off—then came up behind her. If the Syrian guards were going to hit either of them, he intended it to be him. The back of the SkyPak would absorb the bullets, but that "protective layer" was made of lithium-ion batteries—which had a nasty reputation of exploding.

He could not worry about that. He was focused on matching Maya's low altitude and slow speed, as autopilot was not designed to evade enemy fire.

Uzi and Maya were dark objects against an ink black sky, so once they made it another thirty seconds into the flight they should be in the clear until they were close enough to be picked up by the IDF.

Uzi turned to Maya: through the glass of the helmet, the slight instrumentation glow highlighted her features, which did not exhibit fright or fear. Her eyes were wide with wonder: pure joy, like riding a roller coaster for the first time.

He allowed himself a few moments of satisfaction. It had been many years since he was capable of giving his daughter something she enjoyed.

And it had been way too long since she had experienced anything so liberating as flying with the birds.

85

JAFFA, ISRAEL

Hector DeSantos awoke staring at the star-filled sky.

"He's awake!"

Tamar Gur placed a hand on DeSantos's right forearm. "Hey there. How are you?"

He looked at the IV needle protruding from his arm and the bag hanging from the metal support. "Rounds went through, missed major arteries and organs. Kind of a miracle. It's good being in the Holy Land. Someone was watching over me."

"Pain meds kick in?"

"Hell yes. Before they hooked up the IV, it was like the morning after I drank a six-pack but had none of the fun associated with it."

Tamar chuckled. "Thank you for coming to help me."

"You're very important to Uzi—which means you're very important to me. He wanted to come, but we were going in to rescue Maya from Asr Sayy."

"In *Syria*? You're joking."

"Wish I was."

"If you came *here*, what happened to Maya?"

"Benny Herzog went with Uzi. You know Benny?"

"He was the guy who set up my meet with you guys. Did they get Maya?"

"No idea."

"Mr. DeSantos."

They turned to see a squat man built like a tank. He was twenty feet away and approaching with a slight limp. Mossad's Gideon Aksel.

"Director General," Tamar said.

Aksel shook her hand. "Sounds like you two are out of harm's way."

DeSantos managed a weak grin. "We are."

"I know you don't particularly like me, Mr. DeSantos. But Uzi and I have a complex relationship. In many ways, he's like a son to me. A very rebellious son."

DeSantos felt his eyes widen, surprise that could not be suppressed.

Aksel pointed a stubby index finger at his face, and then Tamar's. "Don't tell him I said that. It'll go to his head."

DeSantos and Tamar chuckled knowingly.

"How'd you know we were here?" Tamar asked.

"After Uzi told me that E Squadron operatives were in-country, we located their men and have been keeping an eye on their movements. I figured they were black—and probably doing something we didn't want done."

"But how'd you know that Tamar was kidnapped?"

Aksel gave DeSantos a sideways glance. "Uzi called me. You didn't know?"

DeSantos tried to shift his torso on the gurney—and winced. "No."

"I asked the IDF to dispatch its counterterrorist commando unit. They were coming back from another op about thirty minutes south of here. They're trained to take on complex missions with little to no preparation. Even undercover ops disguised as civilians."

"Impressive," DeSantos said.

Aksel pursed his lips. "Same could be said about you."

DeSantos waved off the compliment. "Please thank them for the help. Impeccable timing. A minute later, the fat lady would've been belting out the coda."

"That commando unit is one of those need-to-know pieces of information. The IDF prefers to deny it exists. Let's keep it that way."

"Good thing E Squadron didn't know they were on their way." DeSantos grinned—but immediately winced as pain sliced through his side.

"We've gotta transport," a paramedic said, approaching the gurney.

DIE TRYING   363

"They never should've attempted this op on Israeli soil," Aksel said. "But that's something our foreign minister will be taking up with Downing Street."

Aksel was speaking English, but DeSantos mentally translated that to: *Israeli shit's gonna hit the British fan.*

"Thank you, Director General, for having my back."

Aksel held out a hand, stopping the medic from pushing the gurney away. "One second," he said in Hebrew. Back to DeSantos: "I've got a request."

"What's that?"

"You and Uzi. Out of my country before something happens I can't fix."

"Soon as the docs say I'm good to go, we're outa here."

"Very good." Aksel patted DeSantos's forearm. "You two find what you were looking for?"

Tamar chuckled—and waited for DeSantos's response.

"I think so," DeSantos said. "I hope so. Time will tell."

86

SYRIA-ISRAEL BORDER

As Uzi and Maya approached the Golan Heights, he could see the watchtowers and their large telescopes. But nothing was trained on them—at least nothing he could see in the darkness.

He only hoped that blindness worked both ways. It was not something he would want to bet his life on.

And yet that's precisely what he was doing.

Uzi glanced at the IDF's overwatch atop Mount Bental. Although sunrise was still an hour away and they were flying too low for radar, he was sure the army's scopes were trained on them.

But no alarms sounded. No shooting erupted.

Maya was clearly unaware of the drama playing out in her father's head. She was taking it all in, looking left and right, up and down. Her arms and legs were moving to the onboard computer as it controlled the thrusters, her altitude, rate of travel, and descent.

Moments later, they had crossed the border and were approaching the kibbutz where Uzi had met Benny's friend, Ilan. Uzi watched as Maya's SkyPak hovered ten feet above the parking lot, then lowered slowly to the ground.

Uzi landed beside her and supported her body while he removed the devices strapped to her arms and legs. She was still dressed in orange prison rags.

Maya did not speak but looked at her father's face as he worked.

After setting her torso unit on the ground, he unfastened his own SkyPak and set it, and his helmet, on the ground. As he stood up, he saw Ilan walking toward them.

"Yo! Where's Benny?"

Uzi shook his head.

Ilan's shoulders slumped and he nodded knowingly. As he approached, he turned his attention to Maya. "So this is the famous young woman all the fuss is about."

"I'm not sure she speaks Hebrew. Or English."

Ilan shook Uzi's hand. "It's good to have you two back in one piece."

Uzi laughed. "I was worried the IDF would think we were enemy infiltrators and fire on us. Surprised they didn't."

"I used to man that post, many years ago. But I still know some people. After you took off, I told my friend, who radioed the outpost. The army was alerted." Ilan laughed. "You really think you would've made it back into Israel alive without clearance?"

All Uzi could do was shake his head. They were here and they were safe. He turned to Maya and gave her a big hug. "I've missed you so much. Sorry it took me so long to find you."

87

ALEXANDRIA, VIRGINIA

The phone rang but Karen Vail was in the midst of a bad dream. She heard it in the distance but incorporated it into the events of her REM adventure.

The second time her handset chimed, Robby moaned and shook her shoulder.

"What," she groaned.

"Phone. Betting on Uzi or Hector."

"Not taking that bet." Eyes still closed, she blindly felt for the device, found it, and answered the WhatsApp call. "Vail."

"Hey. It's Uzi. Sorry to call in the middle of the night."

"Interrupted a bad dream. What's up? Where are you?"

"Israel. But great news—we found Maya and she's safe. We're at a friend's kibbutz. Santa had to deal with something else. Something dangerous. Waiting for word."

Vail sat up and unplugged the phone, then headed into the kitchen so she would not disturb Robby. "That's *fantastic* news. I'm so happy. For both of you. How is she? Where'd you find her?"

"She's been in a Syrian prison for years. And that's why I called. She's withdrawn. Hasn't said much. What do I do for her?"

"Let's state the obvious, okay? I'm not only *not* a practicing psychologist but I haven't even talked with Maya. Big picture? A range of emotions are possible. Impaired memory, disorientation, poor concentration, confusion, flashbacks, even a fear of being kidnapped again. She may be very clingy, hoping that you'll protect her from being taken again. You're her safe place."

"You got that right."

"If she's got PTSD, smells and images could be triggering events. She could have problems sleeping. Anxiety is likely. She might feel helpless. Hopeless. Numb."

"Depression."

"She may even feel guilty because she was rescued. But aside from the emotional and mental health issues, she could have physical problems. Malnutrition. Parasitic or viral infections. I know you don't want to hear this, but we don't know what she's been subjected to. Social isolation, disease. And yeah, physical and sexual abuse."

And losing her mother.

"Am I overwhelming you?"

"A bit."

"Look, people who've been in captivity are taken to medical centers for assessment and treatment *before* dealing with the emotional effects of the trauma. Honestly, you can't be in a better place for managing children and adults with trauma."

"We've got an appointment tomorrow with the Tel Aviv Center for Trauma Intervention. And I'm taking her over to the ER as soon as we're done talking."

"Good. Meantime, most of all, love her. Make her feel safe. Be understanding. *Lots* of patience. Encourage her to express her feelings. Let her know it's okay to feel scared or confused. Or angry."

"Okay."

"We're very resilient beings and she's got you. It's going to take time, probably a lot. *Years*, not months."

"Figured."

"If she hasn't attended school, she probably only knows Arabic— and even just words and phrases she's picked up. She's got a lot of catching up to do. Not to mention learning English. And reading and writing. Math."

Uzi sighed deeply. "Years."

"A *lot* of years. This is a long-term mission unlike any you've taken on. And it'll challenge you like no other. But like I said, she's got you. And you—you should see someone, too. Or maybe a support group. Or both. You've got to look after your own emotional well-being so you can be better equipped to help her."

Uzi did not respond. "Hey. Do you trust me?"

"Always. With my life."

"You'll get through this. It's gonna be a very long road. But you've physically got your daughter back. And each day, little by little, you'll get her back emotionally. Small steps. Some days it'll feel like two forward, three back—but overall, you'll get there."

"Thanks, Karen. You're special, you know that?"

"I think people have used a lot of other, more colorful, adjectives to describe me."

"Before I let you go back to sleep, how'd things turn out with your . . . issues?"

Vail harrumphed. "In the end, I think we'll all be okay. You, me, OPSIG, our country. But it was way too close. Cleaning up the mess, purging the conspirators . . . none of it's gonna be easy. Could get worse before it gets better. But at least you and Hector can come home. And Maya."

"Tell everyone I'm looking forward to seeing them."

"Safe travels, Uzi. Drop me a note after you meet up with Hector, so I know he's okay."

"Will do. And apologize to Robby for waking you guys up." Vail snorted. "Seriously? He's used to it."

88

**HADASSAH EIN KEREM HOSPITAL
JERUSALEM, ISRAEL**

Uzi was waiting in the ER cubicle while Maya was taken for an examination and testing. As Vail alluded, people who have been held captive in less than civilized conditions had to be checked for parasites, viruses, diseases, organ damage, dehydration, and the like. As Uzi stood there staring at the empty gurney, he felt a presence behind him. He turned and saw Gideon Aksel standing there wearing an overcoat and fedora.

"Good to see you in one piece," Aksel said. "That was quite a stunt." Uzi snorted. "Which one?"

Aksel lowered his chin and shook his head, hiding a grin.

"So, Gideon, now that my mind is clear—and free of the stress I've been under for ten days—"

"Not to mention the pain of the past thirteen years."

Uzi pursed his lips. *The pain of the past thirteen years.* "I'm not sure closure is a real thing, but having Maya back is something I never could've imagined." He cleared his throat. "Still."

Aksel drew the curtain closed around them, the ball bearings gliding against the metal track making a whooshing sound. "But something's still missing. That's what you were going to say."

Uzi squinted. "Yeah."

"You want an explanation," Aksel said, removing his brown fedora.

"If anyone's gonna have the answer, it's you. Why'd they do this to me? And who are they?"

Aksel looked down at the hat in his hands. His shoulders slumped and rolled forward. In that moment, Aksel finally began to look his age, the toll of the insurmountable stress of so many years as director general of Mossad taking its physical and mental toll . . . like centuries of running water carving a groove in stone.

Aksel nodded subtly. "You deserve answers. And more. But answers are all I can give you." He still had not looked up from his fedora. "In a way, my friend, this was all my fault."

Uzi folded his arms across his chest. "Go on."

"The head of Iranian counterintelligence. Mehdi Rahmani. He had it out for me for years. Our intelligence, our methods were always superior. We repeatedly penetrated his network, literally and figuratively. Always knew what he was up to. We embarrassed him. Year after year."

Aksel balled a fist, deforming the brim of the hat. "One day, he got even by going after one of our agents. Car bomb. We knew it was Rahmani's work. He was sending a message."

He cleared his throat. "We had to answer, hit him back so hard he'd never dare try that again. So I decided to go after him. Personally. We waited. Patience is important. As you know."

Aksel glanced up at the ceiling, then dropped his gaze again. "Rahmani started having an affair with an Iranian model. We had photos and videos of . . . over a dozen lurid encounters with her."

"That model," Uzi said. "Mossad?"

"Yes." He waited a moment before continuing. Staring at that hat. "I leaked the pictures and videos to the Iranian press." He grunted. "State media. They wanted the story to go away, so they ignored it."

"But you weren't going to let it drop."

"No." He looked at Uzi. "We sent the photos to Rahmani's wife and filmed her as she opened the envelope."

"How—"

"We hacked the cameras inside his house. Like I said, we were always a step ahead."

DIE TRYING   371

Uzi furrowed his brow. He had a sense of where this was going.

"We posted everything to social media. Tiny audience by today's standards, but the story went viral. State media had no choice." He chuckled lightly, almost to himself.

"Rahmani's wife went before an Islamic judge, who ruled Rahmani created difficult and undesirable conditions—according to the Iranian civil code—and granted her a divorce." Askel paused. "Rahmani had accumulated tremendous wealth, mostly corruptly, and she knew how to get at the money. She took it all. And vanished."

"Vanished?"

Aksel bobbed his head. "We may've helped her get away. Into Turkey."

Uzi harrumphed. "So Rahmani came after you."

"Yes." Aksel pulled out a cigarette and lit up. "He figured we were behind everything."

"Gideon, you're not supposed to smoke in—"

He waved his right hand—not to disperse the cloud but to shrug off Uzi's admonition. "Rahmani knew how important you were to me. And he chose to get even by going after your family."

How important I *was to . . . Gideon?*

"And that's why they kidnapped Dena and Maya? To get back at *you*?"

Aksel nodded. "And guess who they recruited to do it?"

Uzi did not need time to consider the question. "Batula Hakim." Hakim, a.k.a. Leila Harel, burned Uzi years later during a mission on US soil that reopened the scar of losing Dena and Maya—and rubbed rock salt in a weeping wound.

"Yes. One of my most valuable double agents." Aksel took a long puff. "Another poke in the eye." He snorted. "They paid her very, very well. Part of that compensation stipulated that she never disclose that Dena and Maya were alive. They were saving that for a time of their choosing, when it would have the most impact and advantage for them."

Uzi's mind was a flurry of interceding thoughts. He couldn't get out a question fast enough. "But Hakim *told me* she killed Dena and Maya."

"So you're saying the double agent lied to you?" Aksel laughed. "No—yes. I mean, she was about to kill me. Why continue the lie?"

"She thought you killed her brother, so she also had personal motivation. The charade of your family's murder accomplished her goal of causing you unending emotional anguish."

"Pain is pain. Murdered or kidnapped, the truth didn't matter."

"Exactly."

Uzi felt bile rising. But the anger was misplaced. Hakim was gone forever. She got what she deserved. Still, it bothered him that so many years later, she still held power over him.

"When did you know this?"

"About Hakim? Or that Dena and Maya were still alive?"

"Still alive."

"Two years later. Give or take. One of our agents got a tip, but we couldn't verify the intel."

Uzi shut his eyes tightly. "Jesus, Gideon. I can't believe you didn't—we were sitting in that limo years ago and you didn't say anything?"

Aksel grunted. "I couldn't. Director Tasset wouldn't sign off on it. And I couldn't argue with him."

Uzi wanted to scream. He took a deep breath instead. "Why not?"

"Because you're a bull in a china shop. Especially when it comes to something close to your heart. It was one of your best character-istics as an operative. And one of your worst. That always had to be considered when you were assigned a mission." He chuckled. "Your family? Are you kidding? Look what happened here, the risks you took despite our *admonitions* to leave it alone." He shook his head. "I'd caused enough damage. I wanted to make it right."

"But you didn't. Thirteen years pas—"

"Yes. Dammit, I know!" He took a long drag.

The curtain parted and a nurse stood there. "Are you crazy?" he asked in Hebrew. "Put that cigarette out!"

Aksel snarled, then dropped the butt to the floor and crushed it with his scuffed Oxford. "Leave us."

The man frowned, then yanked the curtain closed.

"Four missions," Aksel said. "Two by Shin Bet and one by Yamas

DIE TRYING 373

and one by Yamam. We lost three people in the last one. And Tamar lost use of her legs. Our failures were not for lack of effort."

Uzi nodded, sat down heavily on the gurney.

"I'm very, very sorry your family got dragged into it. I'm beside myself over Dena's death. And Maya—" He swiped away a few tears. "Coming after one of my agents to get at *me* . . . They'd never done anything like that. Then again, I went after him. Personally. Like I said, probably all my fault."

"Rahmani was killed in an explosion. A dozen years ago."

"Yes," Axel said. His face was stone, every crease and wrinkle projecting pain. "I had to end this stupid game of tit for tat. Reasoning with him was not an option." He lowered his voice to a whisper. "A kidon was the only way."

Kidon. A Mossad assassin.

"I should've acted sooner. Before he involved your family." Aksel shoved the hat onto his head, then limped a couple of feet to Uzi and rested a hand on his shoulder. His eyes were moist. Seconds passed before he turned and left the cubicle.

Uzi counted slowly to ten.

He wanted to put his fist through a wall.

89

Fifteen minutes after Aksel left him—being alone with his thoughts made it feel like an hour—Maya was brought back to the cubicle.

Uzi tried to engage her in conversation—*Everything okay? Do you have any questions? Do you need anything?* But he only received one-word answers in Arabic. Yes, no, no.

He explained that a close friend of his was recovering on another floor of the hospital and he wanted her to meet him. She did not respond—but she did not object, either.

Five minutes later, they walked into Hector DeSantos's room. He was hooked up to machines and his face was purple and swollen. A shapely nurse was flirting with him—and vice versa.

"Sorry to intrude," Uzi said. "How's the patient doing?"

"And you are?" the woman asked.

"Family," DeSantos said. "It's okay."

She gave Uzi the once-over, glanced at Maya—her eyes lingered a few seconds on the teen's face—then said, "He's going to be fine. He suffered multiple gunshot wounds, but the rounds exited his body. Fortunately for Mr. DeSantos, none of the wounds were fatal. He's on IV antibiotics and pain meds. I'll leave you alone to talk." She winked at DeSantos and left the room—just as Tamar was walking in.

"Whoa," Uzi said. "Look what the wind blew in." He gave her a big hug. "I'm so glad you're okay."

She leaned back and laughed. "You know I'm as tough as they come. E Squadron's got nothing on me. Eight against one? They had no chance." Uzi chuckled.

"You're laughing," she said. "But who's the one hooked up to machines?"

Uzi glanced at DeSantos. "True dat."

"Hey you." DeSantos motioned to Maya. "Come closer. I want to see you."

Maya, holding Uzi's hand, pulled his arm in front of her.

"It's okay, honey," Uzi said in Arabic. "This is Hector, the man I told you about downstairs."

DeSantos tilted his head, studying her face. "I'm a friend of your dad's."

"I don't think she remembers English," Uzi said. "Or Hebrew."

DeSantos operated the bed's remote and raised his torso. "Your dad loves you very much," he said in his best Arabic. "I hope you know that. When he found out you might be alive, he had to come find you." He grinned broadly. "And he dragged me with him."

Maya shrunk back, holding onto Uzi's forearm with both hands.

"That's okay," DeSantos said. "We'll be seeing a lot of each other. You'll get to know me and we'll do all sorts of fun things."

After not getting a response, DeSantos glanced up at Uzi. His knitted brow, the tilt of his head, spoke volumes.

Uzi acknowledged his friend's concerns with a bite of his bottom lip and a knowing nod.

This was going to be a long journey, for sure. But he believed Vail's assessment that humans were resilient creatures and that Maya would recover, no matter how long it took.

Uzi realized that up until a couple of weeks ago, he had been spending his time searching to fill a void left by the death of his wife and daughter. That life was now full of vigor, promise—and challenge.

He would not have wanted it any other way.

ACKNOWLEDGMENTS

As with all my previous novels, the research phase is long and arduous. *Die Trying* presented some unusual challenges. Once again, the dozens of people I worked with provided depth and understanding to the scenes I wanted to write, and the issues involved, including political and religious implications. In addition, those of you who have read my acknowledgments in the past know that I name names of those who've assisted me and their positions. This time is very different because of the subject matter of the story and the state of the world.

When you say to a sworn member of the US Secret Service (USSS) that you're outlining a plot to blow up the president-elect's helicopter (as I did in a previous OPSIG Team Black novel), they get really nervous. While it's fiction, they don't want to be associated with anything that could appear to endanger their mission, their people, or protectees. And one could argue that *Die Trying* is even more aggressive in that regard: attacking the presidential motorcade is a primary ongoing focus of the USSS mission. It's the stuff of agents' regular training—and nightmares. Moreover, the USSS has been the subject of . . . let's call them "high-profile failures" in recent years—a black, blue, and purple eye on their reputation (and mandate). As a result, you won't find as many names called out below.

Lastly, I took some artistic license—sometimes on purpose and sometimes by necessity. In the former category, that was largely due to my pledge to never endanger law enforcement agents (or members of the military) by revealing secrets or sensitive information. This material is provided to me in an atmosphere of trust—which I attempt to maintain. It's why I'm still friends with many of my contacts many years after the first (or only) novel they assisted me with. Thus details may or may not have been altered, changed, or omitted.

As touched on above, the US Secret Service has a very challenging job in protecting POTUS. While I knew a lot about their charge, I now know many more details about how they do their jobs—and how they prepare, both in training and during the performance of their duties. Broadly speaking, some presidents are compliant protectees (Biden) and some tend to flout procedure (Obama, Clinton, Trump), making the detail agents' jobs more difficult. Much of the information regarding the makeup of the motorcade is accurate as of the writing of *Die Trying*. However, where I deviated will remain unarticulated.

The latter category, "artistic license by necessity," involves the distances and details in Jenin and surrounding areas. While I have been to the West Bank, at the time of research it was volatile (more so than at other times), violent, and unsafe. Years ago, while researching *The Lost Codex*, I accidentally drove into an area in the West Bank unfriendly to Americans—and my friend, an Israeli, told me not to stop and "to get the hell out of here." Sage advice, which I followed. For *Die Trying*, I utilized other resources including firsthand accounts, street maps, news photos and articles, unnamed contacts, Google Earth, Bing maps, and contract satellite photo providers (that possessed higher resolution imagery).

With that in mind, among those I can acknowledge, a special hat tip to:

Attorney Gilad Schlesinger, adv, Schlesinger Almougy & Co, law offices in Bnei Brak, Israel, for case law and legal precedent regarding interment of a body buried in Jerusalem. Gilad took time from his busy day to research this issue, which was vitally important to *Die Trying*. I would not have found Gilad without the assistance of Stephan Miller, former adviser for foreign affairs and foreign media to the mayor of Jerusalem (who also assisted me with other issues re: Israel); and Corey Jacobson for putting me in touch with them.

David Weis, rabbi, likewise provided background and information regarding interment and how Israel views it—particularly the governing principles of municipal law vs. religious law and how the former is what matters in Israel's court of law.

Bennett Leventhal, MD, world-renowned child psychiatrist, for reviewing my chapters relative to child trauma and what a young teen would experience in hostile, long-term captivity—and for his suggestions, changes, and referral to an expert in child trauma and disaster intervention.

Tomás Palmer, cryptographer and cyber security expert, for reviewing (a lot of) excerpts from the novel for accuracy regarding EMPs and Faraday cages, electronics, hacking, AI, and related stuff. Tomás is on a different intellectual plane and working with him reminds me that there's an IQ hierarchy in humankind. And then there's the language barrier. One might think Tomás, an American, speaks English. But he speaks what I term cryptographic cyberspeaklish. Thus, he might say, "A lot of attack vectors are left unmitigated because the tap is close in on admin side. And the core OS would be in hardware with integrity watchdog." Fortunately, I'm tech savvy, so although I did not fully understand that, I understood enough to ask intelligent questions to gain clarity. (At least I thought they were intelligent questions.) He also sent me technical papers to read, which began something like, "The OSI Model is a conceptual framework and divides computing functions into a universal set of rules or regulations to support interoperability. There are seven different abstraction layers." Funny, but I only knew of six.

Paul Knierim, DEA assistant administrator, chief of intelligence (ret.), for alerting me to the illicit drug trafficking of captagon by Syrian and other Middle Eastern organized crime organizations. Paul also keyed me in on Harley Davidson motorcycle technology, but most importantly, read the manuscript for consistency and accuracy (and corrected my gun-related flubs, among others). Any errors or artistic license are my doing.

Jeffrey Jacobson, Esq., attorney representing federal agents of all stripes and the former associate general counsel for the Federal Law Enforcement Officers Association, for assisting me with Vail's legal case and FBI offense codes; he looked at comparable discipline meted out for similarly situated employees and estimated the severity of Vail's discipline.

Stan Pollock, CPA and lifelong martial artist in Tang Soo Do (currently a Sam Dan, the equivalent of a third-degree black belt), for his martial arts primer and information on submission choke holds.

Mark Safarik, FBI supervisory special agent and senior profiler at the Behavioral Analysis Unit (ret.) and principal of Forensic Behavioral Services International, for reading the manuscript and providing feedback.

In one of the more odd copyediting issues I've encountered, there was debate over the proper way to handle mention of the 5.11 Tactical company's backpacks, pants, and duffels that the OPSIG operators (and real operators, first responders, and law enforcement officers) use. Since customers and insiders refer to the company as 5.11 and not by its full formal branding, I opted to use the colloquial and avoid the Chicago Manual of Style confusion regarding whether or not to capitalize "tactical." There's no right answer, so I chose the one less confusing. I appreciate the assistance that 5.11 customer service provided in determining the best way forward.

It may not take a village to publish a novel, but sometimes it feels like it. Thanks to the folks at Open Road Integrated Media, including Mara Anastas, vice president and publisher, and Emma L. Chapnick, publishing coordinator, for shepherding my sixteenth novel through production. After thirty years in this business, I never take the complex process for granted.

My editor, Kevin Smith, who has worked with me on fourteen of sixteen books, for his usual stellar work on *Die Trying*. If you look up the term "professional" in Webster's dictionary, Kevin's name appears there as an example (or it should).

My longtime copyeditor, Chrisona Schmidt, who received Most Valuable Person votes for the polish she applied to this manuscript. Predicates, particles, and participles, in a language that seems to possess more exceptions than rules—amid style manuals that are updated too often—require someone to keep it all straight. That's why Chrisona

ACKNOWLEDGMENTS

is my MVP. Can I say that I love my copyeditor? Has an author ever written such a sentence?

Jill Jacobson, my wife and life partner of thirty-seven years, for reviewing the manuscript for timeline accuracy. Between the time zone changes and the different timelines in the storylines, it presented a challenge. I'm horrible with math—I have the annoying ability to add instead of subtract and vice versa (I blame my DNA)—so getting it all correct was no small feat.

ABOUT THE AUTHOR

Alan Jacobson is the award-winning, *USA Today* best-selling author of fourteen thrillers, including the FBI profiler Karen Vail series and the OPSIG Team Black novels. His books have been translated internationally and several have been optioned by Hollywood. His debut novel, *False Accusations*, was adapted to film by acclaimed Czech screenwriter Jiří Hubač.

Jacobson has spent over twenty-five years working with the FBI's Behavioral Analysis Unit, the DEA, the US Marshals Service, SWAT, the NYPD, Scotland Yard, local law enforcement, and the US military. This research and the breadth of his contacts help bring depth and realism to his characters and stories.

Jacobson is currently an FBI Ambassador, helping to further the Bureau's mission and to strengthen its relationship with the broader community.

For video interviews and a free personal safety eBook co-authored by Alan Jacobson and FBI profiler Mark Safarik, please visit www.AlanJacobson.com.

You can also connect with Jacobson on Instagram and Threads (alan.jacobson), Twitter (@JacobsonAlan), Facebook (AlanJacobson-Fans), and Goodreads (alan-jacobson).

THE WORKS OF ALAN JACOBSON

Alan Jacobson has established a reputation as one of the most insightful suspense/thriller writers of our time. His exhaustive research, coupled with years of unprecedented access to law enforcement agencies, including the FBI's Behavioral Analysis Unit, brings realism and unique characters to his pages. Following are his current, and forthcoming, releases.

STAND ALONE NOVELS

False Accusations > Dr. Phillip Madison has everything: wealth, power, and an impeccable reputation. But in the predawn hours of a quiet suburb, the revered orthopedic surgeon is charged with double homicide—a cold-blooded hit-and-run that leaves an innocent couple dead. Blood evidence has brought the police to his door. An eyewitness has placed him at the crime scene, and Madison has no alibi. With his family torn apart, his career forever damaged, no way to prove his innocence and facing life in prison, Madison must find the person who has engineered the case against him. Years after reading it, people still talk about his shocking ending. *False Accusations* launched Jacobson's career and became a national bestseller, prompting CNN to call him, "One of the brightest stars in the publishing industry."

FBI PROFILER KAREN VAIL SERIES

The 7th Victim (Karen Vail #1) > Literary giants Nelson DeMille and James Patterson describe Karen Vail, the first female FBI profiler, as "tough, smart, funny, very believable," and "compelling." In *The 7th Victim*, Vail—with a dry sense of humor and a closet full of skeletons—heads up a task force to find the Dead Eyes Killer, who is murdering young women in Virginia . . . the backyard of the famed FBI Behavioral Analysis Unit. The twists and turns that Karen Vail endures in this tense psychological suspense thriller build to a powerful ending no reader will see coming. Named one of the Top 5 Best Books of the Year (*Library Journal*).

Crush (Karen Vail #2) > In light of the traumatic events of *The 7th Victim*, FBI profiler Karen Vail is sent to the Napa Valley for a mandatory vacation—but the Crush Killer has other plans. Vail partners with Inspector Roxxann Dixon to track down the architect of death who crushes his victims' windpipes and leaves their bodies in wine caves. However, the killer is unlike anything the profiling unit has ever encountered, and Vail's miscalculations have dire consequences for those she holds dear. *Publishers Weekly* describes *Crush* as "addicting" and *New York Times* bestselling author Steve Martini calls it a thriller that's "Crisply written and meticulously researched," and "rocks from the opening page to the jarring conclusion." (Note: the *Crush* storyline continues in *Velocity*.)

Velocity (Karen Vail #3) > A missing detective. A bold serial killer. And evidence that makes FBI profiler Karen Vail question the loyalty of those she has entrusted her life to. In the shocking conclusion to *Crush*, Karen Vail squares off against foes more dangerous than any she has yet encountered. In the process, shocking personal and professional truths emerge—truths that may be more than Vail can handle. *Velocity* was named to *The Strand Magazine*'s Top 10 Best Books for 2010, *Suspense Magazine*'s Top 4 Best Thrillers of 2010, *Library Journal*'s Top 5 Best Books of the Year, and the *Los Angeles Times*'s top picks of the year. Michael Connelly said *Velocity* is "As relentless as a bullet. Karen Vail is my kind of hero and Alan Jacobson is my kind of writer!"

THE WORKS OF ALAN JACOBSON   387

Inmate 1577 (Karen Vail #4) > When an elderly woman is found raped and murdered, Karen Vail heads west to team up with Inspector Lance Burden and Detective Roxxann Dixon. As they follow the killer's trail in and around San Francisco, the offender leaves behind clues that ultimately lead them to the most unlikely of places, a mysterious island ripped from city lore whose long-buried, decades-old secrets hold the key to their case: Alcatraz. The Rock. It's a case that has more twists and turns than the famed Lombard Street. The legendary Clive Cussler calls *Inmate 1577* "a powerful thriller, brilliantly conceived and written." Named one of *The Strand Magazine*'s Top 10 Best Books of the Year.

No Way Out (Karen Vail #5) > Renowned FBI profiler Karen Vail returns in *No Way Out*, a high-stakes thriller set in London. When a high-profile art gallery is bombed, Vail is dispatched to England to assist with Scotland Yard's investigation. But what she finds there—a plot to destroy a controversial, recently unearthed 440-year-old manuscript—turns into something much larger, and a whole lot more dangerous, for the UK, the United States—and herself. With his trademark spirited dialogue, page-turning scenes, and well-drawn characters, National Bestselling author Alan Jacobson ("My kind of writer," per Michael Connelly) has crafted the thriller of the year. Named a top ten "Best Thriller of 2013" by both *Suspense Magazine* and *The Strand Magazine.*

Spectrum (Karen Vail #6) > It's 1995 and the NYPD has just graduated a promising new patrol officer named Karen Vail. During the rookie's first day on the job, she finds herself at the crime scene of a woman murdered in an unusual manner. As the years pass and more victims are discovered, Vail's career takes unexpected twists and turns—as does the case that's come to be known as "Hades." Now a skilled FBI profiler, will Vail be in a better position to catch the offender? Or will Hades prove to be Karen Vail's hell on earth? #1 *New York Times* bestseller Richard North Patterson called *Spectrum*, "Compelling and crisp . . . A pleasure to read."

The Darkness of Evil (Karen Vail #7) > Roscoe Lee Marcks, one of history's most notorious serial killers, sits in a maximum security prison

388 THE WORKS OF ALAN JACOBSON

serving a life sentence—until he stages a brutal and well-executed escape. Although the US Marshals Service's fugitive task force enlists the help of FBI profiler Karen Vail to launch a no-holds-barred manhunt, the bright and law enforcement-wise Marcks has other plans—which include killing his daughter. But a retired profiling legend, who was responsible for Marcks's original capture, may just hold the key to stopping him. Perennial #1 *New York Times* bestselling author John Sandford compared *The Darkness of Evil* to *The Girl with the Dragon Tattoo*, calling it "smoothly written, intricately plotted," and "impressive," while fellow *New York Times* bestseller Phillip Margolin said *The Darkness of Evil* is "slick" and "full of very clever twists. Karen Vail is one tough heroine!"

Red Death (Karen Vail #8) > *Hawaii. Home to picturesque waterfalls. Pristine beaches. And a serial killer who proves as elusive as the island breeze.* When Honolulu detective Adam Russell encounters the body of a woman in her sixties—the second in recent days to inexplicably die of what seems like natural causes—he reaches out to renowned FBI profiler Karen Vail. But even for someone as fluent in the language of murder as Vail, this case is hard to read. Lacking a profile, Vail and Russell pursue an offender who asphyxiates his victims while leaving behind a clean tox screen and no signs of trauma. Perhaps most terrifying of all, if the deaths appear natural at first glance, how many victims have already been overlooked? The queen of FBI thrillers, *New York Times* bestseller Catherine Coulter, calls *Red Death* "A unique and imaginative plot filled with witty dialogue and page-turning intrigue."

OPSIG TEAM BLACK SERIES

The Hunted (OPSIG Team Black #1) > How well do you know the one you love? How far would you go to find out? When Lauren Chambers's husband Michael disappears, her search reveals his hidden past involving the FBI, international assassins—and government secrets that some will go to great lengths to keep hidden. As *The Hunted* hurtles toward a conclusion mined with turn-on-a-dime twists, no one is who he appears to be and nothing is as it seems. *The Hunted*

THE WORKS OF ALAN JACOBSON   389

introduces the dynamic Department of Defense covert operative Hector DeSantos and FBI director Douglas Knox, characters who return in future OPSIG Team Black novels, as well as the Karen Vail series (*Velocity*, *No Way Out*, and *Spectrum*).

Hard Target (OPSIG Team Black #2) > An explosion pulverizes the president-elect's helicopter on Election Night. The group behind the assassination attempt possesses far greater reach than anything the FBI has yet encountered—and a plot so deeply interwoven in the country's fabric that it threatens to upend America's political system. But as covert operative Hector DeSantos and FBI agent Aaron "Uzi" Uziel sort out who is behind the bombings, Uzi's personal demons not only jeopardize the investigation but may sit at the heart of a tangle of lies that threaten to trigger an international terrorist attack. Lee Child called *Hard Target*, "Fast, hard, intelligent. A terrific thriller." Note: FBI profiler Karen Vail plays a key role in the story.

The Lost Codex (OPSIG Team Black #3) > In a novel Jeffery Deaver called "brilliant," two ancient biblical documents stand at the heart of a geopolitical battle between foreign governments and radical extremists, threatening the lives of millions. With the American homeland under siege, the president turns to a team of uniquely trained covert operatives that includes FBI profiler Karen Vail, Special Forces veteran Hector DeSantos, and FBI terrorism expert Aaron Uziel. Their mission: find the stolen documents and capture—or kill—those responsible for unleashing a coordinated and unprecedented attack on US soil. Set in Washington, DC, New York, Paris, England, and Israel, *The Lost Codex* is international historical intrigue at its heart-stopping best.

Dark Side of the Moon (OPSIG Team Black #4) > Apollo 17 returned to Earth in 1972 with 200 pounds of rock—including something more dangerous than they could have imagined. The military concealed the discovery for decades—until a NASA employee discloses to foreign powers the existence of a material that would disrupt the global balance of power by providing them with the most powerful weapon of mass destruction yet created. While FBI profiler Karen Vail and

390 THE WORKS OF ALAN JACOBSON

OPSIG Team Black colleague Alexandra Rusakov search for the spy, covert operatives Hector DeSantos and Aaron Uziel find themselves rocketing alongside astronauts to the moon to avert a war. But what can go wrong does, jeopardizing the mission and threatening to trigger the very conflict they were charged with preventing. *New York Times* bestselling author Gayle Lynds said *Dark Side of the Moon* is "the thriller ride of a lifetime . . . a nonstop tale of high adventure that Tom Clancy's most ardent fans will absolutely love!"

Die Trying (OPSIG Team Black #5) > *This time it's personal.* When Aaron Uziel, head of the FBI's Joint Terrorism Task Force, receives highly protected intelligence that has the potential to throw the Middle East into turmoil, the CIA orders Uzi to stand down because the information could destroy highly sensitive treaty negotiations.

But when Uzi discovers that the intel carries implications that not only impact national security but his own life, career, and family, he cannot ignore it. Uzi enlists the assistance of covert operatives Hector DeSantos, Alex Rusakov, and FBI profiler Karen Vail for a blacker-than-black mission as they travel halfway around the world to verify the intel. But when things turn deadly, involving those at the top of government, Uzi and DeSantos pull out all the stops to track down those responsible for engineering the venomous plan. Or they will die trying.

MICKEY KELLER SERIES

The Lost Girl (Mickey Keller #1) > Amy Robbins suffers a tragedy no one should ever endure: the loss of her young daughter and husband in a deadly accident. Mired in a depressive fog, her successful career vanishes—followed by her life savings and the will to live. But while biding time in a dead-end job, she stumbles on something that upends everything—and lays bare a disturbing truth at the heart of a tragic lie. With fixer Mickey Keller attempting to take from Amy the last hope she has for a return to a normal life, her sister-in-law—FBI agent Loren Ryder—squares off against Keller in a heart-pounding climax that will leave you wondering who are the good guys and who are the

THE WORKS OF ALAN JACOBSON   391

bad. In the words of *Rizzoli & Isles* creator Tess Gerritsen, "Jacobson expertly ratchets up the tension and shows us that the most courageous heroes are those with everything to lose."

SHORT STORIES

"Fatal Twist" ~ The Park Rapist has murdered his first victim—and FBI profiler Karen Vail is on the case. As Vail races through the streets of Washington, DC to chase down a promising lead that may help her catch the killer, a military-trained sniper takes aim at his target, a wealthy businessman's son. But what brings these two unrelated offenders together is something the nation's capital has never before experienced. "Fatal Twist" provides a taste of Karen Vail that will whet your appetite.

"Double Take" ~ NYPD detective Ben Dyer awakens from cancer surgery to find his life turned upside down. His fiancée has disappeared and Dyer, determined to find her, embarks on a journey mined with potholes and startling revelations—revelations that have the potential to forever change his life. "Double Take" introduces NYPD lieutenant Carmine Russo and detective Ben Dyer, who return to play significant roles in *Spectrum* (Karen Vail #6).

"12:01 AM" ~ A kidnapped woman. A serial killer on death row—about to be executed. Karen Vail has mere hours to pull the pieces together to find the missing woman and her abductor—before it's too late. In a short story that reads like a novel straight out of the award-winning Karen Vail series, *USA Today* bestselling author Alan Jacobson sets a new standard for short form fiction.

ESSAYS

"The Vixen" ~ In *Hollywood vs. The Author*, eighteen professional writers who have had experience getting, or trying to get, their novels adapted to film share stories of what went right, what went wrong, as well as who—and what—to watch out for. In "The Vixen," Alan

Jacobson dishes on the many times Hollywood has optioned his books, including a few choice tales on how close he came to seeing Karen Vail on screen—and how his debut novel was adapted to film. Filled with luck—both good and bad—and plenty of humor, Jacobson's essay joins those of Tess Gerritsen, Michael Connelly, Lawrence Block, Peter James, Jonathan Kellerman, T. Jefferson Parker, and more.

More to come

For a peek at recently released Alan Jacobson novels, interviews, reading group guides, and more, visit www.AlanJacobson.com.

THE OPSIG TEAM BLACK SERIES

FROM OPEN ROAD MEDIA

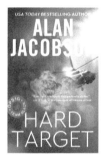

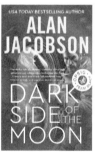
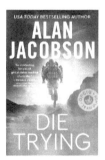

THE KAREN VAIL NOVELS

FROM OPEN ROAD MEDIA

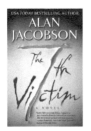  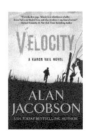

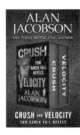  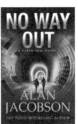 

 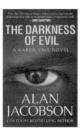 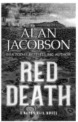

Find a full list of our authors and
titles at www.openroadmedia.com

FOLLOW US
@OpenRoadMedia